D1529094

I AM

The Delta Protocol

I AM

THE DELTA PROTOCOL

Michael Decker

DEDICATION

I like to dedicate this book to all U.S. military personnel active and prior service. Without your service, our hope for continued greatness would not be possible. I would also like to recognize all of the first responders (past, present, and future) for their tireless dedication to preserving public safety and health. The last group that deserves recognition is the average American who faithfully believes in the true meaning of the founding of our great nation. They also have an indomitable spirit that will face and destroy tyranny when it threatens our republic and Constitution.

"We mutually pledge to each other our Lives, our Fortunes, and our Sacred Honor."
-Signers of the Declaration of Independence

Semper Fi

Michael F. Decker

Michael F. Decker

PROLOGUE

The United States has evolved in many ways in its short 244-year history. Our country has never been perfect; no country is. Yet, since its inception, we have been a bastion of hope and freedom never before seen in world history. No other government allowed its governance to be restrained by a piece of paper called the Constitution, but that is what the Constitution was created to do. This Constitution devised by our forefathers was the first in the world's history. It is believed by some that it was divinely inspired. That inspiration allowed a group of upstart colonists, who at the time were subjects beholden to the British King's rule, to forge a new country. These colonists envisioned freedom from subjugation, freedom to own land, freedom to speak without censorship. They also demanded freedom of the press, allowing them to write dissenting articles against their government, freedom of religion, and freedom to chart their destiny. Our founding fathers and the people who believed in freedom's cause had the intestinal fortitude to break the shackles of the most powerful nation on earth. They risked their lives, fortunes, and sacred honor by choosing this course of action.

The words within the Declaration of Independence remind us that we hold these truths to be self-evident, that all men are created equal, that they are endowed by their Creator with certain unalienable rights that among these are Life, Liberty, and the Pursuit of Happiness. Unalienable is a synonym of inalienable, which is defined as incapable of being alienated, surrendered, or transferred.

Our Constitution and Bill of Rights are a template for much of the world's fledgling democracies. Many people worldwide immigrate to the United States, legally and illegally. The laws regarding immigration have changed since our country's inception. In the early 20th Century, immigration was used as a tool to supplement the workforce. We must remember that there was no federal government social safety net. No welfare, no Social Security to rely on. Immigrants who entered the country were usually employed by industries like building the railroad and large dams. They did not become a burden to society through wasteful spending of taxpayer dollars. If people in general and immigrants specifically needed assistance, it was done through family members, churches, neighbors, and charity groups.

People in the United States have lost a vital ingredient in the early development of our country, the ability to be self-sufficient and take personal responsibility for their lives. The bottom line is their rugged individualism. Creating the federal government's social safety net may have begun with compassion for the less fortunate. Still, unfortunately, it has snowballed into a political election gimmick. If a political party tells a block of potential voters they will develop a program or continue an existing program that will pay or supplement a group's income, it usually means they are after their votes. If that group happens to be a large block of voters, then it is likely that those politicians will garner those votes. Add to the fact that the people who oppose the additional spending because of the massive debt the federal government has incurred are now portrayed as heartless racists.

Over the last fifty years, it has been evident that the family structure is slowly eroding. You can see the way children are raised by their parents if they are fortunate enough even to have two parents. You can see the subtle changes within the education system, the changes in perception of the world, and American history. We were once taught how brave and wise our forefathers were and looked in awe at many of America's past heroes. Still, today these people are deemed racist and imperialist. Their monuments and statues were torn down or desecrated.

Faith in God could be seen in many different ways, billboards, holiday displays, and even during a moment of silence after you stood to say the Pledge of Allegiance before the start of class in your elementary school. Unfortunately, this is no longer true. The mainstream network and cable news media have always been somewhat left-leaning. Still, now they have no problem censoring news that does not fit their agenda, even to the extent of lying to the public. As a result, we have protests in major Democrat-run cities that turn into riots, with law enforcement forced to stand by and watch the destruction. Presidential candidates donate money to bail the rioters out of jail if they are arrested. The country has become hyperpolarized. Even the words "Civil War" are used by both major parties and the media.

Now Marxist insurgents and sympathizers have openly challenged the very heart of our country's founding, freedom of speech. They use the narratives like anti-racist, fascist, white privilege, Nazi, homophobic, xenophobic, Black Lives Matter, police brutality, intersectionalism, and cancel culture, to name a few, to dehumanize and disenfranchise people who disagree with them. Although we have many different movements in their primary goals, they all have one thing in common. They are all disenfranchised in some way or another within the society of the United States. They are assembled under the umbrella of Marxism, which is financed by left-wing Socialists. Whether this influence is state-sponsored or homegrown, it spreads throughout our society via professors tenured at higher learning institutions, major news media outlets, Hollywood producers, directors, actors, and social justice organizations. All of these groups help to facilitate the dissemination of Marxist propaganda. This influence is targeted towards our country's strengths, rugged individualism, personal responsibility, and entrepreneurial spirit.

Most importantly is our country's historical relationship with God and religion. This dwindling devotion to faith and the persecution of Christians and Jews from the left and these Marxist insurgents is a recipe for disaster. For the last sixty years, religious affiliations have dwindled in our country.

As religion fades, it is replaced with selfish progressive thoughts and actions allowing society to become less moral in thought and action. Indeed, you can see that the moral fabric of our country is rapidly disintegrating if you believe in the same God as Christianity, Islam, and Judaism do. You have probably asked yourself or others at what point does God say enough is enough? What sin or lack of faith on the part of humanity could merge into a catalyst to spark God's wrath? Well, this is that story.

1

GENESIS

Dr. Norman Peters was a very determined man. Some would call him a genius. The doctor was involved in some of the world's top cutting-edge research, nanotechnology. Dr. Peters pioneered the research to develop technologies and methods to create mRNA sequences that allow cells to recognize them as if they were produced in the body. His whole life revolved around the theory that if he could program nanoparticles, he would have the ability to cure mankind of most diseases, and in all likelihood, even all disorders. The doctor had spent many years researching the problem.

DARPA had understood the concept but wanted the technology for military reasons. The Defense Advanced Research Projects Agency (DARPA) had approached Dr. Peters and offered him a laboratory, a scientific staff, and an unlimited budget to develop the ability to program the nanoparticles. In addition, they wanted him to create the ability to insert the particles into the human body. Once he achieved these goals, he would work on the potential uses of this new technology.

The doctor finally achieved his goals. However, before the experiments were started on the insertion of the nanoparticles into human test subjects, he was contacted by a very influential man.

The man's name was Jonathan Reaver. Reaver was a very wealthy man and also a prominent Congressman. Reaver arranged for one of his trusted advisors to contact Dr. Peters and offer him five million dollars, his own lab, and a budget to complete his work. The catch was that he had to make up an excuse to leave DARPA. Perhaps he could tell them he had to go due to some kind of illness. The man also told the doctor that his work would remain highly secretive.

Congressman Reaver was true to his word. He paid the doctor five million tax-free dollars, set up in an offshore account, and allowed him to work in his new lab without deadlines or any pressure.

The study of nanoparticles was not exclusive to Dr. Peters. Other scientists were also blazing their trail in the field. However, Dr. Peters' research stood out far above his peers because of his ability to program the particles for a specific task before entering the body. His most outstanding achievement is he could then reprogram the particles to do virtually anything from almost anywhere. No one was even close to this breakthrough in technology.

On March 11, 2020, the World Health Organization declared the novel Coronavirus (Covid-19) outbreak in Wuhan, China, a global pandemic.

Dr. Peters explained to the Congressman that this would be the ideal time to introduce his nanoparticles to the world. He explained that several pharmaceutical companies would be franticly producing a vaccine. The use of nanoparticles in humans is not new. What is new is how Dr. Peters intended to program the particles and upload and download commands to the particles once in the body. Dr. Peters explained further that if the Congressman could somehow enable Dr. Peters' access to the production of the vaccine, he could easily insert his nanoparticles into the vaccine without detection.

The Commanding General stood at attention before his exalted leader in an undisclosed location. The General recited the four contingency protocols: One, Alpha: mankind discovering the ability to create human life. Two, Bravo: Mankind has the knowledge and is about to cause an (ELE), Extinction Level Event. Three, Charlie: If mankind's belief in me reduces to below five percent of the total population. Four, Delta: If mankind has the motive, intent, and means to alter his ability to choose between right and wrong and deprive him of free will.

When the General finished, the leader asked,

"I assume there is a problem regarding the contingency protocols?"

The General said, "Yes Sir, actually the fourth protocol, Delta."

The leader said, "General, you are telling me that Dr. Peter's can now program the nanoparticles?"

The General said, "That is correct. Dr. Peters and Congressman Reaver plan to place the nanoparticles within the developed vaccines. They now can program the nanoparticles remotely and at will."

The leader asked, "Do we have eyes on confirmation?"

The General said, "Yes, I had three of my best observing the entire process."

The leader said, "Okay, General, have your legions at the ready, and have the six notified. Then, we will commence with my contingency, the Delta protocol."

The General asked, "Should I notify their leader?"

"No. I have another person in mind for that position. I will notify him personally."

The General asked, "Do you require security for your trip?"

"No, General. I think I can handle it myself, but thank you."

After the General left the room, he said to no one in particular, "Throughout recorded history, he is known by countless names.

Today man is crossing the Rubicon triggering the most destructive power ever known. I AM".

2

STARTING THE DRAFT

Imam Kamal Bari sat in his somewhat spartan office just outside the Fatima Masumeh Shrine in the Iranian city of Qom. The town is a sizeable theological center, with Imam Bari as one of its esteem Shi'a religious teachers and leaders. Imam Bari sat drinking tea while looking over several passages of the Koran for his next class. Bari had spent 40 of his 45 years in constant worship and devotion to Allah, too young to remember the revolution or the Shah. Bari was not part of the political movement. He truly loves God and all the people of the book, which Christians and Jews are also part of. He had never felt any animosity for these religions. Still, with the current regime's power and hardline activities toward his fellow Muslims, Bari had kept his true feelings to himself. It would be dangerous to do otherwise. The Imam drifted in thought back to his early teen years. They were beautiful times. He remembered back on one particular night, while he was sleeping restfully, suddenly he awoke to the presence of a spectral being standing at the foot of his bed. The face was undesirable; the attire was historically old, resembling a sheepherder's robe and sandals.

The being said, "You are one of six." The aberration then vanished.

Franklin Ham is a highly successful leader in the Evangelical Christian Church movement. Franklin is a profoundly religious man. The son of a preacher, he was immersed in the Word of God for as far back as he could remember. Tonight, he worried not about his faith in the Lord but America's faith in God. Since the early 1970s, the U.S. and its people have slowly but indeed turned their faces, attention, and hearts away from God. As hard as he tried to bring the Word of the Lord to as many people as possible, things have progressed to the point that everything was about one's self, not a friend or neighbor, just selfishness. Everyone seemed to not care. If only he could find a way for people to see the Lord's goodness and love as he did.

Franklin sat at his desk inside the den of his home, located in Boone, North Carolina.

The den's walls were paneled with dark rich walnut, adorned with photos of his father, family, and the many missions he had attended all over the world. Many of his most fond memories were those missions he attended in third world countries where he was teaching and spreading the word of God.

The furniture in his office was made of rich leather, black in color. The office contained a couch, a loveseat, a wing-type chair in front of his desk, and his desk chair. He could smell the scent of leather, a relaxing smell that he loved. As Franklin sat, recounting the memories the photos brought to him. He thought back to his teens and the heavenly specter that had appeared to him while he slept. It was something Franklin often thought about. It was the main reason he had offered his life to God. The specter told him, "He was one of six." Franklin's faith told him this was important, but to what end? He bowed his head in prayer, asking for guidance. To his surprise, his prayer was answered in the form of a man. The man was dressed in a royal blue robe. It reminded Franklin of something an ancient Roman aristocrat might wear. The man had a trimmed black beard and wore sandals. The man projected confidence and strength. The man then spoke, "Franklin, I'm Azrael, an Angel of the Lord. The Almighty has chosen you and five others to spread his word to all of humanity. There is another named Michael; the Lord speaks directly with him. He is the leader of the Lord's chosen. Your country and all of humanity are about to be judged. If the Almighty does not feel that your group's progress is sufficient, he will destroy humanity. I will supply you with the time, dates, and locations to meet Michael. Do you have any questions for me?" Franklin responded, "I'm sure I do have questions, but I'm so shocked at your visit that I can't think of any at the moment." Azrael vanished and on Franklin's desk was a piece of paper with the time, date, and location of meeting Michael.

     Dr. Salomon Levi is the founder and leader of the Temple Mount and Land of Israel Faithful Movement, located in Jerusalem, Israel. In his private life, Salomon is an expert researcher and lecturer in Middle Eastern studies, specializing in the history of the national movement of the Kurdish people. He was also an officer in the Israeli Defense Force (IDF). Salomon is a 10th generation Jerusalemite.

Even as a child, Salomon knew that God was calling him to continue the work for the redemption of the people of Israel. As a youth, Salomon was an officer in the IDF and led a company in the Golan Heights during a battle with the Syrian Army in 1958. Salomon was accidentally injured in the heat and confusion of war; he was run over by a tank. Syrian soldiers, trained to shoot any wounded Israeli soldiers, had begun to take over the battlefield. Suddenly, when they were about to fire upon Salomon, they all ran away. Later, these same Syrian soldiers reported to United Nations officers that they had seen thousands of angels around this IDF officer and had, therefore, fled. At this time, Salomon heard the voice of God speaking to him that He was not yet finished with him. Salomon understood this as a divine call to consecrate himself to the work of the Temple Mount.

He feels that the most significant moment of his life, so far, was his participation in the liberation of the Temple Mount and Jerusalem during the 1967 Six-Day War. He believes that at that moment, the circle was closed between his generation and the generation of the destruction of the Temple in 70 CE.

Salomon's movement has painstakingly created recreations of numerous utensils used by the priests during sacrifices and rituals within the Temple. He has individuals that have studied all of the priestly duties and are prepared to continue these duties when the 3rd Temple is finished. Everything has been researched, including the dyes for the colors of the garments to the actual fibers used to make the cloth. The only obstacle is the removal of the Dome of the Rock and the Al-Aqsa mosque located in the Old City of Jerusalem. It is the third holiest site in Islam. The mosque was built on the Temple Mount, known as the Al Aqsa compound. Muslims believe that Muhammad was transported from the Sacred Mosque in Mecca to al-Aqsa during the Night Journey. Islamic tradition holds that Muhammad led prayers towards this site until the 17th month after he migrated from Mecca to Medina. Then, Allah directed him to turn towards the Kaaba in Mecca.

Sitting in his office, Solomon studied the inventory sheets cataloging all the utensils and garments that have been crafted so far and longing to find the Ark of the Covenant. After an hour of study, his mind drifted to his teens when he was visited by the angel who had explained to him that he was one of six. This brought a smile to Solomon's face.

A man sat on the beach near Dam Neck, Virginia, gazing at the stars. It was lonely but soothing. He drifted back in his mind to the many missions that he could clearly recall in vivid detail. These missions spanned 22 years.

A small smile came across his face. All the things that the man had learned, all of the experiences, all the things that he had hoped to do, and all the things he had prayed he would be able to do. These were the thoughts of "Midas" Johnny Black, Chief Petty Officer United States Navy Special Warfare Command, a member of Red Squadron, and the tier-one counter-terrorist unit called the Naval Special Warfare Development Group (DEVGRU) or otherwise known by the uninformed Seal Team Six. The Navy called him Chief, but everyone in the unit called him Midas by his team's name.

At 40 years old, Midas was a lean 200 pounds, mostly muscle with a deadly predator's instinct and fluid movements. He was contemplating retirement from the teams but had no direction to go. Naturally, therefore, his mind drifted back some 25 years when he awoke to a spectral figure that told him he was one of six.

3

UNKNOWN OPPOSITION

Six men sat in a 10,000 square-foot luxury log home, completely self-contained, sitting atop over 400 acres just southeast of Colorado Springs, Colorado. Five of the world's most secretive men sat awaiting the start of the meeting. The host, a sitting Congressman from Colorado, made sure his guests stayed comfortable. For the most part, the men would not be publicly recognized by the average American.

Congressman Reaver asked the assembled group for their attention. "I would like a SITREP (situation report) from each of you. You may begin, Peter."

"Yes, Sir." Peter Billings was head of security for FacePage, America's preeminent social media platform. "To date, gentlemen, we are right on schedule, adding the fact-checking and the advisories to conservative posts have met with little or no resistance. The algorithms I have implemented allow our narrative to trend heavily in all categories. We are ready for stage two whenever I get the word."

"Peter, thanks, and good job." Thomas, can you give us your brief?"

"Yes, Sir." Thomas Wood, a venture capitalist, has a net worth of 35 billion dollars. He also has special withdrawal permissions for an estimated 100 billion dollars at his sole discretion. "As you all know, we have distributed over 10 billion dollars through shell corporations to Democracy Alliance, allowing Mr. Soros to take most of the public heat. The funding to numerous progressive groups and political figures is growing. The amount of local, state, and federal judges has grown and is showing promise, especially in the larger Democrat-held cities. I can also report that the elections of Progressive District Attorneys in our larger cities are due to our donations. Everything is on schedule."

"Thank you, Thomas. Your help is invaluable. As for Mr. Soros, that problem will be taken care of in phase two."

"Dr. Peters, are you ready for your report?" "Yes, Sir, I am." If you remember from an earlier page, Dr. Norman Peters is a brilliant scientist in nanotechnology and neuroscience. He also performed contract work for DARPA, Defense Advanced Research Projects Agency, and headed the breakthrough in brain mapping and introducing nanoparticles into the human body. He was also able to interface quantum computers with the nanoparticles enabling him to program the particles and download data retrieved from inside the body. The programming of the nanoparticles and their retrieval in concert with the quantum-based computers enables data retrieval and exploitation.

Furthermore, it allows the ability to program the nanoparticles for specific tasks within the human body. These programmed particles can be uploaded individually or in mass. Again, their vector into the human body can be achieved by various modes. In this case, it is embedded into the Covid 19 vaccine.

"As you all know, the "China Virus" is now a pandemic. That got several chuckles from the others. China looks to be the culprit from all official sources, another round of laughs. All U.S. vaccines except for the J&J vaccine use my nanoparticles as planned. Our goal is to have 80 percent of the world population have my nanoparticles vector into their bodies. That cannot happen with just the U.S. vaccines. I propose we do a demographic study of the areas worldwide that still need the nanoparticles. Once we identify those areas, we then look at marketing trends in those areas' food and beverage industries. Then we add the nanoparticles to those items. At that point, we should be well above 80 percent.

Reaver looked towards Rich Taylor, his intelligence chief, and asked, "Rich is the Doctor's assessment correct, and can we pull it off?"

Taylor said, "Dr. Peters had approached me with his idea, and I concur with his assessment. We can pull it off with some extra money to bribe the right people."

Reaver said to Dr. Peters and Rich, "Make it happen, gentleman."

"Rich, can you give us a security assessment of the mission?"

"Yes, Sir." Rich Taylor was a former intelligence officer in the U.S. Navy. He left the service as a Commander, transitioning into the Defense Intelligence Agency as an analyst. He was scouted by Congressman Reaver and left government service. "Gentlemen, all reports show our security has not been breached.

Our mission is on schedule. The narrative has taken hold, and all reactions by the government and public are progressing according to the plan."

"Great report Rich, and thank you for your discretion and vigilance. I want you to get Dr. Peters whatever he needs. Thank you all. You will be contacted when we implement phase two."

4

THE BRIEF

The President of the United States of America (POTUS) sat at the head of the conference table in the situation room, beneath the White House. He was meeting with three people. The Director of the CIA (DCI), Susan Hope, Secretary of the Department of Homeland Security Matt Price, and the Chairman of the Joint Chiefs of Staff (CJCS), General James Nolt. The topic was the Marxist insurgency that seemed to be infecting a host of large U.S. cities. The problem was political and Constitutional. The far-left Democrats who hold the majority in the house and a significant portion of the left-leaning news and social media outlets were hell-bent on blocking the President's administration at every turn, anything and everything, including lawsuits, impeachment, or outright lies. They have stopped at nothing to embarrass the President. Now it is the far-left protests in major Democratic-held cities. However, the protests have turned into riots. Rioters and protesters were demanding that the cities defund the police departments.

The President looked toward Director Hope. "Susan, can you shed some light on the origins of these riots?"

"Yes, Mr. President. It is a problem that has plagued our country for over 40 years, maybe longer. It is assuredly Marxist doctrine started by the Soviets, refined by Communist China, and controlled by the globalists. Mr. President, you understand the history as well as anybody. Still, I'd like to include some of the nuances that many are unfamiliar with. I am sure you will understand. This problem was created before World War II. The people involved, or I should say the movement involved, have been extremely patient, and as of this moment, a lot of it is starting to raise its ugly head.

As you know, Sir, these are Marxist/Globalists, but they are using Maoist tactics. These tactics have been in play for generations; our country is just now vocalizing the results of these tactics because they have been ingrained over these past decades with the PC culture and the dialectics used to narrate their ultimate goal. Constitutionally they are well within the boundaries of free speech. The mainstream media is helping them, and I feel this is my opinion. The liberalization of the media and the corporations now owns the media, and corporations are forcing the Progressive narrative on the public. All of the problems that you highlighted during your run for the Presidency and while you have been in office; whether it be immigration or draining the swamp, the Democratic infighting, and the establishment Republicans that try to stop you at every turn, the judges that try to control everything that you try to initiate, because of lawsuits they're all part of this problem whether they are knowingly contributing to it or just have been conditioned to do so. Outside forces are continually attempting to subvert our Democratic Republic system. Mr. President, the Communist Chinese, the Russian government, the Venezuelan government, the Iranian government, and North Korea all have a stake in causing a rift within our population. On the surface, they appear to be succeeding with the spread of the doctrine. In reality, it is a small percentage of Americans that are disenfranchised. The disenfranchised tend to gravitate towards the Maoist/Marxist ideology."

"Question Susan, you came up through the ranks of the CIA, you were a field officer, you were involved in covert operations, what can the CIA do from a legal standpoint within our Constitution to mitigate some of these problems? I want you to sit back and think about that answer for a few minutes while I cover other questions with my other two advisors."

The President said, "General, tell me, how do our forces look right now if we needed to go to war with one or two countries, for example?"

"Well, Sir, we couldn't engage more than one country at a time on a full-scale war. However, I do know, Sir, our war-fighting capabilities have been degraded due to defense cuts from prior administrations. So even though you have boosted our defenses, they are insufficient to be a deterrent if a war broke out now.

I will say, however, that our technological advancements can deal with multiple threats from many countries and nation-states. We will be able to neutralize the nuclear threat and

Communications and command-and-control of numerous countries, even the ones that the CIA director has just mentioned. Still, as far as boots-on-the-ground and controlling large areas of a specific country, we are unable to do that, Sir, one country at a time until the correlation of forces has been trained up."

"Question General, if we had a civil war in our country, would the military support us?"

"Well, Sir, it's been studied. The problem is the General Officer Corps, Sir."

The President said, "Please explain that, General?"

"Mr. President, as you know, prior administrations and prior congress' okayed promotions for a lot of these generals. Well, Sir, I can tell you from personal experience they are not the cream of the crop."

"Okay, General, can you identify the cream of the crop and what strategic places that they are actually in command of?"

"Yes, Sir, I can, and I can have a list for you by the end of the afternoon if that's what you would like, Sir."

"Please do that after we're done with the meeting."

"Matt, you are up to the plate. What would happen to these major cities that are run by these liberal Democrats in the case of a civil war?"

"Mr. President, we've done numerous studies on this very subject. There are multiple scenarios depending on how you want to handle the situation. Containment or offensive operations would determine the strategy and tactics we would use."

"Well, Mr. Secretary, explain to me scenario number one, containment."

"Sure, I can get into specifics or a general overview? It is your preference, Sir?"

"Give me a general concept, Matt."

"Okay, Sir, containment in a nutshell. We would cordon off all transportation in and out of the city; cut electricity, communications, and water into a city. We would allow no one to enter and allow no one to leave unless we sent in military personnel."

The President asks, "Okay, what's next?"

"Well, Sir, within two weeks, civil disorder and chaos would break out in the city. All city government, law enforcement, hospitals, and fire departments would completely break down. The gangs would take over the city. On day 30, there would be thousands, tens of thousands of deaths due to the violence and the lack of food, water, and critical infrastructure services that would not be taking place because of the cut mentioned above in power and transportation. At the end of month two, the city's population similar to Boston would be reduced to 20percent of its original population. Likewise, cities like Portland, Seattle, Spokane, Miami, Cincinnati, Cleveland, Chicago, Minneapolis, San Francisco, and Los Angeles, which is a major port for incoming and outgoing trade, will be completely decimated." Matt finished."

"Thank you for your insight, Matt." The President said.

"Back to you, Susan, what could you do that would eliminate some of this problem without us causing a civil war?"

Susan began, "Sir, we could eliminate or neutralize whoever you prefer, some of the large donors of the insurgency that are multinational, as far as the countries I'm not so sure that the CIA could infiltrate them and do that job, we could generally, but in our experience, we have somebody willing to take the reins of power. But, unfortunately, we have little time or assets to verify the right people, and we would still be taking a chance on the outcome."

The President smacked the table and spoke.

"Well, lady and gentlemen, my hands are tied constitutionally unless we have a Civil War, which I do not want! I will not have this country ruined by these Marxist, Maoist, Communist bastards that have infiltrated this country or were born here over the last several decades! So I'd like for you all to think about how we could do this legally within the Constitution without causing a Civil War if that's possible."

The CJCS spoke, "Well, Sir, I have an idea actually, it's something I've been studying for most of my career, and I'd like to bring it to your attention."

"By all means, General, go ahead." The President said.

The General did just that. "Mr. President, written within the Declaration of Independence, the founders speak of the people being able to form their government if the government has become tyrannical. Sir, no reflection upon yourself, but the swamp is about as tyrannical as you could get!"

"Please go on, General." The President said.

"Sir, my master thesis was in early American history, the Revolutionary War period. Over the past 30 years, I have war-gamed scenarios in which the American populist rises up and takes control of the tyrannical government. In all of my plans except for one, the battle becomes a long protracted war with millions killed, tens of millions homeless, and starving. Of course, the patriots eventually win, but remnants of the swamp still in power remain. Moreover, there is a reasonable probability that a foreign power might try to intercede at some point in the conflict.

As you know, Sir, your office cannot unilaterally take control of the country unless, of course, you invoke Presidential Directive 51, but that would cause civil unrest in itself. As I said earlier, all the scenarios had a high loss of life and property, except for one. The exception is a group of individuals, a large group of individual Patriots of their own volition outside of any government control or your control, Sir. Their mission is to seek out and neutralize the insurgency leaders, media members, corporate owners, or high-profile media members in television, radio, and social media, not to mention the actual CEOs and board of directors of social media platforms. By taking this approach, Mr. President, that leaves you with total plausible deniability from any real action. Constitutionally, you cannot assume that unilateral action on your own without causing a lot of death and destruction. I would say that simultaneously we could have either the CIA or the actual military neutralize a specific country's ability to intercede on behalf of the insurgents. The thing that will reduce the death toll and the destruction is using this large group. They would not engage the civilian population. In addition, the swiftness of the attacks on the target packages will lessen the overall infrastructure damage and remove the possibility of the targets inciting civil unrest or rebellion.

The actual insurgents and the patriots are the only people involved, leaving the military out of the conflict. The group that I speak of is all Patriots! As you know, Mr. President, before my promotion to this office, I was the Commander of Joint Special

Operations Command. I found several that piqued my interest with all the staff plans and contingency plans I have been privy to. With that in mind, I have vetted approximately 2,000 combat-tested Tier One Special Operators and highly trusted Patriots to do a mission like this. I have war-gamed this scenario out with my former subordinate Commanders, and all of them, to a man, believe that this will work. The key to this is your plausible deniability during the operation."

"That's very interesting, General."

But then, the CIA director asked, "May I interject something, Mr. President?"

"Of course, Susan, go ahead."

"I also have a network of former Agency employees who are willing and very capable to assist in this operation, should you find it necessary to implement it. I have 700 former CIA personnel, 500 of whom are former SOG members. The balance is electronic passive and active intercept officers. The President just smiled.

Matt added, "Sir, I also have a group of former Federal protective officers willing to do their duty. My last count was 250."

The President said, "Thank you all. I have some thinking to do. Good night."

5

REVELATION

I left work and just pulled into my driveway at about 0145. It was Tuesday morning. I had just completed my first day of work for the week. I prayed as I usually did, once or twice a day as I sat there. The prayer consisted of: "Hear O Israel the Lord is my God the Lord is one. Please bless, protect, forgive, and continue to guide Lori, Arica, Natalie, Lylah, James, Mom and Dad, Eric and Kim, and Scott and Tammy. Please forgive my sins and guide me to be a better husband, father, and follower of your word. Thank you, Lord, amen." When I finished, I felt, not heard a voice? It was like my whole body was a sound system, not just my ears. It said, "Get out of your truck and come to the rear near the tailgate." Being shocked at the moment, I just complied. After reaching the tailgate, I saw a figure standing beside the rear of my truck. I was startled and reached for the Keltic P-11 9mm in my left front pocket. Before I could pull it, my hand just froze. I could not move it. The figure said, "Relax, Michael. I AM here to see how serious you are about the prayer you just offered to me."

"What? How could you know that?" The figure stepped a few feet closer. I looked at him, her, it, I was not sure yet.

It was dressed in faded blue jeans, well-worn work boots, and a dark color hoodie-type sweatshirt with the hood over its head. The face was somewhat obscured with a not-so-long gray beard. The eyes, they were telling! They were anything but ordinary. The pupils looked like pools of fire, like from a gas range. At the moment, they were a simmering blue flame.

It said, "Are you serious about your prayers?" At this point, I thought I might be freaking out.

I said, "Yes, I am serious."

The voice said, "That is a lot to ask, for giving nothing in return."

I responded, "I know, but they are the most important people in my life." I think this is like a regular conversation, but with who?

I know I'm not dreaming. I'm getting ready to walk into the house. Now the question is, am I crazy or possibly having a conversation with an angel, God, or something else. I remembered in Exodus Mosses speaking with God. He sort of negotiated with God. Should I be so bold? Of course, I would.

I asked him, "Who are you?"

The voice said, "I AM."

I then asked, "Okay, I AM. Why me and why now?"

The voice said, "Because you asked me, and as for why now because I need you."

I'm thinking to myself, "Boy, is Lori going to freak out when I tell her about this."

I asked I AM, "How do I know you are real, a figment of my imagination, or something evil?"

I AM said, "Because of your faith in my Word and the belief in the deeds that I will perform before you."

I asked, "Why now? What can I possibly do for you?"

I AM said, "Man has become too evil. Not just evil but humanity has become self-absorbed, and the people have drifted further from me than ever before. I find it disgusting and completely intolerable because I created man in my image and gave him the ability to have free will, allowing him to choose decisions, good or bad, about his everyday life and spiritual salvation. Now I have a group of people who plan to take that choice away, leaving mankind with no choice but to follow these people's programmed orders."

I said, "What?" I watched the figure's eyes, and they became bright flames with the intensity of a blowtorch.

I AM said, "Let me finish, Michael! I have to make a decision. I need a reason to continue to bless my people. If I cannot find a good cause, I will destroy everything and start anew.

As for you, Michael, you have not followed the law as written or spoken, but when you falter, you ask for forgiveness and continue to try to redeem yourself. I heard you tell your friend Scott that you were a bad person trying to be good. This is the most essential quality for you and all my people: consistency in faith, the will not to quit, and the belief in me. You, Michael, have shown me these traits from the beginning. When you were young, your faith was strengthened by your grandmother and grandfather in your Christian upbringing, followed by your research of the Old Testament, which culminated in your conversion to Judaism. All of these actions are of faith. This was accomplished by you without any formal religious education.

I know you remember when you were 16 when you woke in the middle of the night and wondered if it was a dream? So I sent an angel to stand before you, to relay a message from me, "You are the one."

I said, "I remember. At first, I had thought I was dreaming but woke and pinched myself to ensure I was awake."

I AM said, "I know you have thought about this for many years, wondering its meaning. Before that night, I observed you, along with several others, to discern if you have the qualities I was searching for. So much of your life, Michael, I have given you subtle guidance and a few nudges to prepare you for what I have in store for you. I must tell you, Michael, with a small chuckle, I think you would say, "Give you a heads up." You, Michael, are only the second person I have spoken to directly, Mosses being the first."

I thought to myself, "What the fuck?"

I AM said, "Indeed, Michael, indeed."

I said, "I thought you spoke to several people in the Tanakh." The Tanakh is the Jewish Bible, similar to the Christian Old Testament.

I AM said, "Spoke is a relative term. I communicate to all people in some form, but speaking directly, just two, Moses and yourself."

I said, "I don't know what to say."

I AM said, "Don't worry about what to say. Just listen. I will task you and six others, whom you will direct to communicate my message to the masses and to find, interrogate and then eliminate certain people who will cause irreparable harm to your country and humanity as a whole." Go inside and go to bed now. Tell Lori of our conversation and reflect on what I said for now. I will get back to you."

I said, "Thank you, Lord, and I love you."

I went inside and lay in bed, trying to embrace everything that had just happened. Thinking to myself, I saw no face, but something was there. I just felt or heard the voice in my head and body. I'm not even sure. I know I felt calm and comfortable while everything was taking place. I just keep thinking, why me, and what will my role be?

I woke in the afternoon and readied myself to tell Lori this fantastic story.

When I saw her, I said, "Hey Pookie, remember when I told you about the person standing at the foot of my bed when I was about 16, and it told me I was the one?"

She said, "You're the one all right! You didn't tell me about any person at the foot of your bed. What are you talking about?" I know I told her, but she doesn't remember. So now, I have to explain the story to her first.

I said, "Well, when I was about 16, I was asleep in my room in the basement when I woke with a start. I saw a figure walking towards me wearing a robe with a hood on it, kind of like the garments the three wise men wore. I couldn't tell the color of the robe. I also couldn't see the face under the hood. It stopped about 10 feet away and just stood there. I even pinched myself to make sure I was awake. I stared at it for about 20 seconds, and then it said, "You are the one." That was it. It disappeared. I have always wondered about that vision even now."

Lori said, "You never told me that! Are you messing with me?"

I said, "No, it really happened."

She said, "What do you think it means?" I said, "I didn't know until last night, but I think I do now." After explaining the encounter from last night with I AM, Lori just stood looking at me.

I said, "I'm not sure what that look means?"

She said, "You're serious, aren't you?"

I said, "Yes."

She said, "I believe you. What do you think I AM wants?"

"I'm not sure yet. I'm not sure what I AM is a male, female, or what.

6

REFLECTION AND REVELATION

The President sat alone at the HMS Resolute desk within the oval office. He was thinking about his formative years as a youth. The one thing he always came back to was when he was 15 years old. The memory was still evident. He awoke in the middle of the night startled. There was a man, figure, or spirit, something at the foot of his bed. He was unable to identify clothing or a face.

The figure said, "Do not worry, I'm not here to harm you. I have a message for you. You are one of six." Just like that, the figure disappeared. As the President sat there thinking of that memory. A voice startled him. He looked up and saw a man dressed in a flowing white robe with a dark brown beard and the coldest looking ice blue eyes he had ever seen. The man said, "Do not worry; I AM the angel Gabriel. I've been tasked with sending you a message from God."

The President said, "What? He then pushed a button under the desk to alert the Secret Service. Immediately several agents entered the room. Is everything okay, Mr. President?

The angel said, "They can't see me." The President told the agents everything was fine. He said he must have accidentally hit the button. They said goodnight and left the office.

The President said to his guest, "You have my attention."

Gabriel continued, "You have been wondering about the vision you had when you were 15 and that you were one of six?"

"Yes, I have. What does it mean?"

Gabriel said, "It means that God has a mission for you, and depending on its success, it will determine the fate of your country and mankind."

The President said, "What is it that I have to do?"

Gabriel answered, "There are five others that have been chosen for the mission. I am not at liberty to divulge their identities. However, there is one man whom God has entrusted with the complete knowledge of the real mission. His name is Michael. He will speak for the Lord.

Mr. President, I will give you his particulars and suggest arranging a private meeting. Just so I know that you believe I am who I say I am, I will leave you with this. Your CIA Director, Homeland Security Secretary, and Chairman of the Joint Chiefs of Staff are all under God's grace. You can and should trust them."

7

JUST A SATURDAY NIGHT

Lori and I were sitting in our recliners watching our weekend movie when Rosie, our dog, started barking. I got up to look out the front window and saw an SUV pulling up the driveway.

I retrieved my Glock 19 and put it in the rear of my waistband, and waited for the knock at the door. I was already looking through the peephole when the doorbell rang. It appeared to be two middle-aged, white males wearing suits. They were clean-shaven with short haircuts. My initial thought was the FBI.

I asked who it was, and to my surprise, they identified themselves as agent Hill and Bell of the U.S. Secret Service. They apologized for disturbing us at the late hour but wished to forward a message to us.

Lori put on a robe, and I put on a shirt and invited the two agents in. They produced their identification and were seated.

Lori asked them if they would like a drink. They respectfully declined. Agent Hill retrieved a large manila envelope from his briefcase and handed it to me.

He said, "The President of the United States respectfully requests that you and your wife are his guests at the White House on the Friday after next, for the weekend. All logistics and expenses will be taken care of by the President. If you accept, you will be notified next Friday by phone of the time you will be picked up."

Lori said, "Wow! Are you serious?"

Hill said, "Yes, Ma'am. All of the pertinent information is inside the envelope. If you have no further questions, we will leave, have a good evening, and thank you for your hospitality."

8

KENOSHA, WISCONSIN, 90 DAYS BEFORE THE U.S. PRESIDENTIAL ELECTION

Today in Kenosha, Wisconsin, the news coverage from every major network and all but one of the cable news networks are the same. All reports say that a black man, Donnie Thomas, was shot in the back by a racist Kenosha Police patrolman. The video shows the patrolman in question grabbing Thomas's white T-shirt at about shoulder level. Thomas then attempted to enter his minivan. The patrolman then shoots Thomas in the back with eight bullets.

As a result, a riot began in Kenosha. Fires were started. Businesses were looted and destroyed. The Governor of

Wisconsin made a press statement that the officers used excessive force and should be brought to justice. As information about the shooting leaks to the public, the victim's circumstances are starting to take shape. It appears the victim's girlfriend called 911 requesting police remove her boyfriend from her home. The police department ran Thomas's information through the law enforcement database and discovered that Thomas had been convicted of domestic assault and had an outstanding felony warrant for domestic assault and sexual battery. Police and eyewitness accounts reveal that the officers first requested ID from Thomas, which he refused to show them. He was then instructed to lie on the ground to be searched for weapons, but he refused. Officers attempted to physically take Thomas to the ground. The attempt failed. Officers then used a Taser on the suspect, but he did not respond to the use of the Taser. The suspect then walked to his vehicle and attempted to enter the driver's door. At that point, one of the officers grabbed the suspect somewhere around the left shoulder by his T-shirt. Another officer saw the suspect attempting to reach for an open lock-blade knife and shouted, "knife!"

The officer who grabbed the suspect's T-shirt saw the knife and fired 8 shots into the suspect's back. This information was obtained after the riots started. In its infinite wisdom, the media jumped to conclusions causing the unrest. The Kenosha riot was not the first riot but a part of several riots in Chicago, Seattle, and New York. This did not include the ongoing riot in Portland, which had lasted for the past 70 days. The Portland Mayor refused to allow law enforcement officers to quell the violence. Currently, U.S. Marshals are guarding the Federal Court House.

The rioters made several failed attempts to burn the building down.

9

ANOTHER MESSAGE

After arriving home from work, and sat in my truck for a moment, looking at my cell phone. That is when I felt a voice not heard, but I felt the voice saying, "I'm here, come to the back of your truck."

I got out and went to the rear of my truck and saw an individual dressed the same as before; dark jeans, boots, and a dark-colored hoodie with the hood up. I still couldn't distinguish the facial features, but the eyes were unmistakable. The pupils in the eyes looked like the flames in a gas stove on low, blue flickers dancing within the small orbs.

I AM said, "Michael, are you ready?"

"Yes, Lord, I am."

"Good. I have a lot of information for you and don't worry, you will recall all of it. That is my will."

"Yes, Lord."

I AM said, "I have had messengers reveal themselves to several people who will help in your mission. One is the President of the United States. That is why you were invited to the White House. He has three people from who he requested counsel, the Director of Central Intelligence, the Secretary of Homeland Security, and the Chairman of the Joint Chiefs of Staff. All three proposed a plan to neutralize Senators and Congress members who have been leading your country on this Godless pursuit of Marxism, using it as a means to achieve a one-world government.

They also plan to neutralize the corporate heads of all media formats, including social media and some of the TV anchors of these Marxist media outlets. In addition, the leaders that finance these Marxist groups and the individual leaders of various groups and rioters will also be targeted."

I said, "And he agreed to that?"

"No. The President is taking it under advisement. The angel Gabriel I sent as a messenger told the President that those three advisers could be trusted."

I asked, "Lord, I have a question?"

"Please continue, Michael."

"In reading Jewish commentary, it has been said that Mosses was not allowed into the Promised Land because he killed one of Pharos guards. Is that true?"

I AM said, "No, that is not true. It was just Moses' time to come home. Michael, my wrath is famous throughout history. It is imperative to me to save my people if possible. Your country's people have been faithful believers in me for centuries. In the last 100 years, man has only started to slowly erode the faith in the many religions that believe in me. Now we have many countries and groups that think it is time to destroy my people. I will not let that happen. I could take care of all of this myself, but I want proof that my believers still retain that faith and will help me where they can. Tell the President that I sent you to ease his mind about the horrific things he must do. Tell him that he need not worry about China, Russia, Iran, Turkey, or any other country that he feels is a threat to the United States. I will take care of that problem. I have also had a messenger sent to a current Chief in your Navy Seal DEVGRU. You may deploy him as you see fit. There will be three religious men and a specialist in rebuilding my Temple; I will arrange for you to meet them all. Explain to them my needs, and if they are faithful men of God, they should find a way to communicate my message to the masses. The ones that do not believe in my word will perish. As for the President's plan, I have no problem with killing those people and will not hold the individuals who do it as guilty of blood sin. They are warriors in my name.

You must make sure the President understands that his plan must begin before I intercede with the other countries. On his part, it is a matter of faith in me. Conversely, on my part, it is a test of faith that the President will do the right thing. I will tell you that several unknown groups are behind this movement and are responsible for the Covid 19 virus. They are currently in phase one of the takeover of your country and the blasphemy of my word. The leader of the group is Congressman Reaver. His plan in phase two is the takeover of your country, but more importantly, it is the vaccine for Covid 19. Dr. Norman Peters is a brilliant scientist in nanotechnology and neuroscience. He worked for DARPA, Defense Advanced Research Projects Agency, and headed the breakthrough in brain mapping and introducing nanoparticles into the human body.

Dr. Peters was also able to interface quantum computers with the nanoparticles enabling him to program the particles and download data retrieved from inside the body. With this technology, he will be able to program humanity. Four men report to him. I will give you the necessary information on all of them. As for Congressman Reaver, you cannot kill him when you find him. He is the key to finding the major world financiers behind this entire despicable plan. You, Michael, must be there when they capture him, and you, Michael alone, must interrogate him for the needed information. It will not be easy. You may have to use extreme measures. It will be a tremendous burden on you, but you must do it. I cannot allow someone I do not have direct contact with to gather this information. Once you obtain the names of the people involved, you must dispose of Reaver. I do not want anyone else extracting additional information from him. Do you understand?"

"Yes, Lord. Lord?"

"Yes, Michael"

"Who will protect and take care of Lori, Arica, and Natalie and her family while I'm away?"

"I will, Michael. I think the President will want to keep them at Camp David out of the public eye. I assure you they will all be safe. As for your protection, I will be with you, and I'll bless your Mezuzah. (A Mezuzah is a decorative vessel mounted on the doorpost of your home or worn as a necklace. Within it is small parchment scrolls containing 713 words from Deuteronomy 6:4-9 and 11:13-21; within these verses, there is a literal commandment to "Inscribe them upon the doorposts of your home and upon your gates.")

It will be your strength. Do not take action on the information you obtain from Congressman Reaver. I will contact you and instruct you on how to proceed."

"Lord, I have another question, just to make sure I'm clear on your message."

The Lord said, "Ask it, Michael."

I said, "From everything I have read, and have been taught, whether it is Christianity, Judaism, or Islam, all are monotheistic religions and all worship you Lord. Christianity and Islam have an intermediary between you and the people, Jesus and Mohammad respectively, and Judaism is who you made a covenant. So, are all the other people who have different religions or people who have never known any religion at risk for your wrath? Lord, you said yourself that you alone know the true hearts of mankind. I believe and have the faith that you, Lord, have limitless wisdom and power. As the ultimate judge, is it fair to punish those who have not truly heard or understand your word?"

The Holy of Holies said, "Michael, the three religions you spoke of know my word. The problem is man has interpreted my word to fit his needs. Man has created religions with many deities other than me, man has and is worshiping the earth and nature as a Deity, man is worshiping evil and Satan, witchcraft, and themselves if given enough power!" I noticed I AM's eyes; they changed from a simmering blue flame into an intense orange fire.

"I must cleanse humanity of this rot." I listened to his words trying to understand his frustration.

41

I said, "Lord, I know that I can't fathom even a small portion of your plan. Is it not the leaders of all the religions, good or bad, who have created their personalities, charisma, or outright dominance over the wills of people? Are not leaders of religion to blame for your word not being spread properly? You, Lord, made us in your image, but we are human, imperfect in flesh and will. Isn't that why you allow us to ask you for forgiveness and grant it if you feel sincere? Forgive me, Lord, but how can you punish imperfect humanity if they are taught your word by imperfect men?" I understand that when Moses and the Hebrews made their exodus from Egypt when Moses trekked up the mountain to receive your word and the stone tablets, you spoke to the assembled masses. Was that the only time you talked directly to a group of people?"

The Lord said, "Yes, Michael, the only time. All other conversations were with Moses and you."

I was worried about his potential anger being directed towards me because of the direction I was steering our conversation. I thought to myself, "If he was going to destroy all of humanity, what did I have to lose by asking the question?"

So, I asked, "Lord, why not communicate to all of humanity your intentions and requirements. This will counter all of man's interpretations of your word and the knowledge for those who have not heard your word. After that, if you are not satisfied with the results, you would have no reason to regret your punishment." I AM listened. Now his eyes started to return to a constant blue flame.

He said, "I will consider your words Michael. Is there anything else you'd like to get off your chest?"

I said, "Lord, one more question and a favor?"

"Continue, Michael."

"Lord, I don't know in what capacity I represent you when speaking to the six? Am I a prophet or the Messiah?"

The Holy of Holies said, "If I were your father and asked to relay an important message to another person who would save others' lives would you do it?

"Yes, I would."

I AM continued, "The reason you would do it is that you love, trust, and have faith in your father. Conversely, your father chose you to relay the important message for the same reasons. So, there is your answer, Michael. What is the favor?"

I asked, "Lord, you know I love Lori, and I'm blessed to have her in my life. However, it breaks my heart to see her in pain every day. She is a very good person and deserves to live her life without all of her body's defects that put her in pain every day; can you bless her and stop her pain?

The Lord said, "This I can do, Michael, the other request I'll have to think about."

I said, "Thank you, Lord.

10

DILEMMA

Imam Kamal Bari had just come from an audience with the leaders of the Revolutionary Council. They ordered him to Lebanon to teach the recruits within Hezbollah the inspired words of the Prophet Mohammad. The leaders insisted Bari's lessons be introduced to the recruits. This included spreading the jihad to the infidels and how the Koran demands it. He was trapped. The only thing left to him was prayer. Bari rose from his desk and walked dejectedly to the closet to get his prayer rug. After retrieving the rug, he turned in surprise to see a woman in a flowing robe. It was a deep rich blue. Her eyes were emerald green. Her shoulder-length hair was raven black, and she had a smooth cream-colored complexion. He was speechless.

She said, "Hello Kamal Bari, I am Jophiel. I have a message for you from God."

Bari asked, "Are you the angel who helps the Archangel Michael battle evil in the spiritual realm?"

"Yes, I am. Our Lord has a mission for you. You will meet with two other men of God, and the Lord has chosen a man named Michael to direct you, men of God, to spread his word."

Bari began to cry." How can I do this? I am being forced to Lebanon by the Revolutionary Council?"

Jophiel said, "Have faith Kamal Bari and please take my hand."

CPO "Midas" Johnny Black was sitting on his couch after a long training evolution. He was about to pull the tab on his first of many beers when he heard a knock at his front door. Midas noticed an official U.S. Navy sedan in his driveway. As part of Midas's personal security procedures he has used for the past two decades, he placed his sig P226 in the small of his back holster. The man exiting the car appeared to be a full Captain in dress whites. When the Captain approached the door, Midas greeted him with "Good afternoon, Sir." The Captain replied, "Good afternoon to you, Chief." The Captain pulled an ID case from his blouse to show Midas. The identification stated the Captain was part of the Naval Criminal Investigation Service.

Midas asked, "How can I assist the captain?"

"It's better if we go inside, Chief."

"Yes, Sir, come in, please. Have a seat, Captain. Can I get you something to drink?"

"No, I'm fine, Chief. I'll get to the point, Chief. I know in your line of work, your powers of observation are keen. I want you to remember that in the next few moments. Have you ever discussed the vision you had when you were fifteen regarding being one of six with anyone else?"

Midas became instantly alert.

"No, I haven't, Captain, and how do you know about it?"

The Captain said, "Chief, it was disingenuous of me posing as a Captain." As he was speaking, the man changed his appearance. The Captain said, "Please stay calm, Chief; I have a message for you from God. I am the angel, Raphael. I'm assuming you have a pistol ready to deploy? Let me explain. Normally I would have just appeared before you, but somehow, I think I may have been shot. I was not concerned for my safety, just the noise it would have generated. I wanted to keep this as private as possible."

Midis finally spoke, "What the fuck?"

"Midas, the Lord has a critical mission for you. Five others are part of the six. There is also one other to who all of you will report. His name is Michael. He will be visiting the President of the United States this Friday. You are to accompany him and his wife to meet the President. You will then accompany him to a meeting with the Director of CIA, the Secretary of Homeland Security, and the Chairman of the Joint Chiefs of Staff. Michael will brief you on your mission. At that point, he is your only chain of command. I will arrange travel information to meet Michael this Thursday at 1300 hours. Do you have any questions, Midas?"

"Yes, can you explain what this is all about?"

"The angel said, "I can only tell you that this mission will determine the survival of not only your country but the survival of the human race. Michael will fully brief you on the specifics."

Rabbi Tovia Cohan was in Jerusalem, Israel, sitting at his desk in the office of the Jewish Outreach Program. The Outreach Program is the culmination of the Rabbis' religious studies. Tovia's interest was in reacquainting Jews who have been the victims of conversion by missionaries or cults. He feels that Messianic Judaism does a disservice to Judaism as a whole. Tovia engages Christian and Messianic Jewish rabbis in public debates over their interpretation of the Torah or the Old and New Testaments. Tovia was thinking back to his teens in Brooklyn when he had a message from an angel. He was told he was "one of six."

This is what drove him to serve the Lord all these years. Still, in thought, a man spoke to him. He didn't hear anyone come into the room. He looked up and saw a figure in a long white robe, long black hair, and a neatly trimmed beard. The man said. "Do not worry, Rabbi, I am the angel Ariel. I bring you a message and a mission from God." Tovia smiled, and tears ran down his cheeks.

Tovia said, "I am so happy to hear this. How may I help Elohim?"

"Rabbi, the human race is in the midst of troubling times. Elohim has chosen you and five others to help save humanity. Rabbi, you and two other religious leaders, a Christian, Franklin Ham, and an Islamic clergyman and scholar Imam Kamal Bari, will be tasked with getting a message out to the masses. All of you will meet with a man named Michael, whom Elohim has trusted his instructions."

The Rabbi asked, "Who is Michael."

The angel said, "Well, Michael is an ordinary man. As a young man, he converted to Judaism, and you think, why Michael? I only know that Elohim has chosen Michael to lead this mission because he has faith in him. That is all I need to know and all you need to know."

The Rabbi said, "That's good enough for me."

"As for you, Rabbi, I must get you to Washington D.C., where your group will meet with Michael."

11

CHINESE DECEPTION

The three ministers without portfolios sat secretly in an undisclosed location inside the People's Republic of China. The ministers' names are Chen Liu, Fan Chao, and Ru Ma, all are specialists in the subversion of foreign countries, psychological warfare/propaganda, and cyber warfare. The ministers' have no background in any of the specialties mentioned above. The ministers' are Princelings of the Party's Crown Princes, descendants of prominent and influential senior communist officials in the People's Republic of China. It is an informal and often derogatory categorization to signify those benefiting from nepotism and cronyism by analogy with crown princes in hereditary monarchies. However, today, they are about to reap the harvest from their multi-decades of work. They didn't start the subversion of the United States. The Soviets did. The Soviets began the subversion in the late 1920s, only to add resources and propaganda in the late 1940s. In the 1960s, due to the American liberal's hatred of the government's stance on the Vietnam War, considerable inroads were made with the American youth in those times. These youth grew into adulthood in the 1970s and 1980s. In the 1990s and 2000s, these people began to climb the ladder in their respective professions. Allowing them the freedom to hire and promote like-minded people. This was KGB's most outstanding achievement. They had penetrated multiple social institutions: The media, university professors, lawyers, doctors, and people at various levels of local, state, and federal government. Everything was going as planned. However, things drastically changed when the Soviet Union dissolved. At that point, all that was left were a few hardcore KGB intelligence officers without a job.

The Chinese intelligence community saw an opportunity and seized it. These three ministers were instrumental in recruiting several former KGB intelligence officers whose job was to control agents in the United States, provide funding and propaganda, and foment an atmosphere of dehumanization and discontent among the American population. With the ability of the Chinese government to spend much more money for this cause than the Soviets and the economic powerhouse that China has become, the number of lobbyists and not-for-profit organizations skyrocketed, and the control of power over America's political elite became immeasurable. With the upset election of the Presidency nearly four years ago and the President's Reversal of trade/tariffs with China, the banning of the nuclear weapons treaty with Iran, these men knew they had to act. China has a very close relationship with Iran. Although, it is not publicly reported by the media. Due to America's tight sanctions, Iran's economy is dangerously teetering on total collapse. Iran needs money and weapons technology, while conversely, China needs an inexpensive source of oil and the plausible deniability that Iran's terrorist-affiliated organizations can afford them. The immediate goal of the three was to seduce the Iranian religious zealot Ayatollah Ali Hosseini Khamenei into selling the developed Covid 19 virus for vast sums of money and weapons. The only actual risk Iran would take was using a small detachment of their Quds force soldiers to train progressive elements within the American social justice movement, so they thought.

12

HOOKING THE FISH

Congressman Reaver waited in his penthouse suite at the Ka'anapali Beach Hyatt Residence Club Maui for his visitor. He didn't have to wait long. A knock at his door told him his visitor had arrived. Reaver opened the door to welcome his benefactor. The man before him was small in stature and very solid. He looked twenty years younger than his fifty-eight years, with jet black closely cropped hair and a clean-shaven face. The man's name is Xiang Kao. Unbeknownst to Reaver, Kao is a Colonel in one of the PLA's secret special operations groups, under the command of the General Political Department, which controls the "Three Warfare" of media. These include public opinion war, psychological operations, and legal war. Kao's cover for this operation is to portray an advanced man for a multi-national global concern, whose goals are to advance the progressive ideology through various non-governmental organizations with discrete untraceable funding. "Welcome, Mr. Kao. I hope you had a pleasant flight. Can I get you a drink?"

Kao said, "Congressman, please call me Xiang, and yes, a drink would be fine whatever you're having would be great." They both settled in comfortable chairs with their drinks.

Xiang said smiling, "Congressman, my polling, and PR geniuses' have come up with a truly, innovative grassroots extravaganza of epic proportions. We have done the polling all across the country and have listened to the people on the street. But unfortunately, the BLM movement is losing support. Their support is lower than before the George Boyd murder. Our problem is the violence and looting sprouting from our protests. What we need to do is set an example for the American people. Show the world how peaceful protesting is done by the people who invented it."

Reaver said, "Okay, Xiang, explain it to me."

"We need a historic civil-rights march. Let's take all of the civil rights leaders of the 1960s, along with the leaders in Congress, the Senate, religious leaders, and community organizers. We can allow them to mentor the new generation of civil rights activists. We can pair the veteran civil rights leaders with the new "woke crowd," for example, the freshman Congresswoman's group, the Squad, BLM members, and a huge group of university progressives helping in our cause. This will enable us to have the largest social justice march in our nation's history. The best news of all is that some of the donors love the idea and are willing to bankroll the whole thing."

"That's a hell of an idea! I can sell it if you can have the donors donate some additional money to the political campaigns and the religious leaders' churches."

Xiang smiled and said, "Congressman, I think I can guarantee the donors will gladly donate the additional money. The donors have only one condition. The protest march must be 9 days before the election on Saturday, October 24th in Washington D.C."

Reaver said, "I can make it happen."

13

MIDAS

Lori and I were at home when the phone rang. Lori answered it and said a polite man asked to speak with Michael. Lori told me I had a phone call.

I picked up and said, "Hello."

A man asked, "Michael?"

"I said yes."

"Michael, this is CPO Johnny Black. I was instructed to contact you."

"Hi Chief, how are you?"

"I'm fine. I'm at the airport now and wanted to check in with you."

I said, "Great! Grab your gear. I'll pick you up at departures in 30 minutes. I'll be in a 2014 gray F-150. We'll get some chow at the house." Midas said, "See you then."

I pulled up to the departure gate of the John Glenn International airport after a thirty-five-minute drive. A man waved at me from the curb.

I rolled down the passenger window and said, "Chief?"

He said, "Yes."

I said, "Throw your gear in." Then, as we were driving, I introduced myself, saying, "Michael Stone, Chief, nice to meet you."

He said, "Call me Midas. Is it Mike or Michael?"

"Either is fine."

"Okay, Mike, I don't know about you, but this whole thing is... I don't even have words to describe it. Can you give me a SITREP on what's going on?"

"Well, Midas, this isn't a sea story, and I'm just as surprised as you. So I'll give the scoop as I know it. First of all, I'm just your average American. I did four years active in the Marine Corps as an MP, ended up NCOIC of the base SWAT team, and instructed limited anti-terrorism measures for 8th Marines before their deployment to Beirut after the barracks bombing. After that, I returned to my job with Roadway Express as a Teamster. When my girls were three and five, I started Shorin Ryu karate classes and practiced for 18 or so years, attaining the rank of Yon Dan. Later I became an NRA pistol instructor and studied and obtained my General Amateur radio license. I'm not super religious, but I believe and pray every night. So let me ask you a question? Did you as a teen experience a vision or a spectral visit in the night? Did it tell you that you are one of six?"

Midas reluctantly replied, "Yes, I did, exactly that. What I saw last week just blew me away. I'm in my mobile home drinking a beer, and I see this staff car pull up and out pops a Captain, Navy type. He shows me his ID; he's NCIS. So, I invite him in, and he completely transforms before my eyes as I'm talking to him. This dude is dressed in a BC-era robe and has long hair and a beard. He says he's an angel here to deliver a message from God, I shit you not."

"Chief, I'm not one to one-up a story, but I can't help myself. Check this out. After work, I just pulled in my driveway about 0135, and I felt not heard this voice. It asked me if I was serious about my prayers and then told me to get out of the truck and come around to the tailgate. I go back and there and a figure dressed in blue Jeans, work boots, and a dark-colored hoodie with the hood up. I can't make out the face, but the eyes I'll never forget. The pupils were pools of fire like blue flames; I asked who it was. Its response was, I AM. He spoke of my vision as a teen, and that he had nudged me some through life and that I was the one who would help guide six others in a mission to save our country and humanity as a whole."

Midas said, "You're fucking serious, aren't you?"

I said, "Yep, fucking A, Skippy."

Midas asked, "So, what is my role in this mission?"

"Well, Midas, for now, I'll need your situational awareness and support because when we go to D.C. to meet the President and two cabinet members plus the Chairman of the Joint Chiefs of Staff, I think I'll need it."

When we arrived at the house, it was packed. My two daughters, Arica and Natalie, Natalie's husband James, and my sweet granddaughter, "Little Bit," Lylah, were all there. After introductions, I showed Midas where he would be sleeping. At dinner, I explained to everyone that Lori, me, and Midas would be leaving for Washington D.C. tomorrow afternoon. I didn't get into great depth about the real reasons for the trip. I did say that I was concerned about everyone's safety. There were many questions. I was starting to get pissed. I got up and asked James to join me. When we were alone,

I said, "Look, the bottom line is, do you trust me?"

James said, "Yes."

I said, "Okay. I can't tell you everything yet, but I will. I told James that the girls, Lylah, and he may be taken to a safe place by U.S. Marshals. He needed to have everyone pack some bags as if they were going on vacation for a couple of weeks and to make sure the adults were armed." He looked at me reluctantly and said, "He would take care of it. He asked if his parents were in any danger."

I said, "They will be fine. If I think that there is even a remote chance that they will be in danger, I'll have them protected too." Then, feeling better, James said, "Thanks."

When everybody settled in for bed, Lori and I had some quiet time.

I asked, "Is everything okay?"

She said, "Yes, but the kids were nervous." So I told her what I had told James.

She asked, "What the story with Midas was?"

I said, "Well, he had the same experience I had when he was in his teens. He also had an angel appear before him last week saying he was one of six and to meet with me before we go to Washington."

Lori hugged me and said, "This all so surreal."

I laughed and said, "I bet you never thought we would be part of something like this?"

She said, "No, it never entered my mind, but I still love you."

14

PRE-OPS PLANNING

General Nolt decided if the President was possibly considering his plan, he should meet with his five subordinate commanders of the so-called "Patriot Force." They were meeting at a farmhouse on 500 acres. This farm is in an undisclosed location in North Carolina. The commanders were given the basic breakdown of the personnel and how the assets were to be used.

His orders were as follows: "Gentleman, your men will be deployed in the following manner. There will be ten, 200 man company size units commanded by a Delta O-5 Lt. Colonel or DEVGRU Commander. Each company will have five 40-man platoons, commanded by a Delta O-3 Captain or DEVGRU Lieutenant; the platoons will be divided into 5 eight-man teams, all tier-one shooters. In addition, each platoon will have 20 former CIA signals intelligence, communications specialists, intelligence analysts, case officers, and or (SOG) Special Operations Group paramilitary officers to provide support.

If we run into local, state, or federal law enforcement, we will have 4 man/woman teams per platoon of former DHS personnel to run interference for the ops. They will give us cover should we need it."

"To supplement our forces if and when we may need them are 20 legitimate patriotic Militias across the country, approximately 4,000 strong. These are commanded by former Special Operations personnel loyal to the cause. They will be used as a blocking force, or in the case of targets evading the blocking force, they will be used as trackers. Each of our 10 Companies and the 20 militias will be spaced strategically throughout the lower 48 states."

The General then said, "Men, I must express to you this mission is in the planning stage only. If I decide to give the go order, you will be contacted through secure communications channels with the frag order. This is a profound action we are preparing for. We have the Constitution on our side, as well as the oath you all took to preserve and protect it, as you all know. I want you to go back to your people and plan detailed direct action scenarios on the primary, secondary, and tertiary target packages. Men, get your people trained up. Questions will be entertained if and when we execute the mission. You are dismissed." The General was now satisfied that if the President Green-lighted the mission, the General's men would be prepared.

15

DEPARTURE AND ARRIVAL

At 0700, the phone rang. Lori answered it. After a couple of minutes, she came into the dining room, where everyone was eating breakfast.

I said, "Who was it, honey?"

She said, "It was a man from the Secret Service. He said he and two other Secret Service agents and three U.S. Marshals would be here to pick us up at 0830."

I said, "Marshals too?"

Midas responded, "I'm sure the Marshals are here to protect your family." At that point, everyone started talking. Lori and I looked at each other, and she gave me a slight head nod.

I said, "Listen up, everyone! I want you to listen to me. Don't ask questions, just listen. I will answer your questions when time permits. When I was a teen, I had a spectral figure come to me late one night at the foot of my bed. It said,' You are the one.' It then vanished."

Everyone was just looking at me. I continued, "A couple of weeks ago, after work in our driveway, I was contacted, saw, and talked to, I AM. To make it simple, it was God. He told me six others were chosen to assist me in saving our country and humanity. I don't know why he chose me. He said I wasn't a great Jew, but I kept trying. I couldn't see his face. He was dressed in blue jeans, leather work boots, and a dark hoodie with the hood up. His eyes were like two orbs of fire, dancing blue flames like a gas stove. That is all I can say for now. I'm going to meet the other five chosen people. Midas is number six."

Arica asked, "Who are you, Midas?"

Midas replied, "My name is Johnny Black. I'm a Navy Chief Petty Officer. I belong to a Naval Special Warfare Unit; you probably know the unit called Seal Team Six. I had someone visit me in my teens and inform me I was one of six. Then, several days ago, an angel appeared before me in my living room and told me that God had a mission for me and to meet with your father, and he would give me further instructions." Everyone's eyes grew wide.

I asked James, "Do you have everyone's bags packed and ready?"

He said, "Yes. They are already in the garage."

Two late-model gray Chevy vans and two black Chevy Suburbans pulled into the driveway. The six men introduced themselves and produced identification with badges. The lead Marshal explained that the family would be transported to John Glenn International Airport and board a government Gulfstream, their final destination at Camp David. The Marshal noticed the bags and told us that all of our needs beyond what might be in the bags would be taken care of by the President. The lead Secret Service Agent explained that Lori and I would be driven to the airport, flown to Washington, D.C., and escorted to the White House to meet the President.

I said, "This is Chief Petty Officer John Black. He will be accompanying Mrs. Stone and me." The agent was pleasant and excused himself to make a phone call. He returned two minutes later smiling. He said, "The boss said, give Mr. Stone whatever he asks for."

I said, "Thank you, agent." Then, we hugged and kissed the girls and said our temporary goodbyes.

16

THE IRANIAN CONNECTION

The supreme leader, Ali Hosseini Khamenei, sat in his Spartan office thinking about his alliance with Chen Liu, the Chinese minister without portfolio. It was a cold day in December 2019. The meeting was right in this very office. The man was a Godless infidel, to be sure, but his proposed plan left his country with a lot to gain with minimal risk. The Great Satan had reneged on its treaty with Iran and added sanctions to his country, causing it to collapse financially. Therefore, when a Communist spy within our biological research group reported our success in engineering the Covid-19 virus, naturally, the Chinese approached us. The financial support they offered was immense and badly needed. The plan was to give the Chinese the virus sample to make it more virulent, raise the mortality rate to between 20-and-40 percent, and then deploy it in the U.S. at an undetermined time in the future. The Chinese paid Iran 100 billion dollars for the virus with the agreement that Iran would supply Quds Force personnel for the training of Maoist groups forming in America under the guise of a social justice movement. The Supreme Leader believed the terms favorable towards Iran, allowing for minimal exposure to detection and maximum financial reward. The virus and money changed hands, and the Quds Force cadre started their clandestine insurgency training. In February 2019, the careless infidel Chinese had somehow allowed the virus to escape their bio lab in Wuhan before the virus had been engineered to a higher mortality rate. What is done is done, Insha'Allah. The Supreme Leader picked up the phone and told his assistant to allow his Quds Force commander to enter the office.

General Esmail Ghaani entered the room and said, "As-salamu Alaykum, Supreme Leader."

"Wa alaykumu salām," replied the Supreme Leader.

"How may I be of service?" questioned the General.

"I'd like a status report on your men in Central America.," stated the holy man.

"Yes, Sir!" the General bellowed. "Sir, as you ordered, we have two twenty-man teams. All of which are experts in recon, small weapons, hand-to-hand combat, and explosives. These men are highly motivated and faithful followers of Allah. The men have been training the American insurrectionists. They have finished training and are ready to deploy into the United States whenever you give the order, Supreme Leader."

17

WASHINGTON D.C. THE HAY-ADAMS HOTEL

The three men sat at a table in the "Off the Record" restaurant, just looking at each other. They had never met before, and only one man's name was familiar to the other two.

The Reverend Franklin Ham was the first to speak. He said, "Gentlemen, let me introduce myself, my name is Franklin Ham, and I believe we three are here right now for the same reason, Divine Providence. Who might you Gentleman be?" An older man who was clearly uncomfortable spoke next. "I am Imam Kamel Bari. I have traveled quite a long distance on the wings of an angel, it seems." Finally, the last man said, "It is a pleasure to meet both of you. My name is Rabbi Tovia Cohen, and I believe you are correct, Reverend Ham.

As the three holy men ate their breakfast, they spoke of their lives. They traded stories of how the angels contacted them, how they were told as teens that they were one of six. The Imam's story was much more dramatic than the other two. He was actually brought here on the wings of angels. Though they didn't speculate, they all wondered who the other three were. The Imam asked, "Do either of you know who is paying for our rooms? This hotel is the most lavish place I have ever seen. I don't know about you two, but I could never afford to stay here, and besides, I only have Iranian rials in my wallet." The other two men smiled, not out of malice. It was funny because the Iranian rial was down in value to the dollar. It took 300,000 rials to equal one U.S. dollar on the black market anyway. The Rabbi said, "Do not worry, my friend, the angel who appeared before me said all of the expenses would be taken care of. By whom, I do not know."

Ham asked, "Does anyone know who Michael is? Or what he may have in store for us?" The other two had no idea.

"There is only one thing that all three of us have in common, God or Allah in your case, Kamel. It is the only thing that our various regions completely agree upon," the Rabbi said.

Ham said, "It makes sense. I guess all we can do is wait to be contacted by Michael or another angel" The men agreed.

18

THE WHITE HOUSE OVAL OFFICE

The President sat in a chair across from the fireplace while the CJCS sat to his right on a couch. The DCI and the Secretary of Homeland Security sat on the sofa to the President's left. He started the conversation with a question. "How religious are you three? I'm not trying to pry into your personal lives, but it will have some bearing on how you receive the information a man I have joining us in the situation room will be giving us."

The General spoke first, "Mr. President, it is a personal question. I have throughout my entire career been able to keep my beliefs separate from my troops, superiors, politicians, and especially the media, but to answer your question, Sir, I am a Christian of no denomination but pray to the Almighty as often as I can. I believe that if it was not for the Almighty, this country would have never been formed."

Michael F. Decker

The Secretary of Homeland Security spoke next, "Mr. President, my circumstances are similar to that of the Generals. I am a Christian as well, but I'm Catholic. I, too, believe that our country's founding was due to divine intervention." The CIA Director was last. She said, "Mr. President, I'm also very religious.

Moreover, I am Jewish. You will not find anything in the public record to support this, but I assure you it is true. I also believe that our country's birth and destiny are due to the people's belief in the Almighty, not necessarily a specific religion. "The President listened and finally spoke. " Thank all of you for your candor; there was no right or wrong answer to my question. My own beliefs are similar to yours, but the focus on my beliefs is not what they should be, that is, until lately. This is what my original question is about. You see, several weeks ago, I was approached by an angel. Yes, an angel in this very office.

I was startled when I saw him. I pressed the emergency button under my desk, and Secret Service agents flooded the office. They saw no one, yet the angel still sat there. He told me while the agents were in the room that he couldn't be seen by anyone but me. At that point, I told the agents I accidentally hit the button. They acknowledged my answer and said goodnight. The angel then tells me about something that happened when I was a teen, which no one knows. I had a figure appear before me while I was sleeping. The spectral being, which I still cannot describe, tells me I am one of six. It then vanished. This angel sitting before me in the Oval Office tells me that God has a mission for me and five others, who I can't identify, to save our country and humanity. The angel said that I was to meet with a man named Michael, and he would reveal to me the mission from

70

God. The angel also told me that the three of you presented a plan to me, the same strategy we discussed in the situation room and that I should follow it. Okay, people, if there are no objections and everybody agrees, the 25th Amendment doesn't need to be activated. We will meet our mystery man Michael in the situation room at 1900." They all agreed.

19

JOINT BASE ANDREWS, 1200 HOURS

Lori was seated and looking around. She said, "This airplane is very nice."

So I asked Midas, "What kind of jet is this?"

"It's a Gulfstream G5, an extremely well-designed aircraft platform," Midas replied.

I asked, "What type of training have you had on it?" Midas answered, "I'm rated to fly one, and my team has done hostage take-down evolutions on them. I've even HAHO (high altitude high opening) jumped from them. There is a hatch in the deck."

I asked Lori, "What do you think, Pookie? Want to jump from an excellent flying jet?"

She just rolled her eyes. Then she said, "Hey, are we dressed properly to go to the White House?" I looked at Midas, and he shrugged.

The Secret Service special agent next to us said, "You look wonderful, Mrs. Stone, nothing to worry about."

Lori smiled and said, "Thank you, agent."

I couldn't help myself and said to the agent, "Suck ass!" Everyone laughed.

After landing, we were transported in black Chevy Suburbans to the White House. We entered the White House through the entrance in the South Portico. We were met and introduced to three other Secret Service Special agents, one of whom was a woman, the lead agent on the President's protection detail. She escorted us forward through the Blue Room and then left at the hall across from it. We then entered into the West Wing of the White House. We finally entered a smaller room called the President's Room, now used as a private dining room for the President, while working in the West Wing. We sat there while the lead agent left through another door. Lori looked at the embroidered cloth napkins with the Presidential seal on them.

I said, "That's our tax dollars at work, honey."

She said, "Yes, but see how nice they are." Just then, the door opened, and the President walked through. Midas and I stood up at attention; Lori just sat there.

The President smiled and said, "At ease, gentleman. I wager you two were prior military. Am I correct?"

I said, "Mr. President, I am a former Marine. Allow me to introduce myself, my wife, and my colleague. My name is Michael Stone. Mike is fine if you prefer, and this is my wife, Lori."

The President gently shook her hand and said, "It is a pleasure to meet you, Lori." He shook my hand next and asked who my colleague was.

Midas spoke up and said, "Sir, Chief Petty Officer Johnny Black, Naval Special Warfare Group."

The President shook his hand and said, "Nice to meet you, Chief."

I said, "Sir, Midas, sorry, the Chief is on the Teams, DEVGRU, and is one of the six like you, Sir."

The President said, "Please sit everyone and let's eat some lunch. The food is excellent here." A Filipino steward walked in and took our orders. The President asked about the other four in our little group as we waited. Three of them should be across the street staying at the Hay-Adams, and the fourth was in Jerusalem.

The President asked, "Should they be here?"

I said, "Sir, that is up to you, but I was thinking about possible leaks here in the White House, and it might be more prudent if we relocated to Camp David where there would be fewer prying eyes, besides that is where the rest of my family is."

He thought about it for a few seconds, looked toward his principal agent, and asked, "Andrea, can you arrange that?"

She said, "Yes, Mr. President."

He thought for a moment and told Andrea to contact the CJCS, DCI, and the Secretary of Homeland Security and tell them they would be accompanying us to the retreat.

"Yes, Sir, I'll arrange it now." The President asked me to give Andrea the names of the three men, which I did. We ate lunch, and the President arranged a tour of the White House for us with a very knowledgeable Navy steward. He said he had

74

some business to attend to and would meet us at Camp David in a few hours.

Michael F. Decker

20

NAVAL SUPPORT FACILITY
THURMONT (CAMP DAVID)

True to the President's word, we landed uneventfully at
the designated helicopter-landing pad. I must say it was cool as
hell. We flew in on one of four, Sikorsky VH-60N, "White Hawks,"
from the Marine Corps HMX-1 Squadron. Each White Hawk was
manned by U. S. Marine pilots and crew chiefs. Upon landing, the
facility was secured with a Company of Marine riflemen. I got
goose bumps and started to tear up, knowing I was once part of
such an organization. We waited for the President and his Cabinet
members to deplane. The Crew Chief helped Lori unbuckle and
escorted her off the chopper. Midas and I followed. We were
greeted by a USMC Captain who explained Lori, and I would be
staying in Witch Hazel Lodge, closest to the Presidential retreat,
Aspin lodge. Midas would be staying in Maple Lodge. We were

I AM The Delta Protocol

driven via Humvee by a Corporal. Upon our arrival, Lori was blown away by the beauty of the cabin and its setting. A female Navy Petty Officer stood at the door, who introduced herself as Chief Peterson. She explained that she would be taking care of our needs throughout our stay. Lori and I looked at each other and said, "Thank you, Chief." After we settled in, I asked the Chief if the three men from the Hay-Adams had arrived yet. She explained the men were staying in the Dogwood Lodge, and if I wished to see them, she would have a driver take me there.

I said, "That would be great." So I found Lori, told her where I was going, and kissed her goodbye.

When I arrived at the Dogwood Lodge, the three men relaxed on the front porch.

I walked up the steps and said, "Gentlemen, my name is Michael." I shook hands with Imam Kamel Bari, the Reverend Franklin Ham, and Rabbi Tovia Cohen. They all greeted me warmly.

I began, "People, we have a mission, unlike anything any of us have done up to this point in our lives, more likely, unlike anything anyone has done since Noah was written about." I let the importance of that sink in.

I remarked, "Imam Bari, you are a learned scholar and teacher within Islam. Rabbi Cohen, your quest to bring wayward Jews back to the fold is commendable and your commentary inspiring. Reverend Ham, you and your father, are the bedrock of evangelical Christianity in our country and worldwide. I have none of those accolades. I am a former Catholic who converted to Judaism over thirty years ago. As 'I AM' told me, I was not very good at following his word, but I recognized my sins and continued asking for forgiveness. In a nutshell, gentleman, I am a bad person trying to be good. I have no clue before you ask why the Almighty chose me to lead this merry band. We also have three additional members you have not yet met. The first is Dr. Salomon Levi; he's the founder and leader of the Temple Mount and Land of Israel Faithful Movement. The second man is Johnny Black, he is currently a Chief Petty Officer in the U.S. Navy, and finally, the last man is the President of the United States."

Rabbi Cohen asked, "Michael, do you know why Levi Salomon is part of the six? I ask because I've known Levi for thirty-five years, and if he is involved, it has to do with the rebuilding of the Temple in Jerusalem."

Imam Bari stated, "If this is true, then the Dome of the Rock shrine must be moved or destroyed."

I said, "Maybe, but I have not been told that."

Franklin Ham addressed the group, "People, please! Let Michael explain what he needs from us to fulfill our obligations to the Almighty."

I stood and looked at each of them and said, "I was told directly, in person by 'I AM that his patience is at the breaking point, and he is seriously contemplating destroying all of humanity. Your part of the mission is to create a message that expresses I AM's wishes and intentions. He told me two things regarding the three of you. First, if you are the men of God that you profess to be, you must act like it. Second, you will not mention my name to anyone under any circumstances. You will face I AM's wrath if you do mention my name. When we meet with the President, I will ask if the U.S. government has any advanced communications devices that may help you in your part of the mission. Does everyone understand the dire consequences all of us and humanity will face if we fail?" They all said they understood.

21

TWELVE DAYS BEFORE THE PRESIDENTIAL ELECTION, RED WING, MINNESOTA

The tragic event happened on Main Street, between the Saint James Hotel and the Red Wing Shoe Museum, one block southeast of the banks of the Mississippi River.

Red Wing is a small town, as were many towns in Minnesota. It was a lovely day for October, and the residents were a proud patriotic group of hard-working middle-class citizens. You would think this is out of place in a liberal state like Minnesota. In reality, most rural areas are comprised of Conservative and Independent Americans. The state is run by Progressives because of the large population of Liberals·in the major cities. Today, the people of Red Wing were gathering to show their support for law enforcement and the military by having a parade in their honor. The VFW, American Legion, Shriners, the Woman's Auxiliary, the Mayor and City Council, Boy's and Girl Scout Troops, Miss Red Wing, and the Red Wing High School Band were all represented on various handcrafted floats. The high school marching band filled the streets with music and cheers from the crowd lining Main Street. The festivities were abruptly stopped when three late model, dark, nondescript panel vans pulled into the intersections trisecting the parade.

Twelve Iranian Quds Force commandos dressed in all black, with four men in each vehicle, exited armed with AK-47s. The terrorists began indiscriminately shooting people in the parade. They had no regard for the living. Men, women, and children were targeted. After the shooters emptied their thirty-round magazines, they calmly reloaded another thirty-round magazine and continued the carnage. When the twelve men's magazines went dry, they produced two fragmentation grenades each and lobbed them into the on-looking crowd. There was a total of 720 7.62x39 full-metal-jacketed rounds fired in which 115 people were killed and 75 others wounded. The casualties included men, women, and children.

When the final 12 grenades exploded, the onlookers were cut down like a harvester in a wheat field. The blast killed another 240 and wounded 150 more. Included in the death count were a mother and father and their triplets, who were only three months old. The final casualty count for the town of Red Wing was 355 killed and 225 wounded. It would become the United States' most significant mass casualty shooting in history. The terrorist's vans were abandoned six miles down the road in a small wooded area, with no signs of its occupants.

22

CAMP DAVID, MARYLAND, 1800 HOURS

I returned to the cabin Lori and I was staying in. I explained the details of the meeting I'd just left to her. She could tell I was frustrated and said I needed to calm down. She was correct as always. My mind was swimming; different thoughts were running through it so fast it was a blur. Finally, I began to get dizzy.

Lori asked, "Are you all right?"

I told her, "I think I'm okay. That was a weird feeling!" Right at that moment, I heard I AM's voice.

He said, "Michael, you are doing fine." I asked Lori if she had heard him.

She said, "Yes, I hear him."

I AM continued, "You are fine, Michael, and I wish for Lori to hear our conversation. Listen to me. The odd feeling you just experienced was caused by me imprinting information you may need for your meeting and this mission. When I input the information into your brain, it gets over-loaded. I have thought about what you proposed to me in our last conversation. I still have not decided whether to give humanity a second chance yet, but I will reveal myself at the meeting you are about to attend. Before I make my presence known, seven of my most trusted angels will appear. They are Archangel Michael and the angels Gabriel, Jophiel, Azrael, Ariel, Raphael, and Chamuel. These angels are directed to follow only your orders. Please use them as you see fit. They can achieve unimaginable feats. Just ask the Archangel Michael for whatever you may need. He is my right hand and the General of my legions. I would also like Lori to attend the meeting. I think Lori may be a comfort to you. You are doing fine. I have faith in you."

I replied, "Thank you, Lord." Then, Lori and I left for the meeting next door.

Midas, Lori, I, Kamel Bari, Tovia Cohen, and Franklin Ham sat at a large conference table, easily seating twenty people. There were four Secret Service agents stationed in the corners of the room. I leaned over to Midas, who was sitting on my left, and said in a low voice,

"I need you to observe the body language of all the principles in the meeting. If you need to communicate something urgent with me, just excuse yourself to go to the restroom. I'll follow you."

"Midas said, Roger that."

I leaned into Lori on my right and said, "Feel free to interject any time you think I missed something or any important point that needs to be made."

She said, "I will; you'll do just fine. Love you."

"I love you too."

The door opened, and Andrea, head of the President's Secret Service detail, entered. The President joined next, and everyone in the room stood. CJCS General James Nolt, DCI Susan Hope, and Secretary of Homeland Security Matt Price trailed the President. The President sat at the head of the long table with Hope to his right and the General and Matt to his left. After they were seated, we all got up and moved closer to fill the gap.

The President began, "I welcome all of you here this evening. It appears we have all gathered here for a truly divine purpose. From what I gather from the limited intelligence that an angel supplied to me, our country's future and humanity are at risk of destruction. So, what I'll do now is introduce three of my most trusted advisors to everyone. Then everyone can introduce themselves. Once that is completed; hopefully, Michael can fill in the critical intelligence that the Almighty wishes us to know. So, let's start with our DCI Susan Hope, who is sitting to my right, next is General James Nolt, he is the Chairman of the Joint Chiefs of Staff, and next to the General is our Secretary of Homeland Security, Matt Price."

I guess it was my turn. Not knowing what order I should introduce my people, I relied on my husband's intuition and started with Lori. "I'd like to introduce my wife, Lori." Everyone welcomed her.

"Next is Kamel Bari, he is a learned scholar and Imam from Iran. He was actually plucked from the clutches of the Iranian regime on the wings of angels, so I'm told."

The Imam laughed and said, "It is true, she saved me!" Everyone chuckled, not knowing how accurate the story was.

"Everyone, this is Rabbi Tovia Cohen. The Rabbi is an American who now lives in Jerusalem. He is instrumental in bringing evangelized Jews back into the fold." Everyone greeted him.

"Our next religious scholar, whom some already recognize, is the Reverend Franklin Ham."

The President rose and warmly shook Franklin's hand.

"It's nice to see you again, Franklin. I'm glad you are here."

"Thank you, Mr. President. It's good to see you are well."

I continued, "Ladies and gentlemen, our next man is not a religious scholar but a military man. This is Chief Petty Officer Johnnie Black, currently serving with DEVGRU."

The General said, "Midas, I thought I recognized you. Are you one of the six?"

"Yes, general, it's me, and yes, I'm one of the six. I had an angel visit me along with the rest of us."

Susan spoke up, "Excuse me, everyone, but there are only five of the six present by my count. Lori, are you one of the six?"

Lori replied, "Sorry, Director, I'm just here for moral support."

I said, "We are missing one man, Salomon Levi. He is the founder and leader of the Temple Mount and Land of Israel Faithful Movement. He is the world's expert on all things on the building of the third temple in Jerusalem. Evidently, Rabbi Cohen knows him rather well."

The President asked, "Michael, do we know what role Mr. Levi will play in our group?"

"Mr. President, all I know about him is what 'I AM told me, which was, after the Ark of the Covenant was discovered missing. Man has been searching for it for 2,000 years and has determined that it never existed or it is lost. I AM told me that it is not lost. He knows where it is because he relocated it. He said he would use it to allow a portion of his being to reside inside the Ark for all time when the temple is completed. As for man, I AM seems to think mankind feels that whoever discovers the Ark may think there is some untapped power or advantage to having it. He told me that those thoughts are not true."

Susan asked, "Isn't this the group that has crafted all of the utensils used within the temple if it is built?"

Rabbi Cohen answered, "Yes, Susan, that is true, but there is much more to it. You see, Salomon Levi's movement has craftsmen make the original utensils and have craftsmen build everything from the cloth used for curtains and priestly robes to the altars and the actual stones hand hued by craftsmen to build the entire third temple. You see, everything is ready and stored in numerous warehouses. He even has descendants of the Tribe of Levi training to be Priests for the temple. The only thing stopping construction is the Dome of the Rock. It is located on the same site."

"Okay, people, we are getting ahead of ourselves." The conversations continued.

The President said forcefully, "People! That is enough. Listen to Michael! Continue, Michael."

"Thank you, Mr. President. I am about to tell everyone here today is the exact conversation that I AM and I had. I will also tell you exactly what he told me to relay to you. I will preface this with my background and how I AM made contact with me. If you allow me to relay to you the word-for-word conversation we had in our first meeting."

I began, "I had just pulled into my driveway at about 0145. It was a Tuesday morning. I had just completed my first day of work for the week. I prayed as I normally do, once or twice a day as I sat there. The prayer consisted of, "Hear O Israel; the Lord is my God, and the Lord is one. Please bless, protect, forgive, and continue to guide Lori, Arica, Natalie, Lylah, James, Mom and Dad, Tina, Eric and Kim, and Scott and Tammy. Please forgive me for my sins and guide me to be a better husband, father, and following your word. Thank you, Lord, amen."

After finishing the prayer, I felt, not heard, a voice. It was like my whole body was a sound system and not just my ears."

"Get out of your truck and come to the rear near the tailgate."

"Being shocked at the moment, I just complied. After reaching the tailgate, I saw a figure standing beside the rear of my truck. I was startled and reached for my Keltic P-11 9mm pistol in my left front pocket. My hand just froze before pulling it; I couldn't move it."

The figure said, "Relax, Michael, I'm here to see how serious you are about the prayer you just offered to me."

"What? How could you know that?"

The figure stepped a few feet closer. I looked at the being; I was unsure what I saw, him, her, or it. It was dressed in faded blue jeans, well-worn work boots, and a dark-colored hoodie-type sweatshirt with the hood over its head. The face was somewhat obscured with a not-so-terribly long gray beard. The eyes, they were telling! They were anything but ordinary. The pupils looked like pools of fire like those on a gas range, simmering with blue flames."

It said, "Are you serious about your prayers?"

At this point, I thought I could be freaking out.

I said, "Yes, I'm serious."

The voice said, "That is a lot to ask for and giving me nothing in return."

I responded, "I know, but they are the most important people in my life."

"I think this is like a regular conversation, but with whom?"

I know I'm not dreaming. I'm getting ready to walk into the house. Am I crazy or possibly having a conversation with an angel, God, or something else? I remembered Mosses speaking with God in Exodus; he kind of negotiated with God. Should I be so bold? Of course, I would."

I asked him, "Who are you?"

The voice said, "I AM."

So I asked, "Okay, I AM. Why me and why now?"

The voice said, "Because you asked me, and 'why now,' it's because I need you."

"I'm thinking, boy, Lori will freak out when I tell her about this."

I asked I AM, "How do I know you are real, a figment of my imagination, or something evil?"

I AM said, "Because of your faith in my word and the belief in the deeds that I will perform before you."

I asked, "Why now? What can I possibly do for you?"

I AM said, "Man has become too evil. Not just evil but humanity has become self-absorbed, and the people have drifted further from me than ever before. The most disgusting and completely intolerable reason is that I created man in my image and gave him the ability to have free will. This allowed man to choose decisions, good or bad, about his or her everyday life and spiritual salvation. Now I have a group of people who plan to take that choice away. They will leave mankind with no choice but to follow these peoples' programmed orders."

I said, "What?" I was watching I AM's eyes, and they became bright flames with the intensity of a blowtorch.

In an intense, authoritative voice, I AM said, "Let me finish, Michael! I have to make a decision. I need a reason to continue to bless my people! If I cannot find a good cause, I will destroy everything and start anew. As for you, Michael, you have not followed the law as written or spoken, but when you falter, you ask for forgiveness and try to redeem yourself. I heard you tell your friend Scott that you were a bad person trying to be good. This, Michael, is the most important quality to me—consistency in faith, the will not to quit, and the belief in me. You, Michael, have shown me these traits from the beginning. When you were young, your beliefs backed up by your grandmother and grandfather in your Christian upbringing, followed by your research of the Old Testament, culminated in your conversion to

Judaism. All of these actions are of faith. This was accomplished by you without any formal religious education.

I know you remember when you were 16 when you woke in the middle of the night and wondered if it was a dream? So I sent an angel to stand before you, to relay a message from me, "You are the one."

I said, "I remember. At first, I thought I was dreaming but pinched myself to ensure I was awake."

I AM said, "I know you have thought about this for many years, wondering its meaning.

Before that night, I observed you and several others seeing if you had the qualities I was searching for. So much of your life, Michael, I have given you subtle guidance and a few nudges to prepare you for what I have in store for you. I must tell you, Michael; I AM said, with a slight chuckle, "I'll give you a heads-up, as you would say. You, Michael, will be only the second person I have spoken to directly, Moses being the first."

I thought to myself, "What the fuck?"

I AM said, Indeed, Michael, indeed."

I said, "I thought you spoke to several people in the Tanakh."

I AM said, "Spoke is a relative term. I communicate to all people in some form, but speaking directly, just two, Moses and yourself."

I said, "I don't know what to say."

I AM said, "Don't worry about what to say. Just listen. I will task you and six others, which you will direct to communicate my message to the masses and eliminate certain people who will cause irreparable harm to your country and humanity as a whole. So go on inside and go to bed now. Tell Lori of our conversation and reflect on what I said for now. I will get back to you."

I said, "Thank you, Lord, and I love you."

I went inside and lay in bed, trying to embrace everything that had just happened. I thought to myself, "I saw no one, just felt or heard the voice in my head and body; I'm not even sure. I know I felt calm and comfortable while everything was taking place. I kept thinking, why me, and what will my role be? Okay, everyone, that was my first encounter with I AM."

Matt asked, "I'm curious about what I AM said, 'I will task you and six others, whom you will direct to communicate my message to the masses and eliminate certain people who will cause irreparable harm to your country and humanity as a whole. How do we communicate his word to the masses?"

I responded, "Mr. Secretary, the three religious leaders, and I were just discussing that problem several hours ago."

"Director, I wondered if the Agency or NSA might have some technology to assist us in that part of the mission. General Nolt, I pose the same question to you, Sir? Perhaps U.S. Cyber Command could be of some assistance?"

The Director and the General both looked at the President for permission. The President nodded his assent.

The Director said, "I will inquire with the Director of NSA and people from the CIA directorate of Science and Technology as soon as we are finished here."

The General told us, "I will get a report from the Commander of Cyber Command as soon as we adjourn."

I thanked both of them. Then explained, "In the interest of time, I can tell you may have several questions. Several of your questions will be answered after recounting all of my conversations with I AM. Afterward, we will open the floor for discussion. Does everyone agree?"

Everyone nodded their heads in agreement.

"My next conversation is a little more insightful. I arrived home from work on a Wednesday at about 0130. I'm not sure of the exact date. I would guess about six months ago. I sat in my truck for a moment, looking at my cell phone. That is when I felt a voice, not heard, but felt the voice say, 'I am here, come to the back of your truck. 'I got out and went to the rear of my truck to see an individual dressed the same as before— dark jeans, boots, and a dark-colored hoodie with the hood up. I couldn't distinguish the facial features, but the eyes were unmistakable. The pupils in the eyes looked like the flames in a gas stove on low, blue flickers dancing within the small orbs."

I AM said, "Michael, are you ready?"

I replied, "Yes, Lord, I am."

"Good, I have a lot of information for you, and not to worry, you will recall all of it. That is my will."

"Yes, Lord."

"I have had messengers reveal themselves to several people who will help your mission. One is the President of the United States. That is why you were invited to the White House. He has three people from who he requested counsel, the Director of Central Intelligence, the Secretary of Homeland Security, and the Chairman of the Joint Chiefs of Staff. All three proposed a plan to neutralize Senators and Congress members who have been leading your country on the Godless pursuit of Marxism, using it to achieve a one-world government. They also plan to neutralize the corporate heads of all media outlets, including social media and some of the TV anchors of the Marxist-media outlets. The leaders that finance these Marxist groups and the individual leaders of various groups and rioters will also be targeted."

I asked, "And he agreed to that?"

"No. The President is taking it under advisement. The angel Gabriel I sent as a messenger told him that those three advisers could be trusted."

"Lord, can I ask a question?"

"Please continue, Michael."

"In reading Jewish commentary, it has been said that Moses was not allowed into the Promised Land because he killed one of Pharos guards. Is that true?"

I AM said, "No, that is not true. It was just Moses' time to come home. Michael, my wrath is famous throughout history. It is imperative for me to save my people if possible. Your country has been a bedrock of faith in me for centuries. In the last 100 years, man has only slowly eroded the many religions that believe in me. Now we have many countries and groups that think it is time to marginalize and destroy my people. I will not let that happen. I could take care of all of this myself, but I want proof that my believers will help me where they can. Tell the President that I sent you to ease his mind about the horrific things he must do. Tell him that he need not worry about China, Russia, Iran, Turkey, or any other country that he feels is a threat to the United States. I will take care of that problem. I have also had a messenger sent to a current Chief in your Navy Seal DEVGRU. You may deploy him as you see fit. There will be three religious men and a specialist in rebuilding my Temple. I will arrange for you to meet with all of them. I will explain to them my needs, and if they are true men of God, they should find a way to communicate my message to the masses. The ones that do not believe in my word will perish. As for the President's plan, I have no problem killing those people and will not hold the individuals who do it guilty of a blood sin. They are warriors in my name. You must make sure the President understands that his plan must begin before I intercede with the other countries. On his part, it is a matter of faith; conversely, on my part, it is a test of faith. I will tell you that several unknown groups of people are behind this movement and are responsible for the Covid 19 virus. They are currently in Phase One of the takeover of your country and the blasphemy of my word. The leader of the group is Congressman Reaver. His plan in phase two is the takeover of your country, but more importantly, it is a vaccine for Covid 19. Dr. Norman Peters is a brilliant scientist in nanotechnology and neuroscience. He worked for DARPA (Defense Advanced Research Projects Agency) and headed the breakthrough in brain mapping and introducing nanoparticles into the human body. Dr. Peters was also able to interface quantum computers with the nanoparticles enabling him to program the particles and download data retrieved from inside the body. With this technology, he will be able to program humanity. Four men report to him. I will give you the necessary information on all of them. As for Congressman Reaver, you cannot kill him when you find him. He is the key to finding the major world financiers behind this despicable plan.

You, Michael, must be there when they capture him, and you, Michael, and you alone, must interrogate him for the needed information. It will not be easy. You may have to use extreme measures. It will be a great burden on you, but you must do it. I cannot allow someone I do not have direct contact with to gather this information. Once you obtain the names of the people involved, you must dispose of Reaver. I don't want anyone else extracting additional information from him. Do you understand?"

"Yes, Lord. Lord?"

"Yes, Michael."

"Who will protect and take care of Lori, Arica, and Natalie and her family while I'm away?"

"I will, Michael. I think the President will want to keep them at Camp David out of the public eye. I assure you they will all be fine. As for your protection, I will be with you, and I'll bless your Mezuzah; it will be your strength. Do not take action on the information you obtain from Congressman Reaver. I will contact you and instruct you on how to proceed."

"Lord, I have another question just to make sure I'm clear on your message."

The Lord said, "Ask it, Michael."

"From everything I have read, and have been taught, whether it be Christianity, Judaism, or Islam, all are monotheistic religions, and all worship you, Lord. Christianity and Islam have an intermediary between you and the people, Jesus and Mohammad respectively, and Judaism is who you made a covenant with. So, are all the other people who have different religions, or people who have never known any religion, at risk for your wrath? Lord, you said yourself you alone know the true hearts of mankind. I believe and faith that you, Lord, have limitless wisdom and power. As the ultimate judge, is it fair to punish those who have not truly heard or do not understand your word?"

The Holy of Holies said, "Michael, the three religions you spoke of know my word, although man has interpreted my word to fit his needs. Man has created religions with many deities other than me. Man has and is worshiping the earth and nature as a deity. Man is worshiping evil and Satan, witchcraft, and themselves if given enough power."

" I noticed I AM's eyes. They changed from a simmering blue flame into an intense orange fire," Michael said. "Then I AM said, 'I must cleanse humanity of this rot."

I listened to his words trying to understand his frustration. "Lord, I know that I can't fathom even a small portion of your plan. Is it not the leaders of all the religions, good or bad, who have created the personalities, charisma, or outright dominance over the wills of people? Aren't leaders of the religions to blame for your word not being spread properly? You, Lord, made us in your image, but we are human, imperfect in flesh and will. Isn't that why you allow us to ask you for forgiveness, and you grant it if you feel we are sincere? Forgive me, Lord, but how can you punish imperfect humanity if they are taught your word by imperfect men? I understand that when Moses and the Hebrews made their exodus from Egypt when Moses trekked up the mountain to receive your word and the stone tablets, you spoke to the assembled masses. Was that the only time you spoke to a group of people?"

The Lord said, "Yes, Michael, the only time. All other conversations were with Moses and you."

I was worried about his potential anger being directed toward me because of the direction I was steering our conversation. So I thought to myself, "If he will destroy all of humanity, what do I have to lose by asking the question?"

So, I asked, "Lord, why not communicate your intentions and requirements to humanity. This will counter all of the mans' interpretations of your word and give knowledge to those who have not yet heard your word. After that, if you are not satisfied with the results, you would have no reason to regret your punishment."

As I watched I AM, his eyes slowly returned to a constant blue flame.

He said, "I will consider your words Michael. Is there anything else you would like to get off your chest?"

I said, "Lord, one more question and a favor?

"Continue, Michael."

"Lord, I don't know in what capacity I represent you when speaking to the six. Am I a prophet, or the Messiah?"

The Holy of Holies said, "If I were your father and asked you to relay an important message to another person who would save the lives of others, would you do it?

"Yes, I would."

I AM continued, "You would do it because you love, trust, and have faith in your father. But, conversely, your father chose you to relay the important message for the same reasons. So, there is your answer, Michael. So, what is the favor?"

"Lord, you know I love Lori, and I'm blessed to have her in my life. However, it breaks my heart to see her in pain every day. She is a very good person and deserves to live her life without all of the defects her body has plagued her with. Yet, she is in pain every day. Would you bless her and stop her pain?"

The Lord said, "This I can do, Michael. I'll have to think about the other request."

I said, "Thank you, Lord. "

"Okay, everyone! I've had one more conversation with I AM. It was less than two hours ago. Here is what transpired."

"I returned to the cabin Lori, and I are staying in. I explained to her the details of the meeting I'd just left. She could tell I was frustrated and said I needed to calm down. She was right, as always. My mind was swimming, and all kinds of different thoughts ran through it, so fast it was a blur."

Lori asked me, "Are you all right?"

I told her, "I think I'm okay. That was a weird feeling!" Right at that moment, I heard I AM's voice."

He said, "Michael, you are doing fine."

I asked Lori if she had heard him.

She said, "She did hear him."

I AM continued, "You are fine, Michael, and I wish for Lori to hear our conversation. Listen, the odd feeling you just experienced was caused by me imprinting information into your brain. You may need it for your meeting and the mission. I have thought about what you proposed to me in our last conversation. I still have not decided whether to give humanity that chance yet, but I will reveal myself at the meeting you are about to attend. Before I make my presence known, six of my most trusted angels

will appear, along with their commander, Archangel Michael.
They are: Gabriel, Jophiel, Azrael, Ariel, Raphael, and Chamuel.
These angels are commanded to follow your orders. Please use
them as you see fit. They can achieve unimaginable feats. Just ask
the Archangel Michael for whatever you need. He is my right
hand and the General of my legions. I would also like Lori to
attend the meeting. I think Lori may be a comfort to you. You are
doing fine. I have faith in you."

I replied, "Thank you, Lord."

"Well, everyone, those are the three conversations I had
with I AM. Now I suppose it would be a good time to entertain
questions unless a stiff drink or two is in order before the
questions? So I thought I would interject a little bit of levity before
we began. I looked around the room, and I gasped. Every person
in the room, every person, Secret Service agents, General Nolt, the
President, and even Midas, had tears running down their cheeks. I
looked at Lori and said what? What did I do?"

She looked at me, put her hand on my face, and said, "I
love you! That was the most loving thing anyone has done for me.
Thank you."

Midas said, "Damn, Dude!"

Susan said, "Lori, you are right. That is the most loving
thing I have ever heard." Everyone was wiping away their tears in
some fashion.

Bari spoke, "Michael, you may not have had a formal
religious education, but you are truly wiser than the three of us
supposed religious scholars combined! I'm sure my colleagues
will agree." The other two just shook their heads in agreement.

The General asked the President, "Sir if you don't mind, I'd like to take Michael up on his drink offer."

The President looked at Andrea and asked,

"Would you please see about the drinks, Andrea? I agree with you, General, and we need to make a toast. Michael, it appears you are fully briefed on the General's proposal?"

"Yes, Sir, I have been briefed."

I turned to the General and asked, "General, I understand you briefed your former subordinate commanders on contingency plans if the mission is a go?"

"I have. The order was to have the men continue training on potential primary, secondary, and tertiary target packages and stand by for a FRAGO."

"General, when I get the exact location of Congressman Reaver's compound, would it be possible to detach two of the eight-man teams and put them under the command of Midas?"

The General said, "I don't see any problem with that. However, I do have a question for you, Michael. It is out of pure curiosity. Nothing negative or disparaging is meant by the question. What is your background, you know? Tell us about your career and hobbies."

"Well, Sir, I think it is a fair question, and I'm not insulted. So, I will answer you. I played baseball as a youth. I had hoped to get a scholarship, but that didn't happen. My Dad was a union officer in the Teamsters' local in Columbus, Ohio. He was able to get me hired at Roadway Express as a dockworker. This was in November 1978. I had just turned 18. When the trucking industry was deregulated, I was laid off in November 1979. I collected unemployment and partied for a while. In April 1981, I decided to enlist in the Marine Corps as a Military Policeman 5811. I attended the Military Police School at Fort McClellan. After graduation, I was stationed at Camp Lejeune. I was promoted time in grade to PFC; from that point, I earned meritorious promotions to the rank of Sergeant E-5. My duties involved: Patrolman, gate sentry, dispatcher, breathalyzer operator, and supervisor. At the rank of Corporal, I attended the U.S. Army CID School at Fort McClellan. When I returned to Camp Lejeune, I was promoted to Sergeant in under three years. I was then chosen to be on a special team, working undercover to make drug buys. We also performed CG gate searches and served warrants. The team attended SWAT School and formed two Teams, and I was NCOIC of one of the teams. Once we were on our feet, we began training several police departments throughout North Carolina to create their SWAT teams. Around this time, the Marines deployed to Beirut were blown up in their barracks. These men were from the 8th Marine Regiment. After that incident and before deploying another Battalion from the 8th Marine Regiment, I was ordered to instruct the Battalion in anti-terror and counter-terror operations before the Regiment deployed. The training was good. We thought we had state-of-the-art equipment: CS, Concussion, Smoke grenades, full-size M16A2's, Winchester 12-gauge trench guns, 1911 45 ACP sidearms, M40A1 sniper rifles, and an M-79 Thumper 40mm grenade launcher. After four years, I got out and went back to work for Roadway. I had hoped to be hired by the Columbus Police Department, but after several attempts, I stopped. Lori and I got married.

We have two beautiful daughters, Arica and Natalie. When the girls were 3 and 5, we decided to see if they might like taking karate classes. After they went a few weeks, I decided to go with them. They stayed with it for a few years, but I continued for another 20-plus years and achieved Yon Dan. I had the opportunity to attend an NRA Pistol Instructor Class. A friend and I started giving concealed carry classes a couple of times a month. Now I'm learning the ins and outs of amateur radio. I have a general class license and mess around with UHF/VHF and HF Radios. Lastly, Lori and my granddaughter, I call her "Little Bit," but it is Lylah Rose. That brings us to right here, General, any other questions?"

"I have one?" said Matt.

I said, "Go ahead, Matt."

"This story is incredible! It seems so real, but we have no evidence to conclude that this story is not only probable but possible?"

Susan spoke up and said, "That is correct, Matt, no evidence! That is why it is called faith!"

I said, "People, it has always been about faith or the lack of faith. That is why the world and our country are destined for destruction if we fail in our mission." At that point, there was a sound like a trumpet. I looked around the room and noticed Andrea, along with the other four agents, starting to unholster their weapons, and just like that, the five agents were frozen in place.

Seven figures appeared out of nowhere. All seemed to have black wings taller than their bodies. They were adorned in a mixture of black leather and some unidentifiable chainmail; they each had black leather knee-high riding-type boots and black leather pants, which appeared to have padding on the knees and backside. One was dressed similarly to the others except for a blood-red stripe down the trouser legs and some type of epaulet on the blouse. This man spoke, "My name is Michael, Archangel of I AM's legions. This is the team I AM has chosen to assist you, Michael. They are as follows: Gabriel, Jophiel, Azrael, Ariel, Raphael, and Chamuel. I formally place myself and my team under your command."

Michael, Lori, and all of the angels stood at attention.

I said, "At ease, lady and gentlemen."

I then asked Archangel Michael, "Are there any parameters that I need to know about your team's deployment?"

He said, "Yes, we cannot relay our opinions or give ideas for your planning; we are forbidden to do this. But, except for those two things, we are free to do as you order. I must tell you, Michael, you are the first human who has been given the authority to order me to do anything. That privilege has always been that of I AM and his alone."

That gave me a reason for pause and everyone else in the room.

I asked the Archangel Michael, "How fast could you get Salomon Levi from Jerusalem to here, or is that even possible?"

The Archangel said, "Chamuel, he is assigned to you, is he not?"

Chamuel responded, "Yes, General he is."

"Good, go fetch him most expeditiously!"

18

THE WHITE HOUSE OVAL OFFICE

The President sat in a chair across from the fireplace while the CJCS sat to his right on a couch. The DCI and the Secretary of Homeland Security sat on the sofa to the President's left. He started the conversation with a question. "How religious are you three? I'm not trying to pry into your personal lives, but it will have some bearing on how you receive the information a man I have joining us in the situation room will be giving us."

The General spoke first, "Mr. President, it is a personal question. I have throughout my entire career been able to keep my beliefs separate from my troops, superiors, politicians, and especially the media, but to answer your question, Sir, I am a Christian of no denomination but pray to the Almighty as often as

I can. I believe that if it was not for the Almighty, this country would have never been formed."

The Secretary of Homeland Security spoke next, "Mr. President, my circumstances are similar to that of the Generals. I am a Christian as well, but I'm Catholic. I, too, believe that our country's founding was due to divine intervention." The CIA Director was last. She said, "Mr. President, I'm also very religious.

Moreover, I am Jewish. You will not find anything in the public record to support this, but I assure you it is true. I also believe that our country's birth and destiny are due to the people's belief in the Almighty, not necessarily a specific religion. "The President listened and finally spoke. " Thank all of you for your candor; there was no right or wrong answer to my question. My own beliefs are similar to yours, but the focus on my beliefs is not what they should be, that is, until lately. This is what my original question is about. You see, several weeks ago, I was approached by an angel. Yes, an angel in this very office.

I was startled when I saw him. I pressed the emergency button under my desk, and Secret Service agents flooded the office. They saw no one, yet the angel still sat there. He told me while the agents were in the room that he couldn't be seen by anyone but me. At that point, I told the agents I accidentally hit the button. They acknowledged my answer and said goodnight. The angel then tells me about something that happened when I was a teen, which no one knows. I had a figure appear before me while I was sleeping. The spectral being, which I still cannot describe, tells me I am one of six. It then vanished. This angel sitting before me in the Oval Office tells me that God has a mission for me and five others, who I can't identify, to save our country and humanity. The angel said that I was to meet with a man named Michael, and he would reveal to me the mission from God. The angel also told me that the three of you presented a plan to me, the same strategy we discussed in the situation room and that I should follow it. Okay, people, if there are no objections and everybody agrees, the 25th Amendment doesn't need to be activated. We will meet our mystery man Michael in the situation room at 1900." They all agreed.

19

JOINT BASE ANDREWS, 1200 HOURS

Lori was seated and looking around. She said, "This airplane is very nice."

So I asked Midas, "What kind of jet is this?"

"It's a Gulfstream G5, an extremely well-designed aircraft platform," Midas replied.

I asked, "What type of training have you had on it?" Midas answered, "I'm rated to fly one, and my team has done hostage take-down evolutions on them. I've even HAHO (high altitude high opening) jumped from them. There is a hatch in the deck."

I asked Lori, "What do you think, Pookie? Want to jump from an excellent flying jet?"

She just rolled her eyes. Then she said, "Hey, are we dressed properly to go to the White House?" I looked at Midas, and he shrugged.

The Secret Service special agent next to us said, "You look wonderful, Mrs. Stone, nothing to worry about."

Lori smiled and said, "Thank you, agent."

I couldn't help myself and said to the agent, "Suck ass!" Everyone laughed.

After landing, we were transported in black Chevy Suburbans to the White House. We entered the White House through the entrance in the South Portico. We were met and introduced to three other Secret Service Special agents, one of whom was a woman, the lead agent on the President's protection detail. She escorted us forward through the Blue Room and then left at the hall across from it. We then entered into the West Wing of the White House. We finally entered a smaller room called the President's Room, now used as a private dining room for the President, while working in the West Wing. We sat there while the lead agent left through another door. Lori looked at the embroidered cloth napkins with the Presidential seal on them.

I said, "That's our tax dollars at work, honey."

She said, "Yes, but see how nice they are." Just then, the door opened, and the President walked through. Midas and I stood up at attention; Lori just sat there.

The President smiled and said, "At ease, gentleman. I wager you two were prior military. Am I correct?"

I said, "Mr. President, I am a former Marine. Allow me to introduce myself, my wife, and my colleague. My name is Michael Stone. Mike is fine if you prefer, and this is my wife, Lori."

The President gently shook her hand and said, "It is a pleasure to meet you, Lori." He shook my hand next and asked who my colleague was.

Midas spoke up and said, "Sir, Chief Petty Officer Johnny Black, Naval Special Warfare Group."

The President shook his hand and said, "Nice to meet you, Chief."

I said, "Sir, Midas, sorry, the Chief is on the Teams, DEVGRU, and is one of the six like you, Sir."

The President said, "Please sit everyone and let's eat some lunch. The food is excellent here." A Filipino steward walked in and took our orders. The President asked about the other four in our little group as we waited. Three should be across the street staying at the Hay-Adams, and the fourth was in Jerusalem.

The President asked, "Should they be here?"

I said, "Sir, that is up to you, but I was thinking about possible leaks here in the White House, and it might be more prudent if we relocated to Camp David where there would be fewer prying eyes, besides that is where the rest of my family is."

He thought about it for a few seconds, looked toward his principal agent, and asked, "Andrea, can you arrange that?"

She said, "Yes, Mr. President."

He thought for a moment and told Andrea to contact the CJCS, DCI, and the Secretary of Homeland Security and tell them they would be accompanying us to the retreat.

"Yes, Sir, I'll arrange it now." The President asked me to give Andrea the names of the three men, which I did. We ate lunch, and the President arranged a tour of the White House for us with a very knowledgeable Navy steward. He said he had some business to attend to and would meet us at Camp David in a few hours.

20

NAVAL SUPPORT FACILITY
THURMONT (CAMP DAVID)

True to the President's word, we landed uneventfully at the designated helicopter-landing pad. I must say it was cool as hell. We flew in on one of four, Sikorsky VH-60N, "White Hawks," from the Marine Corps HMX-1 Squadron. Each White Hawk was manned by U. S. Marine pilots and crew chiefs. Upon landing, the facility was secured with a Company of Marine riflemen. I got goose bumps and started to tear up, knowing I was once part of such an organization. We waited for the President and his Cabinet members to deplane. The Crew Chief helped Lori unbuckle and escorted her off the chopper. Midas and I followed. We were greeted by a USMC Captain who explained Lori, and I would be staying in Witch Hazel Lodge, closest to the Presidential retreat,

Aspin lodge. Midas would be staying in Maple Lodge. We were driven via Humvee by a Corporal. Upon our arrival, Lori was blown away by the beauty of the cabin and its setting. A female Navy Petty Officer stood at the door, who introduced herself as Chief Peterson. She explained that she would be taking care of our needs throughout our stay. Lori and I looked at each other and said, "Thank you, Chief." After we settled in, I asked the Chief if the three men from the Hay-Adams had arrived yet. She explained the men were staying in the Dogwood Lodge, and if I wished to see them, she would have a driver take me there.

I said, "That would be great." So I found Lori, told her where I was going, and kissed her goodbye.

When I arrived at the Dogwood Lodge, the three men relaxed on the front porch.

I walked up the steps and said, "Gentlemen, my name is Michael." I shook hands with Imam Kamel Bari, the Reverend Franklin Ham, and Rabbi Tovia Cohen. They all greeted me warmly.

I began, "People, we have a mission, unlike anything any of us have done up to this point in our lives, more likely, unlike anything anyone has done since Noah was written about." I let the importance of that sink in.

I remarked, "Imam Bari, you are a learned scholar and teacher within Islam. Rabbi Cohen, your quest to bring wayward Jews back to the fold is commendable and your commentary inspiring. Reverend Ham, you and your father, are the bedrock of evangelical Christianity in our country and worldwide. I have none of those accolades. I am a former Catholic who converted to Judaism over thirty years ago. As 'I AM' told me, I was not very good at following his word, but I recognized my sins and continued asking for forgiveness. In a nutshell, gentleman, I am a bad person trying to be good. I have no clue before you ask why the Almighty chose me to lead this merry band. We also have three additional members you have not yet met. The first is Dr. Salomon Levi; he's the founder and leader of the Temple Mount and Land of Israel Faithful Movement. The second man is Johnny Black, he is currently a Chief Petty Officer in the U.S. Navy, and finally, the last man is the President of the United States."

Rabbi Cohen asked, "Michael, do you know why Levi Salomon is part of the six? I ask because I've known Levi for thirty-five years, and if he is involved, it has to do with the rebuilding of the Temple in Jerusalem."

Imam Bari stated, "If this is true, then the Dome of the Rock shrine must be moved or destroyed."

I said, "Maybe, but I have not been told that."

Franklin Ham addressed the group, "People, please! Let Michael explain what he needs from us to fulfill our obligations to the Almighty."

I stood and looked at each of them and said, "I was told directly, in person by 'I AM that his patience is at the breaking point, and he is seriously contemplating destroying all of humanity. Your part of the mission is to create a message that expresses I AM's wishes and intentions. He told me two things regarding the three of you. First, if you are the men of God that you profess to be, you must act like it. Second, you will not mention my name to anyone under any circumstances. You will face I AM's wrath if you do mention my name. When we meet with the President, I will ask if the U.S. government has any advanced communications devices that may help you in your part of the mission. Does everyone understand the dire consequences all of us and humanity will face if we fail?" They all said they understood.

21

TWELVE DAYS BEFORE THE PRESIDENTIAL ELECTION, RED WING, MINNESOTA

The tragic event happened on Main Street, between the Saint James Hotel and the Red Wing Shoe Museum, one block southeast of the banks of the Mississippi River.

Red Wing is a small town, as were many towns in Minnesota. It was a lovely day for October, and the residents were a proud patriotic group of hard-working middle-class citizens. You would think this is out of place in a liberal state like Minnesota. In reality, most rural areas are comprised of Conservative and Independent Americans. The state is run by Progressives because of the large population of Liberals in the major cities. Today, the people of Red Wing were gathering to show their support for law enforcement and the military by having a parade in their honor. The VFW, American Legion, Shriners, the Woman's Auxiliary, the Mayor and City Council, Boy's and Girl Scout Troops, Miss Red Wing, and the Red Wing High School Band were all represented on various handcrafted floats. The high school marching band filled the streets with music and cheers from the crowd lining Main Street. The festivities were abruptly stopped when three late model, dark, nondescript panel vans pulled into the intersections trisecting the parade.

Twelve Iranian Quds Force commandos dressed in all black, with four men in each vehicle, exited armed with AK-47s. The terrorists began indiscriminately shooting people in the parade. They had no regard for the living. Men, women, and children were targeted. After the shooters emptied their thirty-round magazines, they calmly reloaded another thirty-round magazine and continued the carnage. When the twelve men's magazines went dry, they produced two fragmentation grenades each and lobbed them into the on-looking crowd. There was a total of 720 7.62x39 full-metal-jacketed rounds fired in which 115 people were killed and 75 others wounded. The casualties included men, women, and children.

When the final 12 grenades exploded, the onlookers were cut down like a harvester in a wheat field. The blast killed another 240 and wounded 150 more. Included in the death count were a mother and father and their triplets, who were only three months old. The final casualty count for the town of Red Wing was 355 killed and 225 wounded. It would become the United States' most significant mass casualty shooting in history. The terrorist's vans were abandoned six miles down the road in a small wooded area, with no signs of its occupants.

22

CAMP DAVID, MARYLAND, 1800 HOURS

I returned to the cabin Lori and I was staying in. I explained the details of the meeting I'd just left to her. She could tell I was frustrated and said I needed to calm down. She was correct as always. My mind was swimming; different thoughts ran through it so fast it was a blur. Finally, I began to get dizzy.

Lori asked, "Are you all right?"

I told her, "I think I'm okay. That was a weird feeling!" Right at that moment, I heard I AM's voice.

He said, "Michael, you are doing fine." I asked Lori if she had heard him.

She said, "Yes, I hear him."

I AM continued, "You are fine, Michael, and I wish for Lori to hear our conversation. Listen to me. The odd feeling you just experienced was caused by me imprinting information you may need for your meeting and this mission. When I input the information into your brain, it gets over-loaded. I have thought about what you proposed to me in our last conversation. I still have not decided whether to give humanity a second chance yet, but I will reveal myself at the meeting you are about to attend. Before I make my presence known, seven of my most trusted angels will appear. They are Archangel Michael and the angels Gabriel, Jophiel, Azrael, Ariel, Raphael, and Chamuel. These angels are directed to follow only your orders. Please use them as you see fit. They can achieve unimaginable feats. Just ask the Archangel Michael for whatever you may need. He is my right hand and the General of my legions. I would also like Lori to attend the meeting. I think Lori may be a comfort to you. You are doing fine. I have faith in you."

I replied, "Thank you, Lord." Then, Lori and I left for the meeting next door.

Midas, Lori, I, Kamel Bari, Tovia Cohen, and Franklin Ham sat at a large conference table, easily seating twenty people. There were four Secret Service agents stationed in the corners of the room. I leaned over to Midas, who was sitting on my left, and said in a low voice,

"I need you to observe the body language of all the principles in the meeting. If you need to communicate something urgent with me, just excuse yourself to go to the restroom. I'll follow you."

"Midas said, Roger that."

I leaned into Lori on my right and said, "Feel free to interject any time you think I missed something or any important point that needs to be made."

She said, "I will; you'll do just fine. Love you."

"I love you too."

The door opened, and Andrea, head of the President's Secret Service detail, entered. The President joined next, and everyone in the room stood. CJCS General James Nolt, DCI Susan Hope, and Secretary of Homeland Security Matt Price trailed the President. The President sat at the head of the long table with Hope to his right and the General and Matt to his left. After they were seated, we all got up and moved closer to fill the gap.

The President began, "I welcome all of you here this evening. It appears we have all gathered here for a truly divine purpose. From what I gather from the limited intelligence that an angel supplied to me, our country's future and humanity are at risk of destruction. So, what I'll do now is introduce three of my most trusted advisors to everyone. Then everyone can introduce themselves. Once that is completed; hopefully, Michael can fill in the critical intelligence that the Almighty wishes us to know. So, let's start with our DCI Susan Hope, who is sitting to my right, next is General James Nolt, he is the Chairman of the Joint Chiefs of Staff, and next to the General is our Secretary of Homeland Security, Matt Price."

I guess it was my turn. Not knowing what order I should introduce my people, I relied on my husband's intuition and started with Lori. "I'd like to introduce my wife, Lori." Everyone welcomed her.

"Next is Kamel Bari, he is a learned scholar and Imam from Iran. He was actually plucked from the clutches of the Iranian regime on the wings of angels, so I'm told."

The Imam laughed and said, "It is true, she saved me!" Everyone chuckled, not knowing how accurate the story was.

"Everyone, this is Rabbi Tovia Cohen. The Rabbi is an American who now lives in Jerusalem. He is instrumental in bringing evangelized Jews back into the fold." Everyone greeted him.

"Our next religious scholar, whom some already recognize, is the Reverend Franklin Ham."

The President rose and warmly shook Franklin's hand.

"It's nice to see you again, Franklin. I'm glad you are here."

"Thank you, Mr. President. It's good to see you are well."

I continued, "Ladies and gentlemen, our next man is not a religious scholar but a military man. This is Chief Petty Officer Johnnie Black, currently serving with DEVGRU."

The General said, "Midas, I thought I recognized you. Are you one of the six?"

"Yes, general, it's me, and yes, I'm one of the six. I had an angel visit me along with the rest of us."

Susan spoke up, "Excuse me, everyone, but there are only five of the six present by my count. Lori, are you one of the six?"

Lori replied, "Sorry, Director, I'm just here for moral support."

I said, "We are missing one man, Salomon Levi. He is the founder and leader of the Temple Mount and Land of Israel Faithful Movement. He is the world's expert on all things on the building of the third temple in Jerusalem. Evidently, Rabbi Cohen knows him rather well."

The President asked, "Michael, do we know what role Mr. Levi will play in our group?"

"Mr. President, all I know about him is what 'I AM told me, which was, after the Ark of the Covenant was discovered missing. Man has been searching for it for 2,000 years and has determined that it never existed or it is lost. I AM told me that it is not lost. He knows where it is because he relocated it. He said he would use it to allow a portion of his being to reside inside the Ark for all time when the temple is completed. As for man, I AM seems to think mankind feels that whoever discovers the Ark may think there is some untapped power or advantage to having it. He told me that those thoughts are not true."

Susan asked, "Isn't this the group that has crafted all of the utensils used within the temple if it is built?"

Rabbi Cohen answered, "Yes, Susan, that is true, but there is much more. Salomon Levi's movement has craftsmen make the original utensils and have craftsmen build everything from the cloth used for curtains and priestly robes to the altars and the actual stones hand hued by craftsmen to build the entire third temple. You see, everything is ready and stored in numerous warehouses. He even has descendants of the Tribe of Levi training to be Priests for the temple. The only thing stopping construction is the Dome of the Rock. It is located on the same site."

"Okay, people, we are getting ahead of ourselves." The conversations continued.

The President said forcefully, "People! That is enough. Listen to Michael! Continue, Michael."

"Thank you, Mr. President. I am about to tell everyone here today is the exact conversation I AM, and I had. I will also tell you exactly what he told me to relay to you. I will preface this with my background and how I AM made contact with me. If you allow me to relay to you the word-for-word conversation we had in our first meeting."

I began, "I had just pulled into my driveway at about 0145. It was a Tuesday morning. I had just completed my first day of work for the week. I prayed as I normally do, once or twice a day as I sat there. The prayer consisted of, "Hear O Israel; the Lord is my God, and the Lord is one. Please bless, protect, forgive, and continue to guide Lori, Arica, Natalie, Lylah, James, Mom and Dad, Tina, Eric and Kim, and Scott and Tammy. Please forgive me for my sins and guide me to be a better husband, father, and following your word. Thank you, Lord, amen."

After finishing the prayer, I felt, not heard, a voice. It was like my whole body was a sound system and not just my ears."

"Get out of your truck and come to the rear near the tailgate."

"Being shocked at the moment, I just complied. After reaching the tailgate, I saw a figure standing beside the rear of my truck. I was startled and reached for my Keltic P-11 9mm pistol in my left front pocket. My hand just froze before pulling it; I couldn't move it."

The figure said, "Relax, Michael, I'm here to see how serious you are about the prayer you just offered to me."

"What? How could you know that?"

The figure stepped a few feet closer. I looked at the being; I was unsure what I saw, him, her, or it. It was dressed in faded blue jeans, well-worn work boots, and a dark-colored hoodie-type sweatshirt with the hood over its head. The face was somewhat obscured with a not-so-terribly long gray beard. The eyes, they were telling! They were anything but ordinary. The pupils looked like pools of fire like those on a gas range, simmering with blue flames."

It said, "Are you serious about your prayers?"

At this point, I thought I could be freaking out.

I said, "Yes, I'm serious."

The voice said, "That is a lot to ask for and giving me nothing in return."

I responded, "I know, but they are the most important people in my life."

"I think this is like a regular conversation, but with whom?"

I know I'm not dreaming. I'm getting ready to walk into the house. Am I crazy or possibly having a conversation with an angel, God, or something else? I remembered Mosses speaking with God in Exodus; he kind of negotiated with God. Should I be so bold? Of course, I would."

I asked him, "Who are you?"

The voice said, "I AM."

So I asked, "Okay, I AM. Why me and why now?"

The voice said, "Because you asked me, and 'why now,' it's because I need you."

"I'm thinking, boy, Lori will freak out when I tell her about this."

I asked I AM, "How do I know you are real, a figment of my imagination, or something evil?"

I AM said, "Because of your faith in my word and the belief in the deeds that I will perform before you."

I asked, "Why now? What can I possibly do for you?"

I AM said, "Man has become too evil. Not just evil but humanity has become self-absorbed, and the people have drifted further from me than ever before. The most disgusting and completely intolerable reason is that I created man in my image and gave him the ability to have free will. This allowed man to choose decisions, good or bad, about his or her everyday life and spiritual salvation. Now I have a group of people who plan to take that choice away. They will leave mankind with no choice but to follow these peoples' programmed orders."

I said, "What?" I was watching I AM's eyes, and they became bright flames with the intensity of a blowtorch.

In an intense, authoritative voice, I AM said, "Let me finish, Michael! I have to make a decision. I need a reason to continue to bless my people! If I cannot find a good cause, I will destroy everything and start anew. As for you, Michael, you have not followed the law as written or spoken, but when you falter, you ask for forgiveness and try to redeem yourself. I heard you tell your friend Scott that you were a bad person trying to be good. This, Michael, is the most important quality to me— consistency in faith, the will not to quit, and the belief in me. You, Michael, have shown me these traits from the beginning. When you were young, your beliefs backed up by your grandmother and grandfather in your Christian upbringing, followed by your research of the Old Testament, culminated in your conversion to Judaism. All of these actions are of faith. This was accomplished by you without any formal religious education.

I know you remember when you were 16 when you woke in the middle of the night and wondered if it was a dream? So I sent an angel to stand before you, to relay a message from me, "You are the one."

I said, "I remember. At first, I thought I was dreaming but pinched myself to ensure I was awake."

I AM said, "I know you have thought about this for many years, wondering its meaning.

Before that night, I observed you and several others seeing if you had the qualities I was searching for. So much of your life, Michael, I have given you subtle guidance and a few nudges to prepare you for what I have in store for you. I must tell you, Michael; I AM said, with a slight chuckle, "I'll give you a heads-up, as you would say. You, Michael, will be only the second person I have spoken to directly, Moses being the first."

I thought to myself, "What the fuck?"

I AM said, Indeed, Michael, indeed."

I said, "I thought you spoke to several people in the Tanakh."

I AM said, "Spoke is a relative term. I communicate to all people in some form, but speaking directly, just two, Moses and yourself."

I said, "I don't know what to say."

I AM said, "Don't worry about what to say. Just listen. I will task you and six others, which you will direct to communicate my message to the masses and eliminate certain people who will cause irreparable harm to your country and humanity as a whole. So go on inside and go to bed now. Tell Lori of our conversation and reflect on what I said for now. I will get back to you."

I said, "Thank you, Lord, and I love you."

I went inside and lay in bed, trying to embrace everything that had just happened. I thought to myself, "I saw no one, just felt or heard the voice in my head and body; I'm not even sure. I know I felt calm and comfortable while everything was taking place. I kept thinking, why me, and what will my role be? Okay, everyone, that was my first encounter with I AM."

Matt asked, "I'm curious about what I AM said, 'I will task you and six others, whom you will direct to communicate my message to the masses and eliminate certain people who will cause irreparable harm to your country and humanity as a whole. How do we communicate his word to the masses?"

I responded, "Mr. Secretary, the three religious leaders, and I were just discussing that problem several hours ago."

"Director, I wondered if the Agency or NSA might have some technology to assist us in that part of the mission. General Nolt, I pose the same question to you, Sir? Perhaps U.S. Cyber Command could be of some assistance?"

The Director and the General both looked at the President for permission. The President nodded his assent.

The Director said, "I will inquire with the Director of NSA and people from the CIA directorate of Science and Technology as soon as we are finished here."

The General told us, "I will get a report from the Commander of Cyber Command as soon as we adjourn."

I thanked both of them. Then explained, "In the interest of time, I can tell you may have several questions. Several of your questions will be answered after recounting all of my conversations with I AM. Afterward, we will open the floor for discussion. Does everyone agree?"

Everyone nodded their heads in agreement.

"My next conversation is a little more insightful. I arrived home from work on a Wednesday at about 0130. I'm not sure of the exact date. I would guess about six months ago. I sat in my truck for a moment, looking at my cell phone. That is when I felt a voice, not heard, but felt the voice say, 'I am here, come to the back of your truck. 'I got out and went to the rear of my truck to see an individual dressed the same as before— dark jeans, boots, and a dark-colored hoodie with the hood up. I couldn't distinguish the facial features, but the eyes were unmistakable. The pupils in the eyes looked like the flames in a gas stove on low, blue flickers dancing within the small orbs."

I AM said, "Michael, are you ready?"

I replied, "Yes, Lord, I am."

"Good, I have a lot of information for you, and not to worry, you will recall all of it. That is my will."

"Yes, Lord."

"I have had messengers reveal themselves to several people who will help your mission. One is the President of the United States. That is why you were invited to the White House. He has three people from who he requested counsel, the Director of Central Intelligence, the Secretary of Homeland Security, and the Chairman of the Joint Chiefs of Staff. All three proposed a plan to neutralize Senators and Congress members who have been leading your country on the Godless pursuit of Marxism, using it to achieve a one-world government. They also plan to neutralize the corporate heads of all media outlets, including social media and some of the TV anchors of the Marxist-media outlets. The leaders that finance these Marxist groups and the individual leaders of various groups and rioters will also be targeted."

I asked, "And he agreed to that?"

"No. The President is taking it under advisement. The angel Gabriel I sent as a messenger told him that those three advisers could be trusted."

"Lord, can I ask a question?"

"Please continue, Michael."

"In reading Jewish commentary, it has been said that Moses was not allowed into the Promised Land because he killed one of Pharos guards. Is that true?"

I AM said, "No, that is not true. It was just Moses' time to come home. Michael, my wrath is famous throughout history. It is imperative for me to save my people if possible. Your country has been a bedrock of faith in me for centuries. In the last 100 years, man has only slowly eroded the many religions that believe in me. Now we have many countries and groups that think it is time to marginalize and destroy my people. I will not let that happen. I could take care of all of this myself, but I want proof that my believers will help me where they can. Tell the President that I sent you to ease his mind about the horrific things he must do. Tell him that he need not worry about China, Russia, Iran, Turkey, or any other country that he feels is a threat to the United States. I will take care of that problem. I have also had a messenger sent to a current Chief in your Navy Seal DEVGRU. You may deploy him as you see fit. There will be three religious men and a specialist in rebuilding my Temple. I will arrange for you to meet with all of them. I will explain to them my needs, and if they are true men of God, they should find a way to communicate my message to the masses. The ones that do not believe in my word will perish. As for the President's plan, I have no problem killing those people and will not hold the individuals who do it guilty of a blood sin. They are warriors in my name. You must make sure the President understands that his plan must begin before I intercede with the other countries. On his part, it is a matter of faith; conversely, on my part, it is a test of faith. I will tell you that several unknown groups of people are behind this movement and are responsible for the Covid 19 virus. They are currently in Phase One of the takeover of your country and the blasphemy of my word. The leader of the group is Congressman Reaver. His plan in phase two is the takeover of your country, but more importantly, it is a vaccine for Covid 19. Dr. Norman Peters is a brilliant scientist in nanotechnology and neuroscience. He worked for DARPA (Defense Advanced Research Projects Agency) and headed the breakthrough in brain mapping and introducing nanoparticles into the human body. Dr. Peters was also able to interface quantum computers with the nanoparticles enabling him to program the particles and download data retrieved from inside the body. With this technology, he will be able to program humanity. Four men report to him. I will give you the necessary information on all of them. As for Congressman Reaver, you cannot kill him when you find him. He is the key to finding the major world financiers behind this despicable plan. You, Michael, must be there when they capture him, and you, Michael, and you alone, must interrogate him for the needed information. It will not be easy. You may have to use extreme measures. It will be a great burden on you, but you must do it. I cannot allow someone I do not have direct contact with to gather this information. Once you obtain the names of the people involved, you must dispose of Reaver. I don't want anyone else extracting additional information from him. Do you understand?"

"Yes, Lord. Lord?"

"Yes, Michael."

"Who will protect and take care of Lori, Arica, and Natalie and her family while I'm away?"

"I will, Michael. I think the President will want to keep them at Camp David out of the public eye. I assure you they will all be fine. As for your protection, I will be with you, and I'll bless your Mezuzah; it will be your strength. Do not take action on the information you obtain from Congressman Reaver. I will contact you and instruct you on how to proceed."

"Lord, I have another question just to make sure I'm clear on your message."

The Lord said, "Ask it, Michael."

"From everything I have read, and have been taught, whether it be Christianity, Judaism, or Islam, all are monotheistic religions, and all worship you, Lord. Christianity and Islam have an intermediary between you and the people, Jesus and Mohammad respectively, and Judaism is who you made a covenant with. So, are all the other people who have different religions, or people who have never known any religion, at risk for your wrath? Lord, you said yourself you alone know the true hearts of mankind. I believe and faith that you, Lord, have limitless wisdom and power. As the ultimate judge, is it fair to punish those who have not truly heard or do not understand your word?"

The Holy of Holies said, "Michael, the three religions you spoke of know my word, although man has interpreted my word to fit his needs. Man has created religions with many deities other than me. Man has and is worshiping the earth and nature as a deity. Man is worshiping evil and Satan, witchcraft, and themselves if given enough power."

"I noticed I AM's eyes. They changed from a simmering blue flame into an intense orange fire," Michael said. "Then I AM said, 'I must cleanse humanity of this rot."

I listened to his words trying to understand his frustration. "Lord, I know that I can't fathom even a small portion of your plan. Is it not the leaders of all the religions, good or bad, who have created the personalities, charisma, or outright dominance over the wills of people? Aren't leaders of the religions to blame for your word not being spread properly? You, Lord, made us in your image, but we are human, imperfect in flesh and will. Isn't that why you allow us to ask you for forgiveness, and you grant it if you feel we are sincere? Forgive me, Lord, but how can you punish imperfect humanity if they are taught your word by imperfect men? I understand that when Moses and the Hebrews made their exodus from Egypt when Moses trekked up the mountain to receive your word and the stone tablets, you spoke to the assembled masses. Was that the only time you spoke to a group of people?"

The Lord said, "Yes, Michael, the only time. All other conversations were with Moses and you."

I was worried about his potential anger being directed toward me because of the direction I was steering our conversation. So I thought to myself, "If he will destroy all of humanity, what do I have to lose by asking the question?"

So, I asked, "Lord, why not communicate your intentions and requirements to humanity. This will counter all of the mans' interpretations of your word and give knowledge to those who have not yet heard your word. After that, if you are not satisfied with the results, you would have no reason to regret your punishment."

As I watched I AM, his eyes slowly returned to a constant blue flame.

He said, "I will consider your words Michael. Is there anything else you would like to get off your chest?"

I said, "Lord, one more question and a favor?

"Continue, Michael."

"Lord, I don't know in what capacity I represent you when speaking to the six. Am I a prophet, or the Messiah?"

The Holy of Holies said, "If I were your father and asked you to relay an important message to another person who would save the lives of others, would you do it?

"Yes, I would."

I AM continued, "You would do it because you love, trust, and have faith in your father. But, conversely, your father chose you to relay the important message for the same reasons. So, there is your answer, Michael. So, what is the favor?"

"Lord, you know I love Lori, and I'm blessed to have her in my life. However, it breaks my heart to see her in pain every day. She is a very good person and deserves to live her life without all of the defects her body has plagued her with. Yet, she is in pain every day. Would you bless her and stop her pain?"

The Lord said, "This I can do, Michael. I'll have to think about the other request."

I said, "Thank you, Lord. "

"Okay, everyone! I've had one more conversation with I AM. It was less than two hours ago. Here is what transpired."

"I returned to the cabin Lori, and I are staying in. I explained to her the details of the meeting I'd just left. She could tell I was frustrated and said I needed to calm down. She was right, as always. My mind was swimming, and all kinds of different thoughts ran through it, so fast it was a blur."

Lori asked me, "Are you all right?"

I told her, "I think I'm okay. That was a weird feeling!" Right at that moment, I heard I AM's voice."

He said, "Michael, you are doing fine."

I asked Lori if she had heard him.

She said, "She did hear him."

I AM continued, "You are fine, Michael, and I wish for Lori to hear our conversation. Listen, the odd feeling you just experienced was caused by me imprinting information into your brain. You may need it for your meeting and the mission. I have thought about what you proposed to me in our last conversation. I still have not decided whether to give humanity that chance yet, but I will reveal myself at the meeting you are about to attend. Before I make my presence known, six of my most trusted angels will appear, along with their commander, Archangel Michael. They are: Gabriel, Jophiel, Azrael, Ariel, Raphael, and Chamuel. These angels are commanded to follow your orders. Please use them as you see fit. They can achieve unimaginable feats. Just ask the Archangel Michael for whatever you need. He is my right hand and the General of my legions. I would also like Lori to attend the meeting. I think Lori may be a comfort to you. You are doing fine. I have faith in you."

I replied, "Thank you, Lord."

"Well, everyone, those are the three conversations I had with I AM. Now I suppose it would be a good time to entertain questions unless a stiff drink or two is in order before the questions? So I thought I would interject a little bit of levity before we began. I looked around the room, and I gasped. Every person in the room, every person, Secret Service agents, General Nolt, the President, and even Midas, had tears running down their cheeks. I looked at Lori and said what? What did I do?"

She looked at me, put her hand on my face, and said, "I love you! That was the most loving thing anyone has done for me. Thank you."

Midas said, "Damn, Dude!"

Susan said, "Lori, you are right. That is the most loving thing I have ever heard." Everyone was wiping away their tears in some fashion.

Bari spoke, "Michael, you may not have had a formal religious education, but you are truly wiser than the three of us supposed religious scholars combined! I'm sure my colleagues will agree." The other two just shook their heads in agreement.

The General asked the President, "Sir if you don't mind, I'd like to take Michael up on his drink offer."

The President looked at Andrea and asked,

"Would you please see about the drinks, Andrea? I agree with you, General, and we need to make a toast. Michael, it appears you are fully briefed on the General's proposal?"

"Yes, Sir, I have been briefed."

I turned to the General and asked, "General, I understand you briefed your former subordinate commanders on contingency plans if the mission is a go?"

"I have. The order was to have the men continue training on potential primary, secondary, and tertiary target packages and stand by for a FRAGO."

"General, when I get the exact location of Congressman Reaver's compound, would it be possible to detach two of the eight-man teams and put them under the command of Midas?"

The General said, "I don't see any problem with that. However, I do have a question for you, Michael. It is out of pure curiosity. Nothing negative or disparaging is meant by the question. What is your background, you know? Tell us about your career and hobbies."

"Well, Sir, I think it is a fair question, and I'm not insulted. So, I will answer you. I played baseball as a youth. I had hoped to get a scholarship, but that didn't happen. My Dad was a union officer in the Teamsters' local in Columbus, Ohio. He was able to get me hired at Roadway Express as a dockworker. This was in November 1978. I had just turned 18. When the trucking industry was deregulated, I was laid off in November 1979. I collected unemployment and partied for a while. In April 1981, I decided to enlist in the Marine Corps as a Military Policeman 5811. I attended the Military Police School at Fort McClellan. After graduation, I was stationed at Camp Lejeune. I was promoted time in grade to PFC; from that point, I earned meritorious promotions to the rank of Sergeant E-5. My duties involved: Patrolman, gate sentry, dispatcher, breathalyzer operator, and supervisor. At the rank of Corporal, I attended the U.S. Army CID School at Fort McClellan. When I returned to Camp Lejeune, I was promoted to Sergeant in under three years. I was then chosen to be on a special team, working undercover to make drug buys. We also performed CG gate searches and served warrants. The team attended SWAT School and formed two Teams, and I was NCOIC of one of the teams. Once we were on our feet, we began training several police departments throughout North Carolina to create their SWAT teams. Around this time, the Marines deployed to Beirut were blown up in their barracks. These men were from the 8th Marine Regiment. After that incident and before deploying another Battalion from the 8th Marine Regiment, I was ordered to instruct the Battalion in anti-terror and counter-terror operations before the Regiment deployed. The training was good. We thought we had state-of-the-art equipment: CS, Concussion, Smoke grenades, full-size M16A2's, Winchester 12-gauge trench guns, 1911 45 ACP sidearms, M40A1 sniper rifles, and an M-79 Thumper 40mm grenade launcher. After four years, I got out and went back to work for Roadway. I had hoped to be hired by the Columbus Police Department, but after several attempts, I stopped. Lori and I got married.

We have two beautiful daughters, Arica and Natalie. When the girls were 3 and 5, we decided to see if they might like taking karate classes. After they went a few weeks, I decided to go with them. They stayed with it for a few years, but I continued for another 20-plus years and achieved Yon Dan. I had the opportunity to attend an NRA Pistol Instructor Class. A friend and I started giving concealed carry classes a couple of times a month. Now I'm learning the ins and outs of amateur radio. I have a general class license and mess around with UHF/VHF and HF Radios. Lastly, Lori and my granddaughter, I call her "Little Bit," but it is Lylah Rose. That brings us to right here, General, any other questions?"

"I have one?" said Matt.

I said, "Go ahead, Matt."

"This story is incredible! It seems so real, but we have no evidence to conclude that this story is not only probable but possible?"

Susan spoke up and said, "That is correct, Matt, no evidence! That is why it is called faith!"

I said, "People, it has always been about faith or the lack of faith. That is why the world and our country are destined for destruction if we fail in our mission." At that point, there was a sound like a trumpet. I looked around the room and noticed Andrea, along with the other four agents, starting to unholster their weapons, and just like that, the five agents were frozen in place.

Seven figures appeared out of nowhere. All seemed to have black wings taller than their bodies. They were adorned in a mixture of black leather and some unidentifiable chainmail; they each had black leather knee-high riding-type boots and black leather pants, which appeared to have padding on the knees and backside. One was dressed similarly to the others except for a blood-red stripe down the trouser legs and some type of epaulet on the blouse. This man spoke, "My name is Michael, Archangel of I AM's legions. This is the team I AM has chosen to assist you, Michael. They are as follows: Gabriel, Jophiel, Azrael, Ariel, Raphael, and Chamuel. I formally place myself and my team under your command."

Michael, Lori, and all of the angels stood at attention.

I said, "At ease, lady and gentlemen."

I then asked Archangel Michael, "Are there any parameters that I need to know about your team's deployment?"

He said, "Yes, we cannot relay our opinions or give ideas for your planning; we are forbidden to do this. But, except for those two things, we are free to do as you order. I must tell you, Michael, you are the first human who has been given the authority to order me to do anything. That privilege has always been that of I AM and his alone."

That gave me a reason for pause and everyone else in the room.

I asked the Archangel Michael, "How fast could you get Salomon Levi from Jerusalem to here, or is that even possible?"

The Archangel said, "Chamuel, he is assigned to you, is he not?"

Chamuel responded, "Yes, General he is."

"Good, go fetch him most expeditiously!"

Chamuel just vanished. The Archangel Michael asked that we move outside to a small clearing adjacent to the cabin to await I AM. We emerged into a clearing with four picnic tables and a barbecue grill surrounded by a giant densely packed pine grove. It was stunning.

I asked Archangel Michael about the condition of the Secret Service agents who seemed frozen in place.

His response was, "Do not worry, Michael, it is temporary. Look around; all of the Marine security detail and civilians here at Camp David are also paused. As soon as I AM has departed, they will be returned to their normal selves without remembering the experience."

"That was reassuring," I AM said. It appeared the group was nervous with anticipation. Everyone was fidgeting and looking about. It was then that a small pillar of fire descended from the heavens, positioning itself at the far edge of the pines. It looked like the depictions of the pillar of fire shown in paintings of the Hebrew's exodus from Egypt. The pillar extinguished, and a single figure appeared. The figure was dressed exactly like the other occasions I saw him. I could hear the group's rapid breathing and sighs while they were transfixed on the figure.

The figure spoke, "I am known by many names: Allah, The Holy of Holies God, Ha Shem, Eloheinu, and The Almighty. My name is I AM. I was not born like humans or my legions of angels. I came into being as I AM. I did not grow up; I do not age. I have no brothers or sisters, nor do I have parents. I tell you this to clarify some of the more imaginative stories told about me over the ages. My first creation was my legions of angels. Though a small percentage had some loyalty issues, they are near-perfect beings in physical prowess and intellect. I believe I've sorted that loyalty issue out. My second creation was Earth. I did work for 6 of your days creating it and rested on the seventh day. It was a glorious creation. My third creation was man and woman. They were created in my image, not physically because I can change my image to whatever I choose."

He continued, "I made mankind see what humanity would do with two fundamental choices. The first was whether to believe in me or other men or self-made deities, and second, the choice of free will, to choose a path that would positively or negatively affect humanity as a whole. The pendulum of that choice has swung in both directions over the millennium. That choice has brought you and me to this juncture. As a result, the world has become evil; the total amount of humanity worshiping me is lower than ever. That is why I stand before you this evening to give humanity one last chance to redeem itself."

Just then, two forms appeared out of nowhere. It was Chamuel and Solomon Levi.

I AM said, "Chamuel, you are running late."

Chamuel said, "Yes, my Lord, Mr. Levi was in the shower when I arrived. So I didn't think it proper to show up with him showing his nakedness. Was that the proper decision, my Lord?"

With a hardy laugh, I AM said, "Yes, Chamuel, it was the right decision."

I AM said, "You three religious men, one a Muslim, a shoot born of your father Abraham and his son Ishmael. One a Christian from the shoot of Abraham and the line of James, and also a bit misguided, lastly, one Jew from the shoot of Abraham, Isaac, and Jacob. You men will tell all of humanity what consequences will befall them if they disregard this final warning. In my discussions with Michael, he has asked me to rethink the sentence of destruction I plan on inflicting on the non-believers. Let me clarify, the non-believers and the people who have inflicted pain, discomfort, and death to others because they have twisted my word to suit their agenda will feel my wrath! An example of this would be Islamic leaders who preach to their people that killing non-Muslims is their right, saying that these actions would please me!"

You could see the blaze in his eyes intensifying as if turning the burner of a gas stove on high. It was terrifying.

I AM continued, "The early Christians did the same thing to Jews, and others they thought were heretics. All done in my name! These atrocities were committed by mere mortals who thought by contriving to subjugate the masses, they could force the people to do their bidding. Now we have a group of men who dare to change my creation! I will not tolerate such men's arrogant behavior. Michael has asked me to punish only the men responsible for teaching words I did not give. He tells me that it is not the fault of their followers who were seduced by these false religious leaders. I am not so sure; I have not decided on their fate. I do fulfill my promises, though. Michael, please bring your lovely wife, Lori, to me."

I looked at Lori, and she nodded her ascent, so I took her hand and walked toward I AM.

23

INTELLIGENCE GATHERING

MUNITH, MICHIGAN

Dog, a member of the Wolverine Guardians, a Michigan militia group, was now sitting inside an older farmhouse in a rural area southeast of Munith, Michigan. His latest intelligence gathering proved that a new militia had moved into his area of operation. Sources confirmed the group comprised thirty shooters of unknown background and twenty support personnel. This was very unusual, considering the Wolverine Guardians had been operational for four years and had selectively recruited members from across the state, now having a membership of twenty. That number included shooters, support personnel, and medical. Something was not right. Dog knew this because he was a retired U.S. Army Special Forces Sergeant First Class, of the famous

Operational Detachment Alpha (ODA), 555, or Triple Nickel. Dog's actual name is Bob Trimmer, and his role in the militia was twofold. First, to exercise his Second Amendment right to bear arms. To be a part of an organized unit that would unite with other like-minded units throughout the country. Should circumstances require action against a tyrannical government? Dog learned this from long experience during insurgency training of indigenous troops in other countries. His instincts were warning him, this new militia was outside of normal operating parameters. He made a call to the intelligence section of the regional command for his unit.

Thirty minutes later, his suspicions were confirmed. It was thought that a group of approximately fifty men had entered the United States, in small groups, over the last six months. These men were tracked from Iran and Chechnya.

The call Dog received next was the most surprising. It was from his DEVGRU Commander. Dog belonged to one of five commands that were not part of the U.S. government.

The Commander spoke plainly, "Dog, I have a sweet piece of ass lined up for you, my boy!"

Dog said, "Hot damn Dude, tell me more."

"Not now, Dog, I'll shoot you a text, got to go, later." The Commander hung the phone up.

Dog knew what to do next. He went into the adjoining room and pulled the new fax from the printer. On it was five sets of five numbers. The first set of numbers referenced the (OTP), One Time Pad code sheet. This sheet has ten separate lines of five groups of five digits. The first group of numbers he received matched with the second line on his code sheet. He then took the five groups of five numbers from the fax sheet and subtracted them from the second line of code numbers, and came up with a new set of four number groups of five numbers each. Now, he had his message to compare the numbers with his number to letter conversion graph.

"Meet n 1hr Delta."

The OTP is completely unbreakable using random numbers, only if you dispose of the code once used. Dog was heading to Randolph Lake, not too far from his current location.

Dog arrived at the designated meet point thirty minutes early. He always liked to recon an area beforehand. Ten minutes later, two men walked up. Dog recognized both men; one was a former Delta Force Captain, who was called Laser; the second man was a DEVGRU Lieutenant called Grunge. They embraced each other.

Dog said, "What's up, fellas?"

Grunge said, "Dog, the intelligence dump you gave command is shit hot. Those thirty shooters are made up of twenty-five Chechen hardline Islamic terrorists with a cadre of five Quds Force commandos."

Dog was surprised, "How in the fuck do you know that, Grunge?"

"Well, you sorry bastard, it just so happens that the Russian GRU put the finger on them. Some Russian Intelligence General made direct contact with General Nolt."

"No shit?"

"It appears the Russians don't want any fallout from what these fuck-sticks plan to do."

"Which is?"

Laser spoke next, "You'll love this Dog; you heard about the march that the progressives and congressional civil rights leaders plan on having in D.C. a week before the election? These fuck-sticks are planning to set up claymore mines along the route and command detonate the mines making Lefty Flambeau. They want it to appear that the right-wing militias perpetrated it as revenge for the Redwing massacre. You know where the terrorists are located, and we just happen to have two teams consisting of forty tier-one shooters on each team, chomping at the bit to get some!"

Dog asked, "No law enforcement?"

"Nope, we would like to take two of the Quds Force commandos for a little chat, but the rest of them, just wack'em."

Grunge spoke next, "The General has given us a go on the planning of the operation. He assured me we would get the execute order from National Command Authority, but both are tied up in a meeting. So I want you to accompany three of my reconnaissance men tonight to do a little sneak and peak. Then, when you return, we will fill in any gaps in our intelligence and hit them at 0400 the next morning, pending a go order."

Dog and his three-man recon team began the sneak and peak at 0445. Moving slowly, they searched for tripwires or any other anti-intrusion devices in two-man teams. They found none while marking their insertion path for the actual assault. Instead, they noted six perimeter guards and one four-man patrol., all dressed in nondescript tactical pants and shirts. All carried AR-type rifles and Beretta sidearms, with night vision devices. The good news was the devices were commercial grade, easily detected by the teams' state-of-the-art NODs (Night Optics Device). The two observed the area for two hours, determining the pattern of the patrols and the frequency of the guard change. They also decided that the Quds Force cadre billeted themselves in the old two-story farmhouse, while the Chechens were housed in the 40'x 60' single-story pole barn, approximately 100 yards behind the farmhouse. Finally, they gathered enough intelligence to formulate a plan.

25

PROOF

A SMALL CLEARING OUTSIDE ASPIN LODGE

Lori and I walked to within arm's reach of I AM.

I AM said in a booming voice, "This Woman, the wife of Michael, is so full of love but has been in so much pain due to abnormalities caused at birth. In good faith and love for his wife, Michael asked me to remedy this."

I AM continued, "I do this now before all of you to show you I AM. Lori, please take my hand."

Lori did. You could now see ten neon blue electric concentric circles surround her. They began at her head and moved toward her feet. Then, they stopped and moved up again.

Lori just stood there silent.

I AM asked the President, "Are the medical facilities here able to do CAT scans?"

The President answered, "I believe so."

"Good, Lori, I want you to inform the President of your doctor's name and phone number and have him fax a copy of your prior CAT scans to compare with the one taken here."

"Yes, Lord."

I AM said, "Now I will demonstrate that I keep my word and the amount of power I can wield to back my word up." I AM bellowed, "Behold! Look toward the heavens, look at the Little Dipper, and see the North Star? Six stars make up the Little Dipper."

Everyone looked at the stars in anticipation. I AM stretched his right hand toward the stars and pointed his index finger.

He commanded, "Look!"

The flames in his eyes intensified, orange in color as they blazed. He made a circling motion with his outstretched arm, and the stars moved in a counterclockwise direction. The faster he circled his arm, the faster the stars moved until they were a blur. Finally, he stopped the motion and moved his arm in the opposite direction just once, and the stars reset to their original position.

There was a gasp from the group.

Several just said, "Impossible." Then, all got to their knees and bowed in deference.

I AM said, "Mr. President, you must make a decision. The General's plan is a good one. I will not allow any of your enemies to interfere with your operation. But, if you choose to do it at all, you must begin your operation first as a sign of faith in me. I, in turn, will fulfill my promise to you. What is your decision?"

The President looked up at I AM and said, "I will order it now, I AM, and please forgive me for anything I may have done to offend you."

I AM said, "Very well." He then turned to Bari and said, "Your religious roots were born of Abraham and his son Ishmael. My word is my word, not Muhammad's. It would be wise for you and your people to remember this."

Bari said, "Yes, my Lord, I will tell them."

"As for you, Franklin, Jesus, although he was a good man, he was not the Messiah. The Messiah has not come yet."

Franklin looked up and said, "Yes, my Lord. I will explain this to my people."

"Tovia, all will come in search of my chosen. They will grasp the corners of your garments, asking for knowledge of my word. My people will teach them my word. I will not hold other people to the standards I expect from my chosen. I ask that they only have faith in me and my word and follow the commandments I gave Moses."

"I understand Ha Shem."

I AM said, "I have faith in all of you. I hope you have faith in me. Michael, if you need assistance, just think or speak Archangel Michael's name. He will be by your side."

I AM disappeared. The Archangel Michael escorted us back to the conference room, and he and his angels also disappeared. The Secret Service Agents were now mobile and acting as if nothing had occurred.

The President spoke first, "General, execute your plan. Then, Susan, support the plan with the people you spoke of. Then, Matt, you do the same."

All responded, "Yes, Mr. President."

He then asked, "Andrea, would you please escort Lori to the medical facility and inform my doctor to call me ASAP?"

"Yes, Sir."

The President then looked at the General.

"Start with that group you told me about in Michigan. I want to see the overall plan for the rest of the operation in the morning. Susan, contact the NSA Director, find out what technology is available to help Franklin, Bari, and Tovia, and explain that I need the information now. Matt, I want you to coordinate with Susan and the General. I want your retired people to run interference if any of the General's or Susan's teams encounter law enforcement personnel."

"Yes, Mr. President."

The President looked at Michael and said, "I have no idea why I'm one of the six, but I truly appreciate that you are leading this. Thank you. Do you have any thoughts?"

"One thing comes to mind, Sir. General Nolt, you will want to hear this, Sir. When we capture Congressman Reaver, which I propose we do in the next day or two, he may be the key to gathering a large percentage of the elected officials on the target list. If I can persuade him to call a meeting of the elected officials involved. If we can do this, we may have an opportunity to neutralize the whole group in a tragic aircraft accident."

The General asked, "What about the loss of life to the security personnel and the pilots?"

"I believe I have a solution to that very problem."

I asked Susan, "I'm sure you have a file on the good Congressmen. If you do, I'd like to see it for Midas and me to determine if there are any ways we may exploit or leverage him during my interrogation with him."

"Sure, Michael, I'll assign someone to it now."

26

WILDCARD

Inside the Red Roof Inn outside Munith, Michigan, a man was anxiously pacing in his room. He was en route to his father's home. His need was to be recognized by his father; this was foremost on his mind. He was an only child and excited to help his father's cause. After speaking to his father's Chief of Staff, he knew his father was backing a social justice March in Washington D.C. a week before Election Day. One of the staffers for his father told him the security for the event was being organized by a group of contractors located in Munith. So, with directions and a contact number, he deviated from his return flight home, and he was waiting for someone from the security group to pick him up. The problem for the security team as they had never heard of a person called Tim Reaver.

After the local Quds Force Commander was notified of the phone call, he knew he had significant problems. The first problem was there was some sort of leak inside their operation. Two, he could not ask for instructions or verify the person's identity due to his operational orders stating no communications were to be made until the completion of the mission. So, he compromised. He decided to collect Mr. Reaver and hold him until after the mission.

Dog had several of his men continue surveillance on the terrorist compound. One of his men thought it unusual for a cargo van to be leaving the compound. All of the occupants leaving were photographed with telephoto lenses, three in total. When the van arrived back at the compound, there was a new face. These photos were sent digitally to Dog's intelligence team. They were sent up the chain of command to a group of former CIA analysts who had just received an entire background file for Congressman Reaver, including photos of his family. Immediately Dog was contacted for verification of the new subject. After verifying the subject 100 percent, Dog was ordered to stand by for further orders.

The new information was fast-tracked to General Nolt. He, in turn, shared the information with the President, the Secretary of Homeland Security, the DCI, Michael, and Midas.

The President spoke first, "Does this change your plans for the strike in Michigan, General?"

The General replied, I'm not sure, Sir, perhaps Michael can help us. He seems to have a lot of assets at his disposal that we do not have."

I looked to Midas and said, "The General is right, what do you think?"

Midas said, "It would be feasible if your new friend, the Archangel Michael, could give us some support."

I said, "Exactly!" I then called for the Archangel out loud, and within ten seconds, he was with us.

The Archangel said, "What can I do for you, Michael?"

I told him of the upcoming operation in Michigan and the Congressman's son being at the location.

I asked him, "Would it be possible for one of the angels to transport the Congressman's son from the compound to a secure location just outside the Reaver's ranch, where Midas' teams will be gathered before our strike? I would prefer that the son be taken before the team's assault, so he is not harmed."

The Archangel Michael replied,

"Yes, we can do that. Consider it done, Michael."

I said, "Great, thank you."

Information gathered by the DHS on the Reaver home was shared with Midas. He, in turn, transmitted the information to the two platoons he was temporarily in command of, along with orders for the platoons to stage at an abandoned ranch, six miles West of the Reaver ranch.

The General told Midas he had just requisitioned four MQ-1C Gray Eagle's, two for Michigan and the Reaver ranch. They should be on station in two hours. The UAVs have a patrol time of twenty-five hours. He also set up transportation from Camp David to the Reaver ranch staging area via Little Creek, Virginia.

I said, "Why Little Creek?"

Midas said, "Michael, my boy, I need my equipment, and I need you geared up. Then, we need to make a quick pit stop at the Team's locker room."

I looked at Lori; she seemed to be taking everything in stride. I walked over to her; we embraced and kissed each other. We said we loved each other. Then, I thought and said, "How do you feel? I mean, you know?"

"I feel wonderful! I can't even say how good I feel. But, I want you to be careful."

"I will. Give the girls and Little Bit a kiss for me."

Midas grabbed a black coffee, and I snatched an ice-cold Pepsi as we walked outside toward the chopper pad. Then, finally, I asked him, "Well, what did you think?"

"Are you fucking kidding me? This is the real deal. I have never in my military career seen a general officer and high-ranking Cabinet officials, let alone a President of the United States, become so humble so quickly. Hell, I was humbled. I know the religious wise men were, and the Archangel Michael and his team are fucking unbelievable! The Teams have nothing on those formidable angel bastards; they can snatch a fucker during a firefight? That shit is a game-changer. To answer your question, Matt was the only one I questioned at first, but after I AM's display and pronouncement. Matt is all in."

I asked, "What kind of comms equipment will we need?"

"State of the art, my brother. Wait until you see my toys." Midas's smile was ear to ear.

27

ONE VOICE

Tovia, Bari, Franklin, and Solomon were given a separate conference room to brainstorm their upcoming message to humanity.

Franklin asked, "How are we going to get our message to the entire world population?"

Solomon answered, "Let the CIA Director worry about that problem. We need to concern ourselves with a unified message. We have just witnessed I AM himself and heard his word."

Franklin said, "Solomon is correct, of course. But, Bari, you and I have been chastised by the Almighty, and I have been humbled."

Bari looked at all three men and said, "Allah has humbled us all. I believe that his words guide us towards our brother Tovia for enlightenment. He will teach us the right path." As the men were coming to grips with their new religious reality, the door opened, and DCI walked in.

Tovia said, "Susan, how nice to see you."

She replied, "Thank you, Rabbi. I have some news that may help you, gentlemen."

They all looked on in anticipation.

She continued, "I spoke directly with the heads of NSA and U.S. Cyber Command. While NSA can help, General James, the Commander of U.S. Cyber Command, says his people can do most of your heavy lifting. Listen, gentlemen, I'm not here to tell you what to say to the masses. I will tell you I'm a very private person, and my religion is part of that privacy. I happen to be a Conservative Jew. As I said, I won't tell you what message to put out to humanity, but I will explain what format you should communicate the messages. The reason for the format is that NSA and U.S. Cyber Command can maximize your coverage with this format. There are two types of formats, voice-only, and video. We can also make transcripts of either. The process is straightforward; decide what the message is, and we record it. I think adding the videos of what happened to the Little Dipper will be vital. We are already getting reports from astronomers around the globe about the anomaly. Our own scientists are baffled; they say an event like that should, by all scientific studies, cause an extinction event. The President has authorized me to assign a protective detail for all of you. You will have at your disposal the multimedia studios here at Camp David. If there is any more assistance you may need, just notify the head of your protective detail."

One by one, the four men thanked the DCI.

The DCI said, "One more thing, gentleman, this is my personal phone number. If you should need anything, do not hesitate to call me day or night."

28

REAVER RANCH

Jonathan Reaver didn't arrive at the pinnacle of his career because he was lucky. No, he arrived there because he was shrewd, calculated, and could gather intelligence on friend or foe, allowing him to predict their intentions well before others. Tonight, the Congressman has a feeling that the financial benefactor, Xiang Kao, was not who he portrayed himself to be. He had no evidence, but the men in his great room should be able to shed some light on the situation.

He asked, "Thomas, can you do a financial forensic audit on Mr. Kao? I'd like to be absolutely positive where his contributions are originating."

Thomas said, "Yes, Jonathan, I can. Actually, I've already begun one. Kao says he has multiple large donors, correct?"

"That is what he has told me anyway."

"Okay, here is the problem; all I could find about financial transfers to Kao was one entity, not multiple donors. The entity appears to be legal as far as U. S. Laws are concerned. The corporation is based in California, but I cannot find out who the board of directors are or what the corporation does to generate income."

Reaver's intelligence officer Rich Taylor spoke up, "I've checked my sources, and I personally checked their data. I have a discreet contact at the FBI Counter Espionage Division. The guy is clean, maybe too clean. My contact is supposed to call me in the next couple of minutes."

The Congressman said, "That is just great. But, people, this does not pass the smell test. I have a gut feeling something is wrong."

Taylor's phone rang, and he excused himself. He returned five minutes later.

Reaver said. "Well?"

Taylor said, "The FBI's information on Kao, if it is his real name, is with a loose connection to the men suspected to be ministers without portfolios in the Communist Chinese politburo."

Reaver said, "Fuck me!"

Taylor continued, "This is not confirmed, but they are said to be Chen Liu, Fan Chao, and Ru Ma. They are specialists in the subversion of foreign countries, psychological warfare and propaganda, and cyber warfare."

"Thanks, Rich. Dr. Peters, is the vaccine deployable at this point?"

The doctor answered, "Yes, it is ready. What do you have in mind?"

"I was thinking of giving it to Kao. What type of vector should we use to get it into his system without his knowledge?"

"I would suggest putting it in his drink."

"Excellent! How long after he ingests it can we take control of his actions?"

"Well, once he ingests it. It will begin absorbing through the stomach lining, and once it enters the bloodstream, it will immediately begin the replication process. To complete the process, it will take approximately 10-24 hours, and at that point, we can take total control of him."

"Are there any range limitations with our command and control of him? If not, where can we set up the control station?"

The doctor said, "All I have to do is pre-program the nanoparticles particles with a scanner and a custom program, and he will become a walking, breathing WI-FI hot spot. I can download his biological data and upload or upgrade commands at any distance. As far as the command center, we can do it here, the lab, or go mobile, whichever you prefer."

Reaver continued, "Those Commie bastards don't understand who they're fucking with! Excuse me, gentlemen, I need to make a call."

After returning from his office, Reaver said, "It's done. Kao will be coming here the day after tomorrow. I told him we needed to coordinate donor contribution lists. Thomas, I need you to attend to legitimize the meeting. Rich, I need you to attend to get a read on Kao and to slip the good doctor's elixir into his drink."

They both agreed.

29

DEVGRU FACILITY OCEANA NAS DAM NECK ANNEX, VIRGINIA BEACH, VA

After landing, we were given transport to a compound. There were several security checkpoints we had to clear. Finally, we entered a large room. It was huge. It had a large bar, several large refrigerators, and an open area with a large sectional sofa for maybe 20 people. Several memorabilia items hung on the walls: An M4 carbine with a short bent barrel. A uniform blouse with a bullet hole in the chest area incased in a large frame and what looked like a life-size wooden Indian Chief.

Midas said, "All of the things on the wall represent trophies from past missions or tributes to fallen Brothers we lost on missions. This is the Red Squadron Team room. We call ourselves the Tribe. The Indian is our Squadron mascot. See the patch with the Chief's head on it? That is our Squadron patch."

I told him, "This is fucking cool. Kind of like a frat house for warriors."

"Yeah, well, let's go get you suited up, then you can be impressed."

We walked to another portion of the complex, where a Chief stood behind a wire-mesh-covered door. Midas greeted him and told him he needed a full kit for urban assault. The Chief asked what size trousers, blouse, boots, and belt I wore. Ten minutes later, he returned with three sets of clothing. Each set had a different camouflage pattern. He also brought out a helmet and told me to try it on. Our next stop was the armory.

Midas asked, "How are your shooting skills?"

I said, "I qualified as an expert with the M16A1 and Sharpshooter with the 1911 45ACP."

"Good!" Midas instructed the armorer to give me a Glock 21, an HK MP7, and an HK416 with a full loadout of magazines, ammo, and suppressors for each weapon, along with a Ka-bar fighting knife. Midas took us to the team locker room. He then sorted my kit out. He said to put on the olive-green uniform. As I was dressing, he also began to dress.

I said, "All of this kit is amazing!"

He just laughed. "Get your shit on, stud. I have two shooters from my element waiting for us at the shoot house. We have time to run through some room-clearing drills."

Midas said, "Here's how we will do this, Michael. Hammer and Slick are swim buddies designated as Alpha 1 and 2. You and I are together and designated Bravo 1 and 2. Alpha enters first, and we follow. Michael, you are the point-man for Bravo. Remember, people, we're loaded with simunitions, so I'm not worried about blue-on-blue fire. Alpha, I don't want 100percent out of you. Leave some squirters for Michael to engage. Michael, engage every target. Don't try to decide if it is a good or bad guy. I'm gauging your raw reflexes. I know you have done room-clearing before, but number three man in, goes right, clearing center, and moving to the first right corner. After clearing center position, put your weapon too low ready, so you don't cover Alpha's man in the top right corner. Once in position, you now cover the door we just entered. Once in position call clear, understood?"

I replied, "Check."

Midas said, "On my mark, people stack up! Three, two, one, execute!"

Alpha 1-point man threw a flashbang, counted to two, and entered right. Alpha 2 entered right behind him, he then button hooked left, and I entered right. I cleared center, lowered my weapon to low ready, and proceeded to the near right corner. Midas entered left to the immediate left corner. Everyone called clear. We stacked up to the next door and made entry. Three shots were fired by each man in Alpha. I entered, starting to clear center, when two man-size popups emerged from a doorway at the center of the room. The HK 416 selector switch was set to 3 round bursts, so I centered on the closest target just above the sternum and squeezed the trigger. The first round hit the point of aim, the second rose to the center chin, and the third center-left just below the nose. I repeated the same on the second target. Midas entered, and we called clear.

Midas stopped the exercise and called everyone over to him.

He said, "Okay, Michael, what was your point of aim, and why did you choose it?"

I looked at Hammer and Slick for any clue, but they were stone-faced. At least they weren't laughing.

I said, "My point of aim was just above the sternum. I chose that point, thinking that the muzzle would raise on shots two and three."

Midas asked Hammer and Slick,

"Well, boys, any input?"

Hammer said, "Sound logic. Was it a lucky shot? Time will tell."

Slick said to Hammer, "You dumb fuck, if it was a lucky shot, how did he do it to 2 targets?"

Midas said, "Michael, that was sound logic, and more importantly, it worked. It isn't how we train, but we don't have time to engrain a new shooting style into you. Nice shooting. Okay, let's start from the top. Michael switch to the HK MP7."

30

Munith, Michigan

At 0330 hours outside the perimeter for the assault on the terrorist stronghold. Two teams of 40 men each were strategically positioned around the perimeter, ready to jump off.

Team 1 was led by a former Captain of "A" Squadron Operational Detachment Delta. His part of the mission was to neutralize the compound guards and the roving patrol. His eight snipers would eliminate the guards with suppressed Barrett Mk22 MOD 0 Advanced Sniper Rifle Systems in .308 Winchester from 100 yards. Each guard had two snipers targeting them for redundancy to ensure mission success. The roving patrol of four men would be neutralized by two, 4-man teams set up in a classic "L" shaped ambush, using suppressed HK MP 7's. Twelve of the remaining 24 shooters would set up a perimeter closer to the compound to kill or capture any squirters, should they escape the death that was about to rain down. He positioned the last 12 of the remaining men to the large pole barn, whose sole mission was to completely destroy the barn and its occupants in the rear of the house. Eight men were armed with tripod-mounted MK47 automatic 40mm grenade launchers, firing High Explosive (HE) rounds. They were positioned with four launchers at the front of the barn and four on the starboard side. One man was set on each end of "L" manned M40 machine guns; the gunners were under complete cover. The two remaining men were armed with HK 416s with EOTech EXP S3 Holographic weapon sights mounted on their rails. More importantly, they had ten grenades each, which were (WP), white phosphorus, and incendiary munitions. The sole reason for their use was to burn the barn and its occupants to ash.

Team 2 was led by a former DEVGRU Lieutenant. He commanded five 8-man teams, all former assaulters from DEVGRU. Three elements would make an entry in three different directions. They would start with flash-bangs clearing rooms to the center of the ground floor. Upon clearing, they will ascend the stairs and continue to clear the top floor. One of the remaining two teams will form a tight perimeter around the house to contain any squirters. The last team is to stand by as a QRF if Team One or Team Two needs additional assets.

The Captain and Lieutenant stood by at the jump-off point, monitoring the two UAVs' video feed. Dog was on the phone, just finishing his call.

Dog had many contacts throughout the country. Many are LEOs, first responders, and firefighters. The plan was to have the local police swat team perform a training exercise several miles from their current location. The exercise simulated several armed men barricaded in an abandoned farmhouse forcing the police to assault it. Flash-bangs, explosions, and gunfire were just what was needed for the real take-down. Dog had just confirmed the exercise was to begin in ten minutes. Everyone was pumped for the take-down. Men began their final rituals: checking magazines, bootlaces, comm connections, and touching whatever lucky talisman they might have before the battle.

A man came running out of the front door in the midst of this. All weapons were immediately trained on him.

A voice over the command net ordered, "Weapons tight! Weapons tight!" These men were disciplined. There wasn't one finger on the trigger of any weapon. The man made it to the middle of the yard when four men came through the door in pursuit. Each man had an AK 47.

The enemy patrol had just walked into the kill box of the 8-man Kilo 1 ambush. The snipers, Golf 1, 2, 3, and 4, all had their scope recitals centered on the guards' heads or chests.

Dog shook his head side to side to clear it. What he saw was impossible. He just stood there, mouth open, watching five man-size creatures dressed in black (and what looked like chainmail adorned on their upper body and arms) swoop in from above with large wings protruding from their backs. One of the creatures snatched the first man running from the four men with AK 47s. It just grabbed the man and flew off. At the same time, the other four creatures descended on the four men with rifles. There was a flurry of wings and some dust as the men were taken, and their AKs were left lying on the grass. Dog looked at the Two platoon commanders and said,

"What the fuck was that?"

The Team One Captain immediately ordered, "All Golf elements and Kilo elements Execute into his tactical radio! Execute! Confirm."

He listened and heard, "Golf elements, execute confirmed."

"Kilo element, execute confirmed."

The Command radio came to life 30 seconds later, confirming all eight of the terrorists were silently killed by Kilo and Golf elements, with zero friendly casualties.

At the Pentagon, General Nolt observed the live video taken from the two UAVs. When the man ran out the front door, the General immediately identified him as the Reaver's son. He instantly broke into the radio command net when he saw the other four men and the angels descend from the heavens like predator hawks.

"Dogwood actual, Dogwood actual. This is Papa actual."

Dog was operating the command net and responded.

"Papa actual, Dogwood actual, authenticate."

"Dogwood actual, Copy, authenticate Mongoose. I say again, Mongoose, over."

"Papa actual, Dogwood actual. Copy Mongoose. Rosebud, continue Papa actual."

"Dogwood actual, Clean Sweep, Clean Sweep, acknowledge. "

"Papa actual, Dogwood actual, I copy."

"Acknowledge Clean Sweep."

The two-platoon commanders looked at Dog. The Team Two commander spoke into his throat mic,

"All Team Two elements. Clean Sweep. Acknowledge."

Team Twos' element leaders acknowledged. Clean Sweep was the prearranged code word for disregarding prisoners, neutralizing everyone.

The Team Two leader ordered his elements to reconfigure. On the orders of both team leaders, the house and barn were simultaneously struck by a fusillade of 40mm grenades. The explosions were thunderous and destructive. Next, several incendiaries and white phosphors grenades were tossed into the buildings. The fire started immediately. Smoke began to filter out windows that were destroyed by the grenade blasts. No one left the house, but two men tried to escape from the barn and were cut down by multiple M40 machine gun round.

31

Camp David, Witch Hazel Lodge

Lori sat with Little Bit on the floor, reading a book. Arica, Natalie, and James sat on the couch watching and talking to each other.

Little Bit said, "Up. Bubbie, up!"

Lori grabbed her and tickled her, and lifted her in the air. Arica and Natalie looked at Lori.

Arica said, "Mom, you are going to hurt yourself!"

Lori said. "I'm fine and continued playing with Little Bit."

Someone knocked at the door, and Chief Peterson answered it.

The Chief walked into the room with the DCI Susan Hope.

The DCI said, "I'm sorry to interrupt Mrs. Stone."

"Yes, he's fine. I didn't mean to worry you. I was just curious how you feel? Has the President's doctor contacted you with the test results yet?"

Natalie asked, "What's wrong, Mom?"

Susan asked in a low voice, "You haven't told them?"

Lori shook her head *no.*

There was another knock at the door.

The Chief announced, "The President's doctor would like to see you, Mrs. Stone."

Lori said, "Please have him come in."

The doctor entered, "I have your CAT scan results Mrs. Stone, and they are quite remarkable."

Lori said, "Everyone, this is Dr. Goodman, the President's Doctor. Your father asked I AM to relieve me from some of my pain. I AM called your father and me forward and took my hand in his, and as he did so, I felt warmth spread throughout my body. That is all I remember of the experience."

Susan said, "There were concentric circles of neon blue light that formed at your head and traveled down towards your feet. They then moved upwards toward your head again."

Dr. Goodman stood amazed at what was said, along with everyone else.

The doctor said, "Perhaps that explains the stark difference in the two CAT scans I compared. The first scan clearly shows numerous structural birth defects and several defects caused by age and wear. The second scan reveals zero defects, none, and no sign of age-related wear. Lori, do you feel any different either physically or mentally?"

"I'm not sure. I don't feel any pain in the places I felt it before. Wait a minute."

She reached up and removed her hearing aids and removed her contacts.

She said, "Dr. Goodman, whisper something to me."

He said, "How do you feel?"

"I feel great! Someone hand me something with small print."

James handed her his watch and turned it over.

"It says serial number 0789931! My eyes and hearing are back!"

Susan asked, "Can you tell if anything else might be different? I have a theory. Concentrate on my words: Your husband is out of the country. Your husband is in Montana."

Lori said, "The first phrase is false, and the second is true. I can feel it, and there seems to be a red hue over the false phrase and a blue hue over the true phrase."

Susan said, "Remarkable! I'd like to try something else. I'm going to let you read the definition of law and then have you read a list of names. See if you can tell if each name is guilty or not guilty of the definition."

Lori began reading the list of ten names and marking guilty or not guilty.

Susan looked at the list. All of the names were people who had been charged with treason in the 18th Century. All were convicted of treason of the ten people, with one being acquitted on appeal. Lori had chosen nine guilty and one innocent.

James said, "It is a miracle! Maybe you are stronger too? Like a superhero. Grab my hand and try to pull me off my feet."

Lori grabbed his hand and pulled, not really hard. James had put his feet shoulder-width apart and bent his knees to root himself. Lori pulled him off his feet, and James almost fell.

Susan started to say something but stopped.

Lori said, "Forget it! I'm not going to be a lab rat."

"How did you know what I was thinking?" Susan asked, "Lori, just one additional test? Please?"

"Okay, just one more test. What is it?"

Susan said, "Just one minute. I'll be right back."

The DCI went outside and called for her bodyguard. His name was Hank Stone.

He had been with the agency for 23 years, most of it with SOG (Special Operations Group). Hank had spent the last three years at the CIA training facility as an instructor in weapons training and hand-to-hand combat. She explained what she wanted him to do, and he agreed.

When they returned, Susan introduced Lori to Hank and explained his background.

Susan said, "All I want you to do is defend yourself from Hank's advancing attack. He will start out slow and advance in speed if you can defend against his attacks. If you can't defend, then we will stop. Okay?"

Lori said, "All right, let's get this over with."

Hank stepped in front of Lori and grabbed her by the left wrist. Lori swiveled her left hand under then over Hank's right hand while adding her right hand to her left for leverage. She then forced Hank's hand up and towards his own body, causing a painful wrist lock which forced him to his knee. They tried it again, only this time Hank put both of his hands around Lori's

176

neck, adding pressure to choke her. Lori drove her left hand up through Hank's extended arms and throat-punched him, causing him to let go of her neck and grab his own neck. She then grabbed Hank, put both of her hands behind his neck, delivered three knee strikes to his groin, and finished with her right foot stepping on the top of his left foot while pushing him backward. He fell back, and if it wasn't for his Danner boots being so tight, she would have broken his ankle.

Everyone looked on in utter shock. Lori was actually startled. She bent down to help Hank up. He looked at Susan, then at Lori. She grabbed him by the arm and lifted him up.

Hank said, "Where did you learn that stuff?"

Lori said, "Mike tried to show me some techniques, but it always hurt when I tried them."

Susan said, "Well, it looks like they work now. What do you think, Hank?"

"They work all right!"

James said, "Damn, Super Mom!"

Natalie, Arica, and Little Bit just laughed.

32

KARVAL, COLORADO

Midas, Hammer, Slick, and I flew to the jump-off point. It was nearing 0001 hours.

We were met by the two platoon commanders temporarily. The Jump-off point was a large ranch owned by a former CIA officer. It was located 30 miles southeast of the Reaver ranch and 20 miles northwest of the small town of Karval.

After arriving at a private airport near Colorado Springs, the team unloaded their gear and reloaded it onto an MH 60 Blackhawk detailed to Midas. They were both former DEVGRU shooters, Trigger and Half-Ass. Midas greeted both with a warm hug and introduced the rest of us. Trigger went on to explain the SITREP (Situation Report). He showed us the UAV photos, current video feed, troop deployment for the raid, and live thermal imaging from the snipers and RECCE teams already deployed. Half Ass explained the number of hostiles inside the ranch. There appeared to be Congressman Reaver, Peter Billings (the head of cyber security for (Face page), Thomas Wood, a venture capitalist, Dr. Norman Peters, a brilliant scientist in the field of nanotechnology and neuroscience, and Rich Taylor, a former intelligence officer in the U.S. Navy. He left the service as a Commander, transitioning into the Defense Intelligence Agency as an analyst, and Chinese male identity unknown.

Trigger asked, "Who's the fuck-stick in the hood?"

Midas said, "Insurance. What are the compositions of the entry teams?"

Trigger answered, "We have five possible entry/exit points on the ground floor, and here they are marked on the overlay. Composition is four (4) man assaulters with a QRF of the same composition standing by if needed. Additionally, we have four scout sniper teams, with 2 men on each team, making 8 men. Also, two UAVs are orbiting, feeding us live video now, and continuing until the conclusion of the operation."

Midas asked, "Is the assault set up for a dynamic or covert entry?"

Trigger answered, "Covert, we've hacked the code for the alarm system, and we are confident our teams can pick the door locks."

"Good. I'd like to capture all of the subjects alive, but remember, Reaver cannot be harmed under any circumstances. Are we clear on that?"

The two Platoon Commanders answered, "Check, Midas."

Trigger added, "Each assault team is equipped with two handguns loaded with tranquilizer darts for non-lethal force."

It was 0100 hours, and Congressman Reaver continued his conversation with his guests; Peter Billings, Thomas Wood, Dr. Norman Peters, Rich Taylor, and Xiang Kao. Everyone was nursing their drinks, following the plan, except for Kao. Dr. Peters nodded at the Congressman, confirming that Kao had ingested the nano vaccine. Peter Billings continued the ruse and bragged about the number of political donations he could secure for the cause, while Kao continued to argue that he had more donors. Finally, it was getting late, and the Congressman suggested that they all should retire and continue the conversation over breakfast. No one argued with the idea. The Congressman showed each man to his respective room and stopped with Rich Taylor at his room.

Reaver said, "Well, what are your thoughts about Kao?"

"Well, he can hold his liquor, that's for sure. He is well versed in political donations and finance, but there are some inconsistencies relating to specific donors and the amounts they donated. It started to become obvious the more he drank. So what are you planning to do with him?"

"I think I'll have the good doctor program him to report back to his Communist masters and kill all three of them. That will send a message not to fuck with my plans."

At 0320, Midas called me, Hammer, and Slick together for our roles during the assault.

Midas said, "Listen up! We will enter behind the assault team entering the front entry door. Once they clear the room, we enter. We wait until they clear each room then we enter. If another team finds Reaver, he will be taken to a secure and cleared room. If we find him, we call in the QRF (Quick Reaction Force). The

QRF will clear the surrounding rooms adjacent to us, and Michael can begin his interrogation. Hammer is point man, then Slick, Michael, and me. We are entering covertly, so no flash-bangs; everyone has suppressors on their weapons. Are there any questions? How about you, Michael, any questions? I'm sure you are nervous, and that is a good thing, just remember the basics; your former training will kick in."

I said, "I'd be an idiot or crazy if I said I wasn't nervous, but this is so fucking cool! Thanks for allowing me the chance to do this with you."

33

ASPIN LODGE, CAMP DAVID, MD

The President sat at the conference table with General Nolt, Director Hope, and Secretary Price awaiting the start of the operation at Congressman Reaver's ranch. His phone rang, noting a call from the Pentagon. The secretary answered and let the President know that General John Mead, Chief of U.S. Space Command, was on the line.

The President said, "Put him through, please. " General Mead, what may I do for you this early morning?"

"Good morning, Mr. President. I apologize for the interruption so early in the morning. I felt you should be aware of some analysis my people have done on the celestial anomaly observed earlier in the evening. According to scientists on our staff and NASA's scientists, we should be experiencing unexplainable weather phenomena all over the globe. Unfortunately, we have seen no such conditions.

The President asked, "Does any of the scientific analysis report a delayed reaction to the weather due to the anomaly?"

"No, Mr. President, the reaction should be instantaneous."

"Okay, General, keep me posted on any further developments and have a video of the event sent to me here via secure satellite. Thank you, General Mead."

"Yes, Mr. President, right away, Sir. Good day."

The President said to the assembled group, "Well, it appears that General Mead and his people, along with NASA, are concerned with the celestial show I AM put on for us. They have concluded that we should be experiencing unexplainable weather phenomena all over the globe, but it isn't happening. So, I asked him to send a copy of the video of the event to us. Perhaps the religious trio can use it for their upcoming presentation to the world. How will they broadcast their message to so many people, Susan?"

"Well, Mr. President, with the combined effort of Cyber Command and the NSA, they plan to hack into every television broadcast station all over the globe, preempt the regularly scheduled programming, and begin broadcasting the religious leader's message. They will also hack into every email address, all of the world's Internet video feeds, and all of its radio stations (these will also be preempted with a voice message). That will leave only people who have no radio, television, email, or internet access. These people will miss the message. In addition, approximately 1.2 billion people have little or no electricity. That's a problem. I have people working on getting information to those people, but I see no way to communicate with them."

The President said, "Okay, that's progress. Have your people continue exploring options."

"General, how is our main operation planning coming? What is it called?"

General Nolt responded. "Sir, it is called Operation Clean Slate. We are in the final stages of selecting target packages. We have all primary targets selected and located, with the personnel designated to engage the targets. Our secondary targets have been selected, identified, and located with personnel designated to engage the targets. The selection of a tertiary target list is near completion. So far, all of the targets on the list have been selected, identified, and located, with personnel designated to engage the targets. We are now firming up the remainder of the list. Completion is estimated to be three days. The mission can commence as early as day five depending on the time of day we choose."

The President asked, "Susan and Matt are your people on the same schedule?"

Matt said, "All of my people are fully integrated into the General's forces and under their command."

Susan spoke next. "Mr. President, my people are also fully integrated with the General's forces. I have a question for you, General, if I may?"

"Anything Susan, what's the question?

"This is just a hunch. Call it female intuition, if on the off chance I AM eliminates, say our primary targets. Do we have a contingency plan to use those shooters to eliminate other hostiles such as the gang infrastructure in our major cities?"

General Nolt said, "We did consider that option, but we didn't have solid intelligence, and pursuing that intelligence through other agencies would raise suspicions."

Matt spoke up, "General, I can provide you with up-to-date intelligence on the ten most dangerous gangs in the United States. I have current reports on gang leaders, estimated membership, locations, and surveillance photos of the leadership. The top ten are MS-13, Latin Kings, 18th Street, Gangster Disciples, Crips, Bloods, Trinitarios, Florencia 13, Barrio Azteca, and the Mexican Mafia. I'll have my people forward the intelligence to you, and you can plan accordingly."

The General responded, "Thank you, Matt, that will fill in a major gap in our contingency planning."

The President asked, "Susan is there any particular reason for your intuition?"

Susan said, "Well, Sir, when I AM spoke to and touched Mrs. Stone. Your doctor stopped by her cabin with the results. I happened to be there when he compared the two CAT scans. It was miraculous! All of her prior skeletal defects from birth are healed. Her eyesight is 20/20, and her hearing is unbelievable. She no longer needed her contacts or hearing aids. She can look at a list of people and tell if they were guilty or innocent for a specific crime. I'm almost positive she can read other people's thoughts, and I asked her if she would let me test her self-defense skills against my bodyguard. She agreed, and we proceeded slowly. She had no training before this because of her ailments. But she actually kicked his ass. So, my assessment is, it is possible that I AM may help us more than he has said once he sees we are committed."

34

GET SOME 0330 HOURS, REAVER RANCH

The feeds from the two UAVs revealed nothing moving inside or outside the house. Thermal imaging from the UAVs also revealed stationary orange blobs consistent with people sleeping in their beds, in relationship with architectural drawings obtained earlier in the week. When the order was transmitted, a man from each entry team began to pick the locks at each entry point. All locks were picked successfully in under 30 seconds. The second order was given 60 seconds later to enter the home. All five assault teams entered simultaneously. The team's movements looked similar to a choreographed dance. The first man entered silently and moved to the right corner of the room, clearing the right and center, then moving along the right wall to the upper right corner of the room facing the center. The second man did the same but moved to the left. The third man moved right and posted on the lower right corner of the room. The fourth and final man moved left and posted to the lower-left corner of the room. The remaining four teams used the same entry procedures when their assigned rooms. This continued into each room within the house until a team discovered a target.

The first man captured was the doctor. He was asleep. He awoke in utter fear with a suppressed Glock 21 pressed into his open mouth while snoring. He was bound with flex cuffs by his hands and feet, gagged, and had a black hood placed over his head. He was then carried over the shoulder of an assaulter like a sack of potatoes to one of six nondescript panel vans waiting in the ranch's driveway.

The second team entered a room across the hall from the doctor's room. Inside was a sleeping Peter Billings. He was lying on his back. He was subdued with a gauze pad soaked with chloroform and then bagged and tagged in the same fashion as the doctor.

Team three entered silently into a room in another wing of the house to find the bed empty. The team leader quickly scanned the room to find light leaking from under the bathroom door. He immediately signaled a halt to the rest of the team. Then, using hand signals, he positioned his men on either side of the bathroom door. When the sleepy Thomas Wood exited the bathroom after taking a much-needed piss, he was placed into a carotid chokehold by the team leader and passed out 10 seconds later due to lack of blood flow to his brain. He was also flex cuffed, gagged, and hooded for transport to the jump-off point.

Team Four entered the room across from Team Three's entry point when Team Three made entry. The first man button hooked right, the second man button-hooked left as the third man crossed the threshold and saw movement under the blanket on the bed to the center of the room. It was later discovered that Rich Taylor was raising a Beretta 92F toward the second man on the entry team. He was immediately shot with a tranquilizer dart in the solar plexus, which caused him to drop the weapon. He was then bagged and tagged like the rest.

Team Five, the team we were trailing, made entry into a room at the opposite end of the wing, where Team Four made their takedown. We posted up across from the room Team Five was now entering. I was next to a door facing the takedown room with Midas to my right, Hammer to my left and Slick to his left on the opposite side of the door. We then heard a commotion coming from inside Team Five's takedown room. It sounded like two bodies slamming into the plasterboard wall. It lasted for about five seconds. It was then that the door beside me opened, and a man emerged with a pistol in his right hand. I yelled "gun!" and turned to my left, grabbing the top of the slide with my right hand and knife hand, striking the man in his throat with my left hand. He released the weapon, and Midas, Hammer, and Slick subdued him. I just stood there. Hammer thanked me, and Midas and Slick just smiled at me.

Team Five exited the room with a man later identified as Xiang Kao. One of team five's men had a bloodied nose. He was cursing under his breath, "The fucker side-kicked me in the face." When I looked down at the man Midas and company had subdued, I said, "You must be Congressman Reaver."

The house was declared clear ten minutes later, and all of the assault elements and prisoners were transported back to the large ranch at the jump-off point.

35

BACK AT THE RANCH

We arrived at the ranch at approximately 0500 hours. All bound and hooded detainees were taken to separate rooms on the first floor and basement. Each detainee was guarded by two operators inside the room and two outside the room guarding the entry door.

Each detainee was seated in a metal chair bolted to the floor before the mission. The detainees were secured to the chair with restraining straps attached to each leg, two around the torso, and a strap on each wrist. The arms were placed horizontally in line with the top of the shoulders and secured to eye bolts in the room's sidewalls. The detainee's flex cuffs and gags were removed. They all sat in total darkness, observed by two operators and a Wyze portable security camera.

Midas and I were currently on a video conference call with the President, General Holt, Susan Hope, and Matt Price.

The President said, "It appears that the two of you look no worse for wear. Can we assume the mission was successful?"

Before we go any further, Michael, your wife, Lori, by all accounts, is doing fine. My doctor diagnosed his CT scan and Lori's past scan. The change is remarkable. It appears that all of her past ailments have been corrected or cured. I'm happy to report this to you."

I said, "Thank you for the news, Mr. President. Could you tell Lori I'm okay?"

"It would be my pleasure, Michael. General Nolt, would you share the intelligence you and your people have discovered about the six men captured?"

The General answered, "Yes, Mr. President. The General split the screen on the video feed, so a photo of a man appeared. This first man is identified as Peter Billings. He was head of security for FacePage, America's preeminent social media platform. He is also suspected of assisting China in systematically identifying anti-communist dissents through China's social media platforms. Once identified, the people are sent to either reeducation camps, tortured and sent to prison, or executed. He is also Reaver's go-to guy for all things social media.

The second photo is of Thomas Wood, a venture capitalist, net worth 35 billion dollars. He is the kingmaker. He creates, supports, and organizes progressive groups with some of the most prominent political donors to the progressive Democrat politicians. These include city prosecutors, local, state, and federal judges, state and federal legislators, and countless lobbyists. All done with donations funneled through offshore shell corporations, supporting all of the above and, in addition, supporting Marxist groups and organizations in the U.S. and Western Europe.

The next photo is of Dr. Norman Peters, he is a brilliant scientist in nanotechnology and neuroscience. He also contracted out to DARPA, Defense Advanced Research Projects Agency, headed the breakthrough in brain mapping and introduced nanoparticles into the human body. He was also able to interface quantum computers with the nanoparticles enabling him to program the particles and download data retrieved from inside the body. The programming of the nanoparticles and their retrieval in concert with the quantum-based computers enables data retrieval and exploitation. It allows the ability to program the nanoparticles for specific tasks within the human body. These programmed particles can be uploaded individually or in mass. Their vector into the human body can be achieved by various modes. In this case, the nanoparticles may be embedded into the Covid 19 vaccine. We have the people at Fort Detrick studying the possibility of embedding these nanoparticles into a vaccine undetected. Obviously, I AM is concerned that the doctor did indeed embed the vaccine with these particles. I've detailed a Platoon of shooters and a couple of specialists from Detrick to look for a lab or samples of the technology from Reaver's home.

Gentlemen, the next photo is of Rich Taylor, he was a former intelligence officer in the U.S. Navy. He left the service as a Commander, transitioning into the Defense Intelligence Agency as an analyst. He was scouted by Congressman Reaver and left government service. We are assuming Taylor is Reaver's intelligence officer.

This photo of our unknown Oriental male is, in fact, Colonel Xiang Kao. He is a PLA Special Forces Colonel who the CIA suspects is a personal attack dog for a group of three Chinese

Ministers, Chen Liu, Fan Chao, and Ru Ma. They oversee a small elite group of Special Forces soldiers who infiltrate foreign countries and recruit potential insurgents sympathetic to Socialist and Communist ideologies. Their mission is to subvert foreign countries, psychological warfare, propaganda, and cyber warfare."

The last photo is of Congressman Reaver. He is a Progressive Democrat. He seems to have numerous high-level connections within our government and international corporate and financial institutions throughout the Western world.

We have several interrogators already available to begin the interrogations. But, Michael, from what you and I AM have stated, you are the only one allowed to interrogate Congressman Reaver?"

I said, "That is correct, General. I AM was explicit on that point. There will be no cameras or recording devices while the interrogation occurs."

The General said, "I understand; I heard what I AM said. Have you ever conducted an interrogation before? I'm not trying to sound critical, but there are many aspects to the procedure, not to mention the psychological effects to the interrogator."

I said, "I understand your concerns, Sir. I've had experience in the Marine Corps with interviews and interrogation, but nothing of this magnitude. I will have Midas with me for consultation if I should need it."

"That's fair enough. Let us know if you need any assistance."

After the video conference, Midas and I walked to the Great Room and sat on a very nice brown leather sectional sofa. Hammer and Slick were there as well.

Midas said, "Stone, that was quick thinking and decisive action you took on Reaver at the takedown."

Hammer jumped in, "Hell yes, it was! I think you saved my ass. How old are you anyway, Stone?"

I said, "It just happened. I didn't even think about it. I just turned 60, Hammer."

Slick busted in, "You are a hard mother fucker for 60, dude."

I said, Thanks, Ass Clown! Now I have to figure out a way to break Reaver. Midas, can you have another chair set up in Reaver's room and put his boy in it? Keep the boy bound, gagged, and hooded, then gag Reaver and take his hood off so he can see his boy."

Midas said, "On my way."

I sat there thinking back on what I AM said to me. "As for Congressman Reaver, you cannot kill him when you find him. He is the key to finding the major world financiers behind this despicable plan. You, Michael, must be there when they capture him, and you, Michael, and you alone, must interrogate him for the needed information. It will not be easy. You may have to use extreme measures. It will be a great burden on you, but you must do it. I cannot allow someone I do not have direct contact gathering this information. Once you obtain the names of the people involved, you must dispose of Reaver. I don't want anyone else extracting additional information from him. Do you understand?"

After that revelation, I thought to myself, "How in the fuck am I going to do this? I thought back to what I had learned as a Military Policeman in the Marine Corps. I learned numerous techniques on interviewing and interrogation, but nothing on this scale. I thought about some of the characters in my favorite novels like Vince Flynn's Mitch Rapp or Tom Clancy's John Kelly/Clark, but this was real, not a fiction novel. It was definitely real.

Midas returned and told me everything was set up. I asked him, "Have you straight-up tortured anyone for information? I made a distinction. I mean torture, not enhanced interrogation?"

He thought about it for a few seconds and said, "Yes, but you have to be careful. You have to really think about it before you do it. You don't want to go in there pissed off and just fuck the guy up without thinking about what your actions will cause. But, on the other hand, if you go all medieval on him, he may just tell you what he thinks you want to hear, not the truth."

I said, "I think I understand, but how do you know where the line is?"

"You don't know where the line is, that's the problem, but if you go in with questions you already have answers to, you establish a baseline for your line of questioning. Then, as you increase the physical or mental stress, you will be able to see if the Congressman is telling the truth or if he is just telling you what he thinks you want to hear. Hopefully, as you are questioning him through this process, you gain more intelligence to continue the process. If you don't obtain more information, you might not know when you cross the line."

"Okay, I understand now. I will tell you something that has to stay between you and me only. I AM has told me that I have to find out who is financing Reaver no matter what. He told me I might, no, I probably would have to do some nasty shit to this fucker, and it was a burden I will have to bear when I'm done getting the information from him. These are his words, not mine, "Dispose of him so no one else can extract any information from him."

"I just need you to tell me to man the fuck up if you think I need it and tell me if you see something that I don't."

Midas said, "I got your six, brother!"

I told him, "Thanks, I mean that!"

He asked, "I gather you're going to start on his son in front of him? If so, I suggest you strip him naked, so when he shits himself, Dad will get the full effect."

I said, "Yes, the son's first, and I'll strip him in front of Dad!"

36

PRESIDENTIAL ELECTION NIGHT

It was 2130 EST, the polls were closed in all of the states that observe Eastern Standard Time, and the remaining states one hour to three hours behind will be closed in three hours. With approximately 60-75 percent of the total votes tabulated within the closed polling places, the numbers show the President was commanding a significant lead in the polls. The percentage of Black votes had almost doubled from the 2016 election. The total of Hispanic votes has also almost doubled. The President and the Republican down-ballot candidates' support has grown across the board in all demographics. It appears that this lead will enable the President to easily win reelection.

At approximately 2200 EST, a phone call was placed by the Speaker of the House to a shadowy but capable IT specialist. Only one word was used in the short conversation, "Mirage."

After the phone call, the Speaker returned to the busy campaign war room in Washington, D.C. The Speaker met with six of her closest allies and told them to begin. Immediately phone calls were placed to the major cities within the swing states, which the Democrats badly needed, to upset the election.

Precinct captains in charge of counting ballots in the major Democratic cities told all of the poll watchers that the counting of ballots would stop and restart in the morning for various reasons.

Before Election Day, Democrats promoted mail-in ballots because in-person voting would be dangerous due to the Covid-19 virus. Before Covid-19 was even heard of, Governors and Secretaries of State in swing states, including Nevada, Arizona, Wisconsin, Michigan, and Pennsylvania, changed their State's voting laws to benefit the Democratic Party. Many of these changes will be challenged by the White House and many average citizens. Multiple irregularities occurred the night of the election, many of which will not become known until four to six weeks after election night. Some of the lawsuits question the Constitutionality of the mail-in ballots. One example happened in a Pennsylvania case. The mail-in ballots were allowed before the election. According to the Pennsylvania State Constitution, the law could only be changed by referendum of the State's voters. Still, it was not taken to the voters, so the claim is that the law was not legal as per the Pennsylvania State Constitution. The election is plagued with irregularities and inconsistencies.

After the phone calls to the respective swing cities, the President's lead in the polls began to erode. This started at approximately 0130 EST. The President had warned the public of the potential fraud that could take place with the states allowing vote by mail ballots to be sent to unsolicited voters.

37

INTERROGATIONS

I entered the room with Congressman Reaver and his son Tim, who looked in his early thirties. I didn't say a word. Instead, I removed my Ka-bar knife hanging on my load-bearing vest and grabbed the front of Tim's shirt. Using the knife, I sliced the front of the button-down shirt open. I then cut around the shirt's cuffs and removed them from the subject. I then slowly cut from the bottom of the trouser legs to the top on each side of the legs. Then removing the belt and buckle, I removed the trousers in two pieces. This left Tim in just a pair of boxer briefs. He was trying to yell but was gagged and unable to speak. I then turned to Congressman Reaver to gauge his reaction. His eyes were wide and accusing. I returned to my work. Grabbing the front of the subject's briefs, I sliced the fabric in half and yanked the cut cloth away, leaving the man naked in the chair. I then removed his hood and a gag. He was frantic, his eyes darting around the room until his eyes fell on his father.

Tim Reaver's arms were bound in such a way as to make moving them almost impossible. The only movement he had was below the wrists and the fingers. His hands switched between closed fists and his palms flat with his fingers extended. I observed a pattern in the son's hand movement, and without warning or saying a word, I grasped the Ka-bar in an overhand grip and ran it through the top of his right hand, pinning it to the top of the chair's armrest. I left it there, still vibrating side to side. Tim let out a blood-curdling scream, and tears ran down his face. He mumbled incoherently and then said, "What do you want?"

I just looked at him for a moment and turned toward his father.

The Congressman was straining to free himself. His face was blood red from exertion. I walked over to him and removed his gag. He began screaming and cursing me. Some of the words were even creative. I let him rant until he finally ran out of steam.

Finally, he asked in a strained but accusing voice, "What do you want? Who the fuck are you? You haven't even asked us any questions yet?"

I asked him, "Do you love your son?"

"Of course I do. What do you want?"

I responded, "Here's the deal, Congressman. I have never actually tortured a prisoner until just now, and I have to tell you, after sticking that knife through your boy's hand, I won't have a problem cutting his balls off one by one, should the need arise. So, I'm going to ask him 10 questions, which he will ask you in turn. If you do not respond, or I feel you are not truthful with me, I will break one of your son's fingers. That is a broken finger for each unsatisfactory answer by you! To be clear, Congressman, I know many things about you and what you've been involved in, all of it bad, so if you want to test me, feel free."

Tim cried and said, "Dad, help me, please!"

I walked over to Tim and pulled my Ka-bar out of his hand, wiping the blood on my trouser leg. I said, "Are we ready, fellas?" They both just looked at me and said nothing.

"Okay, question number one. Tim, ask your father if all of the men captured in your father's home this morning are his employees." Tim did so. The Congressman answered, "Yes, all but one."

I said, "Perfect answer. Are you ready for question two? Who is the man who is not your employee?" Tim asked the question. Reaver answered. "Xiang Kao, a facilitator of financial donations to the Democratic party's reelection campaigns. Although I had suspicions, he was more than that. That was why he was here, to see if I could confirm my suspicions."

I said, "Excellent, so far, so good. Are you ready for question three? Was Dr. Norman Peters working on a vaccine for Covid 19 with the intentions of implanting his nanotechnology into the vaccine, undetected?"

Reaver asked, "If I answer this question can you guarantee me immunity from prosecution?"

I said, "Just a minute, let me check." I pulled out my cell phone and dialed my home number. When the answering machine picked up, I asked the question. Pretending to listen and adding a few yes Sirs, then I hung up. I said, "Yes, it is a certainty you will receive immunity, but only if you truthfully answer the rest of my questions."

Reaver said, "Yes, Dr. Norman Peters was planning to introduce the technology into the vaccine."

I said, "Very good so far, Congressman. Here is your next question. Who are the elected officials taking part directly or indirectly in these Chinese foreign campaign donations, and what organizations received these donations?"

Tim asked his father the questions.

Reaver would not make eye contact with me when he said, "I'm not sure."

I walked to Tim and grabbed his left index finger at its base, and, with my other hand, I grabbed the finger just above the knuckle and snapped it backward, causing an audible crack and a loud scream from Tim.

"Well, Tim, I guess your father only loves you so much."

Tim screamed, "You fucker!"

I said, "Congressman, you know the question? Are you going to change your answer?

He said, "Please! I don't know."

I turned back to Tim and grabbed the same finger on his right hand, and broke it in the same manner. Another audible crack with the accompanying scream, and Tim cried, "Please, Dad, tell him!

I looked at Reaver and said, "Eight more chances then I cut his nuts from their sack."

Looking at his only son, he said, "You are an evil fucker! I have a list in my office safe. It details everything."

"Good, I'm sure you will be happy to give me the combination to the safe. But, then, I think we will take a break and give your son some much-needed medical attention and retrieve your list."

I had Slick, and Hammer remove Tim from the chair, tend to his wounds, and leave Reaver under guard. Then, Midas and I went into an empty room.

I asked him, "Do you have any concerns or criticisms of my actions?"

He said, "No, the important thing is you didn't talk a lot, and having the son ask the questions was a nice touch, especially after you ran that Ka-bar through his hand. How did you come up with that idea?"

I said, Hell, I don't know. It just came to me. Can we have some men go and retrieve the list?"

"They are on the way right now. What's next?"

"I'd like his story verified with the other prisoners, and I want to know more about the Chinese guy."

Each of the other prisoners had a three-man team attempting to interrogate them. All were interrogated; differently. This included threats of prison time, waterboarding, sleep deprivation, stress positions, and loud music. None were tortured at this point. The most difficult was Xiang Kao. The potential breakthrough with him came from the interrogation of Dr. Norman Peters; after being waterboarded, the doctor began to talk.

Congressman Reaver's plan was bold and quite likely possible. Introducing the vaccine and placing nanoparticles in consumer products potentially infecting the entire planet, with the ability to remotely control every human was incredible. The doctor explained how the vaccine was introduced into Xiang Kao's drink just hours before.

The team interrogating Peter Billings, the Chief of cyber security for FacePage, had the easiest job. They put him in a stress position and threatened that when he went to prison for at least 20 years, he would immediately become some gang member's bitch. Billings started to cry and explained how the algorithms were devised, what they actually did, and how the CEOs of the largest social media platforms were conspiring together to bring down the current President and elect one of their own. This information was seditious at best and treasonous at worst.

The team interrogating Thomas Wood used a more delicate approach. They had to supplement the team with a former CIA forensic accountant and a U. S. financial and international finance expert. Woods was sleep-deprived, exposed to extreme temperature changes, and placed in highly uncomfortable stress positions. In addition, one of his interrogators had been used on all of the high-value detainees at Guantanamo Bay, Cuba. Nevertheless, the information gathered proved extremely valuable. The information provided four separate lists: United States donors and donations; Eastern and Western European donors and donations; Middle East donors and donations; South American donors and donations; Central American donors and contributions; and Asian donors and contributions.

Woods was a money-laundering genius. In addition, he possessed a photographic memory, and the details recalled from his memory were remarkable.

It is no wonder Reaver has him on his staff. The names of individual donors are impressive, but the involved nation-states are staggering. Some of the significant nation-states include China, North Korea, Iran, Venezuela, Yemen, Syria, Mexico, and some drug cartels. Surprisingly, Russia is not involved.

Rich Taylor proved to be one of the hardest to break, but he had the most surprising of revelations. Taylor had been exposed to most U.S. military interrogation techniques throughout his career. However, he was not familiar with some of the methods used by the CIA Paramilitary SOG or the tier one organizations such as DEVGRU or Delta's field-expedient interrogation techniques. These were interesting, to say the least. Waterboarding was tried, but Taylor knew they wouldn't drown him if they wanted intelligence. Finally, part of the assault team, a Corpsman said he had an idea.

Doc was a former member of DEVGRU's Red Squadron. He was an assaulter, a corpsman, and a Native American whose tribe was Mandan. This tribe originated from North Dakota. Doc explained his tribe had a rite of passage for their young males into adulthood called the Okipa Ceremony. It began with the young man not eating, drinking, or sleeping for four days. Then they were led to a hut, where they had to sit with smiling faces while the skin of their chest and shoulders was slit and wooden skewers were thrust behind the muscles. Finally, using the skewers to support the weight of their bodies, the warriors would be suspended from the roof of the lodge and hung there until they fainted.

There were other parts of the passage to manhood, but they were not pertinent to Doc's idea. He retrieved his med kit and pulled out a long leather pouch. The pouch was about 12 inches long and 3 inches wide. He opened the pouch, and inside were four rods, each about ten inches long. They had holes drilled in them approximately two inches from each end, used to run paracord through, allowing you to hoist the individual. One end of the rod was in the shape of a point. They looked like darning needles. He said they were made of titanium for strength. He explained that he could make two vertical incisions approximately four inches apart. This allowed the rod to be inserted, point-end first, through the first incision, then under the visible muscle fiber, and back through the second incision. There would be four sets of incisions, two on the back, parallel to the shoulder blades, and two on the front, approximately four inches above the nipples through the pectoral muscles. After the rods are inserted, the paracord is run through all the holes and attached to a pulley to hoist the individual to the desired height.

While the Doc was explaining the procedure, Taylor listened to the entire conversation. It was decided to implement Doc's "Right of passage." He began by injecting Lidocaine into the areas to be sliced as local anesthesia. As each group of two incisions was made, Doc maneuvered the rods into the incision and under the muscle and through the incision on the far side of the area. Although the incisions were somewhat painless because of the anesthesia, threading of the rods was not.

Taylor began screaming and screaming. He asked for a lawyer; his rights were being violated. Taylor demanded the names of his captors. He received no response from the team.

When Doc was finished, he asked Taylor if he was ready.

Taylor said, "Ready for what? You haven't asked me anything?"

Doc said, "You're correct, but the men who interviewed you before I came in asked you several questions, which you refused to answer. So, I will let you decide the order you wish to answer all of the questions because you will answer every one of them."

Doc pulled the rope and hoisted Taylor until his big toes were barely resting on the floor.

38

THE MESSAGE

The three men stood in the studio dressed in their usual fashion, just as they would when leading their respective religious services.

The first to speak was Reverend Ham. "People of the world, God has a message for you. We three humble religious men come before you today to relate to you the word of the one and only God. Nearly everyone in the world has either seen or heard of the cosmic event several nights ago. That event has been speculated upon by scientists the world over. The three of us were present during the event, but more importantly, we were present and observed the cause of the event. The cause was God. God caused the event to prove his existence to the world, so people would heed his warning. The warning, a message really, is this: The 10 Commandments he gave to Moses on Mt. Sinai are your guidebook. When God spoke directly to the three of us, he stated that Jesus, although a good man, is not the Messiah, nor the trinity, upon which the basic tenets of Christianity were founded and taught. This is what God has said."

The Islamic cleric, Imam Kamal Bari, began to speak next. "What Reverend Ham has said is true. I also witnessed the event and heard the spoken word of Allah. Allah also spoke of Mohammad. Allah made clear to me that the Koran, the book we Moslems read daily and use to guide our lives, was written by man, not words stated by Allah himself. Any Muslim cleric or believer who teaches that Jihad is Allah's word is wrong and will be punished for teaching this word. Allah stated, like the Christian Jesus, Mohammed was also a good man, but his words were just that. The words of man, not Allah. Allah stated the people who twist his words for their own benefit will be punished by Allah himself. This punishment is not strictly for Muslims alone. Allah proclaimed he will punish anyone of any religion who has twisted his words to benefit themselves or the organization or religion they represent. For the people of the world who do not know Allah or God, he identified himself to the three of us as "I AM." The time is now to pray to him and ask for his guidance. I feel I may speak for myself and Reverend Ham when I declare that both Christians and Muslims have to change our own religious doctrine. The one thing that Judaism, Christianity, and Islam have all gotten right is that we all believe in the one true God, I AM.

Rabbi Tovia began to speak, "People of the world, it is a troubling time, but one only needs to embrace I AM and his word. Your life will become more fulfilled reading his word. The covenant he has with his own creation is not complex. He wants you only to abide by 10 simple rules. For most of you, they are common sense anyway. I AM is disgusted with the corruption and lies leaders of the world and religious leaders have used throughout history to sway the world's populations to suit their agendas. It doesn't matter to I AM what religion you profess, only that you recognize him as your creator and have sufficient respect for his word.

We tell the world this, to save as much of humanity as possible before I AM brings destruction to those who do not believe in him. This personal belief is only known by two individuals— you and I AM. We are imploring the world to embrace I am now. Do not wait for your religious leaders to say it is permitted, for they may be about to feel I AM's wrath. If you look at your Old Testament and read Zechariah, you will see the will of I AM. I leave you with this, have faith in the Almighty, and the Almighty will have faith in you."

They finished the recording. Salomon Levi was there as well as the DCI.

Reverend Ham asked, "How did it sound?"

The DCI remarked, "It was to the point, but I fear too many people will be hesitant to change their beliefs."

Salomon Levi said, "I believe the director is correct. As soon as this is aired, the religious leaders will start their campaign to make the three of you look like heretics. I do not see this turning out well."

The Rabbi said, "It doesn't matter what the religious leaders say, I AM gave us our mission, and we will complete it. If it saves only 100 people, then 100 people are saved. So it is better to try than do nothing."

39

TAYLOR'S INTEL DUMP

After hoisting Taylor six inches off the ground, his screams began in earnest; they were loud and unending. Doc left him suspended for six minutes and returned him to the ground. Taylor was definitely in pain, although his screams seemed to subside somewhat. After a five-minute break, Taylor was hoisted six inches above the floor for a second time. He attempted to speak, but his words were interrupted by his uncontrolled breathing, he focused on his breathing, and his words became intelligible.

Taylor said, "I can help you, but I need assurances that I will not be prosecuted!"

Doc responded, "That can be arranged, but I assure you that you must fully disclose anything we ask. I can hoist you as many times as necessary to extract the needed information if you don't. Is that clear?"

Taylor said, "Okay, can I have some water?"

Over the next several hours, Taylor revealed Congressman Reaver's plan to win the Presidency in the next election. Reaver has connections with the dominant group of Progressive Democrats and a large portion of the establishment Republicans.

Reaver used these connections to funnel political donations to the power brokers individually and their various nonprofit political action groups. A significant portion of the contributions came illegally from China, Iran, North Korea, and Venezuela. All of the recipients of these donations understood where the source of the donations originated but was unconcerned as long as Reaver laundered the money. The only things the politicians were concerned about were money and continuous power. The ideology that the parties professed to believe in was just window dressing for the two things they all cared about.

Reaver planned that Dr. Peter's vaccine would be rolled out to the world in one-to-six months from now. The vaccine does work against the disease, but at a time of Reaver's choosing, he could program all the individuals who had taken it to do virtually anything he wanted and control the masses. Reaver understood the potential problems from dealing with these foreign nations once President. Still, with the vaccine, and his ability to program those who took it, he wasn't worried- because he could control all of them. Taylor explained how he had been compromised by PLA (MSS), Ministry of State Security, nearly ten years ago. His mission by the MSS was to become invaluable to Reaver and to report intelligence gathered to his handler, Xiang Kao. This intelligence was forwarded to the MSS and then the Chinese

Politburo. Taylor explained that Reaver was suspicious of Xiang Kao. That is why he was found at the Reaver ranch. Reaver had the doctor insert the vaccine into Kao's drink so that Reaver and the doctor could program Kao to go back to his handlers and kill them. Reaver intended an unmistakable message to the Chinese to not fuck with his plans.

Moreover, Taylor explained the involvement of the Iranians, North Koreans, Syrians, and the Venezuelans in depth. These countries Reaver had no knowledge of. The amount of participation of the politicians in the U.S. government was immense. He explained the collusion between the political leaders of Congress, the Senate, lobbying groups, media, and the bureaucracy within the U.S. government, directly or indirectly influenced by the Chinese MSS.

Taylor seemed somewhat relieved about his capture, allowing him the ability to tell his story. However, his relief appeared to be driven by the guilt of being compromised by the Chinese MSS. Taylor also explained that if Reaver did win the election, Taylor would have infected Reaver with the vaccine to gain control of the U.S. government himself, severing all ties with China and its accomplices. Taylor told his interrogators that the lists of people involved in the plot were in Reaver's safe. But only Taylor and Kao knew of the other country's involvement. Doc and the rest of the shooters in the room were horrified at the number of U.S. politicians' participation in the plan.

40

THE LISTS

The samples of the vaccine and its documentation were retrieved and the documents in Reaver's, Dr. Peters', and Taylor's safes by a Platoon of shooters directed by Midas. The documentation and vaccine samples were forwarded to the scientists at USAMARIID for further study. These studies were prioritized by General Nolt. The analyses didn't take long when the scientists knew what to look for. The General called me immediately with the results. The vaccine was indeed capable of being programmed and transmitting biological information from the vaccinated individual and programming the nanoparticles to initiate an unknown number of future tasks. Midas and I also received the files from Reaver's and Taylor's safe identifying all the involved individuals in the conspiracy.

Midas and I found a quiet room to go over the intelligence with the lists from Reaver's and Taylor's safes in hand. We compared the names on the two lists with pen and paper in hand.

The names and positions were nearly identical, although in a different format. Taylor's list had names of countries and leadership involved in the destruction of the United States. Still, each country's involvement was compartmentalized restricting the governments or their intelligence organizations knowledge of the true scope of participation of the other countries. All but one— China. China's MSS operational security was nearly perfect, with one exception, Taylor and the constant threat of his betrayal of the United States. This was the weak Chinese link.

After about 90 minutes of analysis, I asked Midas, "Do you have any recommendations on proceeding with Reaver's interrogation?"

Midas said, "Tell him the names of some key politicians, both Democrat and Republican, and some donors and organizations they donate to. Minus the foreign countries involved. Then tell him the number of politicians and donors on the list, minus the foreign countries. Gauge his reaction."

I said, "I like it."

"Then I lay on the Chinese compromise of his boy, Taylor, and what he planned to do to Reaver?"

Midas said, "Exactly, Stone! You catch on pretty quick for a former Jarhead," Midas said with a laugh.

My response was, "You may suck a dick, Mr. Squid."

We both laughed.

I entered the interrogation room where Reaver and his son Tim were still bound and seated. Tim's stab wound had been cleaned and closed with butterfly strips, and his fingers reset by a former DEVGRU Corpsman.

I said, "Congressman, we retrieved the information in your safe and some other interesting information. As for you and your boy, I hope you are prepared to cooperate with me? Otherwise, let's just say there may be some complications."

The Congressman asked, "What do I need to do?"

I explained some of the key people involved and asked if the Congressman had a prearranged code to have the people on his list meet with him in secret.

He told me that a contingency plan was established to enable 350 critical members of the bureaucracy to meet at his ranch should the need arise. He said he would provide a list of the people that would attend the meeting. He also explained he had contracted a chartered Boeing 747. The 747 would be fueled and ready with 36-hour notification, and with it being Wednesday, they would all arrive Friday evening.

He was extremely helpful, giving me the charter company's name and the names of the 350 traitors.

I left the room and joined Midas again.

"Midas, relay this list to the operators observing the targets. I want to make sure they are complying and heading toward the aircraft when the time comes. I also want Colonel Xiang Kao brought in and seated next to Tim Reaver. Keep him bound and gagged and leave his hood on."

Midas said, "Roger that, Stone."

Midas returned five minutes later with the Colonel, escorted by six Tier one operators. They seated the Colonel three feet away from Tim Reaver, bound, gagged, and hooded. He was in full view of the Congressman and his son.

I asked Reaver, "Do you know who this is?"

Reaver said, "He is Xiang Kao, one of the people I get donations from."

I said, "Is that all you know about him?"

Showing a slight hesitation, he said, "Well, yes."

I said, "Well, Congressman, it seems you are not telling me everything, and I'm not in the mood to fuck around."

"Okay, okay! I suspected that he was more than a donor. I'm not sure, but maybe he worked for the Chinese intelligence service. I just found out. I wanted to send the Chinese Government a message not to fuck with me. So, I had Dr. Peters add the vaccine to his drink. We would then program him to go back to his handlers and eliminate them. That is why he was at my ranch. We had administered the vaccine to him just before you assaulted my ranch. Please!"

"That's better, Congressman.

Did you know that your security guy Taylor, was working for the Chinese MSS? It seems he was compromised by them about ten years ago."

Reaver responded, "No way, I don't believe you!"

I said, "Congressman, it doesn't matter if you believe me! It only matters if I believe you! Your life and your son's life depend on it. Do you know where we found your son? I'll tell you. He was at a farmhouse whose occupants were five Iranian Quds Force commandos and twenty-five, Chechen hardline Islamic terrorists. Are you curious about what they were planning to do? I'll tell you, they were planning to massacre the members of the march you sponsored. Was that your brilliant idea or the Colonel's?"

Reaver looked stunned; he said," Is he telling the truth, Tim?"

His son said, "Yes, Dad. I tried to escape, and they chased me and tried to shoot me."

It was time to hear from Colonel Xiang Kao. I walked over to him and removed his hood and gag. He sat Stone still.

I asked him, "Colonel, I know you have been listening to my conversation with the Congressman. Would you like to add anything?"

He said, "Gweilo fucks!"

I responded, "I think the Colonel just referred to us devil fucks. I asked the Colonel one final question.

"Colonel, do you believe in God? Before he could respond, I unholstered my Glock 21 in one fluid motion and, from point-blank range, pulled the trigger once, blowing blood and brain matter all over Tim. "That was a rhetorical question for those left alive in the room. Congressman, make the necessary arrangements and don't think about fucking me. As you can see, I'm not in the mood." I retrieved the Congressman's cell phone from Midas and handed it to Reaver. I asked Midas, out of earshot from Reaver, to monitor the phone call and have him put it on speakerphone.

I then called General Nolt. I asked him to collect all vaccine samples and all the documentation about the vaccine and have it destroyed. The General said, "What, are you crazy? Why would I do that?"

I said, "General, is the President with you?"

"Yes, he is, but...."

"Let me speak to him, please."

The President came on the line and asked, "Michael, how are things going?"

I said, "Fine, Sir. I asked the General to collect all of the samples of the vaccine Dr. Peters created and all accompanying pertinent documentation and to destroy it. He thinks I'm crazy. I'll tell you what crazy is. I just put a bullet through the head of Colonel Xiang Kao and blew his brains all over the room. That, Mr. President, is crazy. But not destroying all of the information about the vaccine after what I AM told about its creation and how offensive it was to him! That is crazy."

The President said, "I understand, Michael. I will take care of it now." But, before he hung up, I heard him say, "General, I order you to destroy all the vaccine samples and documentation right now! Am I clear?"

The General quickly responded, "Yes Sir, right away, Mr. President."

I chuckled to myself; that felt fanfrickentastic. If Lori heard me speaking like that to anyone, let alone the President of the United States. She would say that is mean or you're a dick. I'll have to tell Midas about that. I'm sure he will appreciate it.

41

FINAL TROOP DISPLACEMENTS

General Nolt explained the final troop displacements to the President, DCIA, and the Secretary of Homeland Security.

The General said, "There are ten, 200-man-company-size units commanded by a Delta O-5 Lt. Colonel or DEVGRU Commander. Each company will have five 40-man platoons, commanded by a Delta O-3 Captain or DEVGRU Lieutenant. These platoons will be divided into five eight-man teams, all tier-one shooters. In addition, each platoon will have 20 former CIA signals intelligence, communications specialists, intelligence analysts, case officers, or SOG paramilitary officers to provide support.

If we run into local, state, or federal law enforcement, we will have 4 man/woman teams per platoon of former DHS personnel to run interference for the ops. They will give us cover should we need it, the General continued.

To supplement the forces, if and when we may need them, are 20 legitimate patriotic militias across the country, approximately 4,000 strong. These are commanded by former Special Operations personnel loyal to the cause. They will be used as a blocking force, or in the case of targets evading the blocking force, they will be used as trackers. Each militia company is 200 men strong; these are also broken down into five platoons of 40 men each. The Platoons can also be subdivided into five 8-man squads. The 20 militias will be spaced strategically throughout the lower 48 states.

The locations of the Companies correspond with the major U.S. cities according to population; around these cities' militia companies are forming a discrete perimeter, with the ability to close access to and from those cities when ordered to do so.

Washington D.C. had three such Platoons assigned with 102 men and women, all tier-one shooters, CIA personnel, and DHS personnel.

One of the assigned targets was a man named Richard Hessler. He was founder, principal officer, and senior managing director of Cinderella Advisors, a Washington- D.C. - based philanthropic consultancy that caters to left-leaning clients. Cinderella Advisors also manages several center-left funding and fiscal sponsorship organizations, including 501(c) (4) Sixteen Thirty-one Fund; 501(c)(3) Middle Venture Fund; 501(c)(3) Honeywell Fund; and 501(c)(3) Wendover Fund. Hessler is closely involved with these organizations, often serving as the founder, principal officer, or board member. In addition, Hessler is closely involved in the Democratic Party and left-wing politics.

He is a former Clinton administration White House appointee and previously served as national field director for the League of Conservation Voters. Hessler later served as a member of the defunct Clinton Global Initiative. These organizations funded pop-up organizations on the Internet too numerous to count or keep effective control over. The four holding companies generated over 400 million dollars annually and controlled several billion dollars of liquid assets. This is termed "Dark money," which fuels leftist politics. Hessler lives in McLean, Virginia, in a 3.5-million-dollar estate. One 8-man squad was assigned to eliminate him. Signals intelligence obtained by the former CIA personnel attached to the platoon continues constant electronic surveillance on the subject.

Another 8-man squad is tasked with eliminating the Speaker of the House, who resides in McLean, Virginia; she is also under covert electronic surveillance. Additionally, the Democrat Minority Leader of the Senate, Democrat Majority Leader, Majority Whip, Assistant Speaker, and Democratic Caucus Chairman all have tier one squads assigned for elimination. Other squads have similar targets, but their targets are lobbyists, leaders of organizations who support or have been compromised by the Communist Nation States. Other primary targets are media corporate CEOs, including social media platforms, television, radio, and print platforms that continually and intentionally produce a narrative that misleads and or suppresses the views of the American public. These CEOs, their staff, and the people presenting the reports to the public are a direct threat to national security and the preservation of our Constitution. Therefore, they are traitors and are targeted for elimination.

These target packages have platoons assigned to them in 50 of the United States' largest cities rated by population. All platoons have secondary and tertiary target packages in the event of compromise, speed of primary target completion, and or shift of mission priorities. Secondary target packages consisted of nonprofit organizational leaders who supported the Marxist/Maoist narrative and provided support for small groups who have incited violence in this year's protest. Donors to these causes were also included.

Tertiary target packages include gang leadership and major drug dealers. Some of the target packages overlapped. These were identified and properly coordinated.

The SF leaders of the militia blocking force coordinate with the company command elements for their respective AOs (Areas of Operation). Blocking the ingress and egress to the major cities was easier than one would think. Using large vehicles and rendering them inoperable in places within strategic locations around the city would cause major traffic backups. Snipers would cause further confusion and chaos."

The President said, "Thank you, General, and God help us."

42

ANGEL 411

I was telling Midas about my conversation with the General and the President. He was there when I made the call but only heard one side of the conversation.

Midas said, "Stone, I have to tell you, in almost two decades in the Navy, I have never seen a senior officer get his balls cut off so artfully by an NCO, let alone a former NCO, and I have seen some artful shit in my day."

I said, "I would have liked to have told him he was a fucking retard, but that was all I could think of.

I think it's time to call my guardian angel."

"You mean Michael? Can you get those angels to replace the security for the VIPs and the pilot and co-pilot, and get the aircraft over some unpopulated area at about 35,000 feet, and the angels just vanish? I'd love to see the faces of those traitorous bitches when they realize that they are well and truly fucked."

I said, "That's the plan. We need to know who and how many will be boarding the aircraft first. In the meantime, let's see what Archangel Michael has to say."

It didn't take long. The angel appeared in about 60 seconds.

The angel asked, "What can I do for you, Michael?"

I explained to Archangel Michael my plan in detail.

Archangel Michael listened patiently, and when I finished, said, "I can do that. First, I must commend you on the imagination of your plan. Do you remember when we first met, and I explained that I would not give you advice on how to do things? This is still the case, but I must remind you that faith in I AM is the number one rule. Depending on the degree of faith in the Almighty, you might surmise that the Almighty may already have a plan for these people, and if your faith in him is not complete, then your plan should be implemented. Do you understand?"

I said I think so. Okay, I have a question? Do you know if my thinking or cognitive abilities may have been enhanced by I AM?"

Michael said, "Of course it has; that is the beauty of I AM's blessings. You, I'm sure, had a certain level of faith in him before being contacted by him, but since that point, your faith has become greater and greater. I'm not sure how it works with humans. Angels, on the other hand, were created as we are now. We don't have a mother or father, except I AM, our creator. So, faith was built into us as part of our creation. When I AM created mankind, a very small percentage of angels became jealous of your creation. To say it was a rebellion. It is wrong. It would be impossible to win a rebellion against I AM. These angels were cast from Heaven to Earth, losing all of their privileges and powers and sentenced to a mortal's lifespan. This is where the Lucifer myth began.

Later, I AM sent a contingent of angels to Earth to help mankind become self-sufficient. These angels were known as the Nephilim. They did help mankind learn many useful things, but they also became jealous of mankind after a while. The Nephilim thought I AM allowed these "Monkeys," a term used for mankind by these angels because I AM seemed to let them do anything they wanted without consequence. At that point, the Nephilim began to interbreed with human women.

The results were offspring that were vastly superior to the average human, having intellect, superior strength, size, and most importantly, not having faith instilled in them because of the inbreeding. This eventually caused an unintended consequence in regards to I AM's plan.

The Stories of the Nephilim inspired the development of ancient Greek and Roman Mythology.

43

THE VOICE

I was sitting at the kitchen table at the ranch, where we interrogated the prisoners. Along with me were Midas, Hammer, and Slick. Slick had made us hamburgers to munch on, as we were all hungry. Slick and Hammer were ragging me about being old and being a Marine. I just laughed and flipped them off. I was trying to come up with a good comeback when all of us heard the voice of I AM. Of course, Midas and I were the only ones who had heard him speak before.

I AM said, "Michael, I see you have retrieved the requested information."

I said, "Yes, I AM. I felt it necessary to eliminate Colonel Kao. He had already been given the vaccine by Doctor Peters and Congressman Reaver. Apparently, Reaver planned to send him back to China to eliminate the PRC leadership by using the software to program the Colonel to do what they wished him to do. So I decided to eliminate him."

Slick and Hammer looked at Midas and me and started to say something, but Midas whispered, "Put a lid on it, now!" After that, they both settled down and listened.

I AM said, "You have retrieved the information I requested. You also ensured that the samples and documentation on the vaccine were destroyed, and for that, I thank you. I want you and Midas and your two teammates to travel to Jerusalem. First, you will meet with Salomon Levi then all of you will meet with the Israeli Prime Minister. He will be expecting you. This is in preparation for the building of my temple, along with retrieving the Ark of the Covenant, which will be placed in my sanctuary within the temple complex. I expect the sanctuary portion of the temple to be ready two weeks from now.

I have heeded your advice about speaking to the whole of humanity and explaining my word to them. I am grateful for our discussion on the matter. When I speak to humanity and explain my needs, I will also pass judgment on all I deem offensive to me and my word. I will allow the guilty to reflect upon their sins for two weeks. They will be unable to exact any form of retribution against anyone during this time. I will also relieve the President and all the operators of the heavy burden of eliminating the primary and secondary targets. I want you to communicate to the President my wishes to shift his operators' focus to the financiers and donors to the Communist insurgency that plagues your country along with gangs and their leadership within the United States. Relay my wishes to him when we are finished here so the operators can adjust their target packages. I will also speak directly to the President. I will have my right hand, Michael and his legions eliminate all who are guilty. We will speak again when you arrive in Jerusalem."

I said, "Thank you, Lord."

Slick and Hammer just looked at us, and then both said, "What the fuck?"

I said, "Don't worry. Midas and I will explain everything."

I then made my call to the President and informed him of what I AM had relayed to me.

After the President received my information, he convened a meeting in the conference room located within Aspin Lodge. In attendance was the CIA (DCI) director, Susan Hope; Secretary of Homeland Security, Matt Price; and Chairman of the Joint Chiefs of Staff (CJCS), General James Nolt, U.S. Army. The President relayed the information he had just received and asked the assembled group if they had any objections to removing the primary and secondary target packages and concentrating the focus of the shooters on the tertiary targets. Director Hope and Secretary Price stated that they had no objections. On the other hand, General Holt asked, "Mr. President, how can we be sure that the primary and secondary target packages will be eliminated? Unfortunately, we only have one opportunity to do this. But, Sir, it is my duty to make you aware of the possibilities, and I do so now."

The President said, "General Nolt, I appreciate your dedication to duty, and I duly note your concern, but the bottom line here people, our faith in God. I've been thinking of all people, not just our citizens. What kind of faith do they possess? They have no knowledge of God sending his angels to seven people in their teenage formative years, and telling them that they will be part of a group, not knowing the other members, or when this would happen and what that group was supposed to do. Those people have no knowledge of I AM making his physical presence known to us. They do not know what message he gave to us. They do not know what he expects us to do. They do not know the price humanity will pay if we fail in our task. Yet some of these people still have faith in God. That faith must be stronger than our own, because we have knowledge of these events, and they do not. I personally have faith in I AM, but is it more than I had before all this started? Definitely more, but is it enough? Only time will tell. General, what are we calling this operation?"

"Mr. President, it is called "Clean Sweep," and Sir, you are correct about the question of faith. I will give the orders to shift to the tertiary target package. Mr. President, it is 1630 now we will be able to commence operation Clean Sweep within 24 hours, but the optimum jump-off time would be at 0330, so 35 hours from now. If you decide to wait, we can start the operation any day at 0330 EST. We need only your order and one hour to begin."

DCI Hope asked, "Mr. President, I would advise that we get you back to the White House, there would be less curiosity from the press and your access to the Pentagon and other agencies would be simpler."

The President said, "I agree Susan. What should we do with Michael's family and Imam Kamal Bari, Rabbi Tovia Cohen, Reverend Franklin Ham, and Salomon Levi?

She replied, "Well Sir, from what Michael said Levi will be traveling to Jerusalem to start the construction of the temple and the three religious men will be transmitting audio and video messages they've created. They can do it from here. Andrea, is there sufficient security here to oversee and protect Michael's family and our other guests?

Andrea responded, "Yes, Madam Director, the Marine contingent is more than adequate, I can also have some extra agents brought in from D.C. to augment the security."

"Thanks, Andrea, I think I will also have five or so SOG agents brought in to help if needed, if that is satisfactory with you, Mr. President?"

The President said, "Then it's settled. Andrea, will you make the arrangements?"

"Yes, Mr. President."

44

NEW MESSAGE

It was time. Michael's question was valid. After making my presence known to the world so many years ago, humanity had already looked to the heavens for some divine guidance or reason for its existence. Cultures varied in their beliefs, unfortunately, they were all wrong. Beliefs varied in all cases, but all were based on multiple deities, not one of these religious beliefs worshiped one single God.

I decided to make my presence known to all. Out of all of my creation, only Abraham answered my call. I made my presence known to him by allowing my angels to make contact with him. It was Abraham who chose me as his God. The people, later known as the Israelites, were to become my chosen people.

Unfortunately, I sent a contingent of angels to Earth, to help civilization progress. These angels were known as the Nephilim, and after some time, the Nephilim became jealous of my human creation. They began to interbreed with human women. This resulted in offspring with superior intellect, size, and strength. This resulted in widespread sin and societal collapse. I made the decision to restart my experiment with humanity. The only way to ensure the Nephilim and their offspring were destroyed was to erase all of humanity from upon the Earth.

I searched my memory for a truly righteous man and his family. Noah came to mind. I instructed him to build an ark sufficient in size to hold a male and female of every animal species along with Noah and his family. Once Noah completed his assigned task, I opened the clouds and let it rain for 40 days and 40 nights. This allowed the entire Earth to be flooded, thus destroying the Nephilim and the rest of humanity. This upset me greatly, destroying the entirety of my creation except for Noah and his family. I vowed to not destroy humanity as a whole again.

Many years later, I made covenants with the descendants of Noah. Then, I made my presence known personally to Moses after freeing the Hebrew people. Communicating with Moses directly, I engraved my 10 Commandments onto two stone tablets for my people to read.

The years passed and my people flourished, but man's sin was flourishing also.

Humanity continued to have free will. Many began to hear my word and had faith in me at one point. But this trend stopped and started to slowly decrease. So I devised a plan should sin overtake humanity again.

My six were contacted by my angels along with Michael. My plan was to eliminate all non-believers and people who did not heed my word. This would allow my believers to remain alive and save me from destroying all of humanity again. This was my thought, until Michael asked, "If the leaders of the religions failed to properly teach my word, or they outright twisted my word for the benefit of themselves or their religion, then is it the fault of their followers for not following your word? Would it be not better to tell all of humanity about you and your word yourself? There will be no excuse for humanity not having faith in you if you do that. At that point, you may punish them accordingly, but I ask you for one chance for humanity, I AM, just one chance."

Michael was correct, I shouldn't have been surprised, and that's why I chose him those many years ago.

Being the Almighty, I was able to defy and modify scientific and natural laws and norms. So, I stopped all of humanity in its tracts, while I imparted my message to them.

There are five messages to five different groups of people: one to Michael, one to the chosen six, one to the brave warriors who have already begun my Holy wrath, one to the Prime Minister of Israel, and one to the rest of humanity. The new messages were:

"To my warriors, you may be believers in me, you may not be. Your actions so far and in the future are sanctioned by your Lord, the one and only God. Your love for your country and for which it stands are key reasons why I hold The United States of America in such high regard, for if the United States did not hold my word in such high esteem, then my jewel— Israel— may not have been founded or still exist. Your righteousness will be guided by my hand. Your deeds will be rewarded in the afterlife, for you have not sinned, but you are the swift sword of the Lord's justice!"

"Hear me, my six! You have pondered your role for many years. Confused I'm sure, as to what it may be. I will tell you now. Mr. President, your courage to fight the tide of change that attempts to corrupt the core values for which your country was founded is admirable. I have seen your intent, it is pure. I will not burden you with necessary deaths for which I asked you to do. My right hand will do the necessary deeds. Order your people to adjust their planned primary and secondary targets to their third choice of targets. These should be the gangs in your major cities, their followers, and the financiers and donors to your Communist insurgency. Clean this plague of evil from your country so you may return to the principles of your founding fathers"

Listen to me, my holy three. I know the struggles you have undertaken in the quest to relay my message. I will make my word known to all of mankind. After Michael's plea to me, I have reconsidered my first response. It was he who bargained with me for humanity's reprieve. I want you to continue your planned transmissions as before, but rescind my original order not to speak about Michael. You may speak of his pleas to me on behalf of humanity, but be vague about his full identity for now. I have further plans for him of which he is unaware. I will take care of the rest."

"Salomon Levi the loyal, steadfast architect of my new temple. I will send you back to Jerusalem with an angel. When you arrive, your Prime Minister will prepare a path for you to start my new home. Within two weeks, you will complete my sanctuary and place my ark within the sanctuary for part of my being to rest for all time. Salomon, I will tell you the location of my Ark of the Covenant."

"Midas, you are a true and faithful warrior. Continue mentoring Michael, both of you will travel to Jerusalem in two weeks to see me. I will give you further instructions at that time."

"Prime Minister, you are the current caretaker of my jewel, Israel. I will send a man, Salomon Levi, to you and two Americans. One is named Michael and the other Midas. In addition, an angel will appear before you during this message as a sign of my existence. You are to facilitate all the needs of these three men in the preparation of the building of my temple. I want you to consult with the President of the United States about this message, my plans are known to him."

"To the people of the world, this is your father and creator. Depending on your religion, I go by many names, but my name is I AM. I have no mother or father, nor do I have siblings. I was not born like you. I just AM. I do not age like you. I created everything you see, the Earth you live upon, all of the creatures, plant life, the sun and the moon, the whole universe. After I created the Earth, I created the angels, they are almost perfect beings. I then created mankind. I wanted mankind to go through life with free will. I wanted humans to be able to make their own choices in life, good or bad, without dictating their actions of behavior by me. After a while, I understood that this approach was incorrect. At that point, I made myself known to the world. The only response I received was from Abraham. So, you see, I did not force myself upon the world but was chosen by Abraham. He then listened to my word and spread it far and wide. All of this is documented in the Jewish Bible.

Many religions, most of which bear some symbolism to my word but do not explain all of my words. I will explain my word in the simplest of terms. I handed Moses the Ten Commandments that I engraved into Stone myself. I expect everyone to follow these Commandments. In addition, I also want you to observe the Sabbath. I toiled for six days creating the Earth, but I rested and reflected upon my creation on the seventh day. You too may toil for six days, but you will do no work on the seventh day. This seventh day will commence at sunset on Friday evening and last until sundown on Saturday evening.

I expect you to do no work and reflect on your shortcomings during this time. You should seek forgiveness and guidance from me. I also expect you to show kindness and charity to the widows and orphans of the world. If you have sinned by not following my Commandments, ask me for forgiveness with a prayer, or just conversation. If the sin was against a specific person, you must ask them for forgiveness first. They do not have to grant you forgiveness. If that is the case, you may ask me for forgiveness, but only after asking the person you wronged first. After that, you may ask me for forgiveness through prayer for all sins you may commit other than to a specific person. I'm not concerned with the name of your religion. Still, I insist that the religion must be true to my word and it must not add other humans or alleged deities as an intermediary between mankind and me. That has been a problem for thousands of years. Religions and their leaders have used their interpretations of my word to enrich themselves, and their religions. They used these interpretations to murder millions of people for thousands of years. I will punish those among you who have perpetrated this crime. It is an abomination in my eyes.

I am a loving God and a generous creator; my covenant is simple. Your religion is based on a misinterpretation of my word to the Christians. Jesus was a good man, but not the Messiah, and definitely not a person to be worshipped and portrayed as a savior cleansing the world of sin. I can assure you I did not send him for that reason. I am your Father, your Creator. I do not need anyone as a go-between me and my creation. All of the people of the world have direct access to me. You need only to open your hearts and pray only to me.

Muslims of the world, your book is based on Mohammed's life, deeds, adventures, and rules. Mohammed's words are also a misinterpretation of my word. I did not pronounce Mohammed a prophet. Although many of your religion's tenants are admirable, the words are not mine. I AM abhorred that Jihad is something you think you must do to make me happy. I will personally address a group, person, or religion if I think my wrath is warranted. I am your creator and judge overall. My creation will not judge others for sins they perceive are against me or my word. Those who have called for this have sinned in my eyes and will be punished accordingly.

To the Jews with whom I have made my original covenant, your Bible is pure and has stood in its original form and words since its inception. I have chosen you to be the teachers of my word. Be mindful of others' lack of knowledge and help those who wish to learn. The faults I find in you are few, but you must allow those who seek knowledge of your religion to attend temple service without a charge. If a person voluntarily contributes to the temple that is fine. But do not compel them to pay. I'm not concerned with magnificent temples, just a place where my chosen can gather and hear my word and worship.

To those religions which are not Christian, Jewish, or Muslim, I put you on notice: I am the Lord your God, your father, and creator. Believe in me and have faith in my word. Find my teachers that will help you to understand.

To those who have no knowledge of me. Look to any religious Jew and ask them to guide you on how to open your heart and understand the meaning of my word.

Israel, including Jerusalem, are my jewels to all of humanity, for a part of me will reside within the temple sanctuary forever. The United States of America has been her protector since her inception. The United States birth was not an accident but by my hand. The forefathers of this great nation were divinely inspired by me. The Constitution which these men wrote is a road map with the goal being that the rights of the people were given to them from their creator, I AM, not a government or a man, this is paramount. There are forces aligned against this idea. Those forces I will punish. This Constitution should be a model for the world to emulate because I have inspired its creation.

To those that feel they need not commit to my word or show true faith in me. You will be judged when I take up residence within the temple sanctuary. As I said, I created everyone with free will. You may choose freely to truly believe in my word or not, but you will pay the consequences if you freely chose to not believe in me and my word. This is humanity's last warning. I know what is in every person's heart and soul. Although, I would expect the current places of worship will become crowded, if that becomes the case, do not worry. Gather where you can; gather in your homes, and in parks, I am everywhere. I will hear you. Rejoice in my word, seek my guidance.

I will hear you. Do not persecute those who you feel are not following my word. It is not your role to cry blasphemy. I will judge, not you!

The righteous Jews will be my teachers to the world. They will help guide everyone to know me and my word. They are bound by a higher standard regarding my word. Everyone else is not bound by this higher standard, just the simple rules I stated before. Seek out my teachers and learn about me. That is the role of my chosen teachers. Three men will become known to the world, a Rabbi, an Imam, and a Reverend. I have appeared before these men and spoke directly to them. They will form a troika. A bridge from old man-made beliefs to this new dawn. They are not Prophets, nor men to be worshiped. They are men I deem holy. They will oversee the training of religious schools that will teach men and women the process in which I want my word taught. This institution of higher learning will be built within the temple complex.

I have made known that my temple in Jerusalem will be rebuilt. The Ark of the Covenant will have a permanent home inside the temple's sanctuary. This is where a piece of my being will reside for all time. The sanctuary will be finished in two weeks. The temple itself will be completed at a later time.

I must tell all of you my initial plan was to unleash my full fury upon the world due to the lack of faith humanity has shown me if it wasn't for one man who had the courage and forethought to actually debate the merits of my wrath with me. I would have laid waste to most of humanity. He alone asked that I give humanity a chance by speaking directly to the masses and explaining what I expect from you as my children and to let you hear from me, not others. This I am doing now. Everyone must understand that I am a loving God. Your good deeds toward your fellow man make me proud of my creation. These deeds and the discipline to follow My Commandments are all I ask. Doing this will allow families, communities, countries, and the entire world to live in peace and harmony. This will enable me to bless the world with plentiful bounties like water, crops, weather, and many other blessings that a father would bestow upon his children.

I know people will fall short of achieving perfection when following my words. That is expected. Most importantly, they realize their error and ask for forgiveness while trying to better themselves. The world I envision for the faithful is beautiful, bountiful, peaceful and full of love and fellowship. As a token of my love for my creation I now eradicate this man-made Covid 19 virus from humanity.

As for the ones I have judged guilty. You are undeserving of forgiveness and redemption, you will pay with your lives and souls. You will be unable to change your destiny no matter how hard you try. You will be incapable of retribution no matter how hard you try. Your words explaining your innocence will go unheard. Then, you will have two weeks to ponder your fate. At that time, I will extinguish your life, and you will turn into a pile of dust wherever you may be.

Humanity will observe the dust piles and know I AM. Do not remove the dust piles. Wait for them to scatter into the wind of their own accord. This I command of all of you.

45

WE HEAR YOU, LORD

After the message people all over the globe began to reflect upon the word sent to them directly from I AM. Many people actually looked around and saw their families for the first time. What they saw was something more important than their job, how they were perceived by others, how they were conditioned by the Government, media, and the social issues people were expected to endorse.

The people in countries with totalitarian leaders and basically disavowed religious activities were affected the most, simply because they were forbidden to engage in religious activity. It started with the individual families. They actually spoke to each other about the blessings and the word of I AM. These small families compared their feelings with grandparents, uncles, aunts, cousins, and in-laws. The conversations grew, and neighbors became involved. Soon neighborhood religious meetings began to spring up everywhere.

In China, for example, billions of people who have been repressed in speech, thought, and religion, began to come together in one common cause, I AM.

Throughout Asia, the Middle East, Africa, Central America, South America, North Korea, Russia, and her satellite States, people whose families for generations have been repressed by dictators felt a sense of freedom unknown to them until now. They didn't storm the Capitals or Presidential palaces. Instead, they came together in small groups at first to speak of I AM. Then, the groups became larger and larger, filling open areas. There were no formal organizations or formal prayers. Instead, they spoke of freedom, looked to the heavens, and spoke to I am in their own heartfelt words.

The authorities were perplexed, they also heard I AM speaking to them, explaining his love for all and the freedom of free will, so instead of repressing the crowd, they became part of the congregation that was forming right before their corrupt leaders' eyes. They too had heard the voice of I AM and knew in their hearts they had but two weeks to live. They also knew that as much as they wanted to lash out at these rebellious people, they were powerless to do so. They could do nothing but look forward to their deaths in the distant future.

The Vatican was in turmoil. They too had heard I AM. For many, it was clear that though their hearts were in the right place, the doctrine that they had taught and practiced for millennia was misguided. The true believers in God, who revealed himself as I AM. They have no problem facing the truth. The pretenders who used their religion as a tool for power, control, and financial reward had different thoughts, but thoughts were all they had.

They were also unable to do anything for I AM's word and power were absolute.

Around the globe, Muslims were gathering in small family groups relating their experiences and feelings during I AM's revelation. Many felt the burden of duty to Mohammed and his word lifted. They now knew the truth that I AM spoke in their hearts and souls. It was no longer Allah's word but I AM's word.

The Clerics, Imam, and Mullahs who preached the word of Mohammad, not for its content, but for a twisted interpretation that fit a narrative that allowed them to subjugate the less literate and incite violence and revolution towards the enemies of their choosing were not happy with I AM's words. Through their own twisted faith, these men knew enough that I AM would doom them for using their religion the way they had. It was a terrifying feeling to know in their hearts that the very words they had used to control and incite their followers would now condemn them to death in two weeks, and they also were knowledgeable enough to realize that forgiveness was not an option.

There were a few leaders who attempted to disregard I AM's will. With just the thought of ordering retribution against the Almighty's word, a pain so intense as to cause a blood-curdling scream escaped from these leaders' mouths. The pain was so intense as to make a normal person pass out, this was not allowed for these men. Instead, they had to suffer from the wrath of the Lord.

In the United States, families came together and spoke of what I AM had told them all. They were excited there was no longer a divide or rivalry between the numerous religious denominations, everyone knew the rules, I AM had told them directly. They all talked about their forefathers, how wise they were with I AM's help. It really was so simple, yet everyone overlooked the simplistically. The Declaration of Independence said it. "When in the course of human events, it becomes necessary for one people to dissolve the political bands which have connected them with another, and to assume among the powers of the Earth, the separate and equal station to which the Laws of Nature and of Nature's God entitle them, a decent respect to the opinions of mankind requires that they should declare the causes which impel them to the separation.

We hold these truths to be self-evident, that all men are created equal, that they are endowed by their creator with certain unalienable Rights that among these are Life, Liberty, and the pursuit of Happiness. That to secure these rights, Governments are instituted among Men, deriving their just powers from the consent of the governed, --That whenever any Form of Government becomes destructive of these ends, it is the Right of the People to alter or to abolish it, and to institute new Government, laying its foundation on such principles and organizing its powers in such form, as to them shall seem most likely to affect their safety and happiness. Prudence, indeed, will dictate that governments long established should not be changed for light and transient causes. Accordingly, all experience hath shown that mankind is more disposed to suffer, while evils are sufferable than to right themselves by abolishing the forms to which they are accustomed. But when a long train of abuses and usurpations, pursuing invariably the same Object evinces a design to reduce them under absolute Despotism, it is their right, it is their duty, to throw off such Government, and to provide new guards for their future security. Such was the patient sufferance of these Colonies, and such is now the necessity which constrains them to alter their former systems of Government." These men were blessed by I AM.

There was a patriotic fervor that spread throughout the citizenry. The vast majority of the citizens realized the true meaning of their forefathers. Different religions and their sects no longer mattered. I AM and his word was the only thing that mattered, and I AM alone guided their country's forefathers to create the Declaration of Independence and the U.S. Constitution. These documents allowed the people all the freedoms they needed and the power to choose who represented them in their Government.

All of the people who were targets of operation "Clean Sweep" heard I AM, but many in their own arrogance believed that they were true believers in God's word. They thought that they were safe from his wrath. For them, it was an opportunity to have I AM clear out their opposition. So, they just waited.

The shooters and other members of the operation "Clean Sweep," received the general message and their special message from I AM. Many had tears running down their cheeks. They were a proud group and inspired by the message. The entire group had no doubt of the mission from a Constitutional standpoint, but their morale only soared with the personal sanction from I AM.

Many of the owners of the major media platforms were torn. Most who had no religious affiliation were torn between I AM actually being real or are the right-wing Government using some secret military/CIA programming to send this message. The same was true with the major news media anchors and personalities. The news narrative continued to be the same, but with an anti-religious bias.

46

CLEAN-UP AT THE RANCH

Midas, Slick, Hammer, and I were preparing to return to Camp David, but there were a few loose ends I needed to tidy up. So I asked Hammer and Slick to retrieve Thomas Wood, Dr. Norman Peters, and Rich Taylor, and transport them bound and gagged to where we held Congressman Reaver and his son Tim.

Midas asked me if I was going to eliminate all of them. I nodded yes. He said, "I know you have to do this Stone, but I can help you."

I said, "I know you would help Midas, but I AM said I should do it, so I will."

All five men were seated in a small circle in the room where I had interrogated Congressman Reaver and his son Tim. All were bound and gagged. Midas interrupted me and brought in five hoods, he explained how it would cause less mess. The hoods were placed on all five of the men. Without waiting to think about what I was about to do. I walked behind each man and shot a suppressed 230 Gr. FMJ 45 ACP round into the back of each man's head. I felt no remorse or guilt; I was numb and felt no emotions. With that done, we gathered our gear to board Blackhawk helicopter for a short hop to an Air Force base approximately 50 miles to our North. We would fly to Joint Base Andrews and board another Blackhawk to Camp David.

We arrived at Camp David five hours later. We were tired and I just wanted to see Lori and the rest of my family.

We were met by a squad of Marines at the chopper pad. The Squad leader Corporal Mets informed us he would drive us to the lodge where Lori was staying. It didn't take long, the Humvee stopped in front of the lodge. We thanked the Corporal and retrieved our gear, looking up at the porch, I saw Chief Peterson who welcomed us back. We walked into the Great Room. To my surprise, Lori, Arica, Natalie, James, and Lylah were all sitting talking to Imam Kamal Bari, Rabbi Tovia Cohen, Franklin Ham, and Salomon Levi. Lori ran and hugged and kissed me when they saw us, followed by Arica and Natalie. James gave me a hug and shook my hand, little Lylah ran up saying, "Grandpa!" I grabbed her up and gave her a big hug and kiss. Saying, "That's my Little Bit."

I introduced my new shipmates. When everyone was introduced, I asked Solomon Levi, "It is Dr. Levi, correct?"

He said, "Yes, it is I have a doctorate in Ancient Hebrew History."

"Okay, doctor, have you contacted your Prime Minister?"

"I have. The PM called this morning. I spoke to him after his conversation with your President. I'd like to get back to Jerusalem as soon as possible."

I called for the Archangel Michael and he appeared in less than a minute. After I explained what I needed. He agreed, so he and Dr. Levi vanished on their way to Jerusalem.

I asked the three remaining religious men if their audio and video broadcasts were completed and ready to be aired.

Rabbi Cohen said that they had just finished editing two hours ago and the broadcasts were ready to be transmitted. He also informed me that the broadcasts could be aired remotely.

I said, "Okay, gentlemen, get with our CIA liaison here and have him arrange for a government Gulfstream and security detail to transport you to Jerusalem. Explain to him that Imam Kamal Bari has no passport and make the necessary arrangements, also have him book three suites at the Herbert Samuel Hotel because we'll be joining you later and if you need any clothing for the trip have him arrange that also."

They agreed and left to see the CIA liaison officer.

I asked Midas, "What do you think we'll need for the trip?"

He thought about it for a minute before responding,

"I have contacts and friends in Shayetet 13, they are DEVGRU's counterpart in the Israeli special force's community, and they will help us with supplies we can't take with us. So I would like to activate my squad, that's six more men, we have two already, so we have a total of eight. If we can talk the General or the President into it. If we can do that, we can deploy with all our gear and fly over in a C- 130 or a Gulfstream that would be better and covert. We could then cover our mission as a training exercise. With the additional men, we would be almost self-sustaining."

I said, "You're the expert, Brother. Make your list and I'll make a phone call. Whatever we do I need to eat, shower, and get some sleep. You, Hammer, and Slick also need to get chow and rack time."

I looked at Lori and smiled, then said, "I'm starving, how do we get food?"

Lori said, "The Chief will order it from the galley, I think that's what it's called? Do you want pizza or steak?"

I said, "Either one is fine, I need a shower."

After a badly needed shower, I called General Nolt. I explained to him what Midas needed. I was surprised that he was very cooperative. He explained he would speak to the Secretary of Defense and have JSOC cut orders for Midas's squad to train with The Israeli Special Forces and land at Lod Air Base, part of Ben Gurion Airport. He told me to tell Midas to collect what gear he needed from Little Creek and a Blackhawk would pick us up tomorrow at 1500, and go from there to Little Creek to pick up the men and gear, then on to Joint Air Base Andrew to board a G5 to Lod. Finally, he told me that the President had spoken to the Israeli Prime Minister and the Prime Minister has extended to me full cooperation with all of his country's resources. Then he said that he and the President wished us all good luck.

I said, "Thank you, Sir," and hung up.

After eating pizza and steak, Lori and I sat down to relax.

She said, "You look like you enjoy the military stuff."

I said, "I did but I'm too old for it."

"How do you feel about killing those men at the ranch?"

"What? What men?"

"Look, big buddy, when I AM touched me, he not only fixed me physically but I can tell what people are thinking and if they are telling the truth or not."

"Are you serious?"

"Yep, so how do you feel about killing those men?"

"I really don't know. I AM said I needed to do it, that I might not like it, but it was a burden I had to shoulder. I didn't like doing it. So I just did it."

Lori said, "I'm glad you're okay. But, guess what else I know? Don't guess, I'll just tell you. You, big buddy, will become the President of the United States."

"What? You're crazy, Pookie."

"No, I'm not crazy, when I AM passes judgment on humanity in less than two weeks, he will create a large vacancy in the House and Senate, just in the federal Government. The state and local governments will be affected also. Don't ask me how I know, I just do. 221 Democrats in the House and 211 Republicans, with three seats still vacant. There are 50 Democrats and 50 Republicans in the Senate. There are 23 states with Democrat Governors and 27 Republican Governors. I think that only five or ten Congress people will survive. In the Senate four or five will survive. As for the Governors, 12 will survive, all Republicans. The Governors appoint Senators when there is a vacancy before an election. All of the newly elected administration will not survive. The bureaucracy in the federal Government will be cut by 70 percent. The lobbying groups will be cut by 80 percent. The Supreme Court will lose members. Top command leadership in our military will be also affected.

I'm impressed. How do you know all of this?"

"I told you. After I AM healed me, I became more aware. Call it a 6th sense. The President understands some of the implications because of the change in target packages that Operation Clean Sweep was planning to initiate. Since I AM relieved him of two-thirds of the mission responsibilities. I'm sure the General's intelligence is not as accurate as I AM's. There's bound to be more people targeted, don't you think?"

"Yes, I agree. How are the kids doing with all of this?"

"Well let's just say Natalie and James are asking questions about being Jewish, they even had Rabbi Cohen cornered asking him questions. He was happy to help them."

"I'm glad to hear that. I'm beat, how about you?" She nodded and we went to bed.

47

DEVGRU FACILITY OCEANA NAS DAM NECK ANNEX, VIRGINIA BEACH, VA

The four of us climbed out of the Blackhawk assigned to transport us. The crew shut it down, secured it, and said they would be in the area. Midas led us to Red Squadron's team room. When we arrived, twelve or so men were lounging around. A Master Chief, two Lieutenants, and a Commander came over to us. The Master Chief was the first to speak.

"Midas, what in the holy fuck have you been doing, and why did the Secretary of Defense call the JSOC Commander and in turn call Commander Lott at 0300?"

Midas said, "Good to see you too Master Chief! What did the Honorable Secretary of Defense have to say?"

"I don't know Midas, that's why I'm fucking asking you?"

"Well Master Chief, I guess it is a need-to-know situation and you must not need to know."

"Listen here, tadpole!"

The Master Chief was interrupted by the Commander.

"At ease Master Chief! Midas, could you bring you merry band of fucktards to my office?"

Midas said, "Yes Sir!"

We followed the Commander to his office and he had us all take a seat.

Commander Lott began, "Midas, I'm officially giving you your warning orders, whatever the fuck they are. Here is what I know: the President calls the SECDEF and orders him to get you six more men, any equipment you think you might need, make sure your VIP is taken into town, and allow him to purchase any clothing he might need with a credit card sent by the President himself. Then the President tells the SECDEF to supply you with a G5 and a pilot and co-pilot to transport you and your men, equipment, and Mr. VIP here to the Air Force base at Lod in Israel. So naturally, the SECDEF calls the JSOC Commander and orders him to do what the President says, and I get a call at 0300 ordering me to take care of the problem. Interestingly, the National Command Authority seems to be the only person in authority who may know what's going on!"

Midas looked at me. I said, "Commander, my name is Mike Stone and I'm not at liberty to brief you on the operation. Not knowing is good in your case, because all of your superiors have no knowledge of this operation, only the President. Commander, I will satisfy your curiosity without getting your ass in a crack." The Commander looked me up and down and then raised his eyebrow in curiosity.

I said, "Commander are you a religious man? At least now that you had your one-on-one with the big guy upstairs?"

The Commander said, "To answer your question, Mr. Stone, I'm way more religious today after that conversation."

I said, "That's a good thing Commander. Midas and I have met the big guy and spoken to him personally. Actually, he requested our presence in Israel, that's why we are here and, on our way there. You see?"

The Commander looked at Midas like he was thinking, is this guy full of shit, or what? Then Midas gave the Commander a thumbs up. After that, the Commander had no further questions.

Midas gave Slick my sizes for trousers, boots, shoes, sports coat, boxers, and a hygiene kit and told him to buy enough for two weeks. He then had Hammer get the additional six men, inventory the gear they would be taking, and loaded it onto the G5. He also told him to load a full kit for me.

During the flight to Lod, Midas introduced me to my new teammates. First, I met Doc, who obviously was a Corpsman and also trained as an intelligence specialist. His skills were ELANT, electronic intelligence, SIGINT, signals intelligence, interrogation, and espionage.

Then there was Rooster, whose primary skill set was weapons. He was an expert in all small arms use and was a skilled armorer. His secondary skillset involved communications, including radio, satellite, and microwave, and repair and encryption.

Nightmare, was the detachment's operation's specialist, his duties involved planning, route reconnaissance, and tactics. His secondary skill was scout sniper.

Pyro was the detachment's explosive specialist, his skill set covered anything that involved explosives, including creating explosives from household chemicals to traditional military-grade explosives. In addition, he could build explosives or disarm explosives, including IEDs and nuclear explosive packages. He was also the assistant detachment leader under Midas.

Bigen was a man small in stature, whose primary skill set was hand-to-hand combat. Along with that skill set was his proficiency in using and employing bladed weapons, the garrote, and booby traps. His secondary skillset was explosives.

Spade was the primary Scout Sniper and escape and evasion expertise as his secondary. He could pick locks, hotwire any vehicle and crack safes. Midas said he was the best sniper in the Squadron.

As for Hammer, his primary skill set was communications, including military radios, HF radios, UHF, satellite, and VHF radios. In addition, he could repair all radios and build and deploy any wire antenna. His secondary was weapons.

Slick was a Jump Master as well as an underwater scuba specialist. His secondary skill set was as a Corpsman.

Midas explained that these men were all experienced operators, with as many as 15 deployments (and as few as 5) as part of Midas' detachment. As a result, Midas was confident his team could handle it, not knowing the precise mission the team was heading toward.

We really had no idea what I AM had in store for us, only that he had requested our presence. Dr. Levi had called me, informing me that the sanctuary part of the temple construction was underway. All of the materials used for the second temple's construction had been painstakingly researched and handcrafted by master craftsmen who specialized in the second temple construction techniques. The beams, hand-hued stones, altars, containers, lavish draperies, walls, floors, doors, and utensils had already been crafted during the last ten years and stored in the Institute's warehouses; always secured guarded for their protection. The Priests and Ark Bearers are all volunteers. All have submitted to DNA tests proving they are direct descendants of the Levi tribe. All are experts in the rituals and traditions concerning the operations of the sanctuary and tabernacle. The Priestly Source (or simply P), was painstakingly adhered to. In general, the priestly work is concerned with priestly matters, ritual law, the origins of shrines and rituals, and genealogies all expressed in a formal, repetitive style. It stresses the rules and rituals of worship, and the crucial role of priests, expanding considerably on the role given to Aaron (all Levites are priests, but according to P only the descendants of Aaron were to be allowed to officiate in the inner sanctuary). It is not a secret that the Institute is continually reconstructing implements for the 3rd temple, and has devised plans to use them when necessary. What is not known publicly is the fact that 90 percent of the materials, including stones for walls, wooden beams, all utensils, gold and silver plating, cloth, and fabric for the different chambers within the temple, and the priestly garments to be worn inside the sanctuary, are made and stored in a secured, undisclosed location just outside of Jerusalem.

Construction began immediately after clearing the Dome of the Rock grounds. As for the sanctuary, the detailed plans for the temple showed its location outside of the Dome of the Rock grounds.

Dr. Levi explained that a consensus of all the leading religions in Jerusalem agreed that the Dome of the Rock would be dismantled and all relevant parts of the structure saved for future use. Therefore, the wall of the temple complex will begin except for one wall. The unfinished wall will tie in with the others, but a large corridor will temporarily be created for construction and disassembly of the Dome of the Rock. Upon completing the buildings inside the walls, the temporary corridor will be removed and the final wall completed.

The site for the sanctuary and tabernacle had already been cleared and construction would commence in the morning. Dr. Levi also informed me that the Israeli Prime Minister requested Midas and I meet with him upon arrival. Therefore, a car and security detail will be standing by at Lod for our arrival.

48

THE UNDETERRED

A small cell of Islamic terrorists met in a spartan back room in a restaurant on the outskirts of Jerusalem. What was unusual about the cell, they were from three separate terror organizations, none of which were friendly with each other. Representatives from Islamic Jihad, Hezbollah, and the Iranian Quds Force (or Jerusalem Force) were in attendance. All of these men had heard I AM's message, and none believed it to be true. These men knew in their hearts the message was not from Allah but an evil trick created by their mortal enemy Israel, or the "Great Satan," as they referred to the United States. They saw the religious leaders of their faith kowtow to their mortal enemies, publicly supporting the dismantling of the Dome of the Rock to allow for the construction of the Jewish pigs' temple. This, they vowed, would never happen!

There were various operational concepts discussed between the three men. All of the conventional terror operations from kidnappings, car bombs, aircraft hijackings, and bombs in large public areas were all discussed, but none of these plans could stop the dismantling of the Dome of the Rock.

These men were not affected like the leaders of countries that had received I AM's edict; so, the amount of damage they could do to a large population or another country was discounted.

After hours of boasting of each organization's past exploits, the Qud's Force representative proposed the idea of killing all of the Levi priests. These men were needed to fulfill the duties inside the tabernacle, for, without the priests, the sanctuary and the tabernacle could not be used. Furthermore, it would take decades to identify and train new priests. With such a large time frame involved in identifying and training new priests for duty within the temple, it was believed that a negotiation to cease the dismantling of the Dome of the Rock could be achieved. The question was, what type of operation would be needed to achieve that goal. The group decided that only one man was ruthless and cunning enough to carry out the mission. This man was Jabril Kader. His name was known to very few people. No intelligence agency had a photo or fingerprint of him. He has used aliases for the past ten years but has engineered, planned, or taken part in seven spectacular operations. He killed over 500 Westerners and Jews in these operations and wounded or maimed more than 2000 men, women, and children. These three men were part of a group of six people in the world who could contact him.

When we landed at Lod, we were met by three black Chevy Suburbans; each contained a driver and two security personnel. The head of the security detail introduced himself to Midas and me. His name was Avi. He explained he and two of his men would escort us to see the Prime Minister. Midas asked about his men and equipment? Avi explained that it was taken care of, there was a secure area for the equipment at Lod, and we could post a couple of our men there to guard it if we wished. The other men would be transported to the hotel. He also explained that the team was permitted to carry concealed weapons and encouraged us to carry them. But, of course, Midas and I would have to relinquish the weapons before meeting the Prime Minister.

We arrived at Beit Aghion, the official residence of the Prime Minister. It is located at 9 Smolenskin Street, on the street corner of Balfour Street, in an upscale neighborhood of Rehavia, situated between the City Center and the Talbiya neighborhood.

Before entering, we submitted to a security search and were then ushered into the Prime Minister's office. He greeted both of us warmly. The Prime Minister had four men sitting at a large conference table. He introduced them as Tov, Defense Minister; Avi, Mossad Director-General; David, Israel's Chief Rabbi; and Dan, General of all Israeli Defense Forces. We all shook hands and were shown where to sit. The PM asked about our flight and our accommodations. He explained his conversation with our President and his meeting with Dr. Levi.

The General explained that the Commander of Shayetet 13 would be meeting us at our hotel when we returned after the meeting.

The Rabbi asked, "Are you Jewish, Mr. Stone?"

I said, "Yes, I converted to Judaism 31 years ago."

The Rabbi asked, "What makes you qualified to be a representative of the President of the United States, no less, of I AM?

The room became quiet, but everyone seemed to be curious.

I said in a low, calm voice, "Rabbi, I'm not sure what your question is, but if it is why I'm here and not someone else. I'll tell you, all of you."

I said, "I AM chose six people for reasons only he knows. He chose me to lead and organize the six, again because he only knows. I know that Rabbi, you are not one of the six, so I do not answer to you, Rabbi! I only answer to I AM. Is that clear enough for you Rabbi?" The room became deathly quiet. No one said a word.

"What would you like us to do for you, Mr. Prime Minister?"

The Prime Minister explained how Israeli military troops had set up a perimeter around the new temple site and units of Shayetet 13 were positioned around the sanctuary and tabernacle location. It appeared that the Muslims that are worshipers at the Dome of the Rock and the leaders in charge of the area are helping dismantle the buildings on the Dome of the Rock, with no protesters involved.

Midas asked, "Mr. Prime Minister, we know that is unusual considering the history in the area, but understandable, after I AM sent his message. Are there any security threats that the military or the Mossad is concerned about?"

The Mossad Director-General said, "We are always concerned, especially with changing the landscape as we are about to do. I believe the defense minister has the same concerns. The problem we are having is intelligence or the lack of intelligence. There is no chatter whatsoever. The perimeter is secure. We have all known threats under surveillance. So where will you wish to deploy your men?"

Midas said, "Let me speak to the commander of Shayetet 13 when we return to the hotel and we will do a recon of the potential target areas. After that, I'll let your people know where we intend to locate."

The Prime Minister said, "Thank you, gentlemen. You will have my country's total cooperation, let my people know your needs and we will make sure those needs are taken care of. If there are no more questions, I'll have my security detail drive you to your hotel."

When we arrived at the Herbert Samuel Hotel, Midas contacted the Shayetet 13 detachment commander. He was waiting in one of the four suites for which we had made our reservations. The commander, a young Major, handed Midas a folder and told him that inside was an intelligence report on a man named Jabril Kader. However, they have very little information on him and no known photo. The reason for the folder is just a gut feeling— no solid intelligence. The commander also told us that the equipment we have at the airport is under guard by his men and Midas's two men left behind to guard it was en route to the hotel as we speak. He handed Midas an ID card to present to his guards when we decided to access our equipment. We both thanked the commander and he left.

We both read through the folder. Operationally, this guy was a ghost. He was purported to have been involved in several high-profile terror attacks against Israeli targets and U.S. military targets. However, it was all conjecture on the part of Israeli intelligence, and the U.S. intelligence community had zero speculation.

Midas said, "I'm worried about this guy. It's a gut feeling, but I pay attention to those feelings."

I said, "Okay, let's get the team together and figure out how someone could stop the construction of the sanctuary. If we figure out how it could be done, then the *who* isn't so important?"

We called a team meeting. Doc, Rooster, Nightmare, Pyro, Bigen, Spade, Slick, and Hammer sat around the room with Midas and me. Midas explained the tactical situation to everyone and said we need to think outside the box on this mission and identify what situation could stop the sanctuary's construction. I asked Dr. Levi to join us. Dr. Levi explained that all material things for the temple and sanctuary were redundant. He had two extra articles for every material piece.

Nightmare spoke next, "What about personnel? You have people trained for specific roles within the temple, correct?"

Dr. Levi thought about it and said, "Yes, we have trained specialists for every duty within the temple."

Nightmare said, "Okay doctor, which of these personnel are the most important, and without them, could stop construction of the sanctuary or temple?"

The doctor replied, "All personnel manning the temple require a large amount of training, most have university degrees in ancient Hebrew history and have studied at a rabbinical school.

Twenty-four men make up the priests that have various duties within the temple. These men are relieved just before the start of the Sabbath on Friday evening by another group of 24. There are also the 71 men who compose the Sanhedrin, they are a group of scholarly sages who make up the council that determines Jewish religious law, and all rule, within the temple complex. They actually reformed in 2005 in anticipation of the building of the third temple. The priests are by far the most difficult to find and train. First, we must establish their linage through DNA tests to determine if they are, in fact, descendants of Moses' brother Aaron from the tribe of Levi. Then they must volunteer for rabbinical school. After they complete that, they're sent to an advanced course on ancient Hebrew history, geared solely on the priestly duties within the temple. Then they must continue their studies to gain an intimate knowledge of the practices within the sanctuary and tabernacle. It takes approximately 10 years to find and train a priest, if everything goes smoothly. Sadly, we only have 50 qualified priests in total, there are another 30 in the pipeline, but it will be three years before they are qualified."

Nightmare said, "The priests are the potential target. Without them, no sanctuary, or tabernacle."

Everyone agreed.

I asked, "Dr. Levi, where are these men housed?"

Dr. Levi said, "The men stay in a large apartment complex within a rabbinical school East of Jerusalem. They are under constant guard by the Sayarot, an Israeli Defense force Special Operation Force.

Unknown to the public, these men are under just as much security as our nuclear weapons program."

Midas said, "Thank you, Dr. Levi. We will call you if we have further questions."

Midas continued, "All right people, time to put your operational brain housing groups in gear. Nightmare, contact our friends at Shayetet 13. Tell them I need maps of the rabbinical school complex, the apartment building layout, detailed maps of the routes in and out of the area, and the routes to and from the school to the sanctuary. I need to know all modes of transportation to be used, and the security package used to protect these men. I also want Shayetet 13's threat assessment of potential terrorist activity concerning these men. Also, drop the name Jabril Kader to their intelligence people and gauge their reaction."

49

WASHINGTON D.C.

In Washington D.C., the President and his administration were under intense pressure to concede the election. This pressure is being brought to bear by the left, major media outlets, and social media outlets. I AM's message didn't seem to affect these groups. They were relentless in their ongoing attacks. Republican Congressman and Senators who seemed to support the President and his policies had no problem turning on the President, even though their constituents enthusiastically endorsed him. Members of the presidential administration began to distance themselves from him. The media outlets, Democrat politicians, Hollywood, social media, CEOs of major corporations, and professional sports organizations attacked the President. These groups never once acknowledged the message from I AM. The information about I AM was only disseminated through the White House, alternative social media, alternative news outlets, by word of mouth, and different religious organizations.

On the other hand, the American people understood the message from I AM and could see for the first time the stark contrast between the propaganda being perpetrated by the left and the media outlets. The lack of coverage relating to I AM's message seemed to be the straw that broke the camel's back. Crowds gathered in front of all the major media outlets' headquarters in all major cities in the United States. Crowds also gathered in Washington D.C. in front of the Capitol building complex. The groups were peaceful but passionate and loud.

The Mayor of Washington D.C. immediately called the Secretary of Defense, demanding the National Guard be activated and sent to disperse the mob. The Secretary of Defense had personally seen the group gathering and explained to the Mayor that the people gathering were doing so peacefully. He had no intention of violating the people's Constitutional right of free assembly. The Mayor hung up on him and called the Speaker of the House. She was told by the Speaker's aid that she was at lunch and would the Mayor like to leave a message? The Mayor hung up on the aid also.

People continued to spill into the Capital complex area and the mall. People sang God Bless America and impromptu speakers spoke about the Constitution, and I AM.

At a news Headquarters in Atlanta, Ga., people continued to gather outside. They then began to go inside the buildings, not forcing entry, just calmly walking in. Soon the lobbies filled, and people continued to flood into the building; soon, all the floors of the buildings were full of citizens chanting, "We the people!" At this point, security was called, but there was nothing they could do; some of them joined the people. CNM was on the air live when the anchors were startled as the studio began filling up with people. Several group members began asking the anchors why they were not reporting on I AM's message? The people were not threatening in any manner. The anchors were frozen in their seats and did not answer the question. The male anchor that seemed tough on camera began to cry and curled up on the floor in the fetal position. The famous female anchor stared blankly at the camera while she went into shock. The cameras kept rolling. Two of the people drawn into the headquarters, a man and a woman, who happened to be journalism students at Georgetown University, rolled the woman anchor aside, grabbed another chair, and seated themselves at the microphones. They then began interviewing others about the I AM's message.

While waiting for Nightmare to return with the intelligence we needed, I caught the headlines and live video feed on CNM News. I told Midas to check out the T.V. coverage. I then called Rabbi Cohen in the suite next to us.

I said, "Rabbi, this is Stone. Turn on CNM." He did as I asked.

I said, "I believe it's time to upload your broadcasts. Do you concur?"

The Rabbi said, "All three of us have been following the coverage. It appears groups are gathering worldwide, all with a similar theme. We will upload the broadcasts immediately. One of us will keep you updated on the progress."

"Thank you, Rabbi."

I said to Midas, "These groups are forming worldwide, as focused as they appear to be, they have no central leadership. That is about to change."

Midas said I'm really not surprised at the formation of the groups, especially within the countries that have repressed the populists' freedom of speech and religion. You're right about the need for central leadership and guidance. We need to fill that void before someone else does."

Rabbi Cohen called the groups' CIA liaison, who notified DCI Susan Hope. The DCI then notified the NSA and U.S. Cyber Command to begin the broadcasts.

What the world first heard and then saw were three religious men standing dressed in their usual fashion just as they did when they led their respective religious services.

The first to speak was Reverend Ham, "People of the world and children of God. We three humble religious men come before you today to relate to you the word of the one and only God. My name is Reverend Franklin Ham; to my left is Imam Kamal Bari, and to my right is Rabbi Tovia Cohen. Nearly everyone in the world has either seen or heard of the cosmic event that happened almost three weeks ago. That event has been speculated upon by scientists the world over. The three of us were present during the event, but more importantly, we were present and observed the cause of the event. The reason was I AM.

I AM caused the event to prove his existence and heed his warning to the world. The notice, a message really, is this: The 10 Commandments he gave to Moses on Mount Sinai are your guidebook. When I AM had spoken directly to the three of us, he stated that Jesus, although a good man, is not the Messiah, nor the trinity upon which the basic tenets of Christianity were founded and taught. This is what I AM has said."

The Islamic cleric, Imam Kamal Bari, began to speak next. "What Reverend Ham has said is true. I also witnessed the event and heard the spoken word of I AM. I say this because all of Islam has used Allah as the name for our creator. When I AM had spoken to us, he said he had been called by many names, but he said his name is I AM. So now I will call him I AM. I AM also spoke of Mohammad. He clarified that the Koran, the book we Muslims read daily and guide our lives, was written by man and is not words given to Mohammad by I AM himself. Any Muslim cleric or believer who teaches that Jihad is I AM's word is wrong and will be punished for teaching this. Like the Christians' Jesus, I AM stated that Mohammed was also a good man, but his words were man's words, not I AM.

I AM, proclaimed solemn declaration of intent. The people who twisted his words for their own benefit will be punished by I AM himself. This punishment is not strictly for Muslims alone. I AM proclaimed he will punish anyone of any religion who has twisted his words to benefit themselves or the organization or religion they represent. For the people of the world who do not know "I AM," the time is now to pray to him and ask for guidance. I feel I may speak for myself and Reverend Ham when I declare that both Christians and Muslims have to change our own religious doctrine. The one thing that Judaism, Christianity, and Islam have all gotten right is that we believe in the one true God and that God has made his presence known to us. He is I AM. Rabbi Tovia Cohen will guide us in the teaching and understanding of I AM's word"

Rabbi Tovia Cohen began to speak, "People of the world, it is a troubling time, but one only needs to embrace I AM and his word. Your life will become fulfilled reading his word. The covenant he has with his own creation is not difficult. He wants you only to abide by 10 simple rules. For most of you, they are common sense anyway. I AM is disgusted with the corruption and lies leaders of the world and religious leaders have used throughout history to sway the world's populations to suit their agendas. It doesn't matter to I AM what religion you profess, only that you recognize him as your creator and have sufficient respect for his word.

We tell the world this to save as much of humanity as possible before I AM brings destruction to those who do not believe in him. This belief is only known by two individuals, each one of you and I AM. We are imploring the world to embrace I AM now. Do not wait for your religious leaders to say it is permitted, for they may be about to feel I AM's wrath. If you look at your Old Testament and read Zechariah, you will see the will of I AM. I leave you with this, have faith in the Almighty, and the Almighty will have faith in you." I AM has also instructed the three of us to explain to all of humanity that one man stood between the almost complete destruction of humanity and I AM. His name is Michael. He and he alone chose to plead with I AM for a second chance for humanity and for I AM to speak directly with all of humanity and explain what he requires from his creation.

50

KEYSTONE

Nightmare and Slick retrieved maps and blueprints of the building where the priests were housed. They also obtained the routes from the secure apartments to the Sanctuary. Nightmare explained the reaction of the Shayetet 13 intelligence officer when he brought up Jabril Kader's name.

Nightmare said, "The man was not shocked but was hesitant to give him further information."

Midas and I decided to check out the route personally. We drove a nondescript Ford Explorer, supplied by a Shayetet 13 member with whom Midas had already trained. The traffic along the route wasn't congested, although the roads within the city proper were barely wide enough for our vehicle. Midas explained the streets were 1000's years old and were made for carts, not cars. However, we noticed two potential choke points along the route due to the roads' width and the three-story buildings adjacent to the roads' width. I marked the positions on the map. Upon arrival at the secure apartment complex, we saw visible security around the building but no physical barriers to prevent a suicide car bomber from ramming the building. We stopped in the apartment complex's parking lot and waited for one of the security personnel to approach. The man approached and asked us to identify ourselves. Midas explained the vehicle belonged to his friend Tommy Aluf. At the mention of the name, the security man said, "The security around the building comprised all Shayetet 13, and Tommy was their NCOIC."

Midas then asked, "Are you or your team familiar with the route we just took and the potential choke points?"

The man said he was familiar with the route and the choke points. However, he said they were a concern for his team.

I asked, "What is the mode of travel to transport the 50 men to the sanctuary?

The man explained, "The team had planned on using two commercial buses for transport, but due to the heightened threat, the Shayetet 13 leadership were exploring other options."

Midas asked, "What about the IDF's newest armored troop carrier?" The man didn't know of the plans concerning those yet.

I asked Midas about the IDF's troop carrier, and he explained the Namer (Tiger in Hebrew) carries a crew of 11: commander, driver, gunner, and eight troops. The gunner's remote-controlled weapon station can be fitted with a 7.62 mm or 12.7 mm machine gun or 40 mm grenade launcher.

He explained we would need at least seven to carry everyone, but fourteen would be a good safety redundancy and other armored escorts evenly between the Namers.

Midas asked, "What about precautions in case of a truck bomb?"

The Security man said, "The first apartment building was made to look occupied, but in reality, the priests were quartered in two buildings further back in the rear, allowing a sufficient buffer against a truck bomb."

We thanked the Shayetet 13 team member and drove off to finish our route reconnaissance. The route from the rabbinical school to the Sanctuary had no choke points. We looked around for probable locations to plant a bomb or plan an ambush as we sat there. The closest any vehicle could get to the Sanctuary was 50 yards, and that distance of ground was covered with construction debris. The priests would have to cover that distance by foot.

51

JABRIL KADER

The Quds Force representative had made contact with Kader. Kader wasted no time agreeing to the proposed operation after the representative told him of the money he would receive. It was 2.5 million dollars upfront and another 2.5 million dollars if the operation was successful.

Kader had many aliases and many contacts in the Middle East. His plan was simple. Actually, he had already planned for a similar operation like this one. He already had enough explosives staged in a nearby safe house planning for the other operation. He also had two contacts working for the construction crew clearing the grounds where the Sanctuary was now being built. His two contacts had assisted two more of Kader's men in placing the explosives in the exact spot where the two Americans were observing. Kader obtained the explosives CL-20, a new explosive first developed at the naval test range at China Lake. The current state-of-the-art military explosive is HMX at the cost of about U.S. $100/kg. CL-20 is considerably more powerful than HMX, demonstrating about 40 percent deeper penetration in steel blocks. The additional power results from faster detonation velocity (9,660 m/s compared to 9,100 m/s for HMX) and larger density (2.04 g/cc compared to 1.91 g/cc for HMX). The CL-20 was formed into thin, brick-like shapes. Each brick was centered inside a 10-gallon steel drum, surrounded by 12.5 mm steel ball bearings. There were 20 drums spaced 5 feet apart and 4 drums deep. This covered an area 25 feet by 20 feet. Upon detonation, each drum would be electronically detonated. Before detonation, an actuator would release a large spring propelling the drums out of their holes to three feet above the ground, sending 400 12.5 mm steel ball bearings in a 360-degree radius. 8,000 ball bearings would explode into a 100 square-yard kill radius.

The explosives had been planted the night before, and Kader's construction contacts had expertly covered the explosives with construction debris. Kader lowered his binoculars, started his car, and returned to his safe house. He had to make plans for one last detail before being comfortable implementing his operation.

The President and General Nolt were finalizing the start time for Operation Clean Sweep.

The question was whether to do it now or wait until I AM began showing his wrath. They decided to call Michael to see if he had any input.

I answered my phone, and the White House switchboard operator said, "Is this Michael Stone? I acknowledged. She said, "Please hold for the President."

The President came on the line and said, "Michael, how are you? The General and I were just discussing when to begin Operation Clean Sweep. We wanted your input to begin it now or wait until I AM begins showing his wrath. What do you think?"

"Mr. President, I have actually thought about your question. While waiting might seem prudent because logic says to wait until the herd is thinned. Starting now will show I AM we are committed to our roles. After all, it is only four days ahead of I AM's deadline, and anyone who might object will most likely be gone before they can attempt to cause problems. It will also show the nation and the world that we will no longer be held hostage by these people. We, the people, should control our destiny rather than hope that I AM will clean our mess up. That is my recommendation, Mr. President."

The President was silent then responded, "Thank you, Michael, for your candor and advice. We will begin Operation Clean Sweep in 12 hours. That will be 0300 EST.

52

OPERATION CLEAN SWEEP

The President informed General Nolt to proceed with Operation Clean Sweep. The General acknowledged the command and made a phone call to Clean Sweep's operational command. The commanders acknowledged the General's order and began transmitting the warning order for the beginning of the operation.

All subordinate units received the warning orders and began infiltrating their assigned target areas.

At 0230 EST, all units acknowledged they were in place.

At 2300 PT, inside the city of Compton, California. Two 8-man teams were set up outside the separate headquarters of the Bloods and the Crypts. They would attack their targets simultaneously. Three squads of the reserve S.F. component were called to set up a perimeter in a one-block radius surrounding each target. Each squad split into two elements of four men. Both elements placed claymore mines 20 feet from all possible exits from the target buildings. The other 4-man teams used 40mm grenade launchers to fire "Willy Pete" white phosphorus rounds through several windows of the target buildings. It didn't take long for the second and third stories of the buildings to begin burning. Once the fires started, numerous people ran to exit the buildings' ground floors in a panic. With smoke-filled eyes and while coughing, they stumbled into the kill box of the claymore mines and were immediately shredded into piles of dead meat. The casualties that resulted were 25 Bloods killed by the claymores and 13 killed by gunfire when the fires became too intense, and they tried to exit. An estimated 19 more were burned to death inside the building.

A similar fate befell the Crypt headquarters. Again, thirty gang members died due to the claymores, 15 were shot dead, and an estimated 20 burned inside the building.

In Chicago, the main organized gangs comprised the Gangster Disciples, Vice Lords, Black P. Stones, Latin Kings, Black Disciples, Maniac Latin Disciples, Spanish Cobras, Almighty Saints, Spanish Gangster Disciples, Four Corner Hustlers, and the Only Drillas Allowed. These gangs are the main source of gun violence in Chicago. There are upwards of 100,000 gang members in the city, giving it the title of the most gang-infested city in the U.S. Major concentrations of these gangs are in the following metropolitan areas of the city: New City, Chicago Lawn, Englewood, King Drive, Cottage Grove, Auburn Gresham, 95th Street, and a small stretch on the South Side with areas like Princeton Park, Rack City, 093, Nate Ville, and Roseland.

For this large operation, 3 platoons of 120 men were required. Surveillance and detailed reconnaissance had led up to this moment. Finally, with the assistance of the former CIA signals intelligence specialist and the former DHS agents who would provide cover for the shooters, should local law enforcement be alerted? The teams were ready. There were enough personnel to provide one 8-man squad to assault the gang buildings and snipers for overwatch while the teams entered. All of the assaults were similar. This was due to the close confines and the urban environment. The tactics used were basic CQB, which meant close quarter battle tactics used by tier one operators to prosecute HVT's high-value targets like Fallujah, Iraq. Breaching charges were used to blow doors open or shotguns to blow the hinges off entry doors with 12 gauge breaching shells. Once the entry doors were breached and the assaulters tossed in flash-bangs, the 8 men began servicing targets and clearing rooms.

In some cases where entry was available through a second or third story window or door, the team split into two 4-man elements, working from the top-down and the bottom-up, clearing the building. All weapons were suppressed HK Mp7's, using the smaller H&K 4.6×30 round, except for the 12-gauge shotgun to breach the entry door if necessary. 13 different gang headquarters were assaulted with zero friendly casualties 290 hostile gang leaders from 13 other gangs were neutralized. All teams completed their missions in less than five minutes and safely exfil the target areas.

Major cities with dense populations and uncontrollable gang violence across the country were targeted. Cities with minimal gang activity controlled by local law enforcement were not targeted. It is estimated that 27,000 gang leaders and members were eliminated, with approximately 1,000 tier one shooters in less than 90 minutes.

The other half of the force targeted financiers and donors to the Communist insurgency plaguing the country.

The rules of engagement had to be determined. It was decided that if the spouse was connected to fundraising or the Communist party, they would also be eliminated. This was investigated by former DHS agents and former CIA analysts attached to Operation Clean Sweep. If security was present, they were deemed hostile because of their voluntary association with the target.

Major donors and financiers in the top 50 major cities of the United States, the leaders and second-in-command members of the Communist party, and any off-shoot groups financed by them. All were part of the target packages. The totals of the target packages were over 800 men and women.

Eliminating these targets used much less manpower than the gangs. The majority of the assaults were done by 4-man teams. They eliminated perimeter guards, bypassed alarm systems, picked locks, entered the homes in a tactical line, cleared rooms, eliminated interior guards, and neutralized the targets. If children were present, they were searched and locked in an interior space for release when the team departed the target area. There were a couple of close calls when security guards attempted to defend their sponsors, but no friendly casualties. Finally, shortly before 0530 EST, all targets were neutralized, with zero friendly losses and only three injuries from sprained ankles.

Operation Clean Sweep may have come to a successful conclusion. Still, it was just the beginning of the ignited fireworks by the left-leaning Democrats and the (in-name-only) Republicans. It was Wednesday morning, two days before I AM's wrath. The major news media and social media were demanding answers to the murders of thousands of people the day before. No one knew who or why the murders happened. There wasn't even a total body count yet. The media was speculating on several theories, but it was only speculation. They were adamant that the United States Justice Department investigate the mass killings. As the day progressed, two or three groups were targeted; one group was composed of gangs and their leaders, the wealthy donors to Democratic Progressive causes, and the third, leaders of not-for-profit organizations that promoted social justice issues. Social media went berserk. Thursday at about 1300, a group of Democrat lawmakers from Congress and the Senate held a press briefing on the killings. They were demanding an investigation by the FBI into the mass murders. They were also demanding the President make a statement regarding the massacre.

The President's advisors and cabinet members asked the President's Chief of Staff if the President would make a statement. It was interesting that several Republican governors said that the killings of gangs and their leaders may be outside the law and our justice system, but the governors would not mourn their loss. The governors of Florida and Ohio, who have experienced rampant gang violence in Miami, Jacksonville, Cleveland, and Cincinnati, actually hinted at pardons for the perpetrators.

Hammer came into the room Midas and I were staying in and told us of the killings and divide the country was experiencing over the issue.

I looked at them and said, "I bet the pole numbers skyrocket for those two governors in the next day or two."

Midas said, "I agree, but there might be fewer people to poll." Then he laughed. He then asked me when I thought I AM would act?

I said, "I don't think he'll do it on the Sabbath. So, I figure tomorrow before sundown, but that's just a guess."

Midas said, "The Sanctuary is complete except for locating the ark. Has Dr. Levi said anything to you about it?

No, he hasn't. That doesn't worry me as much as the feeling I have about the safety of the priests. Are there any updates on the potential threats on our priests?"

The rest of the team entered the room. Midas's men had just finished doing P.T.

Midas said, "Nightmare, are there any updates from our brothers in Shayetet 13?"

Nightmare responded, "Yes, Chief, their operations NCO and I became cozy after tipping back about a case of beer. I asked him about the threat from Jabril Kader. He was hesitant at first but gradually started telling more. Kader was an informant for the Mossad 20 years ago, and then he just fell off the grid. Mossad wrote him off as dead. As the years progressed and a new wave of attacks began in Israel, Mossad started hearing rumors about a terrorist everyone called the ghost. The intelligence on the ghost was compartmentalized within Mossad. A couple of former Mossad agents went through selection for Shayetet 13 and passed.

This is how the operation's NCO got a whiff about Jabril Kader. So, these Mossad agents knew of Jabril Kader's existence and his alleged terror attacks. The Ops NCO is worried, but Mossad doesn't want Kader's relationship with them discovered. They did arrange to use the heavily armored troop carriers to transport the priests tomorrow. Other than that, the government or the Mossad feels there is no other credible threat."

Midas said, "Fuck! Did they request us to deploy anywhere specific?"

Nightmare said, "No, they didn't even mention deployment."

53

THE WORLD T MINUS 1 DAY

Around the globe, people were speaking of I AM. Many sought out Jewish temples and their rabbis in the quest for knowledge about I AM. Others talked with Jewish friends. Social media was full of posts requesting that they be added as friends to known Jewish blogs or individuals. Churches and Mosques worldwide asked rabbis of nearby temples to be guest speakers at their places of worship. Those who could not make contact with anyone Jewish began a frantic online search for the tenants of Judaism. Over the last week, the search terms; Jews, Rabbi, temple, Judaism, and Old Testament were the most sought-after search phrases on the Internet. Large portions of the world's population actively sought I AM's word.

The mega televangelists were somewhat worried. Their subscriptions, donations, tithes, and audience ratings were cut nearly half in 10 days.

Professional football games' attendance declined considerably since some players had decided to take a knee and not stand for the national anthem. As a result, people pooled their money and began donation drives to rent several stadiums during the week. These stadiums allowed people to gather and hear the word of I Am from multiple religious speakers from several different religions. There had been seven such gatherings since I AM had spoken directly to the people. There were also 3 other similar gatherings planned but were stopped by Democrat mayors in the cities where the stadiums were located.

The crowds continued to grow around the capital complex. The crowds continued to be peaceful; it was almost festive. People were gathered in large groups listening to speakers, talking about I AM's message, our founding fathers, their relationship with I AM, and the wisdom he bestowed upon them. There was much talk about how they drafted the Constitution and started this fledgling nation amid the great empires of the time. They questioned why our current leaders made professions of politics and entered their terms with average incomes, always promising change and a better country, only to leave office without making change for the better and becoming millionaires.

The media for years denigrated candidates who came from the outside and just wanted to serve the public because they were not politicians. They would say, "How can they run the government without experience?" Finally, after hearing this for so many years' people began to believe it. Now they were questioning that idea and felt used by the career politicians. The President had made several appearances with the groups, telling them that their questions were valid, and continued their peaceful vigil. He also began and ended his visits with a prayer to I AM.

The left and the media portrayed the mob as domestic terrorists and the President as an insurrectionist. Congress demanded he stopped the gatherings and threatened to impeach the President for a second time. When questioned by the media about the charges, Congress lobbied against him. He would smile at them and tell them to have a great day.

Rabbi Cohen, Reverend Ham, and Imam Bari started having virtual services broadcast worldwide. At this point, there had been three such services since I AM's message. The Israeli government arranged a large sports stadium to host the next service, which was to take place on Monday after I AM showed his wrath.

The sanctuary and tabernacle were completed with one day to spare. It was incredibly beautiful, and the detail was magnificent. Solomon Levi explained that he had transported enough priests from the rabbinical school to man the sanctuary. He had accomplished this by having the men dress like construction workers and brought them in grouped in twos and threes over the past three days. The priests were stationed at the entrances to the tabernacle, and the others were within the tabernacle, the Holy of Holies. These men stood where the Ark of the Covenant should be resting; the others were stationed around the altar, where the sacrifices were to occur. A fog appeared to fill the tabernacle chamber as we stood admiring the intricate carvings and gold and silver plating. We stood transfixed when the fog began clearing several minutes later. Apparently, the long-lost ark was now sitting in its proper resting place. Dr. Levi started to cry tears of joy for I AM's gift. People began to move towards the ark. Dr. Levi shouted to stop, stay where you are! Do not get any closer or touch the ark. He explained that it would mean certain death for just anyone to come into contact with the ark.

The ark was truly beautiful with the out-stretched wings of the two cherubs of gold on top. As everyone stepped back from the ark, a shofar blasted, and a second later, Archangel Michael appeared with his six angels. They surrounded the Ark of the Covenant in a protective circle, and when the circle was complete, a pillar of fire descended from above and covered the ark.

The Archangel Michael said, "I AM has just placed part of his being inside the ark for all time, and he will begin cleansing evil from the earth at 12:00 noon. It is now 9:00 a.m. You have two hours to retrieve the rest of the priests before this happens."

I asked the Archangel Michael, "We are concerned about the security for the rest of the priests. I'm sure we can transport them to this location, but they must travel about 50 yards in the open when they dismount the armored vehicles. So if there is an attack, we are sure it will happen there. Do you have any suggestions?

"You know I'm not allowed to give suggestions, Michael, but I do see the need for your concern. I can tell you to remember your conversations with I AM. Do you remember what he told you about your own protection? If you do remember that, plus your faith should enable you to protect the remaining priests."

Before I could thank him, the angels vanished.

Michael F. Decker

54

THE GAUNTLET

Midas and I just had started discussing the situation when Midas's tactical radio crackled. It was the Shayetet 13 command net. They transmitted that all available units needed to respond to a grade school west of Jerusalem. The on-site security was taking heavy fire by an unknown number of heavily armed men. Several of the attackers had entered the school and killed an unknown number of teachers, and we're taking more than 100 children ages 7-to-11 hostages. The demands were unknown at this time.

Midas looked at me and said, "It's a diversion! They are going to hit us here." Then, he called the detachment, "Listen up, Pyro on me, Spade and Nightmare deploy your long-range rifles. Set up positions for views of probable sniper hides and look for anyone that could possibly detonate an explosive device within sight of our location."

Pyro came running to us.

294

Midas said, "I'm taking the rest of the team to the rabbinical school. We will escort the priests here. You heard my orders to the two snipers. Keep your eyes open for someone with a remote detonator. I think our friend would like to see his work done in person. Michael, try to figure out how to protect the priests once we get back. I'm rolling."

I told Pyro that the round-trip travel time from the rabbinical school to here was (give or take an hour) depending on the composition of the convoy; it could take another 15 minutes. He agreed. I had no idea what to do. So, I prayed for the safe transport of the priests and the safe return of my new friends. We waited and observed. I knew that terrorist cocksucker Kader couldn't start the ambush without seeing the priests.

Midas called on the radio 40 minutes later and said, "Pyro, we are en route with the package. The Minders all left for the crisis area; the only additional manpower is the drivers, ETA 20 minutes. Copy?"

Pyro answered, "Acknowledged Boss, standing by."

I suddenly felt the need to call Lori. So I dialed her cell number, which I miraculously remembered. She answered, and I said, "Hi, Pookie. Are you doing okay?

"Yes, we're fine. What are you doing?"

"They are getting ready to open the sanctuary, and we are waiting for the priests to arrive. They should be here any minute. I just wanted to hear your voice and tell you how much I love you."

Lori said, "That's sweet, but what's wrong?" I had forgotten she could detect a lie after I AM healed her.

"Nothing is wrong. I just wanted to check in; the team is waving for me now. Tell everybody I send my love and give Little Bit a kiss for me. I love you. I'll call later, bye."

I think I was about to cry.

Lori hung up, worried. Then, finally, she got everyone together and turned on the T.V.; they were supposed to be covering the opening of the sanctuary live.

The only thing I could think of was what the Archangel Michael had said to me, "Remember what I AM said to do about protecting yourself, and have faith, and you should be okay." So I thought about what I AM had said to me.

He said, "As for your protection, I will be with you and bless your Mezuzah. It will be your strength." I said to myself, "There could be worse ways to go out. I pray this works!"

Spade called on the radio and said Midas was about 2 minutes out.

I asked for a Sit Rep. Spade, and Nightmare said, "No targets yet."

I told Pyro to secure the inside of the sanctuary, and he complied.

The news media was the first to arrive. I didn't have time to warn them because Midas and the convoy pulled up right behind them. I called Midas on the radio.

I said, "Listen to me! I'm coming out to the armored vehicles. While I'm walking out, have the team flex cuff one arm of each priest to the next priest in line. When they are all flex cuffed, have each team member flex cuff themselves to the priests. When I get there, have the first group come to the rear ramp. I will flex cuff one of my hands to the first man in line. Only then let them exit the vehicle. I will escort the line to the next vehicle and repeat the process until everyone is connected to me. That includes you, Midas. It is our only chance to protect everyone if that fuck stick tries something. Do you copy?"

Midas answered, "I copy you, you goofy fucker. If it works, I personally will pay for us to get drunk. Listen up, team! Do everything Stone just said by the numbers. Sound off." The team acknowledged.

They were ready when I arrived. The priests were scared and kept talking in Hebrew. Finally, I got loud and told them to shut the fuck up! They must have understood me because they didn't say another word.

I told Midas and the team my plan. They looked at me. One of them said *that's* the plan? I said, "It's all I got."

Midas said, "Listen, ladies, the only easy day was yesterday." Surprisingly they all laughed. What a bunch of weird fuckers, I thought.

Midas called the snipers for a SitRep.

They replied, "Nothing yet."

He said, "We are moving." They clicked their mics in the affirmative.

We started moving across the 50 yards we needed to cover. We were at the halfway point when Spade came over the radio, "I have movement 700 yards to your 5 o'clock atop a 3-story building. Far-right window. No shot."

Nightmare said, "I have eyes on target, firing!"

Spade said, "Hit! Fuck! He hit the remote!"

Nightmare said, "Taking a second shot! Kill! Target is down."

It was too late. We took two more steps, and a large explosion ignited all around us. There was no sound, just smoke and debris blocking our vision.

The news media was broadcasting live, and the reporters were taken aback when we dismounted the armored vehicles with 30 priests flex cuffed to one another. They were attempting to speculate on the reason for this when two rifle shots got their attention. All the media immediately tried to find some type of cover. One cameraman kept the camera fixed on our group when an enormous explosion filled the camera's viewfinder. The networks back at their respective headquarters looked in shock at the carnage.

My family watched the whole thing in abject horror.

Midas and I looked at each other.

Midas said, "Keep moving!" So we did and made it to the sanctuary entrance, where Pyro opened the door and guided us inside.

I asked Midas to confirm that Kader was dead. Nightmare confirmed it.

I said, "Okay, I have to make a call. Then I have to see if I shit myself."

I called Lori and told her I was fine. Don't believe what you just saw on T.V. I'm fine. Love you. I'll call you back when we get this sorted out."

Midas found me. He asked, "Did you shit yourself?"

I said, "No, but I should have."

He said, "Good! I'm calling Shayetet 13. We are leaving for the hotel when they get here, and I will pick up the bar tab."

We made our way back to the hotel. It took Shayetet 13 about 30 minutes to relieve us. They had captured or killed all the terrorists at the school and confirmed that the attack was used to draw assets away from the sanctuary. We were sitting at the hotel bar working on our second round of drinks when Slick motioned for us to look at the big-screen T.V. It replayed the entire encounter we had just been involved in. You could clearly see Midas and me leading the priests toward the sanctuary. At the halfway point, the explosion was visible.

Midas said, "What in the fuck?" All of us saw it clear as day. When the explosion started, you could see an invisible dome over all of us. It began at the halfway point, covered the distance to the sanctuary, and included the entire sanctuary. You could see debris from the blast bouncing off the invisible shield and piling up around the shield's perimeter. People in the bar began looking at us.

Hammer said, "He who hesitates is usually fucked!"

Midas said, "What the hell are you talking about, Hammer?"

I said, "It's a quote from Stephen King's book, "Under the Dome." Nightmare said, "Another pop-culture book expert. I like that."

I said, "Time to go, ass clowns. Let's head for our rooms."

We all gathered in Midas and my suite. The team just looked at me.

I said, "Listen. I AM blessed the Mezuzah I wear on this gold chain." I showed them. "Anyway, he said it would protect me. So, the only thing I could think of was to connect everyone to me. I was hoping that everyone connected to me would be protected."

Midas said, "Well, Bro, thank you. It sounded and looked like one hell of a detonation!"

As a toast, the team thanked me and downed whatever they were drinking. I was definitely getting a buzz.

Nightmare said, "We are getting popular with the local population. I think it's time to beat feet, Frogmen."

Midas agreed, "Call the pilots Nightmare. It's time to go home."

55

JUDGMENT

The weather changed dramatically all over the globe at 1200 hours, Zulu time. The sky looked as if a major thunderstorm was forming. Weather forecasters and astronomers were reporting a never-before-recorded phenomenon, an unscheduled eclipse of the sun. Then, it became totally dark everywhere in the world.

It started simultaneously around the globe. It was first noticed by people watching the news anchors on CNM as they began another round of trash talking about the President and his devoted followers. Suddenly, the man and woman behind the news desks vanished into a pile of dust with just their clothes left sitting in their chairs. Next, people changed channels to other major news outlets and saw more clothes and piles of dust in the anchors' chairs.

I AM's judgment completely decimated all the major mainstream news outlets that had long ago decided to lie to the public was good for their bottom line. Included in this group were the CEOs, their boards of directors, most of their families, all of the producers, directors, and media personalities who had helped to spread the lies.

The CEOs of most social media platforms, their boards of directors, the people who wrote the code for their algorithms, and their fact-checkers all met with I AM's judgment.

Several European billionaires were meeting in a posh mansion on the outskirts of Zurich, Switzerland. Attending the meeting were representatives of 50 NPOs, (nonprofit organizations) who support and donate funds to groups that support Socialist views and doctrine. The goal of these groups is to form a narrative that is anti-American and portrays the U.S. Constitution and its founders as racist slave owners. Some of these groups have been major participants in the sponsorship of riots that have been seen in U.S. cities during the past year. These groups also finance the campaigns for district attorneys in many of the larger, progressive U.S. cities. These D.A.s have actually dropped charges on large groups of these rioters.

These men and women sat drinking, eating, planning, and congratulating each other for their accomplishments and future plans until a holy vengeance swept the mansion, and everyone attending no longer existed. The entire estate was filled with piles of very expensive clothing, and human remains turned to dust.

The Chinese Politburo was meeting in full session. On the agenda was the current insurgency being manipulated by these men through the MSS, Ministry of State Security, and the leaders of the PLA, which stands for the Peoples' Liberation Army. The Chairman of the Communist Party requested the presence of the heads of the MSS and the top generals of the PLA. When all the men were in attendance, and the questions began in earnest from the Chairman and the other Politburo members, it was at that very moment that all their decades of planning vanished. Every man in the room died, and all that remained of their dreams were piles of dust and clothing.

Along with these men throughout China and abroad, all officers within the PLA, all voluntary members of the Communist Party, including state and local leaders, every scientist involved in the development of weapons of mass destruction, biological and germ warfare, and cyber espionage died where they stood or sat. The entire Chinese Communist system was destroyed. Communist China's estimated population was 1,439,323,776 billion, approximately 18.5 percent of the total population. The number of people involved in religious worship, whether Christian, Jewish, or Muslim, practicing their religion legally or illegally totaled 100,000. If you add to the total number of people who heeded I AM's word, the total amount of survivors remaining is 287,964,755 million people. In her great wisdom, China lost nearly 80 percent of its population in the blink of an eye.

The leaders of Iran in every sector of government, military leaders, terror organizations that Iran supports, and religious leaders who used I AM's words to subjugate their people and others, along with those who did not recognize I AM's warning, all died in place. This allowed a new generation of younger people who listened to I AM to fill the political void.

Mother Russia did allow for religious freedom to a certain extent. But, like the countries already mentioned, the leadership at the highest levels died along with nearly 30 percent of the total population, leaving only 100,000,000 people alive.

North Korea was interesting in retrospect, a country of 25 million populated with peasants for the most part. The Communist leadership treated them as slaves. They had no communication with the outside world. The city of Pyongyang was the complete opposite of the rest of the third-world country. It was modern. It was also solely populated with the privileged class of North Korea, totaling more than 3.25 million people. The Army consisted of approximately 1.5 million men. About 250,000 were serving in the PLA's officer corps from that number. The number of high-ranking Communist Party members was estimated to be 200,000. For unknown reasons, the so-called peasants of North Korea enthusiastically listened to I AM. The total death count was a scant 5,000,000 million people, including the government's leadership, the population of Pyongyang, the entire officer corps, and the high-ranking Communist Party leaders.

In fact, every Communist, totalitarian, dictatorship, theocracy, every government that suppressed the people's freedom was killed.

The countries that respected their citizen's freedom were not without casualties for the most part. There were citizens and politicians within those governments who actively sought to reduce the liberties of their citizenry. These individuals were sought out by I AM and forfeited their lives.

We were about 30 minutes into our almost 16-hour flight when Hammer came up to Midas and me.

He looked alarmed and said, "Boss, we have a no-shit problem!"

Midas said, "What is it?"

"The pilot and co-pilot are gone."

We went to the flight compartment as fast as we could. But, unfortunately, the flight crew was gone. So the only thing left was the pilots' uniforms and a pile of dust in their seats.

Midas checked the instrument panel, decided that the plane was on autopilot, and let out a sigh of relief.

He said, "All right, I can fly her. But I'm going to need another set of eyes up here. Stone you up for it?"

I said, "Sure, I'm game."

In Washington D.C., the House of Representatives voted on a spending bill in session. All 435 members were present. They were hurrying the vote so the Senate, which was also in session, could vote on the bill and send it on to the President. CSPAN 1 and 2 were carrying both votes live.

The Speaker called for yea or nay votes and afterward announced the yeas had won it. At that point, a Republican from Indiana requested a recorded roll call vote. As the vote started live on CSPAN, 430 members of Congress died at the exact same time everyone else in the world died. The sole surviving members of Congress were 5 Republicans.

In the Senate, the Minority leader was in the middle of an impassioned speech regarding immigration when I AM's wrath filled the Senate chamber. The Minority leader and 44 of his fellow Senators died right then. Just dust piles and expensive suits remained. It was the same with the candidates who had won the election in November. This included the Federal government, Congress, Senate, the newly-elected President, and Vice President, moreover, State government, State Representatives, State Senators, Governors, and Lt. Governors, State Treasurers, State Auditors, Judges, and local election winners from school board to Mayor. But the major disaster happened in the Federal government and the State governments. In Congress, the 4 remaining members had just won reelection, and one Congressman who had won his first term was all that remained of Congress. The Senate also had 5 living members who had won reelection. Of the 50 Governors, only 20 survived, all from Red states. This posed a problem. The Governors of each state are required to appoint the Senators for their states if a vacancy needs to be filled.

The Supreme Court lost 4 members, the Chief Justice and three Associate Justices.

The military hierarchy was also affected. Several Generals, Colonel's, Lt. Colonel's and Admiral's, Captain's, and Commanders died. Still, these men and women were primarily administrative and not part of the combat arms for the most part. The problem will be promoting junior officers into senior positions since the Senate must advise and consent to the names of officers submitted for promotion if promoted above O-4.

The White House was put on total lockdown per the Secret Service. At 1500, three hours after I AM began his judgment, the President called a meeting of his National Security Council within the Situation Room. His National Security Advisor, Pete Miller, was present. Miller gave the President the latest intelligence that was known at the time. So far, all that was known was the United States was safe from any likely foreign intervention. The military's alert readiness status was at DEFCON 3. This level was presented to the President by the Secretary of Defense. The code word for this was "Round House." It is a level above DEFCON 2, normal military force readiness. DEFCON 3 is a ready alert status above normal readiness. Many of the United States' strategic missile submarines are constantly in this ready state, but the rest of the armed forces are not. It allowed the Air Force to prepare aircraft to mobilize within 15 minutes. DEFCON 2 & 1, for the most part, pertains to the likelihood or probability of attack or retaliation with nuclear weapons.

Miller updated the President on the number lost in the Senate, the House, and the Supreme Court. He also explained the problems in reinstituting all three.

Vice President Paul Times spoke up, "Mr. President, I think under the circumstances you need to consider invoking Presidential Directive 51. The continuity of government is paramount with the virtual destruction of two-thirds of our government." Miller agreed also.

The President said, "Pete, make it happen. You're right as usual, Paul."

With the Presidential directive ordered, the President (for all intents and purposes) became the Government of the United States.

The President called his Press Secretary into the Oval Office. The President smiled when his Press Secretary, Sheila Long, entered the room.

He said, "It's nice to see you, Sheila. I'd like you to make a statement to the White House press pool.

She said, "Yes, Mr. President. But it seems there are only 3 of them left alive. The rest are just piles of dust with their clothing in the seats where they were sitting."

He said, "I see. Okay, have Peter Miller give you the pertinent information on what we know and announce that I will personally be giving a statement this evening at 6:00 PM. Sheila, also tell the networks I will require their statement coverage. Because of what I AM told us, please ensure that the dust piles remain in place."

"Yes, Mr. President."

56

THE AFTERMATH

We were all tired after the 12-hour flight from Israel. Midas did a fine job flying, and I just sat there watching him fly and making sure we both had plenty of coffee. What had happened in the outside world was far from our minds, as we had no access to the news coverage.

We arrived at Andrews Air Force Base at about 0030 and were met by a Blackhawk and her crew for the short hop to Camp David. Once there, a Sergeant and his driver met us there who were polite and transported us to our assigned quarters in a large black panel van. I said my goodbyes to the team and told Midas I'd see them in the morning. I told him not your morning, my morning, about 10:00. He laughed.

I started for the front door when Chief Peterson opened it and greeted me. After exchanging pleasantries, she showed me in.

Lori was there reading a book. She jumped up and gave me a big hug and kiss.

She said, "I was so worried about you. Is everything okay?"

I said, "Everything is fine, Pookie. I missed you."

She told me that after the live coverage at the sanctuary and the video broadcast by the three religious men, someone on Facebook identified you. Then more people recognized you and started asking questions on social media platforms. They speculate that you are some kind of prophet who has God-given powers. I called Kim to see if she would feed and water the dogs, and she said she would. I explained to her about your involvement in everything.

She said news media trucks and reporters parked on the road outside our house.

I said, "I guess the cats out of the bag."

She told me that Scott called Eric and wondered where you have been.

Lori said, "I called Scott and told him. He said I should have someone with authority call QPS to excuse my absence. She told me that she called the President.

The President said he would take care of the problem. Then, he asked for the number he should call. A few minutes later, he called back and said he spoke to someone in the Feeder department, and they were very cooperative. They told the President that all you had to do was put yourself back in service whenever you decided to come back. I also called Carl and told him what the President told QPS."

I said, "Good move. Thanks, Pookie. I guess we should head home. I don't have anything else to do, and please remind me to call Mom on the way home."

Lori said, "Okay, I will, tell the kids. When do we leave?"

"Tomorrow, I would think? I'll call and ask."

I called the President but was told he was in a meeting. So instead, I was transferred to his Chief of Staff. He introduced himself as Robert Outts. He said how honored he was to speak to me and that the President had only good things to say about me. He told me the President wanted me and my family to come to the White House 2 weeks from that day for a celebration the President wanted us to attend. He also noted that the Secret Service would pick up my entire family and transport us to the White House and back, adding that everyone would be staying in the White House, not at Camp David. I told him that sounded great and we would be looking forward to it.

I told him of my concern with the news media parked in front of my house. He said not to worry about it. The President would ensure my family's privacy. He told me a Blackhawk would pick us up at 1400 tomorrow and fly us to Andrews, and a Gulfstream 4 would fly us to Columbus, and U.S. Marshalls would drive us home. He thanked me again.

The meeting the President was attending was with his full Cabinet. In addition to the Cabinet were the surviving Congressman and Senators. The main topic was the implementation of Directive 51. The President wasn't asking for opinions. Instead, he was informing the group of his decision. Another topic was the fall of the dictatorial, Communist, and Theocratic governments and what could be filling the void. The

President was taking this topic under advisement. Finally, a topic was brought up by the head of the CDC regarding Covid 19. The doctor stated that tests being sent to the CDC were thought to be positive but turned out to be negative. He further noted that his colleagues had reached out to medical facilities throughout the U.S. and other countries, and all reported similar findings.

The President asked, "Did you draw any conclusions in your findings, Doctor?"

Mr. President, it is too soon to be definitive, but if this trend continues, it may indicate the virus has disappeared.

The President asked, "Is it possible that I AM removed the virus?"

The doctor said I would say that is a logical statement. There is no scientific explanation that I'm aware of."

The President said, "Doctor, please keep us informed."

The judgment I AM met out was an equal-opportunity justice. The criteria were simplistic: you were killed for the oppression of other people, for religious, personal, greed, or power reasons. It didn't matter your race, religion, ethnicity, or gender. Others included in this were participants in the removal of freedom and liberty from countries around the globe. The population of the earth was approximately 7.8 billion people. After I AM's judgment, there remained 5.5 billion people, roughly the world population in 1987. The approximate death toll of the world population was 28 percent or 2.2 billion people.

The amazing fact was that 100 percent of the entire population had faith in I AM for the first time.

This revelation was unique. It meant that everyone had a belief in I AM in common.

The next morning, we said our goodbyes to the staff at Camp David. Midas and the team were waiting for us at the helicopter pad. We exchanged handshakes and Bro hugs.

Midas said, "I have to give it to you, Jarhead. We are going to miss your sorry old ass."

I thanked all of them for the experience and flipped Midas off as I went through the hatch to the chopper.

The flight home was enjoyable. Everybody was talking about what had happened. I was just happy to finally relax.

Arica and Natalie came over to me, and Natalie said,

"Daddy, we want to apologize to you."

I said, "For what?"

She said, "Well, we have always been proud of you." Arica said, "You know your Marine macho stuff. We always say you are annoying, and we always believed what you told us, but thought maybe you exaggerated your stories a little."

I said, "Really, I didn't know that."

Natalie said, "After all that has happened. We just wanted you to know how proud we are of you."

I looked at my two girls and hugged them tightly while fighting tears.

I said, "Thank you, girls. I love you both so much." Lori and I were holding hands when she leaned over and kissed me.

She said, "We're all very proud of you."

We finally pulled into our driveway in two black Chevy Suburbans. We got out, and the Marshals helped us with our luggage. Two Marshals grabbed a footlocker-sized pelican case and took it in the house.

I asked the lead Marshal,

"What's in the pelican case?"

He said, "There are three of them." He then handed me a note.

I opened it. It read, "Here you go, you old fuck stick. Just something to remember us by. Two is one, one is none. It's your kit; you dumb Jarhead, and some ammo." It was signed by Midas.

Once in the house, I opened one of the cases. It was a complete loadout, H.K. 4-16 with ACOG sight and suppressor, a Glock 21 with a suppressor, 10 magazines each, body armor, night-vision goggles, Safari land tactical thigh holster, and Steiner binoculars.

The other case held the same loadout. The third case was full of ammo, 5.56 and 45. ACP hollow point rounds. There must have been 7,000 or 8,000 rounds of each caliber. I was stunned but very happy.

I called Rabbi Cohen, interested in the progress of the temple. He told me the sanctuary and tabernacle was complete. The temple was about two-thirds complete, and it was estimated to be another two to three months to complete. He told me of the university where he and the other two wise men were teaching. At capacity, many people wanted to become teachers of I AM's word. He asked me if I AM had spoken to me lately?

I said, "No, why?"

He shuddered and stammered and then said, "Do you remember telling us that I AM said not to mention your name?

"Yes, I remember; he was pretty adamant about it."

The Rabbi said, "When I AM sent out his message to everyone, he sent a separate message to the three of us. Mainly that we should still send the broadcast to the masses, but he also said to mention your name. He wanted the world to know how you pleaded with him to give humanity a second chance. So I AM told us to add your first name only to our broadcast and nothing more.

His reason was that he had future plans for you.

I said, "That makes sense now. People on social media have identified me, and there are media outlets parked on the street outside my home."

"I'm sorry, Michael, we were just following orders."

"Don't worry about it, Rabbi. Please give my best to the other two wise men."

Michael F. Decker

57

RECONSTRUCTION

I went back to work. I saw Scott and explained what had happened. He was extremely interested in what I had to say. Of course, being a smart ass not unlike me, he said, "Sign me up."

It was Thursday, and we were readying for our trip to the White House when Lori said she had a surprise for me. She said to look in the closet.

It was a new suit. It was a wool blend; black with subtle blue pin striping, something I've wanted for a long time. I gave her a hug and kiss and thanked her.

She said, "Okay, I have some questions for you."

"Go ahead," I told her.

"What is your position on protecting the Constitution?"

"What do you mean?"

"Listen to me very carefully. Your position is that the States should hold an Article V Convention. During the

Convention, you propose to protect the Bill of Rights by stating that these amendments and rights are forever unchangeable by word or intent."

"I agree with that. But, first, how did you learn all this, and second, why do I have to tell anyone my position on it?"

Lori said, "You don't pay attention very well. I told you that you will be President of the United States. A President must let the public know what positions they will take on various issues."

"So, you think this weekend is the beginning of my campaign?

"Yes! I know it is."

It was nice flying to Washington D.C. Me, Lori, and two Secret Service Agents were the only passengers on the G4. We landed at Andrews and were driven to the White House in a black Chevy Suburban. When we arrived at the entrance, one of our agents asked if we were carrying? I told him we both were. He explained the firearms policy at the White House and asked us to let him secure our weapons until we left. He said he would make sure they were returned, and we agreed.

We were met by the Chief of Staff. He introduced himself and began an in-depth tour of the White House. When we finished, he showed us to the Lincoln Bedroom where we would be staying. Before leaving, he handed us an itinerary for the evening, which began in about an hour. We heard a knock at the door, I answered it. Standing in front of me was a Navy Steward. He asked if he was disturbing us and said he had refreshments and snacks if we were so inclined. I asked him to come in. The cart had a minibar with a silver ice bucket and crystal tumblers. Next to this was an iced silver bowl of shrimp cocktail, cut chunks of cheese, and crackers. The Steward introduced himself as Thomas and said he was there to ensure our stay was pleasant. He asked if he could fix us a drink. He thought it was our first visit and some newcomers were a little nervous so a drink my help. Lori said, "Yes, please." After Thomas made our drinks, I handed him the itinerary the Chief of Staff had given me.

"Thomas, could you fill us in on this itinerary?"

He said, "Sure, Mr. Stone.

After Thomas explained the itinerary to us, there was a knock at the door. Lori answered it.

She called to me, "Mike could you come here?"

I saw a U.S. Marine Captain in dress blues standing inside the door when I left the bathroom. He introduced himself as Captain Horton. He explained he was to escort us to the East Room for a ceremony. Protocol dictates that he escorted Lori to the threshold, and he will announce our presence.

I said, "I understand, Captain. Pretty cool, huh, Bren?"

Entering the East Room, we could see that people were already seated at tables in front of a raised platform with a lectern in the middle. We were escorted to a large table with seating for twelve. Reverend Ham, Rabbi Cohen, their wives, Imam Kamal Bari, Dr. Solomon Levi, and Midas were sitting at the table. They all treated me warmly.

The President was announced, and everyone stood to the Marine Corps band playing Ruffles and Flourishes. Then, the President walked to the lectern.

The President began, "Ladies and Gentlemen and all the rest of this great nation. We are here tonight to honor six great men and their extraordinarily unique leader. I can count myself part of the six men but by no means include myself as part of their greatness. By being a part of this group of men, I can recount from witnessing firsthand the uncommon valor, the steadfastness of their character, and their undying devotion to God and this great nation, the United States of America. Before I begin their story, shall we bow our heads for a moment of silence to reflect on our own deeds and pay respects to I AM.

It may sound like an epic fantasy novel when I begin this story. But, I assure you it is factual. Imagine back in time when you were in your late teens, comfortably sleeping in your bed when you suddenly awaken for some strange reason, you're not scared, and you appear to be fully awake. Now you see a spectral figure at the dark end of your room. The figure is dressed in a long robe, similar to those worn in biblical times. At this point, you wonder if you are dreaming. Whether you pinch yourself or something else, you try and figure out if you are actually awake. At that point, the figure tells you that you are one of six and disappears. As you get older, you think back to that moment from time to time and wonder what it meant? Can everyone picture this in their mind?

Let us fast forward to four months ago. You are now an adult, pursuing your career. Perhaps you're married and raising a family when a spectral figure appears before you again out of the blue. This time the figure identifies him or herself as an angel with a message from God. The message was straightforward. In my case, the angel satisfactorily established himself by recounting the specter that appeared before me that night in my bedroom when I was 16. He told me that I was one of six chosen by I AM to help an unknown leader save humanity and this country. The angel identified the leader as Michael.

Michael was to make contact with the other six, and as a group, we were to find and interrogate a group of people who had greatly offended I AM. This group of people had devised a plan to insert nano partials into the vaccine the United States was developing for the Covid 19 virus. The other aspect of I AM's mission was to inform as many people around the globe that I AM was disappointed in humanity because of their loss of faith in him and their inhumanity to mankind. This part was spearheaded by three religious' leaders, Reverend Franklin Ham, Imam Kamal Bari, and Rabbi Tovia Cohen. Their responsibility was to inform humanity of their shortcomings and renew their faith in I AM before he pronounced his judgment. This was no easy task. But isn't that what religious leaders have attempted to do since the beginning of recorded history? I may be getting ahead of myself in recounting this part of the story. I digress.

I contacted Michael and arranged for him and his family to visit Washington D.C. Once they arrived, they had an additional person with them, Johnny, another member of the six. We met briefly, and it was decided that since Reverend Franklin Ham, Imam Kamal Bari, and Rabbi Tovia Cohen were also in town, we would all travel to Camp David to get acquainted. After we got situated, Michael began to tell us about his personal conversations with I AM and what I AM expected us to do.

The President recalled what I had told the group at our first meeting. He also told the assembled guests within the East Room that he had a meeting recording if anyone questioned the story's validity. He then recalled the appearance of the six angels proceeding I AM, revealing himself to all of us. Next, the President asked the assembled guests if they had seen the celestial anomaly. He explained that the seven of us had been witnesses to the event and explained to everyone how I AM pointed to the grouping of stars and said, "Behold," I AM pointed at the stars. Then he began a circular motion with his outstretched index finger. The President continued, explaining everything except Operation Clean Sweep.

The room was quiet during the President's explanation.

When he finished, he asked five men to join him at the front of the room. The Vice President joined the President. The President read a short description of the requirements for the medal he was about to bestow upon these men. Then he placed the second-highest medal a civilian could receive from a grateful nation, The Presidential Citizens Medal, these he placed around the necks of the recipients. The Vice President stepped up and placed the same medal around the President's neck.

The assembled guests stood and applauded.

The President then called me up to the front of the room.

He said it is my honor to award Michael Stone with the highest award any civilian may receive from a most grateful nation, the Presidential Medal of Freedom. He placed the medal around my neck and whispered, "Thank you, my friend."

58

CLARITY

After the ceremony, I was looking forward to speaking to the three wise men and Dr. Levi about the progress of the Temple and the new school. I also wanted to see Midas and thank him for the goodies. When the President's Chief of Staff, Robert Outts, walked up and said that the President would like to speak to me in the oval office. Lori and I got up to follow him. He turned and said, "Just you, Michael." For some reason, it hit me wrong.

I said, "Lori come with me!"

He looked at me, then at Lori.

He said, "If you insist, Michael."

I said, "I do."

Outts led us into the Oval Office. The President stood and greeted us.

He said, "How good to see you, Lori. How have you been?"

Lori smiled and said, "Very well, Mr. President, thank you for asking." The President then greeted me and shook my hand.

He said, "Please have a seat on the couch. Thank you, Robert that will be all."

Outts looked dejected.

A Navy Steward came in and asked if we would like some refreshments. Lori said she would enjoy a Long Island Ice Tea. I said, "Tequila, neat, please." The President said, "The usual Juan, please." After pleasantries were exchanged, the President looked at Lori and said, "The Director of the CIA, Susan Hope, told me you acquired some additional abilities after I AM healed you. I have a question for you. Why do I want to talk to Michael?"

Lori said, "Because you want him to be the next President." She said it without hesitation. I looked at both of them. Then the President said, "Will he be the next President of the United States?"

She said, "Yes, he will." He smiled.

I asked, "Sir, why?"

The President said, "First we need another round of drinks, Juan another round please." It only took two minutes for the drinks to arrive.

The President said, "There are several reasons, Michael. First, I ran for President because I thought the country was heading in the wrong direction. The people wanted change, I did that to the best of my ability, and you see what happened. The swamp fought me at every turn, even my own party. These people have entrenched themselves so deeply into the system that it is harder than you might think to uncover them. I'm getting off-topic. Excuse me.

I have absorbed everything they could throw at me and am still standing, but at a cost.

Michael, whether you know it or not, you are a natural leader. You have no problem accessing a situation gathering the proper resources to manage the situation. Then once you have decided on a course of action, you don't debate or delegate responsibility. You take decisive action. You damn sure are not a politician, and this country has been given a second chance by I AM. I'm truly saddened by the deaths worldwide and especially those of our own citizens, but I know that in the long run, if those deaths didn't occur if I AM did not intercede, this country was heading towards civil war. The resulting casualties would be many times greater than I AM's judgment. Michael, this is the first time in human history that the total of humanity has faith in one God, I AM. Every person in this country has that faith. With that faith comes an understanding of personal responsibility and self-sufficiency, which was becoming a real problem until I AM intervened.

I said, "It is human nature to want to be taken care of. For most of us, it is just a thought. The real problems are that the politicians pander to these people and make unrealistic promises to garner their support. Truthfully, it's not just the Democrats. It's the Republicans too. It is too easy for people to receive money or some type of benefit from the government. I have no problem ensuring people in need have a safety net."

The President said, "You are correct, Michael, and I feel the same way. For the last four years, I've tried to navigate all the barriers preventing the implementation of those very ideas. This is why you will be so effective. Look, Michael, I AM eliminated several major obstacles impeding this country's potential greatness. One, the fake news media; two, all of the hard-core Communists and their sympathizers; and three, a majority of the special interest lobbies supported a Socialist or Communist government. People are united right now because of I AM, and guess what? They believe that you, Michael, interceded on their behalf, asking I AM for a second chance for humanity. Over time people will start to lose this united bonding with I AM. Unfortunately, that is human nature. That is why you need to do this now rather than later.

I can give you some advice that I learned the hard way if you like, but in reality, all you need to do is let the governors and their constituents know your vision for the country. Then, they will listen and elect the right people. You must do this now. We have to have another election, and you will take my place as the nominee. At this point, if I wanted to run, which I don't, you would beat me. Trust me when I tell you this.

This will be the only time that the Constitution can be protected forever. Term limits could easily be implemented, the size of this bureaucratic swamp could be virtually cut in half. There are so many possibilities afforded to you right now. By asking I AM for a second chance in forgiving humanity, you also allowed our country a second chance to preserve the Constitution and our form of government, and most importantly, freedom and liberty. Tomorrow I want you to sit in on a Cabinet meeting. In addition to my Cabinet, the remaining Congress and the Supreme Court members will attend. Toward the end of the session, the White House press pool will be allowed in to ask questions. So be prepared, I'm sure they will have questions for you. As for you, Lori, is there anything I have said that is not true?"

Lori said, "Mr. President, everything you say is true, and the timing is also critical."

The President said, "Michael, one asset you have that I didn't is Lori. With her newfound abilities, she should be able to ensure that the appointments you make are loyal to your ideas and the right choice for the position. Michael, one piece of advice, when you pick your Chief of Staff, choose a person you have personally known for many years. That person does not necessarily have to agree with you in every instance, but they do so in private when they disagree with you. Everyone else must believe that your Chief of Staff is unwavering in his or her loyalty to you. This is something I have not yet found."

The East Room was again the room for the meeting, but it was arranged differently. The President, Vice President, and the Cabinet members were all facing the center of the room. The remaining Congress and Senate sat at a table to the left of the Cabinet, and to the right were the remaining Supreme Court Justices. This formed a horseshoe-type table arrangement. The guests were seated at the opposing end of the Cabinet. There were four empty seats to either side of the President and Vice President for guests to come up and speak with the assembled group.

The President spoke first, calling for a moment's silence for the country's dead. He then asked the Secretary of Homeland Security, Matt Price, to read the country's death toll.

Matt Price said, "Thank you, Mr. President. The total number of deaths of Americans to date is very comprehensive. The count was conducted by state and local law enforcement.

According to I AM's wishes, medical records from coroners were excluded, but the numbers are firm. The population of the United States was approximately 350,000000 million people. Statistics show that 75 percent of the population was religious. This included Christians, Muslims, and Jews. Although the religions are different, they worshiped the same God. The other 25 percent either were not religious, agnostic or atheist. Their religions worshiped another God entirely. Of this group, 10 percent changed their views and actions after hearing I AM's message, and the remainder died. So, 15 percent of our population, 52.6 million people, also include others who were believed to have been killed due to I AM's judgment.

The President's National Security Advisor, Pete Miller, spoke next.

Miller said, "As all of you know, the President has enacted Directive 51 to help guide our country through these troubling times. The only changes this far are the President making or delegating decisions made by the Legislature and the court systems. There have been no changes in either of these bodies to date. The President hopes that the directive will only be in place for a short time until we can again have elections for Congress and determine the line of succession in the states without governors to appoint Senators for their respective states. We are monitoring the progress of the line of succession as we speak."

The next speaker was the Director of the CIA, Susan Hope.

She stated, "Mr. President, through contacts with our embassies around the globe, we have made contact with several parties who not only have the support of their citizens but also wish to renounce their former government's policies. Iran is one of those countries. Imam Kamal Bari has been instrumental in the negotiations with these leaders. China is another country; due to the horrific losses to the population, there has been positive contact with Taiwan. And the unification of the former PRC with the Taiwan government is almost assured. North Korea is also informal negotiations with the South Korean government in hopes of reunification. Russia has made formal contacts with us to normalize relations in hopes that we can help foster true democracy within their government. All these contacts were made outside of the Department of State's purview due to the potential security concerns involved in negotiating with these unknown individuals until they are properly vetted. The Department of State had experienced a disproportionately higher casualty rate than other government departments, leaving the department unable to execute its assigned duties effectively. After consultation with the Secretary of State and the President, it was decided that the CIA take the lead role in identifying and negotiating with the potential leaders.

There were three speakers in the next update, Imam Kamal Bari, Rabbi Tovia Cohen, and Reverend Franklin Ham. They each gave an assessment of the effect that I AM's words had on humanity as a whole. The Reverend said, "Humanity as a whole has received the word of I AM with surprising enthusiasm. The downfall of this enthusiasm is that there is no guidance other than the words he spoke. The words are sufficient in their meaning, but it would be better to have people trained in teaching those words. We have established a higher learning school inside the temple complex for that very reason. I'm happy to report an overwhelming number of people who have volunteered to attend this school and teach I AM's word.

Rabbi Cohen spoke, "We are also happy to report the financial donations to expand and operate the school is unprecedented. People, or should I say humanity, have unselfishly opened their wallets to donate to this cause." The assembled group stood as one and applauded.

The Secretary of the Treasury, Scott Webber, was next to speak.

Webber said, "As a whole, the country is stable. We will, however, have a period of adjustment while our manufacturing sector begins rebuilding factories. With the losses in the PRC, the number of goods produced there will be in short supply until we reestablish our manufacturing sector. It is estimated it will take nine months to regain that production level."

Senator Wood raised his hand to ask a question.

"Yes, Senator Wood. Do you have a question?"

"I do, Mr. Secretary. Why do you assume the manufacturers will return to the United States rather than relocate elsewhere?"

The President answered the question.

"Senator, the answer to your question is that it is all about money. It may be more expensive to rebuild and produce goods here than elsewhere, but the overall cost of transportation and logistics will offset those costs. I will propose incentives similar to those already enacted, with one exception. If the manufacturers decide to import their products rather than produce them here, an import tax or duty, whatever you want to call it, will be imposed on their products. The imposed impositions will exceed the total cost of manufacturing their products here. I'm being cynical, of course, when I say just money. But, you see, Senator, since I AM's message and judgment, people feel a sense of responsibility to themselves, their families, their country, and by extension, to all humanity. So, this sense of responsibility, one would think, should be expressed toward their fellow Americans as well. This will also factor in a company's decision-making process.

59

MEDIA EXPOSURE

The meeting adjourned for lunch. The President asked Lori and me to join him in his private dining room adjacent to the Oval Office. We had finished eating and started to discuss the itinerary of the second portion of the meeting. The Archangel Michael appeared in the blink of an eye, seated at our table. The three of us looked at the new guest in surprise, but not as surprised as the first time we had seen him appear this way. The Archangel Michael greeted all of us and explained that I AM had dispatched several angels to worthy individuals in countries who lost their leadership due to his wrath. It was explained to these individuals that I AM wished them to lead their respective countries with his blessings and remember what is expected of them. He explained I AM's a pleasure at the work the six had accomplished.

The Archangel Michael then said, "As for you, Michael, I AM's plan is that you will become the next President. Your country must become a shining light to all other nations. I AM understands your thoughts about how to pursue your country's destiny. You will have ample support. Your lovely wife, Lori, has been blessed by I AM. She will help you. You, Mr. President, I AM understands your sacrifices to this point and is grateful for your selflessness in helping Michael attain the office of the Presidency. Your faith has grown during this journey, Michael. I AM is pleased that you used that faith to save the priests and your team. Continue in your faith as it will serve you in the future. I must go now, but I am still available to you if you need me."

Then he was gone, and the three of us just sat looking at each other.

The President said, "Well, nothing more needs to be said. Let's do this, Michael."

The three of us entered the East Room. The President gestured for us to sit to either side of him. The Sergeant of Arms called the meeting to order. The original people were in attendance with the addition of the White House press pool. However, due to its disproportionate causality rate, the press pool was supplemented by eight new faces.

The President began, "Ladies and gentlemen, I have a major announcement to make. As you all know, I have implemented Presidential Directive 51. This directive gives me extraordinary powers over our government's legislative and judicial branches. Of course, one man should not have that much power. Nonetheless, it is necessary to sustain the continuity of government.

I have decided to begin the process of a new Presidential election immediately. Under the directive's current authority, I will order the People's House of Representatives election and the Senate's unfilled seats. Ordinarily, the states' governors would fill these seats until an election is held, but not this time. This process will start today when I sign the order after this meeting. Campaigning for the election will be short compared to past elections. The actual Election Day will be thirty days from today. This is so the winning Presidential candidate will be able to be sworn into office as we have in the past.

With that said, I will not be running for the office of President. There are many reasons for this. But that can be discussed at a later time. However, I will tell you that I will wholeheartedly endorse Michael Stone as the next President of the United States of America."

The guests were stunned at the President's revelation but stood in applause. But unfortunately, that was a different story, and only five of the ten present applauded but did not stand.

The President waited for the applause to die down.

He said, "Michael, please join me up here. I'm sure the press may have some questions for you."

I stood and walked to the microphone. Ten of the reporters were waving their hands to ask the first question. I pointed to a woman in the second row.

I said, "I apologize, Ma'am; I don't know any of your names." She was from CNM and told me her name. Then, she asked what made me qualified to run for the presidency.

I said, "This." As I pulled out a copy of the Constitution I had printed and carried for several years, I said. Not able to see what it was from across the room, she asked what I was holding.

I said, "It is a copy of the Constitution that I always carry. I asked her if she had read it. I then told her about the qualifications to be eligible to run for the Presidency. I told her I was older than thirty-five, along with being a naturalized citizen.

The next question was from an older man with NBD. He wanted to know why a person who has no political experience should be elected President.

It always bothered me when politicians are asked a question and, in all reality, they never answer it. They just dance around the periphery. "You are correct. I am not a politician, nor do I want to become one. What does a politician produce for society? They pass legislation, but do they write it or even read the final product? The answer is no. Here is how it works; a special interest group contacts the Congress member, either in person or through a lobbying group. This group explains that they— or one of their donors— would like to make a sizable donation to the Congress person's campaign if they would support (or sponsor) a certain bill. The bill's framework is already in draft form from the special interest groups' high-priced lawyers. The Congressional aids add to the bill, which usually includes money or the Congress persons' other big donors. The bill becomes so large that no one has time to read it. It is then put to the vote and the Speaker, or the Majority Leader in the Senate, tells their members to vote for it, still unread, of course. So, you tell me what is so special about being a politician?

A woman reporter shouted, but Mr. Stone, how will you know how to run the country?

I said, "I'll answer your question. But in the future, please wait until you are called on. The job description of the President includes protecting and defending the Constitution of the United States, to protect our country from foreign aggression, and to ensure that citizens retain the ability to pursue three basic rights; the right to life, the right to liberty, and the right to the pursuit of happiness. The third right is not a guarantee of happiness, just the right to pursue it. Moreover, all of the tools are there. It's up to the individual's determination and hard work to achieve the degree of happiness they are pursuing.

I picked a quiet woman in the rear of the press pool.

She said, "Thank you, Mr. Stone. Were you present in Jerusalem at the sanctuary when it was attacked?"

I said, "Yes, I was."

"Is it true that you stopped a terrorist attack attempting to murder the priests assigned to sanctuary and tabernacle?

"I think you give me too much credit Ma'am." I'll take one more question. You, Sir, go ahead."

"Mr. Stone, are you a prophet for I AM?

60

PRESS COVERAGE

The next day there were many stories about me in the major media and social media. Reporters were trying to discover more information about my past.

The video of the blast at the sanctuary clearly identified me. The stories varied in theme. One read, "Michael pleaded with I AM to give humanity a second chance. Let him give the United States a second chance."

Another said, "Michael is the people's man. Moreover, he shows his disdain for politicians just like the rest of us."

Another said, "Michael negotiated with I AM and was heard. What more needs to be said."

They interviewed everybody they could find, they had copies of my DD-214, a copy of my NRA Instructor certificate, and a copy of my Yon Dan Certificate signed by Master Moore.

This was a major undertaking, to say the least.

After talking with Lori, I explained what I thought I needed to do to pick competent people. I wanted people passionate about their job and someone who has had experience in the field they'll be working in. I asked her if she could tell if the person was sincere or may have other motives. She said she could tell. My first concern was establishing my inner circle. The first people to come to mind were Eric and Scott. I needed to contact them.

The next day started with a breakfast meeting with the President and the senior member of both the House and the Senate. The two men introduced themselves as Congressman Jeff Tolan and Senator Tom Wells. They seemed eager to hear my ideas on policy. Before beginning that conversation, I asked the President how he could have the election so quickly. The President explained that under the authority of the Presidential Directive 51, he was able to make decisions for the Legislative and Judicial branches of government that are normally under those two branches of government's purview. He also said that he had discussed his plans with the remaining members of Congress and the Supreme Court Justices. All had agreed it was the best course for our democracy. Congressman Tolan explained that with the losses of state leadership, it was best to allow the surviving governors to choose their respective senators while holding an election for senators in states where the governors had died.

Senator Wells asked, "Michael, what do you think of our political system?"

I looked him in the eyes and said, "Senator, I think our form of government is one of mankind's greatest achievements and our Constitution. On the other hand, the people running our government are worthless parasites. It would be illegal for anyone who has held an elected office from dog catcher to senator to ever run again if I had my way. Before you say anything, I know a few good people are serving or have served in the past, but to ensure cancer has been eradicated, they should all go. I think the word 'politician' and the profession labeled as such is, and should always be, derogatory in nature."

The President said, "I told you two he was blunt."

The Congressman and the Senator smiled and then laughed.

The Congressman said, "Semper Fi Devil Dog. You see, Michael, both of us are prior service. I was a Grunt Lieutenant in the 8th Marines, and Wells was a Dogface Lieutenant with the 5th Special Forces Group. We both left the military to start a manufacturing business, but we couldn't do it here, and we weren't moving overseas. So, we ran for office to try to change things. We agree with you. My question is, how soon can we start rebuilding our manufacturing base so we can get the hell out of here?"

I asked, "What about the rest of your colleagues?"

Tolan said, "They are on the same page."

I asked, "How can we change the Bill of Rights so no one can fuck with them in the future?"

Wells said, "That, we can help with."

The President said, "There are two paths, Michael. The states can call for State Constitutional Convention, or two-thirds of Congress can propose an amendment and vote for it. Your best bet is to make sure the people understand your intentions and that they vote for people with similar views in Congress. Michael, we are meeting today to give you every opportunity to do that. The three of us are prepared to pay a considerable amount of money to make sure the people understand your intentions. You will owe us nothing now or later. This is the only time in history when we have had a good chance to fundamentally change this political cesspool. If I understand you correctly, you want permanent protections for the Bill of Rights, manufacturing brought back to this country, term limits, lower taxes, smaller government, and all the baggage that comes with it. Is there anything else?"

"Yes, Social Security. I want it fully funded and kept in its own account without any access. I want all of the bullshit money spent on other countries to stop unless we get something in return. I want the open borders closed. Why would we give money to countries to help their citizens if they turn around and send them here as illegal immigrants?"

Tolan said, "Look, Michael, everything you have said we all agree with until now none of it was possible because of the progressive stance on many of the policy objectives. Now it is a different story. We will not tell you what policies to champion. Instead, we will try to explain some of the hurdles involved in implementing some of them. All three of us have enough money in our PACs to finance your election, and we are here now to commit those resources to your campaign, no strings attached. Personally, and the President and Senator Wells agree, you need to pick people around you who are not part of this establishment cluster-fuck we call D.C."

I said, "That was my plan, I want people who have been successful in the private sector and have shown leadership in their respective fields, and I don't mean academia. I want people who can and have done the work. I want people who don't want to stay in office but just want to do their patriotic duty for the American people and go back to their usual professions."

61

UNIFICATION

The two weeks before I AM's judgment brought families and communities together. It expanded, bringing small towns, large cities, and whole states together. Their belief in I AM was part of it, but it brought a sense of individualism and personal responsibility back to the American people. They understood that life may be more challenging, becoming self-reliant, but also knew that to allow the government to take care of them was impossible.

The way the news was presented was totally different. What was left of the board of directors decided to actually give the facts on a given story and let the viewer's come to their own conclusions. People were on a quest to understand the meaning of I AM's words. They were told to look towards the Jewish text (the Talmud) for guidance and were also told to reference the 10

Commandments. As long as they did that and remembered to give charity to widows and orphans and observe the Sabbath from Friday at sunset to Saturday at sunset, all would be well in I AM's eyes. This they did. The respect for others became quickly apparent in actions and words. People were told of the school for teaching I AM's word in Jerusalem. Many called for information, and many decided to attend the learning center. As a stop-gap measure, many heads of current churches and mosques began teaching the basics of the 10 Commandments in their services until they understood what I AM wanted.

All of this left the adult citizens of the United States hungry for a national leader and local and state leaders who conformed to what the people understood. When people heard that Michael was running for President, they were intrigued. They went to their attics and pulled out old history books. In those books, it was said that people from all professions and walks of life used to run for political office as a civic duty allowing them to give back to a nation that had provided them with liberty and the ability to pursue happiness. They didn't do it to enrich themselves or gain power. It was a duty and a burden they gladly shouldered to thank a grateful nation. They understood that the same school books their children brought home from school no longer spoke of such noble acts.

Wealthier Americans immediately saw the need for factories in the United States. They understood two things: the demand for products that the Chinese could no longer produce and our country's strategic position when China imported the vast majority of our goods. The second reason was simply that it was good for business.

Investors were researching potential products needed for the American public not only for their everyday needs but products that were essential to the United States national security, such as pharmaceuticals, medical gowns, gloves, face masks, plastics for the wrapping of meat and cheese products, plastic containers for water and other numerous goods, metal cans and metal lids. None of these products had been produced in the U.S. for a long time but were exclusively made by China.

Investors who took a long view could see prices for these goods would rise, but they also saw a new group of buyers in the future; the factory workers. This group of people had been virtually extinguished beginning in the middle 1970s. It was a large group of consumers. They made far more than the current service industries. In fact, before the factories went overseas, fast food restaurants were primarily staffed with high school students learning the ropes of a structured work atmosphere. There was no such thing as career jobs in those industries unless you wanted to become a manager. So employment should increase, as should the cost of living. Michael's name was spoken in those circles as well.

Before the first scheduled rallies for Michael to appear, the media covered groups of citizens calling for people to vote for Michael. This included candidates who were currently running for other elected offices. They adopted, "We want real Americans, not politicians," as their battle cry.

The remnants of other boards of directors, small as they were, could see which way the wind of public opinion blew after losing 65 percent of their market share. So the remaining members decided to use their social media platforms to allow their clients the right to free speech and individual opinions. The only caveat was that such speech would be banned if posted to cause specific violence or a crime. As a result, some boards decided to sell their platforms to more conservative investors.

After the meeting with the President, Congressman Tolan, and Senator Wells, Lori and I flew home. I had to talk with Eric and Scott, and after I spoke to them (depending on their answers), I knew I would be very busy expressing my views to the American people. I didn't know exactly how, but the three men I had just met assured me they would handle the particulars. I asked Lori what she thought about these future plans so far.

She said she was excited about it, but she knew my Presidency was a foregone conclusion.

I said, "What am I to make of you? Super senior advisor to the President?"

She laughed, "No. First Lady is fine, Big Buddy."

I called Eric and Scott and told them to bring Kim and Tammy over for a cookout. I told them we needed to discuss something important.

62

ELECTION NIGHT

Lori and I decided to stay at our home during the election. It was much more comfortable, and we would have other family members there along with Eric and Kim and Scott and Tammy, so we had a cookout and made drinks and had some beer. The only additional people were Eric's and my protection detail. Combined, that totaled 15 men and women. I tried to get them to relax, but relaxing wasn't in their job description.

Everyone was watching the returns on the news. I asked Eric and Scott to grab a beer and follow me outside to the patio.

We sat down. I said, "To a better country." We all touched cans. I continued, "This is it, guys. It's game time. We have a better chance to change this country for the better than anyone before us, except Washington and Adams."

"Eric, how did your security briefings go? I'm sure they were interesting."

Eric said, "I can't believe everything they told me. I've never even heard of some of these things. How did you know about all of these things? I've heard you talk about some of them over the years."

I said, "Most of the security issues involving other nations have been happening, or we're starting to happen, many years ago. I love history and the military, so I learned a lot about how nations act or react under certain conditions when I read about them. Knowing the history and not forgetting historical moments or decisions can save time and heartaches."

Scott said, "I talked to the Assistant Director's and Secretaries of the FBI, CIA, Homeland Security, Department of State and Treasury. You were right, they all want to be promoted to the next level, and they all told me how they segregate the personnel who aren't part of their game plan. They are all scum bags. They don't give a rat's ass about anyone but themselves. So at least we know where to contact the people who may care."

Eric added, "I had people calling me from several government agencies testing the waters to see if they would still have a job. What a bunch of suck asses."

We all laughed. James brought us another beer and brought us up to speed on the election returns. It was a foregone conclusion that Eric and I would win. The returns confirmed that we had surpassed the 270 thresholds with 350 electoral votes 188 votes were remaining. Moreover, the House election returns revealed that close to 95 percent of the candidates winning by a large margin were all average Americans, not politicians, and all fiercely supported the agenda I had proposed. The remaining 5 percent were not politicians, but their leads were not as large as the others.

I said, "Guys, we are about to make history, good or bad. Only time will tell. Things will get extremely busy leading up to the swearing-in. Scott; did you find a place to live yet?"

"Yes, Tammy found us a brownstone condo in a decent neighborhood."

I said, "Good. I'm glad you found a place."

Just then, Lori came out and handed me the phone. She mouthed, "It's the President."

I took it and said, "What can I do for you, Mr. President?"

The President said, "Congratulations, Michael. Actually, I should say congratulations, Mr. President-Elect. I'm extremely happy that you won. I'd like you to bring Lori and the rest of your family to the White House. I have planned a celebration in your honor. I have already made the arrangements and notified your protective detail. After the celebration, I'd like to have you and Lori stay here for a couple of weeks. There are many things I may be able to assist you with before the transition."

I said, "Thank you, Mr. President that is very considerate of you. I will inform everyone."

I turned to Lori and said, "Tell everyone to pack a bag; we are going to the White House. You and I will be spending a week or two there." Then, I turned to Eric and Scott and said, "You two are also coming."

The final election results were tallied before taking off in a Gulfstream 5 from John Glenn International Airport. The total seats up for election for the House of Representatives were 435. Every one of them was won by people who had not been politicians. They consisted of doctors, teachers, policemen, firemen, small and large businesses owners, health care workers, auto mechanics, salespeople, hairdressers, barbers, coaches, truck drivers, lawyers, carpenters, bricklayers, contractors, and many others, but none were politicians. The 45 seats up for election in the Senate mirrored the Congressional choices, but again no politicians. This could not have been better news. My duty was to ensure that the new group knew my position on the issues and convince them to vote for the changes.

The news media reported the results and speculated whether the new Congress and Senate would agree to my proposed changes. From the early polls conducted and interviews with some of the winners, it appeared they agreed and supported my proposals.

After landing and being transported to the White House, we were greeted by an agent on the President's security detail. We were escorted to six different rooms, which would house the family for the next night or two.

The President requested Lori, Eric and Kim, Scott and Tammy, and I meet with him in the Oval Office several hours later.

Once situated, we were all served drinks. The President said,

"Congratulations to all of you for your victory. Michael and Eric, your election win was historical. Your uncontested election was a first. Not since George Washington in his first two terms has anyone won a Presidential election unopposed. As for the Congressional and Senate seats, it was unprecedented that all were average Americans with no politicians being elected. This by itself ensures you a mandate for change, Michael. With those two unprecedented wins, Congressman Tolan and Senator Wells can help shape the agendas for the House and Senate. No other President in history has had a chance to change things like you will have Michael, and I know you will make changes for the right reasons. That is why I'm so happy for you. The offices both of you are about to enter is a rather exclusive club, but it will be a major change from your current life. The benefits for the jobs are outstanding, but along with those benefits come some stifling restrictions. The two of you, along with your wives, will no longer be able to do anything for yourselves. The White House staff will take care of everything, including your meals, snacks, beverages, laundry, and housecleaning, pressing your clothing, shining your shoes, grocery shopping, washing your car, and getting your gas. Every time you leave the grounds, you will have a security detail. When you walk from one room to another, the Secret Service will be monitoring your movements. To a certain extent, the same will go for your family. I'm just trying to prepare you now so it will not come as a big shock."

"My first bit of unsolicited advice for Michael and Eric is to have a tailor from Brooks Brothers come and do a fitting for both of you. I'm sure you are going to need some suits and accessories. My recommendation is to have at least 8, possibly 10 suits, 15 dress shirts, ties, 5 or 6 pairs of dress slacks, and 4 or 5 pairs of dress shoes. Next, have them fit you for 2 tuxedos for formal occasions and several pairs of socks. Brooks Brothers will give you a substantial discount, perhaps even do it for free, plus they like the publicity. I'll talk to them. The owner is a friend of mine. As for your wives, they will have every women's wear designer offering their clothing for each of them to wear at no charge."

Thank you, Mr. President, for your insight and generosity."

Eric said the same, and the women were all smiles.

The President said, "It was nothing; like I said, you will be a member of an exclusive club, and please, all of you call me Don."

"We will be celebrating this evening in the East room, dinner, orchestra, and many Washington insiders. Before you get excited, I don't want you to pick any of them for your administration, but they don't know that. I'd like you to continue the same strategy you have Eric and Scott do. By the way, that is a very good strategy on your part. I'm just allowing you to speed the process up. You'll have them all in the same room. Think of it as your own personal entertainment package." The President laughed. "I will definitely be entertained knowing you are about to run it up in all of them. That reminds me, I have an election gift for all of you. I'm sure you may not have anything to wear tonight with the short notice I have given you about the celebration. I would normally apologize, but I have a solution, and it is my gift for all of you. First, you ladies will be accompanied by a female Secret Service agent and a few other agents who just happen to have a discriminating taste for the attire you should wear this evening. She will take you shopping as a gift from me."

Lori, Kim, and Tammy all thanked the President.

The President said, "As for you three, my man from Brooks Brothers is standing by in the next room to take your measurements; you would be surprised how fast they can make three suits when the President orders them to."

"As I said, it is my gift to all of you, so the only thing I want to hear is, thank you."

Everyone thanked the President.

63

THE CELEBRATION

True to his word, the President was correct about Brooks Brothers. All three of our suits were made one hour before the celebration, including fitted dress shirts, cufflinks, ties, shoes, and socks. It was amazing the speed at which this was done, and the wives also scored big with their designer gowns, shoes, and matching purses. They all looked beautiful.

All of us were escorted into the East Room, with the ladies escorted by U.S. Marine officers as our arrival was announced. I scanned the room to see seating for 100, a small dance floor, and an orchestra playing classical music. White House stewards continually walked through the crowd with trays of drinks. The President met with us after we entered. He explained that he would personally introduce us to the people we needed to meet. He said we should come up front, and a reception line would be formed. As the individuals came up, the President would introduce them to us. Then, after dinner, we could strike up conversations with the people we wanted to get information from.

I had thought a lot about how I wanted the United States to be perceived by the world, and it was not how the State Department had been running things. I didn't like that many at Foggy Bottom felt it necessary for other nations to like us. Personally, I could care less. But, if they were friends and traded fairly with us great, but friends or not, if they didn't deal fairly or threatened our security, then it was time for them to learn that the United States of America was not the world's benefactor.

After the receiving line, we sat down to a very nice dinner. During the dinner, I separated the names of the people I thought we needed to pump for information into three groups. I would speak with one group while Eric and Scott talked to the other two groups.

The first people I spoke with were the Deputy Attorney General and the Deputy Director of the FBI. Both men were very eager to answer my questions. First, I asked about their careers and aspirations. Then I asked about their subordinates, the stellar ones, and the problem people. They explained how they had mentored the stellar ones. Then went on to explain that a few of their people refused to go along with the program, explaining further how they segregated them from the chain of command. I told them I had heard good things about them and said someone would be in touch.

I watched Eric and Scott work the room. It looked like they were enjoying themselves. I saw a Marine enlisted man at the bar. As I walked over, I noticed he appeared to be a Sergeant Major in the Marine Corps. I addressed him as "Sergeant Major," stringing out the R and omitting the G. The last time I was in the presence of the Sergeant Major of the Marine Corps was in 1984 at Camp Lejeune when I was part of a personal security detail for him and the Commandant.

He turned and faced me. He said, "I'm sorry, Sir, I didn't realize it was you."

I smiled and asked, "Is the proper term Sergeant Major or has the Corps come up with a new name?"

He smiled and said, Sergeant Major, is just fine, Sir. But, unfortunately, the Corps has changed a lot since 1984 and not all for good."

"Well, Devil Dog, how about we grab a beer, and you can tell me a sea story."

The story he told was very interesting. Sergeant Major Tim Owens enlisted in 1988 as a 0331 (Grunt basic infantryman), spending most of his career in the 8th Marine Regiment/2nd Marine Division. He was stationed at Camp Lejeune, North Carolina, but deployed to various locations. I was curious how his career path enabled him to be the highest-ranking enlisted Marine in the Corps. He explained that he went to selection for Force Recon and became a member of the Company-size force as an E-5 Sergeant in 1990, just to take part in Operation Desert Storm. At the time, his unit was part of a unit called SRIG. SRIG's mission was to provide surveillance, reconnaissance, intelligence, counter-intelligence, electronic warfare, air and naval gunfire liaison, tactical deception, maritime direct action, and secure communications to MAGTFs, (Marine Air-Ground Task Force). Force Recon was the ground reconnaissance piece of the unit. After serving in Force Recon, he became a First Sergeant in the 8th

Marine Regiment. After that, he became the Sergeant Major of the Regiment and was later promoted to Sergeant Major of the 2nd Marine Division. He explained that the officers became very political when he was SgtMaj at the Regiment. He had not experienced this in his career before that. However, when he went to the Division level, it was worse. He told me that the last hard-core General officer he knew was Commandant of the Marine Corps Al Grey.

I told him, "I remember General Grey from when he was a Major General commanding the 2nd Marine Division. He was a hard-core fucker."

The Sergeant Major said, "Mr. Stone, I was promoted to the position because the Commandant's inner circle needed a former recon Marine with the General to appease the more conservative Marine officers. I knew that going in, and I'm not proud of it. However, the truth is that every Marine officer above the rank of Major is basically a politically-correct type officer, not a warrior. So Sir, this is going to be a problem for you."

I said, "Sergeant Major, I've known that for many years now, basically since the Clinton administration took office. It is not just the Corps; it's the whole military. So my question to you is, do you know where all the good officers are stashed and do you care enough about your country to help me find them?"

The Sergeant Major smiled a broad smile and said, Mr. President-Elect, it is an honor to help you and my duty to do so."

I said, "Thank you, Sergeant Major. I'll put you in touch with one of my people. Semper Fi."

I spotted the President and walked over to him.

I asked, "Mr. President, would it be possible to meet with Director of the CIA, Susan Hope, Secretary of Homeland Security Matt Price, and CJCS General James Nolt in the next day or so? I'd also like to ask you if you had planned on initially placing someone else in Treasury but were politically unable to do so?"

The President said, "Sure, Michael, we have a meeting in the morning; why don't you bring Eric and Scott, and we can discuss my Treasury choice."

64

SECURITY BRIEFING

Lori and I were up early for me anyway, having a nice breakfast.

She said, "So this is where we'll live for the next four years?" I said, "Yep, just a different bedroom and no cleaning for you. You are not even allowed to help clean the place."

She said, "Yes, but I can tell them the places they missed."

I rolled my eyes. "If I bring some of my Cabinet choices to you, can you tell if they have an ulterior motive other than what's in their job description?"

"I think I can. How it works, I think, is, I kind of read their minds. It's a vibe. I don't have to be at the meeting. I could just come into the room for a moment to see you or say something to you."

"Okay, we'll put that to the test real soon, so think about how you want to do it. I have a meeting to go to down the hall. Love you."

Andrea was outside the door when I left for the meeting. She said, Good morning, Mr. President Elect."

"Good morning, Andrea. Are you escorting me to the meeting?"

"Yes, Sir, Follow me, please."

"Andrea, you might think this an odd question, but do you really enjoy your job, and if you do, where do you see yourself in 5 or six years?"

"Well Sir, to answer your first question, I love my job. As for 5 or six years from now, the procedure is that I will be rotated off of the Presidential Protective detail to a training billet or another assignment. Is there a specific reason for the question?"

"Actually, there is Andrea. I'd like to give you 3 options. One is to follow normal procedures. Two is to remain at your current position as Head of my Security Detail, and three is to become my Director of the Secret Service. I don't need an answer now, but think about it."

"Thank you, Sir. I will think about it."

The meeting was held in the Situation Room. Everyone stood and greeted me. Eric and Scott were already there and had been introduced to the others.

The President began by singing the praises of the DCI, Susan Hope, Secretary of Homeland Security Matt Price, and the CJCS General Nolt.

I said, "Mr. President, you are preaching to the choir. If you and I are vouched for them, they're staying on my team, as long as they are willing."

"Thank you, Michael. I have to say they are extremely loyal."

I said, "No need to thank me, Mr. President. Here is what I want to accomplish, lady and gentlemen. I want to disable the Department of Homeland Security. Matt that doesn't mean you're out of a job. I also want the post of Director of National Intelligence removed. I can't see why we can't go back to having the DCI in charge of Intelligence dissemination. That would be you, Susan. I will give you a fair warning that the games played by all of the intelligence communities will not be tolerated. The responsibility is yours, Susan. The money we save by reducing these assets will be used to pay off the debt. I also want the NSA reined in. Zero tolerance for any gathering of SIGINT, ELINT, or other intrusive electronic intelligence gatherings of U.S. citizens. Matt and Susan, I expect the two of you to work together to make this happen and give me multiple options for where Matt will be most useful.

General, I have a specific mission for you. I want you to meet with the current Sergeant Major of the Marine Corps and give me options and a plan to remove and replace the officer corps from LtCol. and above. There may be exceptions; I will decide that on a case-by-case basis. Those officers have become too political. They must remain apolitical. I want line animals and shooters running the commands, not a bunch of political ass kissers. When you have accomplished this, we can discuss a suitable position for you, or you may remain at your current post. I know for a fact, General, since you are a shooter yourself, you have a plan to do just what I suggested. Are there any comments, questions, or criticisms?"

DCI Susan Hope spoke first. I have to agree with your reasoning. I would only add that if the intelligence departments fail to perform as you propose, I feel that you should allow the DCI statutory authority to remove intelligence personnel for just cause. As far as the speed at which we can switch back to prior procedures, it could happen within a week of notification.

I said, "Thank you, Susan."

Matt Price spoke next. "First of all, thank you for your confidence. As you probably already know, many of the personnel in the agencies under my direction will still be on the payroll because of their duties with their parent agencies. The cost savings would primarily be actual DHS personnel and DGS supervision and the building structures we use. It will still be considerable cost savings. I can give you a report on the proposed cost savings by the end of the week, Mr. President."

"I know this is a lot to ask of you, Matt, but I trust you. I would also like you to formulate a plan to present to Congress, which reduces the bureaucracy at the Justice Department and allows department heads to progressively discipline personnel for not adhering to written policy. Additionally, I want to formulate a course of action to rid the FBI of all personnel regardless of their position if they fail in their institutional responsibilities. I know they have the Office of Professional Responsibility as their in-house internal affairs department, but that's not working out very well. Explain to the assistant directors and the SACs that I will replace the OPR people with U.S. Marshals to review their conduct if that is what it takes, but wait until you have developed a plan. I authorize you to implement it first."

Matt said, "Yes, Sir."

General Nolt spoke next. "Sir, I see you have zeroed in on an institutional problem our military has had since the mid- 90s. I have no problem helping you clean this mess up. In fact, Sergeant Major Tim Owens and I go back quite a few years and see eye-to-eye on many things.

"Glad to hear it, General; I thought you two were cut from the same cloth."

The President spoke next, "Michael, you are taking the bull by the horns. Can you, lady and gentlemen, update Michael and me on what's happening in your areas of responsibility?"

The DCI went first, "Mr. President, the country we used to call the People's Republic of China no longer wishes to be called that. There is no decision on a permanent name as of yet. We have initiated Intelligence gathering and direct negotiations with the new leader, Dishi Lo. He came to power by being an influential leader in the underground Christian religious movement. He has stated to our Cultural Attaché that he has no ill intent toward us and wishes that we send over some of our nuclear proliferation experts to examine China's nuclear arsenal and to safely dismantle it, and to ship it back to the U.S. Our Cultural Attaché is negotiating with the Taiwanese government at the moment in search of some sort of reunification with the mainland. Dishi Lo insists that he will not continue the negotiations until we render his nuclear arsenal safe and remove it completely from China's soil.

North Korea's people have control of the country and are requesting emissaries from the new university in Jerusalem to guide them on what I AM would want them to do. We have been in contact with the Israeli government, and they are willing to finance the travel and protection of the emissaries. I believe Rabbi Cohen will be one of the emissaries. In the meantime, they also request assistance in securing and dismantling their existing nuclear and chemical weapons.

The Russian Federation is now under the control of the leader of the Russian Orthodox Church. He is Patriarch Kirll of Moscow and all Russia. He is personally involved in consultations with Rabbi Cohen.

The Mexican, Central American, and South American drug cartels were decimated by I AM.

There also was a large percentage of the corrupt Mexican government killed. There has been a movement of the population supported by the Catholic Bishops there to form a reform government. They are requesting through their news media that citizens do not migrate from their country and that Mexican citizens who illegally and legally emigrated to the U.S. return home to help rebuild their beleaguered nation."

Eric said, "That's incredible, all of it."

The President said, "Yes, it is. Think of the possibilities when people have faith. Thank you, Susan."

Matt spoke next, "Mr. President, all of the protest and civil unrest around the country has stopped. Crime in the country is in decline. The daily shootings in Chicago have also declined, though there is still some gun violence, from citizens shooting the remnants of gangs trying to re-establish themselves in the city. Local law enforcement has reported that there may now be fewer than 100 gang members within the city. These statistics are similar in many of our major cities. With the loss of leadership in these large cities, the elections allowed regular citizens to be elected. The citizens have a newfound respect for the rule of law and law enforcement in general. There is a shortage of college and

University Professors after I AM's wrath. The gaps are being filled by former professors who were ostracized for being conservative. I received a report from the Justice Department concerning the states and federal prisons' population. With the two combined, we had approximately 1.5 million prisoners incarcerated. I AM's day of wrath reduced the total population to approximately 700,000. That's an almost 60 percent reduction, with most of the reduction being state prisoners."

The President said, "Thank you, Matt."

The CJCS spoke next, "Mr. President, our forces, as you know, have returned to their normal readiness levels. The military as a whole has lost thousands of personnel since that fateful day. We have lost many general officers who have held key commands and many more General and Field-Grade officers who were commanding Battalions and Regiments and administrative posts within the Pentagon. I think it is important to note that this attrition will solve some of President-Elect Stone's concerns with the leadership challenges within our military. As you know, we cannot promote officers above the rank of 0-6 without the advice and consent of the Senate. We have no intelligence at this point to concern us of aggressive intent of other foreign nations."

"Thank you, General. That is all, people. Michael, Eric, and Scott, I'd like a word with you."

After the others left, the President said, "Michael, what you are planning will not be easy, but long overdue. I believe with the state of the world and our nation to date, in time, you have the best chance to pull this off. You appear to understand what needs to be fixed. To answer the question you posed to me earlier about my Treasury choice. I had to choose him for political reasons. I knew, just like you, what needed to happen, but I didn't have the support from my own party to do what was right. My first choice was a man named Tiddus Blue. He is not a politician; he is a fixer. Over the years, I've seen this man take companies destined for bankruptcy and turn them around. This guy was born to do this kind of thing. He can smell waste from a mile away. I'm not telling you to pick him, but do yourself a favor and let him show you what he can do on paper. From his report, you can set parameters for him."

I said, "I thought it was something like that. With all of the so-called speed bumps out of the way, I should at least see what numbers he can show me. If it's not too much trouble, set up a meeting, Sir."

The President said, "Michael, I'd like to pardon everyone involved in "Operation Clean Sweep." The problem is the pardon won't cover state laws. Do you have any thoughts?"

I said, "I've been thinking about that also. Does the Justice Department need to know about the pardons?"

The President said, "Normally they are involved, but no statute says they have to be involved."

"Good. Have all of the pardons written up. I will write one for you. I have an idea that if Congress passes a law stating that all crimes or acts of violence were perpetrated because the motive was of a political nature; it will become an exclusively federal crime with no state or local jurisdiction. I think I can have that law passed. After it is passed, I will have a pardon written for you, Sir."

The President said, "That might just work, Michael. Thank you."

"Sir, I have a question? Did you have anyone working on changing the civil service rules or laws concerning government employees? I don't want to run into problems with the bureaucracy becoming the resistance as you incurred."

The President said, "I did have a study and plans for just that problem and numerous other problems, but from a political standpoint, and of course my own party causing me problems, I never had a chance to implement them. Since you have no such problems with Congress or the Party, I will give you a copy of my studies and plans for you to take note of."

"Thank you, Mr. President. I promise if I make use of your plans, I'll make sure to give you the appropriate credit."

65

ADDITIONAL PLANNING

There was so much to be done that I wanted to repair. It was daunting. The meeting with Tiddus went well. He agreed to do a report on the changes I wanted. He said it would be a week or two before it was complete.

Eric and Scott were with me in the Situation Room. The President graciously allowed us to use it in the interim.

I said, "So you see the problems we will have?"

Eric said, "Yes, So many decisions or changes to make in so little time, with little information to make a good decision."

Scott said, "I thought it would be easier than this. Being an armchair quarterback on past politicians' decisions was stupid."

I said, "It will be hard, but we will do it. We have enough information to get some of the people in place. I don't give a fuck who comes up with the answers. Listen, for us, this whole thing is not political. I will give credit to anyone who deserves it. I don't have to look good. The only thing I care about is the welfare of the country. We've narrowed down candidates for Justice, Treasury, and the State Department. We have the CIA. I'm going to talk to Midas when he arrives. He might have some leads for the Director of the FBI. He should be here in the next ten minutes. He will help, along with General Nolt, in the realignment of the military and possibly have a good idea for a Secretary of Defense. When we pick people for positions, I'm hoping I can have them help with some of the less important posts. We must pick the right people for the major positions to trust that they will make the right choices for the less important positions because less important doesn't necessarily mean not important. If the wrong people are in those positions, they could possibly halt or slow down the progress we are trying to make."

A light on the desk phone had lit up red. I picked it up. I listened and said, "Send Midas in, please. It's Midas."

Midas entered, and everyone was introduced. We gave each other a bro hug.

I said, "I need to use that brilliant Squid military mind."

Midas said, "You know I would normally have a smart ass come back, but it appears I'm at a disadvantage seeing how you've been bumped up a few notches in the chain of command. What can I do for you, Sir?"

"First of all, cut the Sir, shit, you are among friends. Second, I need your opinion on the state of the current officer corps in the entire military."

"Well, that is a big bone to chew on. You know, as I do, 0-1's are idiots and need constant supervision from NCOs. 0-2's have learned some lessons from their NCOs and are starting to become good officers, but enough to be dangerous to their troops. 0-3s have learned the proper lessons and are willing to ask advice from their NCOs while gaining maturity for their role as a leader. 0-4s are a new ball game. They are understudies for their 0-5 or 0-6 bosses for the most part. That could be good or bad. If their boss is a good one and they emulate him or her, it's good. If the boss is bad and they emulate them, it's bad, but sometimes the 0-4 sees these bad traits and rejects them and becomes a better leader. 0-5's by this time, it is a career, so it's time to suck up to get promoted. Some may be good officers, but many are willing to compromise their integrity for promotion. Not all of them, those who don't compromise their integrity, truly love their job, and promotion no longer matter. They become hopelessly disgruntled and either resign or continue to press on. 0-6 and above is basically a political animal. A small percentage of them made it to the top without becoming political, but they are rare. Why do you ask?"

Scott said, "Isn't that a bleak description of our military leadership?"

I said, "Yes, it is Scott, but it's true nonetheless. The reason I asked is those were my thoughts. Also, I just wanted to verify them with someone I trust still in military service. Midas, I need to unfuck that political mindset in the military leadership. It almost sounds like I need to grab officers from the 0-4 ranks and have them promoted before they can be contaminated."

Midas said that would be one way to do it. Some of those would be missing the Command Staff Officers course. For the Army, that's the Command and General Staff Officers Course. For the Navy and Marine Corps, it's the Naval War College, and for the Air Force and I guess Space Command, it would be the Air

Command and Staff College. All are geared to allow tactical leaders to learn a strategic view of the battlespace. The courses last for 10 months for all three branches of service."

I asked, "What would you recommend I do to unfuck this problem?"

Midas said, "Stone, I see you're serious about this. Look, I'm a shooter; on the teams, we benefit from a nearly no-rank structure when we plan an OP. What that means to Eric and Scott is that everyone on the team has input into the mission's planning regardless of rank. During a planning brief, we have to consider not only tactical considerations but also strategic ones. The U.S. military's tier-one units plan the same way, the D-boys, the Raiders, and the Air Force's 24th Special Tactics Squadron. All plan the same, and most of the operators are NCOs, so planning isn't an officer-exclusive club."

I asked Midas, "Have you heard of a Marine senior NCO named Tim Owens?"

Midas thought and said, "I've heard sea stories about a Gunny Owens; he was a legend in the Force Recon community. Is that Marine you're talking about?"

"Yes, I didn't know he was a legend, but he is the current Sergeant Major of the Marine Corps. I met him at the celebration thing the President had for us. He's not happy with the officer leadership either. I'd like you to meet with him and General Nolt to figure out how to fix this senior officer bullshit. In addition, research the possible fixes for promoting qualified senior NCOs. Promoting an E-8 or E-9 to a 0-5 or 0-6 is not normal, but is it possible? Do you have any problems with General Nolt?"

Midas said, "No problems, especially after you tightened him up a while back. I can work with them. During WWII, senior NCOs were promoted to 0-4 through 0-6. Hell, they even promoted civilians who worked in jobs critical to the military's mission, directly to 0-6 and Flag rank. It looks like I'll be busy, Stone; I'll take my leave."

"Thanks, Midas."

Eric said, "He's on Seal Team Six?"

"Yes, but it is called DEVGRU or Naval Special Warfare Development Group, and believe me, he knows his shit."

Scott said, "A good man to know in a pinch. What was all the pardon talk about with the President?"

I said, "You guys know most of the story. But, you don't know that a congressman and a doctor planned to use nanoparticles infused into the vaccine to control human behavior. That was the last straw for I AM. He told me specifically to interrogate the congressman and everybody involved with him and identify the person or persons involved in financing the operation to spike the vaccine. He said I was the only one who he trusted to interrogate him. Once I retrieved the necessary information, I was to eliminate the congressman and the others with him. Midas and a couple of his men, along with some other Special Operations shooters, took down his home, and I did what had to be done."

Eric said, "You mean…"

"Yes, I did what I AM told me to do. Enough said, and the whole affair is extremely classified. I hope you both understand that."

They both said they understood.

66

BUMP UP

I'd already decided on two of my appointments, but this third choice was a little out of the box. Scott found the 42-year-old Sammie Cole. After Cole graduated from the U.S. Naval Academy in 1994 in the top 10 percent of her class. She requested the U.S. Marine Corps as her service branch and became a Naval Aviator, flying F-18 Super Hornets. In 2000 she left the service as a Major. She then received her master's degree in International Relations from the Fletcher School at Tufts University. She then applied and was accepted as a Foreign Service Officer for the U.S. State Department. She then requested two back-to-back hardship postings in Bangladesh and Uganda, filling several roles in both embassies.

As Cole progressed in her career, she specialized in several diplomatic functions, from international law to weapons proliferation. In 2015 she drafted a position paper outlining the pitfalls of being too accommodating during negotiations. The draft, although true, was not received well by the Foggy Bottom elite. Regardless, she was still being considered for promotion to Assistant Secretary of State for Trade. Unfortunately, while meeting with a Chinese trade delegation, she was aggressively assaulted by one of the male members of the delegation. During the assault, Cole grabbed the Chinese man's genitals. She twisted and pulled with such force and ferocity that the man's penis was torn from his body and he bled out in the garden where the meeting was held.

The State Department was under so much pressure from the People's Republic of China that they removed Cole from the promotion list and relegated her to a job supervising and teaching new Foreign Service Officers the rules about sexual harassment.

This is how Scott ran into her. He became lost in the halls and stopped by and opened the door to ask for directions. Cole was the person who helped him. When he found the office he was looking for, he mentioned Cole's name to the Under Secretary. At this point, the Under Secretary started to laugh and gave Scott the short version about Cole. It appeared to Scott that the State Department was happy how they fucked up Cole's career. Scott told me about the incident, and I pulled her record. Now I'm about to interview her for a job with General Nolt and Midas.

The General and Midas entered the suite that Tolan had supplied me.

I said, "Welcome, gentlemen. I wanted you here to sit in on an interview I'm about to have with a woman who may be our new Secretary of State. Feel free to ask her questions that may pertain to her overall job description. I have you here because I trust both of you, and you have more current insight into geopolitics than I have at the moment."

The General said, "Thank you, Sir, but it is out of the ordinary that two military people are consulted for State Department issues.

I said, "That's true, General. I like to think outside the box when possible. I think General MacArthur said, "The soldier above all others prays for peace, for it is the soldier who must suffer and bear the deepest wounds and scars of war."

Midas said, "Very nice, Stone."

Lori knocked on the door and entered with Sammie Cole.

All of us stood when they came in.

Lori said, "This is Sammie Cole. We've had a nice talk while you guys were in here telling stories. She seems like a very nice person."

I said, "Thank you, dear. Sammie, have a seat and make yourself comfortable. My name is Mike Stone; this is John Black and General Nolt."

Sammie said, "Thank you, Sir, and gentlemen, it's my pleasure to be here."

I said, "Sammie, I've reviewed your record, and quite frankly, I'm impressed. Would you give us an overall assessment of the State Department?"

Sammie said, "Sir, in two words, it's a cluster fuck!"

The General choked and spit up his drink, Midas started laughing, and I smiled.

Midas said, "Could you be more specific?"

Sammie said, "Sure, 90 percent of the diplomats don't understand the word no. I have never seen one serious negotiation. There are no boundaries established at the start of a negotiation, and it's a sin if you hurt someone's feelings. They are like the people who go to a car dealer and pay the sticker price for the car without haggling over the price."

I asked, "How can it be fixed?"

She said, "If you really want to know, Sir, many people need to be fired."

The General asked, "How would you accomplish that, young lady?"

As an officer, she said, "General, you know leadership comes from the top, but the NCOs are the enforcers. So, to fix this, we need like-minded department heads to lay down the law and get rid of the diplomats who have interests other than the country's good."

I asked, "Are there enough good NCOs to head the departments?"

Cole said, "Mr. Stone, they have me working out of a broom closet, and I'm not the only one. I can guarantee that 50 people like me are scattered in broom closets throughout the State Department. So if you choose me to be one of the department heads, I can assure you my troops will be squared away."

I said, "That is very confident of you, Major. Perhaps you can help me with a couple of appointments I've wanted to make?"

She said, "Yes, Sir, I'd be happy to help."

I said, "Good! General Nolt, I want you to become my Secretary of Defense. Don't say anything yet. Hear me out. Of all the senior officers active today, you still hold true to being apolitical. I cannot say as much for many of your contemporaries, and more importantly, I trust you. Now tell me you will do it."

The General said, "Sir, I'm honored that you would consider me competent enough to be in charge of our armed forces. I will accept your offer and give both you and our country 100 percent."

I said, "Thank you, General. Midas, you are not getting out of here without a scratch. I need you also. I want you as my National Security Advisor."

Midas said, "Stone, I mean Sir, I'm just an enlisted squid."

I said, "Midas, I'm just an old enlisted Jarhead. Are you telling me you can't handle the job?"

Midas said, "No, Sir, I can handle the job."

I said, "Good, then you'll do it?"

Midas said, "I'd be honored, Sir."

I said, "As for you, Major, I don't need NCOs at State. I need leaders. Are you up for the Secretary of State post, or is that too much for you?"

Cole's mouth hung open at my response.

As she pulled herself back together, she said, "Thank you, Sir, you won't be sorry."

I said, "Great! Here is how I see these appointments, all of you at some time in your careers have bitched or moaned about the useless leaders we have had over the years. I want people who have actual experience in their respective job, not some political appointment or some academic who has a theory about how to do it. I said the same thing about Congress and the Senate. I want you to run your departments like a business and make a profit. You may streamline your departments as long as they are revenue-neutral. I only ask you to run any new proposals for your departments by me before you implement them. I also want you to take out the unnecessary trash as you do this. There is plenty of waste in your departments.

Sammie, I'd like to see those qualified out of the broom closets."

Sammie said, "It will be my pleasure, Sir."

67

COST CUTTING STRATEGY

We prepared for the cost-cutting meeting with the Secretary of the Treasury designate Tiddus Blue.

Matt Price, Eric, Scott, Midas, and Sammie Cole was in attendance. Matt explained his numerous conversations with the executives in charge of the FBI. Matt explained that the upper echelons of the FBI feel that President-Elect Stone's proposal to cleanse the FBI of alleged political leaning as opposed to apolitical leadership within the FBI was exaggerated, and they had no intention to comply with the President Elect's request.

I said, "Matt, thank you for verifying what I thought their answer would be."

Matt said, "Sir, they are truly out of control, insubordinate bastards!"

I smiled at his comment and said, "Matt, you have been extremely loyal and have performed excellently. How would you like to become my Attorney General?"

"Sir, thank you for your confidence in me, but..."

Matt was cut short by Eric,

"Matt! There are no buts! You both accept the job, and do your best to represent the American people, or you don't. So man the fuck up and quit whining."

Everyone in the room looked at Eric. He had never raised his voice in a meeting before.

I looked at Eric; he was sitting to my right.

I said, "My man!" and fist-bumped him.

I looked at Matt and said, "Matt, I think you better answer Eric's question. I think you may have pissed him off."

Matt's face flushed red. He looked at Eric and said, "You are correct, Eric. There should have been no hesitation in my answer. I would be honored to accept the job."

Midas said, "Mr. Pres... I mean Stone; I may have someone you might want to look at for the post of FBI Director."

I said, "What's his background, and does he or she have any experience?"

Midas said, "Yes, he does have experience, but I'm going to have to explain. I personally know this man. He was in my BUDS class in 2001. Interestingly, he was an FBI special agent starting in 1991 after getting his law degree from Ohio State University. He later became a member of HRT (the FBI's Hostage Rescue Team). During an investigation, which was part of his other duties, he uncovered evidence of criminal activity within the office of a U.S. Congressman. While pursuing the evidence,

Special Agent James Hoover was told by his SAC and several other upper echelon FBI Executives that he was to stop his investigation.

He was outraged at the order and resigned from the FBI.

He then became a District Attorney for the City of Columbus, Ohio.

After the attack on the Twin Towers, he enlisted in the Navy, where I met him during BUDS training.

Five years ago, Chief Petty Officer (Hammer), James Hoover's element, was engaged in a firefight in a village in Afghanistan. Several of his men were ambushed just outside the village and killed. During the firefight, three of the terrorists were taken prisoner. The remaining terrorists who occupied the village told Hammer if he did not release the prisoners, two of which were HVT's (High-Value Targets) and leaders of the group, the terrorists said they would kill everyone in the village. The village contained approximately 200 men, women, and children.

Hammer refused the demands. Consequently, the terrorist killed everyone in the village. Afterward, Hammer and his men killed the remaining terrorists.

Hammer was relieved from his command pending an investigation by the Naval Investigation Service. The investigation cleared Hammer and his men of all charges. Three weeks later, a liberal congressman on the Judiciary Committee had the FBI investigate the incident. Hammer was relieved again and ended up resigning from the Navy. There were no formal charges brought forward. He now runs a survival camp in the Mountains of Idaho.

Scott said, "So you believe Mr. Hoover has sufficient experience to run the FBI?"

Midas said, "I do, Scott."

Matt finally spoke, "Hammer has enough experience and expertise to run the FBI, but so do others. The quality that I like most about him is that the FBI, for reasons I can only assume are not up to their self-proclaimed incorruptibility, fucked Hammer on two separate occasions. So I think he will have ample motivation to clean that rat's nest out."

I said, "Midas, can you call him? I'd like to speak with him?"

Midas said I have him in a holding pattern. I'll call him now."

Midas spoke to Hammer for about 30 seconds and handed the phone to me.

I said, "Mr. Hoover, this is Mike Stone. I'd like to make a proposal to you, and I hope you are willing to serve your country again. Midas has been explaining your career to me, and I find it fascinating and disappointing. But, I'll get to the point. I need someone to grab the FBI hierarchy by the balls, take them out of the Hoover building, and put their asses on the street."

Hammer said, "Sir, Midas told me you wanted to shake up the bureau, and if you need me, I will relish the task."

I said, "Great! How soon can you get to DC?"

"Well, Sir, after talking to Midas, I decided to come to D.C. I'm in the lobby of your hotel as we speak."

I looked at Midas, and he winked at me.

I said, "Hammer, stand by. I'll have someone come down and escort you up."

Matt said, "I'll get him since he'll be working for me."

I said, "Matt, please grab Tiddus on your way back. I think he is in the café."

Matt said, "Will do, boss."

I said to the group, "Let's take a short break and give the others a chance to get up here."

When everyone arrived, I made a short introduction to Mr. Hoover and explained we would talk at length after our meeting.

I then said, "Tiddus, please give us an overview of our financial state."

Tiddus said, "Yes, Sir. Our national debt is 30 trillion dollars, with this year's revenue of $3.863 trillion for FY 2021. Income taxes will contribute $1.932 trillion. Another $1.373 trillion will come from payroll taxes. This includes $1.011 trillion for Social Security, $308 billion for Medicare, and $43 billion for unemployment insurance. Our current budget is $4.829 trillion dollars. The U.S. government estimates it will receive $3.863 trillion in revenue, creating a $966 billion deficit for Oct. 1, 2020, through Sept. 30, 2021. We all know this is unsustainable, and for how long, we don't know. So our main priority will be to cut spending. Next is the passage of a balanced budget amendment. To attain these two goals, we have to cut our current budget. A 25 percent across-the-board budget cut would save us $1.20725 trillion dollars a year, but with the $966 billion deficit, we save $200 billion.

The true net budget should be 3.62175 trillion dollars after a 25 percent cut, leaving a $242 billion savings.

I've made studies on several Cabinet Departments. If we were to abolish the Department of Education, the IRS, and the

Department of Homeland Security, still allowing 50 percent of DHS budget to remain for their personnel to go back to their parent departments, the country would save an additional $177 billion annually. In addition, reducing the budget by 50 percent for the Departments of International Assistance, Other Independent Agencies, and General Services, and accounting for a 25 percent pay cut for everyone but the military and law enforcement agencies, there would be an additional $109.6 billion saved. All totaled that is nearly $527 billion in savings annually. That is over one-half a trillion dollars per year to pay down our 30 trillion debts. Sir, one thing I forgot to list here was the amount of funding allowance given to both Congress and the Senate for their staff. They are handed over 950 million dollars per representative up to 18 staff members. That totals almost 650 billion dollars. I might suggest cutting that staff and its funding by 50 percent and saving an additional $325 billion totaling 825 billion dollars. The good news is when we pass these cuts and other budget items and submit our first budget, we will have cut the budget by 2.75 trillion dollars and 2 trillion every year after that."

I said, "Tiddus that is pretty comprehensive. So, it's a federal employee reduction of 500,000 employees?"

Tiddus said, "In raw numbers, yes, when your Cabinet secretaries take the helm, they may reduce that number further depending on how efficiently they run their departments."

I said, "Here is what I want to do. Some of you have ideas that you would like to implement within your departments but don't know if they are feasible until you get there. The others who currently hold positions already in their respective departments or have seen firsthand how they operate will better understand what changes they can affect. So, I'll start with the latter group for their opinions on the changes proposed and if they feel they can add to our country's savings. Susan, would you give us your assessment?"

Susan Hope said, "Sir, I fully agree with your premise of cutting the Federal government. As for the CIA, there are some personnel changes I'd like to make. We are very heavy on the administration side. I'd like to reduce that number but add it to the operations side of the house. At worst, it would be revenue-neutral. I do see us cutting some personnel."

I said, "Thank you, Susan. General, can you give us some insight into your plans for the Defense Department?"

"Mr. President Elect, we obviously need to cut spending. I will be continuing a constant review of our allocations and keeping savings at the top of our priorities."

I said, "Thank you, General. Sammie, do you have any comments or recommendations?"

Sammie said, "Sir, I agree with the cost-cutting strategies we've discussed. As for my department, I feel the State Department has more people than necessary. Once I take command, I'm sure I can make some additional reductions."

I said, "Thank you, Sammie. Eric, what's your opinion? Before you answer, Sir, this applies to everyone in this room. Just call me Stone. You can resume the more formal title of address."

Eric said, Okay, Stone, you know I feel the same way you do about the cuts. I plan on having my staff study the spending of all of our departments and determine if and where we can make additional cuts."

I said, "Good, I'm interested to see what you come up with. Scott, do you have anything?"

Scott said, "I do. Our country has lost about 52 million people. How many of those were Federal employees, not counting military or law enforcement? Tiddus, do you have those figures?"

Tiddus said, "I believe I do, Scott. Just one second. Here it is. It looks like 526,000, or 1 percent of U.S. deaths. So if we deduct the number of Federal employees who died from the 25 percent personnel cut, we could hire 34,000 additional employees or just add that to the savings, which for the average Federal Employee, including benefits, is approximately 123,068 dollars multiplied; that by 34,000 equals $4,184,322,000."

Scott said, "So we are not looking at putting 500,000 people out of work then?"

Tiddus responded, "Theoretically, some of those people will need replacing depending on their particular job."

I said, "Although the deaths we have had recently are tragic, the unemployment numbers aren't as bad as I had imagined. Midas, do you have any comments?

Midas said, "I do, Mr.... I mean, Stone. I think we are long overdue in cutting the number of people employed by the federal government. I will be assessing my department in hopes of reducing the number of chiefs so I can have more people doing the job."

I said, "It seems we are all on the same page. I'll take our recommendations to Senator Wells and Congressman Tolan. Scott, did you find out if it was okay for Mom to stay in the White House?"

Scott said, "It is fine, there's precedent for this, Presidents Grant, Truman, and Eisenhower had Mothers-in-law stay in the White House."

I said, "Great! The inauguration is in two days, everyone. Try to get as much accomplished before Wednesday, but save some energy for the festivities. That is all I have."

68

CONGRESSIONAL INPUT

Eric, Scott, and I met with Senator Wells and Congressman Tolan inside a secure room within the capital complex. After exchanging greetings, I said, "Did you gentlemen review Tiddus' proposal?"

Tolan said, "We did, and it is long overdue. I've had several meetings with the incoming Congress. Everyone appears to be on board. Senator Wells and I have drafted bills for everything we have spoken about from making the Bill of Rights unchangeable as a Constitutional Amendment, making Social Security untouchable for any general spending, new election verification laws, a balanced budget amendment, an overhaul of disciplinary practices for federal employees, revocation of the Patriot Act, an overhaul and the complete restructuring of the FISA Courts, term limits, a bill imposing a 10-year waiting period for Congress and Senate members leaving office before they can except any type of revenue from a lobbying group, and removing the Department of Education and the Department of Homeland Security from the Cabinet. I also have a bill to remove the IRS when we pass the Federal sales tax. Both of us have Congress and Senate members designated to sponsor and co-sponsor the different bills on their first day in session."

Senator Wells said, "Michael, we need to do this as fast as possible because some of these members will start to oppose your ideas just to gain their own personal power sooner rather than later. It's just human nature. Never forget this."

I said, "I know that's true, and I won't lose sight of the possibility. Thank you both for your hard work. Do you think I should host a welcoming ceremony for the new Congress and Senate, maybe have my Cabinet appointments mingle and reinforce the need for my proposed policies?"

Tolan said, "Sadly, there is no venue large enough to accommodate that large of a group. I'm not sure it's ever been done. Maybe we could host a joint session of Congress the night after your inauguration, and we could invite you to speak. Afterward, you and your people could mingle with the Congress and Senate members. What's your opinion, Senator Wells?"

Wells said, "I think that is a great idea, Congressman. Michael, we both are impressed with the nominees you have chosen for the Cabinet posts. However, I guarantee the lobbyists in D.C., at least the ones still alive, are in a panic over your choices."

Tolan said, "I also wanted to assure you that the bills that will be introduced are brief and concise and, as you said, "Short enough to read during a commercial break."

I said, "Gentlemen have you found a path to allow me or the Secretary of Defense to remove officers in the military for conduct other than apolitical behavior and promoting junior officers several ranks below the outgoing officers, to a rank commensurate to their new post?"

Wells said, "Michael, you will be the Commander in Chief of the entire U.S. Military. You can order it or have the SECDEF order it." Tolan agreed.

Scott asked, "Congressman Tolan, have you or the Senator received any opposition of the President Elect's policies from lobbyist groups?"

Wells said, "I have Scott. They really haven't had a chance to influence the new members yet. Many of the "Globalists" was part of I AM's purge, but many different types of lobbyists are willing to pay big money for influence. That's why doing all of this now is so important." Tolan agreed with his colleague.

I said, "One final request, gentlemen. I'd like a law passed regarding political violence. I'd like it to be under Federal Jurisdiction exclusively, regardless of where the crime was perpetrated."

Both men acknowledged the request and put it on their list.

The meeting ended, and we returned to my room at the Hay-Adams. We were looking over some notes when the Archangel Michael appeared right between Eric and Scott, seated on the couch. I wish I'd had a camera ready when it happened. The startling surprise of the two was priceless. The truth be told, it scared the shit them. Both of them looked at me speechless. I started to introduce them to the Archangel when Michael introduced himself to them.

Michael then said, "The Holy of Holies would like a word with the three of you."

I said, "Thank you, Michael."

I AM appeared sitting in a leather armchair across from Eric, Scott, and the Archangel Michael. He was dressed in the same attire I had seen him before jeans, leather work boots, a black hoodie, and a worn brown leather bomber jacket. His face was still obscured by the hoodie and the shadows from the lighting. You could make out the outline of a short gray beard and the ever-present fire-like eyes.

I was standing beside the couch facing him when he said, "The three of you will have a big day Wednesday, and I have every confidence in all of you, fulfilling your oaths to your country's citizens and me. I wanted to impress upon Eric and Scott that they should support Michael, and advise him, but remember that my hand guides him and you.

Michael, I wanted to personally thank you for your unsolicited faith in me and my words. This faith has enabled you to save the lives of my priests, your men, and the sanctuary tabernacle complex, and for that, I thank you.

The three of you are about to embark on a historical journey. Of course, the free will I have granted mankind will play a role in your journey, but with your choices and the policies you are proposing, I have great confidence that your journey is heading in the right direction.

Scott, I know your faith has grown, not that you didn't believe in a higher power, but you were more inclined to believe if you had some proof. Obviously, you changed your mind, or you wouldn't be here. What changed your mind?"

Scott said, "I AM, Michael, and I have had many long conversations about many topics, including theology, politics, and history. His view of religion was different from all of the mainstream religious dogma. The one thing that struck me was the consistency of his views. Every time I asked questions about Judaism, he would answer my question, and if he didn't know the answer, he'd tell me that. Although he didn't know all the answers, he still retained unwavering confidence in his faith. I also wanted to have that confidence when you spoke to the world; that sealed the deal for me."

I AM said, "Scott, take my hand."

Scott held out his hand.

I AM grasped Scott's hand, and Scott felt a warmth flow through his entire body.

I AM said, "As a token of my faith in you, I have healed your eyes. Remove your glasses."

Scott did as he was told, and to his astonishment, his vision was better than ever without his glasses.

Scott said, "Thank you, Lord, for everything."

I AM said, "Eric, you are next. I also have faith in you and know you have faith in me. Come here and grasp my hand."

Eric complied and grasped I AM's hand. He, too, felt an indescribable feeling of warmth radiating through his body.

I AM said, "Eric, you will now have great confidence when speaking to people, individually or in large groups."

Eric said, "Thank you, Lord that means a lot to me."

I AM said, "Michael, come to me and take my hand."

I did as I was told. I then felt the warmth flowing through my entire body.

I AM said, "Michael, I have already blessed Lori, but now I bless you and your daughters Arica and Nicole and your granddaughter Lylah. Lylah will become a great leader in the years to come. She will make your family proud, and also me."

I said, "Thank you, Lord."

I AM said, "Michael, when you asked me to speak directly to my creation, I was hesitant. What I mean is I have never hesitated regarding any decision I have made. This hesitancy was an entirely new concept and feeling to me. I now realize that even a supposed all-knowing, all-seeing being like me can learn, and for that, I am grateful. All of you will now leave here blessed in special ways by me. However, with that blessing also comes responsibility for your actions. Remember that!"

Just like that, I AM was gone.

The Archangel Michael remained and said, "Michael, I'm still charged with helping you if you need me." Then he vanished also.

Scott said, "That was incredible!"

Eric said, "We have been truly blessed."

I said, "I agree with both of you. Now we need to fix our country."

69

EPILOGUE

Today is the big day. My family, including Mom and Tina's family, were present. Everyone looked wonderful. I asked the President who organizes the Inauguration. He told me it was organized by the Ceremonials Division, part of the State Department. He said it was all arranged down to the smallest detail and the President had enough on his plate, so he doesn't need to worry about arranging functions. There's even an Official Protocol Officer to inform the President who is who as far as foreign diplomats and heads of state are concerned.

The President said, "Michael, everything is taken care of for you. All you have to do is lead the nation and make executive decisions. At least that is what you are supposed to do. I'll tell you this, though, at this level, the President's level, mistakes can cost lives, international incidents, and economic problems and, possibly wars. It is something to keep in the back of your mind at all times."

I said, "That's all?"

He laughed and said, "That's enough, believe me."

It is on January 20th at 11:50. I'm now standing in the front row with guests of the Inauguration Ceremony. Eric is now taking his oath of office for the Vice Presidency of the United States. Kim is on his right, and an Associate Justice of the Supreme Court administers the oath. At this moment, I'm filled with a combination of joy, hope, determination, and above all, faith. Everyone applauded after the oath.

Rabbi Tovia Cohen began an invocation before my oath. When he finished, I stood and helped Lori up and my mom. We stood across from the Justice with Lori and Mom to my right and Arica and Natalie, along with her family, on my left. I looked at the President standing in the front row, and he gave me a big smile and a thumb up. I gazed at the assembled guests and out to the mall, from the West side of the Capitol building, where thousands of Americans stood watching the ceremony, wondering what kind of leader I would be for their country?

Rabbi Cohen stepped up to Justice Brown.

The Rabbi said, "Michael, this was my great grandfather's Tanakh; my family and I would be honored if you would use it today."

I said, "Rabbi, I am honored by your gesture; thank you."

I placed my left hand on the Tanakh and raised my right hand.

Justice Brown said, "Mr. Stone, please repeat after me: I, Michael Stone, do solemnly swear that I will faithfully execute the

393

Office of President of the United States, and will to the best of my ability, preserve, protect and defend the Constitution of the United States, so help me God." Congratulations, Mr. President." I repeated it slowly, after every sentence, and then the Justice shook my hand. Lori hugged and kissed me, and my girls did the same, and Little Bit gave me a big hug. I was fighting back the tears of joy. Finally, my mom came up and hugged and kissed me. She said, "Your Dad and I are so proud of you." I hugged her again, wiping my tears on her shoulder.

Andrea, now the head of my Secret Service Protection Detail, whispered, "Excuse me, Mr. President, Senator Wells and Congressman Tolan would like a private word with you."

I said, "Lead the way, Andrea."

We walked into the Capitol Building with several more agents with us. Andrea stopped at the door, knocked, and entered. Half of the agents stayed with me, and the other half cleared the room. I walked in, and both men stood.

I said, "What can I do for you, gentlemen?"

Tolan and Wells said together, "Good afternoon, Mr. President.

Wells continued. "Mr. President, we wanted to notify you as soon as possible that we have several bills for your signature if you wish, Sir."

Tolan said, "Mr. President, Congress, and the Senate have officially been in session since January 4th, and we have been busy. The following bills are ready: The Bill of Rights Protection Amendment, the Federal Employee Responsibility Act; the revocation of the Patriot Act; and the removal of the Director of National Intelligence along with the National Military

Authorization Act. In addition, we've passed a new bill called the Heartland Act Too. Mr. President, you may not be familiar with the Heartland Act. Let me explain. It addresses two key issues that you wanted to be changed. The first issue is the hardening of the electrical grid against solar flares or EMPs. Corporations involved with the electrical grid are mandated by law to begin hardening their structures within 30 days or face major fines or possible jail time. The cost of the improvements cannot be passed on to consumers. It must be funded with the profits of the corporations. The second part of the bill addresses the manufacturing of critical goods within the United States and the import and export of trade goods. As a result of Covid 19, Americans have seen and experienced shortages and potentially disastrous scenarios where possible hostile nations could reduce or even cut off critical manufactured products or materials. These products run the gambit from pharmaceutical preparations and other vital health care items to textiles, computer equipment, silicon chips, plastic lids, fertilizer, and containers for everyday use. Mr. President, we import 41 percent of our total imports from China. The bill will allow companies who choose to build and manufacture goods in the U.S. a lower income tax rate than previously allowed. The alternative is to mirror the trade practices of the country exporting goods to the U.S., along with an additional tariff for corporations with U.S. citizens on the board of directors. By mirroring the export country's trade practices, the U.S. will level the playing field regarding trade policies of governments who export more than they import from the U.S.

The following Cabinet posts have been abolished: Department of Education, the IRS, and the Department of

Homeland Security. The Small Government Act covers a 25 percent reduction in all federal agencies except for the military and law enforcement. The following departments have additional budget cuts of 50 percent: Departments of International Assistance, Other Independent Agencies. General Services and the staff allotment for Congressional and Senatorial aids will also be cut by 50percent. The Bill of Rights Protection Amendment and the Balanced Budget Amendment needed two-thirds of Congress and the Senate to pass. The vote was 90 percent for both bodies. Right now, the states have the proposed amendment before them. The time-limit given them was 30 days for an up or down vote. There are 20 days remaining. I personally think it will pass, but we have to wait and see. Congratulations, Mr. President."

I was stunned. I responded, "Thank you, gentlemen. Should I sign them now?"

Wells said, "No time like the present. We even have extra pens for souvenirs of the momentous occasion."

There was a White House photographer taking photos to memorialize the event.

The rest of the day was completely filled. I met with several members of the White House staff. I was introduced to Colonel Gibbs, the primary pilot for Marine One. He discussed emergency evacuation procedures for Lori and I should the need arise. There were three balls planned for tonight starting at 2000 hrs.

The last briefing before the ball was with an Air Force General and a Major.

The General said, "Good evening, Mr. President. First, I would like to apologize to you, Sir, this briefing was to take place this morning, but I understand you had other pressing business. I asked the General to begin the briefing. The General removed a plastic card the size of a credit card and handed it to me.

The General continued, "Mr. President, as you can see, there are two columns of numbers. I would like you to pick one number grouping from either column. Once you choose a grouping, note its position on the card and point out the grouping to me. This card is called 'the biscuit,' the numbers are called the 'gold code.' In the case of a nuclear release, Sir, the Major here or one of the other rotating service branch aids will open this briefcase. This will enable the Secretary of Defense to be notified of a pending nuclear launch. He will then authenticate that you, Mr. President, are giving the launch order. Authentication is verified by your chosen gold card numbers on the biscuit. Once the order is deemed valid, the Chairman of the Joint Chiefs Staff is notified. At that point, you will be given several options for the strike. Depending on the target, the options consist of the size of the weapons yield, air or ground detonation, and the number of weapons to be deployed. After your decision has been made, Sir, the appropriate orders will be given to the units that will deploy the weapons. The Major will accompany you with the football everywhere you go. When you are in your office, the dining room, or your bedroom, a military aid with the rank of O-4 or higher will be in close proximity to you. Do you have any questions, Mr. President?"

I said, "Just one, General. What's your name, Major?" I asked, turning to him.

The Major came to attention and said, "Sir, Major Thomas Workman."

I shook the Major's hand and said, "I always like to know the people I'll be working with; nice to meet you, Major Workman." I shook the General's hand and said, "That was a good briefing, gentleman. Thank you. If you excuse me, I have a hell of a job ahead of me. But right now, I will meet the First Lady for a dance at the Ball."

The end

AUTHOR BIO

Michael F. Decker's debut novel *I AM The Delta Protocol* is a uniquely credible representation of the headlines surrounding the 2020 Presidential elections,

Decker's previous service as a U.S. Marine and a Military Policeman, along with being the NCOIC of the base SWAT team at Camp Lejeune. This experience combined with his fascination with the inter-workings of government and extensive knowledge of American, and military history allowed him to deliver an authentic and detailed portrayal of this exciting and hard-hitting political thriller.

Decker's motivation for writing the novel is his contempt for the mass media, progressive movement, social media censorship, and the incursion of the far left attempting to remove our Constitutional rights and destroy the country.

Made in the USA
Monee, IL
07 April 2022

94186392R00239